Evelyne Morris was born in England towards the end of WW2, in 1944, but she comes from an international cultural background. Her grandparents were French/Italian and Maltese/Greek, and she was brought up in a college with foreign students from all over the world – Europe, the Far East, the Middle East, Africa and South America. She has a brother and sisters-in-law from Spain, France, and Japan, and she has daughters-in-law from Brazil and South Korea. She started writing after retirement, and this is her second novel.

This book is dedicated to my late brother, Dr Roger Chambers, who not only encouraged me in my writings, but also often talked to me about the time he spent in Jamaica in the 1970s as a paediatrician, caring for babies and small children amongst the poorer communities.

Evelyne Morris

COMA

AUSTIN MACAULEY PUBLISHERS™

LONDON • CAMBRIDGE • NEW YORK • SHARJAH

A CIP catalogue record for this title is available from the British Library.

ISBN 9781788489799 (Paperback)
ISBN 9781788489805 (Hardback)
ISBN 9781788489812 (E-Book)

www.austinmacauley.com

First Published (2018)
Austin Macauley Publishers Ltd
25 Canada Square
Canary Wharf
London
E14 5LQ

Part One

Chapter One

It had been a long day, full of nothing in particular, and Detective Inspector Lavinia Hobbs was looking forward to going home, a quiet Friday night in. She was a tall, good-looking black woman in her early fifties. She was also very experienced in her work, having spent over twenty-five years 'on the job', most of it in CID. As a black woman in the police force, her promotion to the rank of DI was extraordinary, and she was very proud of her achievements.

But just ten minutes before the end of her shift, a call had come in about a car on fire at Westover Common. Usually it would have been her sergeant who would have responded to the incident, but because the car was a new and outrageously expensive Maserati Quattroporte GTS, and not the usual joy-rider's choice of easy pickings, she decided to take charge.

Outside it was dark and stormy, and the rain was now falling down in sheets as she ran to her car parked at the far end of the car park. Why had she left her raincoat in her car today? She usually brought it into the office with her. Soaking and now thoroughly fed up, she drove down the county lane passing Westover Wood, towards the reported burning of the Maserati on the adjacent Westover Common.

She knew that there would be a log fire burning and a hot meal waiting for her at home. James, her husband of only six months would be waiting for her with his cheerful chatter and never-ending understanding of how difficult it was for her to let go of the grisly details of her job. How could she talk about the two little children who had been found last week in a shallow grave up on Greystone moor? How could she talk about the harrowing interview she had been forced to have with the children's shocked and grieving

9

parents? Her boss, Detective Chief Inspector Henry Ericson, was sure that the father knew more than he was letting on.

Same Evening, 8:15 p.m.

As Lavinia was musing over these things, she wished that she had sent DS Oliver to Westover Common after all. How she wanted to be home again, sitting in front of that log fire. She was struggling to see ahead as she peered through the rhythmic swishing of her windscreen wipers into the dashing rain beyond. Then appearing out of the rain-soaked bushes at the side of the road, she saw what looked like a bundle of rags. Was there some movement? Or was it just the wind moving the rags? She pulled up sharply and hurriedly dragged on her raincoat before opening the car door. Taking a deep breath, she stepped out into the wind and rain to examine the bundle.

"Christ Almighty!" she exclaimed out loud, "It's a woman, and she's covered in blood!"

Her mobile phone was already switched on to the police emergency channel. She crouched over the body to see if the woman was still alive and felt a very faint pulse in her neck. "DI Hobbs here," she said, "I need an ambulance here on the B2060 between Westover Wood and Westover Common. I have found a woman who is barely alive and needs immediate help. Tell them that she is bleeding heavily from a head wound. I shall escort the ambulance to the hospital and attend to the woman there. I also need DS Oliver to organise a murder back-up team to examine the scene here and see if it is possible to trace this woman's movements. It could be a hit and run or she may have been attacked in Westover Wood and was able to crawl to the roadside. It could be attempted murder. I was on my way to investigate the burning of a Maserati on Westover Common. This should also be followed up as the two events could be linked. Let me know when to expect the ambulance. This lady needs urgent attention."

Chapter Two

Same Evening, 8:55 p.m., Wallchester General Hospital

Forty minutes later, Lavinia entered the chaos of the A&E department of Wallchester General Hospital. Always when she visited the hospital, she thought of her late mother, Mary, who had come from Nigeria to work there as a nurse and had done so for over twenty-five years.

Taking off her rain and blood drenched coat, she was shown to a side ward where she found a tall and very good looking black doctor of about forty attending to her victim. "Good evening," he said in a deep, warm voice which, she thought, had a light Caribbean accent. "I am Mr Akami, a consultant neurologist, a specialist in head and brain traumas. I am assessing this lady's head injury. Are you related to her? Do you know what happened to her?"

(Akami, Akami my love. Have you come to save me again?)

DI Hobbs gave a brief look at his identification badge, Alexander Akami, it read. "No, I'm sorry, I'm not related," she replied, "and I don't even know who she is. I am Detective Inspector Lavinia Hobbs, and I found this lady by the roadside with that horrible wound to her head, Doctor. Do I call you Mister or Doctor? Have you been able to assess her injuries yet?"

(Lavinia. Are you my Lavinia, my faithful black slave who cares for me?)

"As a consultant within the hospital, I am called Mister, but I know that it can be confusing, so I would be quite happy if you address me as 'Doctor'," said Mr Akami.

He bent over to look closely at the woman lying in the bed. "This lady does have a significant wound at the back of her head and she is drifting in and out of consciousness all the time. I believe that she may have an intracranial hematoma, a bleed between her

11

brain and her skull, which means that we will need to have it drained as soon as possible. I am having her transferred to our intensive care unit to have her put into a medically induced coma so that we can scan her skull and brain to confirm my diagnosis. Although I am not a forensic specialist, it seems to me that the scratches on her arms and legs from her crawl through the woods are superficial and she does not seem to have any defence wounds. One hit and she was down…"

As he was talking, a uniformed police constable, who was stationed outside the door of the side ward, came in.

"Ma'am," he said, walking towards Lavinia, and handing to her a large evidence bag, "I have just been given this woman's handbag. It was found by the forensic team some fifty metres away from where they believe her body was left by her attacker. They do think that they have found evidence that she was dumped by a car by the lake and somehow, with that awful head injury, she managed to crawl to the edge of the woods where you found her."

"Thank you," said Lavinia. "Has the team found anything else that might give us any idea what happened in Westover Woods, or whether this attack is linked to the burning car on Westover Common?"

"I don't think so, Ma'am," replied the constable. "Sergeant Oliver, who is in charge of the search team, says that the constant rain this evening has washed out most of the possible evidence, how she was attacked, the car tyre tracks and her tracks. He said that he will contact you directly if there is any more news from there. He also said that he sent two DC's to the Common. The Fire Service has dampened down the fire, but the petrol tank in the car had exploded and the vehicle is virtually destroyed, including its number plates, so they have not been able to identify the owner as yet. They will check the chassis' number when it has cooled down."

"Okay," said Lavinia. "You can get back to your guard duties. I don't want anyone, other than hospital staff, coming into this side ward or the intensive care unit when she has been transferred, until we know what has happened to this lady. I feel sure that whatever the reason we are dealing with an attempted murder here."

As he left the room, she sat down and after pulling on a pair of latex gloves; she pulled out of the evidence bag a pretty, pink leather handbag. "Phew," she whistled silently through her teeth, "Louis Vuitton. She's a lady who must be loaded!" She opened the handbag and rummaged inside. "Ah ha! Got you!" she muttered to herself as she pulled out a fat matching pink wallet. She opened it up and found £165 in notes, and several credit cards.

"Well! I don't think that she was mugged. Dr Akami," she said out loud, "your patient's name appears to be Mellissa Harris, and she is 28 years old. This photo on her driving licence seems to be her. How badly is she injured, and when do you think that she will be awake enough for me to interview her? Can I talk to her before you put her into that deep coma, while she is just plain unconscious? Can she hear us talking and will she be able to take anything in?"

"She can probably hear us and maybe take in significant words or names," replied the doctor, "but I don't think if she were to come around, that she would be either lucid in her speech or understanding us in anyway. There can be no interviewing for some time." He pointed to some marks on her left cheek. "Look – she has some bruising on her face, making me think that she was hit, probably by an open hand. Her head injuries are a puzzle. On the surface there are all sorts of leaf debris which she must have picked up when she crawled through the woods, but deeper down the wound is clean. I think that she was hit before she reached the roadside, even before she was left in the woods. I don't think that she was hit by a car. The scan will tell us whether there is blood in or near her brain. We must also wait until the swelling goes down before we can examine her head wounds more thoroughly."

"We have a forensic team working at Westover Wood, and I hope that we will soon have the answer to the puzzle of how and where she was attacked, and how she came to be in Westover Wood," said the detective. "You say that she is to be put in a coma. How much is she aware of her situation right now? If she hears us talking, can she take anything in, or respond by moving her eyelids or, say, a little finger?

As they were talking, a tall and attractive young man in his early thirties walked into the side ward. Lavinia thought that she recognised him but could not quite place him. She got up and went towards him.

"I am Detective Inspector Hobbs and I'm sorry sir, you can't come in," she said, trying to usher him out. "This is a restricted room and the constable at the door shouldn't have let you in."

"I am Mellissa's husband," he said. "I'm Charlie Harris." All his speech started coming out in a jumble of words. "What has happened to my wife? Why is her head covered in bandages? Is she going to recover? Is she able to talk and say what happened? All I know is that she pinched my car and went off in the rain."

"Of course, Charlie Harris, better known as Detective Inspector David Holland. I thought I knew your face!" Lavinia was surprised and somewhat taken aback to be talking to a made up version of herself. Oh, those handsome blue eyes and lanky blond hair. No wonder half the women in Britain were 'in love' with him. She pulled herself together. "You will have to ask those questions of Dr Akami here. He will be able to explain your wife's condition. I am Detective Inspector Lavinia Hobbs," she repeated, "and I am in charge of the investigation to find out…"

(I can hear them talking. Why can't I move? I can't even blink my eyes. I can hear Charlie. Does he still want to hurt me? Oh! Akami I can hear you too. My beloved Akami. Have you come to save me again? Am I back in Jamaica? Back with my love, in Jamaica?)

Chapter Three

29 December, 1831
Silver Bay, Jamaica

(I am heavily pregnant and the baby is due in about two weeks' time. But I cannot rest, I have to run away from the murderous mob which is attacking my home. I am gasping and struggling to breathe. This is partly due to fear, but also because of the vile, acrid air that is filling my lungs. The usual fabulous setting of the Jamaican sun is obscured by the thick, black plumes of smoke coming from the storehouse. I am choking on the stench and sticky sweetness of burning sugar that is filling the air.

The storehouse, the cane crusher and the whole season's crop of sugar cane is on fire; and now the wild mob is throwing burning torches into the windows of my home, the plantation house.

I should not be discovered as they will surely kill me and my unborn baby. From my hiding place and shelter behind this huge oak tree I look back at my home, called High View. The home where I have lived almost in isolation for three long years. How I long for my real home back in England. I even plan to bring back two of the former slaves that I have freed, Akami and Lavinia. Not just slaves but, apart from Lucy who lives far away in Kingston, my only real friends. And Akami is my own true love too.

The mob is being led by one of our slaves, Lucas; the only slave from Silver Bay and the one who killed Peter Frobisher. It was to hunt down and catch Lucas that Charles and Jack Frobisher left me unprotected.

I recognise only Jeremiah in the mob of slaves from the neighbouring plantation who are surrounding the building. Why is Jeremiah here? He knows me well, and he must remember that it was I who saved his dying boy, Samson, after he had been bitten by a brown recluse spider. I not only saved Samson's life, I also persuaded his owner, Thomas Chamberlain, to re-house Jeremiah and his family away from the swamps that teem with deadly snakes and spiders.

The mob is now surrounding the plantation house and is chanting and stamping in one of their ancestral African tribal dances. The women are ululating, becoming more and more frenzied.

I can hear the horses in the stables screaming as the stables are set on fire, and I am powerless to help them; and now I see my Sheba, my darling dog Sheba, who never hurt a living soul running for her life. Fear of the noise and smoke made her stray from her usual place at my heels. I feel compelled to watch as one of the men capture my faithful pet dog, my beloved Sheba. Oh no! Oh God help me! I am helpless to save my pet. I am paralysed with fear and agony as I watch a frenzied man slit her throat in one swift movement. A soft bark leaves her body as she dies. I want to but I cannot scream out. I must remain calm and make no noise. I must not endanger the life of my baby. I want to block out the viciousness of the act but I let out a low moan as all the men smear Sheba's blood on their bodies. They have not heard me. I'm still safe here behind the tree. They have set fire to the veranda and the tall white pillars of the portico and now the flames are gradually reaching right up to the second floor of the house.

All of a sudden there is a popping sound followed by a noise that sounds like a clap of thunder and the whole building is becoming engulfed in flames that shoot high into the sky, the smoke adding to the dense blanket which is obliterating the last of the sunset.

I am desperately afraid. "Akami... Akami, where are you?" I cry silently. Where are all our own slaves? "Akami! Akami!" I am terrified and now I call out loud. "Akami, where are you? Take me away! Hide me! Save me and this baby who is soon to be born."

I know that my own slaves love me and that Lavinia and Akami will protect me from the wild mob. I am terrified of these frenzied slaves from the neighbouring plantations. Slaves who think that freedom is coming at last; and emboldened by the preaching of the Reverend Sam Sharpe of Montego Bay, they have been killing all the white people they can find. Now they are continuing their wild dancing around my home. The sparks and ashes are falling fast and with a gust of wind the upper branches of my protecting oak tree catches fire. The mob is still dancing around the burning house and no one has heard my call. Still unseen I run into the wild hibiscus bushes which scratch my arms and legs. Through the smoke and fires, and the burning homestead trees that are crashing down, Akami reaches my side, and gathers me up and his big, strong arms, holding me tight.)

She hears a new voice, a woman and one she did not quite recognise. Was it the Lavinia she heard before?

"...I am in charge of the investigation. Your wife is seriously injured and Dr Akami is attending to her. You were saying that she drove off in your car. Is that a Maserati Quatrroporte by any chance?"

Before Charlie Harris could reply, DI Hobbs saw a movement out of the corner of her eye. "Her finger is twitching," she said addressing the Doctor. "Do something Dr Akami. She's coming around. Can I speak to her?"

(And now a deep warm voice. A well-remembered voice. Akami! Akami! I know that you will save me, my love!)

"No. No one can speak to her," said Dr Akami. "She may twitch a little, but she is still deeply unconscious. In a minute or two we will be taking her to the Intensive Care Unit and putting her in a medically induced coma. She will be kept alive by life support machines while my team and I assess and attend to that nasty head wound, which will include scanning her brain to see if there is any permanent damage."

"Wait a minute!" said Charlie Harris. "I don't want her to be taken to the ICU and hitched up to those awful robot-like machines."

(She was deeply unconscious, but somehow she could still hear and even recognise some of the voices of people talking around her. Akami, my beloved Akami. And that was Charlie talking. He was asking, no demanding in that awful way of his, that they should not move her. Not take her to the ICU? What's that? Not put me on machines? What machines?

She tried to touch the little golden cross at her throat and found that she couldn't move her hand. Please, Jesus, protect me. He is as hateful as that other Charles.)

Inspector Lavinia Hobbs gave Charlie Harris a good, hard look. "Why would you even resist putting her on a life support system? Or trying to save her? The doctor said that putting her into a coma is the best way to save her."

She turned to Dr Akami. "Did I really see her little finger move? Could she come around naturally without being put in an induced coma? Can you please tell us again what the future holds for Mrs Harris? I thought that you doctors were always saying that someone in a coma can, sometimes not only waken and recover but that a full recovery and return to normal life is not impossible."

"That is true," said Dr Akami, "but with Mrs Harris we still do not know the cause of her head injuries, and how much trauma her brain has received. As I have already told you, we have to wait until we have scanned her brain and the swelling has gone down before we can make a full assessment of her injuries and whether she will recover. What I am sure about at present is that her brain is active. There is no question of whether or not we put her into a coma and on life support machines. That little twitch shows that she is alive and strong enough to recover. It is just a matter of keeping watch over her and to be ready for the first signs that she is going to wake up."

Two porters and a nurse came in to move Mellissa's bed to the ICU. "Thank you, Nurse Bingham," said Dr Akami, "my assistant neurologists are on stand-by and are waiting to receive you in the ICU, ward 2. I shall be following you up as soon as I have finished talking to the detective and Mrs Harris's husband."

Lavinia had been looking at Charlie Harris as Dr Akami was speaking. Did she see a look of fear rather than relief come into his eyes? A second later he was the all concerned and loving husband, taking her hand as she was being wheeled out of the room.

"Can you hear me darling Mellissa, I am here to look after you. Please wake up soon. We can still go to Jamaica as soon as you are well again."

Dr Akami, who was just about to talk to DI Hobbs, spoke to Charlie. "Were you planning to go to Jamaica?"

"Yes," Charlie replied. "Mellissa has recently found that someone with the same name as her maiden name, that is Mellissa Goodchild, married a sugar plantation owner in Jamaica who owned the Silver Bay plantation in western Jamaica and lived through the slave uprising in the 1830's, just before the slaves were freed. She intended to go and find out all that she could about this Mellissa Goodchild and to discover if she is related."

"That is so interesting," said Dr Akami. "I am Jamaican. My great grandfather was a slave who lived through that uprising and I am pretty sure that I have heard mention that he was on the Silver Bay plantation. My two grandparents were children when their parents left Jamaica to come to England in 1948. They sailed on the 'Empire Windrush'. They were part of the first mass migration of Jamaicans to England. I was born here but I still feel Jamaican." He paused for a moment, deeply lost in thought.

Then he continued. "Well, enough of that. Mr Harris, Detective Hobbs. We will get Mrs Harris settled in the ICU. The anaesthetist will put her in a deep coma and we scan her and do all that we need to right now and I will ask you both to leave us to do what needs to be done before you come up to the ICU. You will both be able to come in there when we are ready for you."

(Jamaica. Silver Bay, Jamaica. That's it! I remember Silver Bay…)

Chapter Four

London, 1827

I am back here in London, long before I went to Jamaica and how I came to go there. Yes, it was Silver Bay. I am only nineteen and I am being introduced to Sir Jonathan Harrison. At this time, I am assisting my father, Doctor Roger Goodchild, at his clinic in Harley Street, London. I am my father's only child, and as a woman, I am unable officially to train as a doctor, so my father is teaching me himself. Most of the time my role is as a chaperone to his wealthy female patients, but my father is a good instructor in anatomy and he teaches me every time he has an unusual case. He is a great believer in the use of leeches to withdraw tainted blood from the body and even in maggots to eat away at putrid flesh to leave a clean wound!

His patients are mostly society and aristocratic people, and most of their complaints are everyday illnesses: colds, influenza, aches and pains and an occasional broken bone. He also holds a free charity clinic every Friday two and a half miles across London from here, in St Bartholomew's Hospital, which they call St Barts. I also assist him there and I learn so much more. The poor people of London have so many real illnesses and suppurating wounds that need attention. It is my personal belief that the main difference between the health of the rich and the poor is not only the food that they eat, but most of all, their cleanliness and the conditions in which they live. If a rich man, living in a good clean home injures himself I can clean the wound, wrap it in clean bandages and give the wound time to heal. If a poor man has a similar wound even if I clean it and wrap it in clean bandages, somehow the filth that he lives in will seep into that wound and make the flesh rot. Cleanliness has to be the answer to having a healthy life.

The women who attend our private clinic in Harley Street particularly trust my father and consult him in all aspects of 'female ailments' including monthly menstruation and pregnancy problems. This is when I am most useful. Most of these patients will only let me, as another female, touch their persons, and my father will stand behind the screens explaining their conditions and instructing me in what to do.

My father and I meet Sir Jonathan Harrison when he brings his wife, Lady Amelia, to my father's practice when she is suffering with very debilitating headaches and migraines, and the troublesome effects of going through the ladies 'change of life' – the menopause. Sir Jonathan and Lady Amelia are very pleasant people, and my father and I are soon invited to their country home in Oxfordshire where we meet their three sons. Their eldest son, also named Jonathan, is due to inherit his father's title together along with the bulk of his wealth. Then there is Anthony, already a Captain in the Oxfordshire Regiment of Horse, and finally Charles, a very handsome young man of twenty-two who is exploring the possibilities of working overseas in the British Caribbean territories. Oh! He is so handsome…

Chapter Five

Saturday, 23 January, 2016. 10:00 a.m.
Westover Police Station

Charlie could hardly believe what was happening. How many 'interviews' had he done over the past four years in a 'room' just like this one? He was already well into the fifth series of 'Inspector Holland'. Sitting in a small, drab studio set room with bright lighting and no windows, with just one table and four hard chairs, grey walls and an obvious see through mirror.

Now he was on the other side of the table being interviewed by the real version of his own make believe self. He laughed silently in his own boyish manner, so beloved of his fans.

But he was actually in a state of confusion and shock. What had happened to Mellissa was really just an accident, he hadn't meant to hurt her. He had just got over exasperated with her wilfulness. If only he checked her properly when she had fallen and not assumed that she was dead. That was his biggest mistake. And Panic! Taking her to Westover Wood! How could he have been so stupid? How could he explain it all? Could he keep up the pretence that he knew nothing. How...? DI Hobbs was talking and DS Oliver, sitting at her side, was staring at him in a very concentrated and alarming manner. He had hardly heard what the DI had been saying in the last couple of minutes. Charlie was beginning to sweat.

"Yes, Mr Harris," she said. "But this is real and we are investigating what I believe to be the attempted murder of your wife."

"Am I being charged with murder? Shall I telephone my solicitor?" he asked aggressively, "You can't really believe that I would hurt Mellissa. I love her and I want, just as much as you, to catch the bastard who did this to her. I am sure that they just wanted the Maserati, and she was attacked so that they could steal the car."

"Yes, Mr Harris. Just be calm and let's slow this down a little," said Lavinia in a very soothing tone. She had been warned of his irrational and explosive temper. His star status making him think that he should be treated differently from everyone else. "First of all you are not being charged with anything. We are just having a little chat about you and Mellissa. It was very difficult for us to have a proper talk in the hospital, so I thought that it would be easier for us all to do it here."

She went on, "I am still just at the first stage of my investigation, and all I want from you is a little background knowledge about you and your wife. Where you met? How long you have known her? What she is like? How is your marriage, etc.?

Let's start at the beginning. When and how did you meet?"

Charlie took a deep breath and relaxed into his chair. He ran his fingers through the famous blond hair in that casual manner of his that got all the girls, young and old, wanting to touch him. Ready to adore him and believe every word he uttered. He made it look as though it was an action he did without realising, but actually it was completely calculated, done to get that exact reaction. "I don't know why you would think that it is relevant, but I met Mellissa two and a half years ago when she started work on the set of 'Inspector Holland'. She was a runner and a researcher. Very good at her work, very focused and very popular with the team. In fact, Larry Holmes was very much in the running to be a serious boyfriend, and I was quite jealous of him. I didn't know it then, but she had already fixed her eyes, her beautiful brown eyes, on little old me." He smiled with his boyish, charming grin. "I was smitten with her almost as soon as we started dating and I asked her to marry me within six months of our first date. We were married on 20th June 2014."

"Yes, I remember seeing it on the News. Very charming and beautiful you both looked." Lavinia paused a little and then continued. "How come, if she was so good at it, did she give up her job as TV researcher?"

Charlie hunkered down in his chair and fiddled with the buttons on his jacket. "Well," he said. "I wanted to have a family as soon as possible. She wasn't quite so keen, but we did start trying for a family straight away." He laughed. "That was fun too, you know!" There was even a smirk now.

"That's quite unusual." said Lavinia. "It's normally the girl that wants the hubby and baby scene."

Charlie managed to look shocked and indignant. "Detective Inspector Hobbs," he said in his famous David Holland voice, "you are a prejudiced woman!" Then he paused for a moment and laughed. "Sorry, I shouldn't have said that. I can't quite believe that this is all serious stuff. No, I am sure that there are just as many men married to career girls who resist having babies as there are girls married to men who want to put off the whole dirty nappies and night crying scene. Anyway we weren't having any luck and I persuaded Mellissa to give up the job, which involved hours of rushing around being busy, busy, busy all the time. I loved having her at home all to myself. I was always jealous of the other chaps at work trying to chat her up, knowing full well that she was married to me."

Hm, thought Lavinia. *A jealous and controlling husband. How far does this 'loving' husband exercise control over his darling wife. His beautiful possession?*

DS Oliver spoke up. "You mean," he said very carefully, "that the real reason you wanted her to give up work was to get her away from anyone else, especially men, claiming her attention?"

Charlie bridled, and the handsome blue eyes flashed with icy coldness. "No. That's not right. It wasn't like that at all. All I wanted was for her to relax at home and not have the daily stress of working in a film studio. You know we make one, two-hour episode of DI David Holland every ten days, and there are eighteen episodes in each series. We work very long hours and the pressure is relentless." He paused for a moment, and the two detectives gave him time to collect his thoughts and continue.

"Anyway, it wasn't long after that that we started talking about taking a Caribbean holiday to get away from everything and really chill out at the end of filming this series. I don't know why, but we settled on Jamaica, and I bought her some travel and history books about the island. It was just to satisfy her curious mind and give her something else to think about.

Then she came across her maiden name, Mellissa Goodchild, spelt in that unusual way of hers with two ells in Mellissa, who was both a slave owner and an abolitionist, and she got caught up in the Christmas slave revolt in1831; and she was off again! She went on and on and on about there must be some connection with her and all her research instincts were up and running again. I wasn't getting a look in!"

There's the jealousy again, thought Lavinia. "Do you mean that you were now jealous of her attention being diverted from you once again?" she asked.

"No. It wasn't like that," Charlie started to get annoyed once more. "But we did argue a bit about it."

"Did you hit your wife Mr Harris?" asked the Sergeant, without smiling and looking at Charlie Harris directly into his eyes.

"No. I did not!" Charlie was angry again. He knew that he was lying, but somehow he had come to believe his lie. He stood up and was making for the door. "I would never touch a hair of her head. Do you hear me? I love her with all my heart. I would never hurt her. Now I think that it's time for me to leave this interview. Next time we talk, if there is to be a next time, I will have my solicitor with me."

Lavinia looked at her sergeant and frowned a little. "Well, I think that we will leave it here for now," she said quietly.

"Do you mean I can go?" asked Charlie.

"Yes, but we will still continue our investigations, so don't go off anywhere."

Chapter Six

Saturday, 23 January, 2016, 4:00 p.m.
North London, England

Once Charlie returned home everything that had happened came back to him vividly, and he realised that he was now in deep trouble. Christ! That bloody DI. She's on to me! Fuck. Fuck. Fuck. How can I get out of this?

She wasn't breathing. Oh my darling, what did I do? I was certain that she had no pulse. I was panicking. The love of my life was dead! I didn't mean to slap her that hard! I don't do domestic violence. I have never hit her or any woman before. Oh God! God! God! She must have hit head on that pointed corner bit of the marble kitchen worktop as she fell. How I wish that I had never suggested that bloody holiday in Jamaica or bought her that fancy travel book. Once she had spotted her maiden name, Mellissa Goodchild in the potted history she completely blotted out of our everyday life, and I got angry. She just wanted to find out about that Mellissa Goodchild, whose plantation house was burnt to the ground by slaves. She just would not let go and kept going on and on about wanting to 'trace her roots' in Jamaica? We were fighting, OK? And I hit her, OK? I did not mean to kill her! I love her.

Oh fuck! Fuck! Don't panic. Think!

The next time they call me in I might even be arrested. That DI will say that I murdered her. I couldn't hide Mellissa at home. I really thought that she was dead and I had to get rid of her body. But where? Come on. I had to think. Where? I have played a police inspector for eight years now. DI David Holland. Why didn't I think of a script! Clever DI Holland! What would he be looking for? What clues and traces of a crime would he be picking up? What could I do so that I wouldn't get caught?

Well, I panicked. Why didn't I check her body more closely? How could I have missed a pulse, even if it were only faint? How could I have been so stupid to take her to Westover Wood and dump her there? I took her down the track to the lake. I was sure that they wouldn't find her for days. No one goes there in the wintertime.

Oh God, she was so heavy! Much heavier than she looked! It must be what they describe as 'dead weight'. No, I mustn't laugh. Get serious. They are on to you. It was cold and dark, and I had to get on with it quickly. I was lucky that none of my neighbours were out and about. Just as well the house and driveway is not overlooked by any of them. That's what TV star money can buy – a soap star house in the green belt, in its own grounds. Very private! Not quite a footballer's lifestyle, but not bad for an East End boy!

God, how could she have been so heavy? She's just a tiny thing. But I did get her into the boot of my car. I had to use my car 'cos her car is not big enough to fit her body into. It's a ten-minute drive to Westover Wood, so I expected to be back before people started coming out for their Friday night fun. If I had met anyone, I would have pretended that I was looking for her. She had telephoned me when I was on the set yesterday afternoon. I'll say that she telephoned to say that she was leaving. I remembered to take her handbag. She would never have gone off without a handbag. Why didn't she take her own car? I'll say that she found the spare keys of mine, then she waited for me to go into the house, slipped out without me seeing her, and then she took mine. My brand new Maserati! Just to spite me! Yes. So I used the spare keys.

Oh God! It was awful. I looked at my shoes. They were plastered in mud. I thought that it would get all over the car. Then I remembered, there was a spare pair in the boot. Then when I opened the boot I saw all the blood. How could there be so much blood from such a little wound?

I had to get rid of the car. My super new Maserati. Cost me one thousand and eighteen K, and her blood was all over the boot. First place the cops would be looking at. Then it started raining! Oh hell! What the heck could I do? I decided to torch the car.

Chapter Seven

London, 1827

My father is always calling me his beautiful and clever daughter, but when I look into the mirror in my bedroom all I see is a short and dumpy girl with dark blond hair, and pretty brown eyes set in a plain round face. I'm sure that the beauty and charm that Charles Harrison and his parents see in me is that I am the only child of a very wealthy man, a widower with no other demands on his money, his wealth making up for his lack of any aristocratic breeding. Not quite of their standing in society, but not 'trade' either. They know that I will have a very sizable dowry. My knowledge of medicine does not matter to Charles at all, except that I will be able to look after him when the family buys the sugar plantation in Jamaica, which is almost the whole topic of their conversations. And, of course, my knowledge of medicine might keep the valuable slaves that come with the plantation, healthy and strong enough to do their work.

Needless to say, I have fallen head over heels in love with Charles Harrison, and I do believe that he loves me too, and not just my dowry. And very soon our engagement is to be announced in all the society newspapers. My father tries to explain to me how life will be living on a sugar plantation, the horrible lives that slaves are forced to live, working in the hottest of climates from dawn till dusk They are treated like cattle, he says, possessions that can be bought and sold, away from friends and family. He has even heard of small children being sold away from their mothers if the mothers are required to satisfy their masters in lascivious ways. But there is a lot of talk nowadays about the abolition of slavery, and those slaves on the plantations will become indentured servants and labourers. I hope that it happens because I can see that Charles and I can make their lives better.

I am too much in love to listen to my father and Charles tells me that his plantation is to be a haven of good treatment, a semi-paradise for the three hundred odd slaves who live there. No one will be whipped, or badly treated. They will have lives very similar to our own servants and tenant farmers, he says. Families will not be broken up and sold away from the plantation. He says that the only way to get good harvests is to have all the slaves working together in happy unison, eating well and living in contented family groups. And I believe him!

"It's only because you are afraid of losing your assistant that you are saying all these horrid things about Charles," I cry to my father.

"No, darling," he says, taking me in his arms and kissing me on the top of my head, the way he used to do when I was a little girl. "I have been aware for some time that you will soon be ready for marriage and will want a home of your own. I was even hoping that young Doctor Martins might please you and then you could both be partners in my practice."

"How could you even think that father," I reply quite crossly. "You know that I don't like even being in the same room as Dr Martins, what with all his snifflings and coughings and sallow spotty skin!"

"I know," sighs father. "I have realised that you two have no liking for each other. But, in anticipation of you leaving me I have already been talking with midwife Braxton about the possibility of her joining our practice and teaching her to extend her training into general medicine the same way that I teach you."

I am really angry now. "Mrs Sally Braxton!" I exclaim. "The widow next door! I know that since mother died two years ago she has been trying to replace her in your affections. She never stops with all her simpering and invitations to supper. And now you suggest replacing your daughter too! How dare you!"

"I have been doing so just because I really do recognise your need to marry and have a home of your own," repeats my exasperated father. "But I never, in the world, expected that home to be on the other side of the world, and you living in nightmare conditions."

I am moving. I am moving. What is happening to me?

Chapter Eight

Saturday, 23 January, 2016, 1:00 p.m.
Wallchester General Hospital

DI Hobbs, DS Oliver and Charlie Harris found their way to the anti-room outside Ward 2 of the ICU having travelled there from the Wallchester Police Station together. There they met again with the consultant neurologist, Dr Akami who confirmed that Mellissa was now under complete medical sedation, a medically induced coma.

"Inspector Hobbs, Mr Harris," said Dr Akami, "before you enter the ICU, I must prepare you for what you will be seeing. You and Mr Harris must not be frightened or concerned when you see Mrs Harris. The scan showed that she did have a bleed between her skull and her brain, but fortunately we have been able to drain it away. As well as the bandages now enveloping her head, she has now been intubated, which means she has had a tube inserted down her throat linked to a machine which has taken over her breathing. She has been anesthetised by way of a needle inserted directly into a vein in her neck which has a tube attached with a controlled drip of anaesthetic. A consultant anaesthetist and her team will be monitoring Mrs Harris at all times, day and night so that she cannot be over sedated.

You will also see a tube inserted into her chest, leading to her stomach, which is delivering a feeding fluid directly. Food has been reduced down to its simplest form, the main basic elements of what we eat as life sustaining food; mostly water and in that water is suspended a calculated quantity of essential minerals, plus the basic building blocks of food; fats, carbohydrates, proteins and vitamins. She won't be needing any nappies as she won't be producing any faeces, but she does have catheter inserted directly into her bladder to drain away her urine which is collected into a bag on a stand next to her bed.

"Yuk!" Was Charlie's response. "So, can I go in now?" he asked. "I am not worried about all the tubes and things. I just want to see my wife."

"Yes, you can go in now," said Mr Akami, "but mind what I said. I'm sure that it will still be a shock for you."

And, giving a backward smirk to Lavinia and the DS, he left them in the anti-room to go into the ICU.

Once Charlie had left the room Lavinia spoke to the consultant. "Dr Akami," she asked, "do you now have a prognosis for Mrs Harris; how long she will be in this coma, and how soon you will be able to bring her out of it?" While she understood what the doctors needed to do to keep Mellissa alive and bring her back to full consciousness, she was eager to get on with her police investigation and get the details from her victim directly. Straight from the horse's mouth as it were!

"I also need to know," she continued, "how safe she will be here. We still don't know why she was attacked and by whom. I'm not convinced that her attacker could be stopped from coming in here and interfering either with her medication, or tampering with all those life supporting machines."

"DI Hobbs," replied the consultant in a deep and rather hurried voice. He was now anxious to get on with what needed to be done, and not waste his time talking to the police, especially as there was nothing that he could achieve while his patient was under sedation. "As you know this is an ICU ward, and she will have to have twenty-four hour monitoring for the next few days. She will not be left alone at any time, and there will be no opportunity for anyone to come into this ward to do her any harm. In fact, the only non-hospital persons who will be admitted will be yourself, your sergeant and, of course, her husband."

"Is she dying?" asked DS Oliver.

"No." said the doctor. "She is not in any direct danger for the present. But she is in that deepest stage of coma from which she will either return to us in the next few days or she might stay this way for months, even years."

"And I am no further on in my investigation," sighed Lavinia. "Dr Akami, will it be alright if my sergeant, he is Detective Sergeant Oliver by the way, for him to stay in the ward if he sits in a corner? I am still very concerned about Mrs Harris' safety. I still think that there is a possibility that whoever did this to her may try and prevent her from waking up."

Dr Akami looked at the DS, Lavinia's right hand man. He was a young man of about twenty-eight, slightly scruffy and slightly overweight. *You could do with a lot less food and a lot more exercise*, he thinks!

"Good afternoon, Sergeant," said Dr Akami. "I really don't think that Mrs Harris will be in danger here, there will be me and my nursing staff in and out of the unit, at regular times, all day and night. The room will have a constant flow of highly trained ICU nurses, none of whom will leave the patient unattended at any time. There will also be anaesthetics team, who will monitor Mrs Harris at least three times a day and during the night, plus myself and my team of neurosurgeons. I don't want unnecessary people who will add extra clutter to the ward and possibly bring in unwanted germs and bugs. We have to keep our patients in the ICU as risk free from possible infections as we can, but I have no objection to you sitting in the anti-room outside here as long as you don't get in the way."

"Thank you, Doctor," said Sergeant Oliver.

"Before I leave," said Lavinia, addressing her sergeant, "I would like to have a quick update on how I think the case is going."

She turned to face the consultant. "Thank you Dr Akami for all you help and your patience with us. Thanks. We'll leave you to your patient. But please call me, or get my sergeant to call me if there is any change in Mrs Harris. Good or bad." She smiled her thanks as Dr Akami left them to follow Charlie into the ICU.

Once they were settled in the comfortable seating in the anti-room, Lavinia spoke confidentially to DS Oliver. "I think that there are only two viable options to what has happened to Mrs Harris. First is that she wanted to punish her husband for his petty-minded jealousy, pinch his car and get it all muddied up and spoilt. And then there just happened to be one or more individuals up in Westover Wood who see an expensive car and a woman at the wheel driving erratically. And on the spur of the moment he or they decide to take it from her. When she has stopped the car, they open the driver's door, pull her out and wallop her one. Then they take the car and leave her in the wood, where she crawls the 200 metres to the roadside where I found her.

Problem No.1, what did they hit her with? The doctors and the forensic team agree the main wound is even and clean.

Problem No.2, having gone to all that trouble and committing GBH, attempted murder even, why did they then take such an expensive car to the Common and set it alight? Were they feeling guilty? Did they lose their nerves? It's all a bit unlikely, isn't it?"

Before the DS could reply she carried on.

"This is my other theory, and the one I think more likely. I think that Charlie Harris and his wife have a real ding-dong of a fight, and that he hits her, slaps her face, or something, and she falls hitting her head on something with clean, with sharp edges. Remember what the doctor said, that there was bruising on her face as well as the head wound. I am in the process of getting a search warrant so that we can have a forensic team search the house. Difficult job because he's rich and famous and has a huge following. And by now he will have a skilful lawyer looking after his interests.

But for all his protestations of love, I think that he did it. Then he panics, thinks that he has killed her, puts her in his Maserati because her car is too small to get a dead weight body into. He drives her to Westover Wood and leaves her by the lake thinking that no one will find her until springtime. No one usually goes down by the lake in the winter, it is often flooded and extremely muddy.

Then he goes back to the car and sees that it is covered in blood, the inside or the boot, or wherever he placed her. He panics again and all he can think of is driving a couple of miles to Westover Common and setting the car alight to get rid of all the evidence. Completely incinerate it. Over £100,000 would you believe! His insurance will pay up!

I think he did it and I think that he might return here at some quiet time, maybe at the dead of night, and interfere fatally with his wife's monitoring and life-saving equipment. Remember the doctor said that he would be one of the few privileged people allowed to visit and have access to her. Even if she is attended by at least one person, day and night, I don't think that it would be impossible for him to trick one of them to leave the room for a minute or two. Then 'bingo' he does the dirty deed! That's why, Sergeant Oliver I want you to stay on your guard. Constantly. No going off to the coffee machine or to buy cakes from the café unless you have a proper replacement. Constable Withers is still out side in the corridor, so you must work with him."

"Yes, Mam," said the Sergeant. "I think that I agree with you and I shall take all the precautions necessary to make sure that Mrs Harris remains safe."

Part Two

Jamaica, 1829
Silver Bay Plantation

Chapter One

18 July, 1829

Kingston

They stood hand in hand on the foremost deck, watching the magical sunrise in the eastern skies. "Look! Look Charles," whispered Mellissa, afraid of breaking the spell. "I can see a smudge on the horizon. It must be Jamaica."

It was, and as they sailed nearer and nearer the smudge became a jewel. An emerald set in the sparkling blue sea. The blues and greens of the waters seemed almost luminescent. Fishes and dolphins accompanied the ship as it made its way towards the port, the dolphins riding on the bow waves at the front. Gradually the details of the island became clearer; the high central mountains, the tops still covered in morning mist, the wonderfully different shades of greens, reds and purples of the jungle which covered the island on all sides, and then the buildings of Kingston becoming more and more defined. Birds of all kinds, especially gulls were accompanying them into the harbour, shrieking and whirling about the ship in a noisy but exciting welcome to their new home.

Charles and Mellissa were excited. After four weeks at sea they were ready to disembark. They were standing amongst their luggage at the rail watching all that was going on in the busy harbour as the ship was manoeuvred into its docking place. Half an hour later, having taken leave of Captain George Truman, they stepped off the ship and into the bustling port of Kingston. Before Mellissa could take in the sights and smells of her new surroundings the stifling heat onshore hit her as if she had walked into a brick wall. There had been many hot, extremely hot, days during the crossing, but there had always been sea winds or even just light breezes to take the edge off the heat coming directly from the scorching sun. Now it was relentless and Mellissa could hardly take in anything for want of fresh, cool air to breathe in. She staggered on the quayside and Charles took hold of her arm.

"Steady on, Old Girl," he said and held her tightly.

"It's so hot," she gasped, "I can't breathe."

"You'll get used to it in a couple of days," Charles said with a chuckle and gave her an encouraging squeeze around her waist.

"Couple of days!" Mellissa exclaimed. She was in a near faint. Her lightest lawn cotton dress, which aboard ship had felt like whisper floating around her, was already hanging like a damp rag and sticking to her heavily perspiring body. "I don't think that I will ever get used to it."

She tried to take in the strange sights and smells of Kingston, the high mountains which formed a background to the Port, and everything around her, but the flies and other biting insects were astonishing and completely unexpected. They buzzed around her so vehemently that she had to use the full veil on her hat to protect her face and eyes, blurring her vision even more. There were ants crawling all over her shoes and up her legs. Ants that started to bite and sting. She looked like a mad woman as she tried to brush them off while swatting at flies around her head. She had read so many books about the animals, birds, plants and even insects of Jamaica, but nothing she had read had prepared her for the astounding quantities of flies and ants that seemed to be everywhere. She felt that she was under attack, and Charles tried hard not to laugh. She felt faint and smothered as she wrinkled her brow in disgust. *I hate it here already,* she thought.

A well-built man of about forty years stepped forward. He was wearing a grubby off-white suit and broad brimmed straw hat, which shaded his unpleasant pale green, almost colourless eyes and his heavily wrinkled face. The white skin of his face and hands were tanned to a leathery brown.

"Mr and Mrs Harrison?" he enquired, taking off his hat to reveal a startling white bald head. "I am James McBride, the overseer for Silver Bay." He spoke with a strong Scottish accent, which Mellissa found hard to understand. She did not know why, maybe it was the accent, or the eyes, but she took an instant dislike to him.

"I have the carriage standing by to take you to the plantation," he said. "It's more than sixty miles from here so we will need to stop overnight, and I have arranged for you to stay at the home of my friend, Mr Jardine who lives near Mandeville, which is halfway between here and St Elizabeth. St Elizabeth is your nearest neighbourhood town, and the Silver Bay Plantation is five miles further on."

He looked at his new employer and his wife and thought that they did not look as if they had the stamina needed to live in Jamaica, especially on a plantation so far away from any townships, and where they would hardly ever meet up with any other white folk. *That Harrison looks like an arrogant bastard to me,* he thought to himself, *an English high and mighty 'Milord'. And she looks as though she would rather be anywhere in the world than be here right now. I think that a strong puff of wind would blow her over. I don't suppose they know about the hurricane season which will be starting in a couple of months or so.*

McBride had hoped that when the Johnstons sold Silver Bay, the new people would remain in England, like so many other plantation owners, and leave him as boss in charge of their Jamaican money maker.

Oh well, he thought, *I had better get used to them if I want to keep my position and all the money making extras that go with it that only I can make happen. Although it makes my skin crawl I must keep myself humble and polite. Hopefully they will be like the Johnstons who turned a blind eye to my 'enterprises', and left most of the running of the plantation to me.*

He put his hat back on. "Mrs Harrison," he continued in a servile voice, "it will be much more comfortable and cooler for you once we are on our way. The movement of the carriage will bring you some relief from the heat, and from the flies and the ants too. The weather here in Jamaica is normally much cooler than this. Unlike England, we don't usually have a huge change of temperatures during the year. But it is just that this particular week an unexpected and unusual hot spell has arrived. I'm sure that it will cool down in a couple of days and the temperature will return to normal."

"That will be a relief," gasped Mellissa. "I can barely breathe at all."

He handed them up into the comfortable open carriage, with two beautifully groomed matching bay horses in the traps, and took from the front seat a water skin to give to his new boss. "Here," he said with a cheerful, but false looking smile, "take a drink from this. I filled it up not long ago from a crystal clear mountain stream." He handed it to Charles who took a deep gulp. The water was sweet but had warmed up somewhat. He pulled a face and passed the water skin over to Mellissa.

"Here you are, Old Girl," he said. "Take a swig of this. It's wet and warm, but it's better than nothing!"

"Thank you Charles," she said, "but I must rid myself of the ants first." She was twisting about in her seat and trying, unsuccessfully, to brush them away.

"Abraham over there," said McBride, "will put all your luggage on the wagon and will follow us back to Silver Bay." He pointed to an aging black man who was standing quietly in the background holding the reins of another two horses. The Negro had a bent back and a head of tightly curled white hair which had a large bald spot in the centre, and a look of complete weary servitude on his face. The horses he was holding were attached to a large wagon, and were impatiently pawing the ground, ready to be on their way again.

Mellissa lifted her veil and looked at Abraham. *Oh dear,* she thought. *He does not look as though he is strong enough or fit enough to lift those heavy boxes which we brought with us. McBride should have brought a younger, fitter man; this one should be on light duties. I must see what I can do for him when we get to the plantation. I hope that Charles and I can make some difference to the lives of our people there.*

She put up her parasol as soon as she was settled into the carriage. A comfortable light breeze picked up almost immediately, and she breathed a sigh of relief. She lifted the veil and folded it back on her hat, keeping it secure with a large, gilded hat-pin and looked around. It was the first time that she really noticed her surroundings. The port was bright and bustling, quite unlike the drizzly port of Tilbury outside London, from which they had left England. Almost all the workers here in the port were Negroes, mostly men but there were a few women there too. At home in London, Mellissa had hardly ever seen or spoken to any black people. Those few that she had met were usually the maids or servants of her father's patients and the few she had seen loading the ships in the London docks; and now it would seem that she would be surrounded by them, hardly a white face to be seen. She felt a little uncomfortable and just a little bit frightened too. Almost all the talk since she had met the Harrisons had been about Jamaican plantations, sugar cane and slaves, but somehow she had failed to realise what the reality would be. To be almost entirely surrounded by black faces, and especially how it would feel to 'own' men and women. She looked behind the carriage and saw Abraham preparing to drive the heavily laden wagon which was now behind them. *I, no, we own that man. He belongs to us in the same way that all these horses belong to us!* She shivered with revulsion.

She tried to put those thoughts to the back of her mind as looked across the port to the town beyond. Lots of timber houses of all shapes and sizes, some in straight lines and some just scrambled together, with a background of that huge and very beautiful mountain range. Contrasting with the town and the mountain backdrop was the glimmering blue ocean; every view in every direction was stunning.

McBride climbed up into his seat at the front of the carriage and started to drive into the town. They drove through a market where many black women, dressed in brightly coloured cotton dresses and headscarves, were selling their wares. There were clusters of small children around them, some working alongside their mothers and the smaller ones running and tumbling around the market place. Many beautiful examples of local handicrafts, exotic fruits of all kinds, most of which were completely new to Mellissa, were on display. It was so colourful a scene, so exciting, that Mellissa found that she had recovered enough to want to get down from the carriage to take a closer look at the strange and fascinating things and people all around. A Negro woman with a small baby slung in a red and blue coloured shawl across her back approached the carriage. "Here, lady," she said, her Jamaican accent sounding pleasantly strange to Mellissa's ears, "would you like to try my sweet oranges, only half a penny for three."

Before Mellissa could reach out for the tempting fruit, one she actually recognised because she had eaten oranges at Christmas time in London, McBride turned around in his seat and roared at the woman. "Clear off, you nigger bitch. Take your filthy hands off the lady!" Simultaneously he swiped at her with a short whip which caught her across her proffered arm, and she dropped her fruit.

"Oh! No!" Mellissa called out. She was startled and angry. "Don't…"

"You cannot let any of these black bastards take advantage of you, especially the freed ones," shouted McBride. "They know that you are newly come to the island and they will all want to take advantage of you, and rob you blind."

"But…!" exclaimed an outraged Mellissa. Charles stopped his wife from saying more with a quiet squeeze of her hand. "Please Mellissa," he said quietly, "don't make a fuss. We don't want delays. Let's just get on our way to our new home."

Mellissa contained her disappointment in her husband for not standing up to McBride, and her anger at the cruelty of McBride as they continued on their way through the colourful streets of Kingston. She was wondering how soon they would be able run the plantation on their own, and get rid of him. Then in a side street Mellissa saw a different kind of market. Here, chained together, were two black people dressed in rags, a man and a woman who looked roughly between the ages of twenty and thirty. They were being pushed and pulled towards low wooden platform. The woman was completely overcome with tears. The man had his arms around her and held her as closely as he could while they were dragged onto the platform. Now a rather shocked Mellissa asked in a quiet voice, "What's going on there?" Although she was somewhat afraid that she already knew what the answer would be.

"John Sexton is selling his house slaves, man and wife together. He is preparing to go back to England and needs to raise as much cash as he can. He will sell them as a pair if he can find willing buyers, but if not, they will be sold separately," said McBride, quite matter-of-factly, with absolutely no feeling at all. It was as if he was talking about selling apples!

"Oh no! Can we not buy them Charles? It would be cruel to separate them," cried Mellissa. She glared at McBride, her dislike of him now showing openly.

"My sweet darling," replied her husband. "We cannot buy up every slave that we see being put for sale. You have come to settle into our own plantation, not to play the charity goddess. We don't even know yet how the plantation is supplied with workers or how it is run."

He did not see the grimace that his overseer had on his face. McBride was thinking, *how dare the little rat question the running of the plantation knowing that it is my job. I can do it very well without his interference!*

Mellissa had started to cry. "I thought that it had become illegal to sell slaves now. That everyone was starting to treat them as workers, proper human beings and not slaves."

"That is not going to happen," said McBride, who was listening to their conversation. "The niggers will stay as slaves. What has become illegal, unfortunately, is the slave trade from Africa, not the owning and selling of niggers already living here." McBride was now showing his resentment at the interference, as he saw it, of the goody, goody preachers back home in England. "I have nothing but contempt for those softy abolitionists living in softy England. They are trying to ruin the way of life of those of us living and working in the colonies to bring them the very luxuries, such as sugar, coffee and tobacco that they rely on and use without thinking how those luxuries are produced."

Charles saw interesting times ahead! Did he agree with his new overseer or would they soon be clashing in opposing arguments? He saw that he would have to tread a careful line between his wife and the Silver Bay overseer.

There was an uncomfortable silence as they left Kingston behind and followed the road which ran alongside the coast. The water was sparkling blue near the white sands of the beaches, and a deep green further out. The beaches were divided from one another by rocky outcrops and stands of palm trees. Mellissa broke the silence. "Charles," she said, "what are all those green lumps clustered around the top of the palm trees? They are palm trees, aren't they?"

Before Charles could answer McBride turned his head around and answered for him. "The palms here are coconut palms," he said, "and the 'green lumps', as you call them, are coconuts, the fruit of the palm tree."

"Fruit?" queried Mellissa. "They look as hard as cannon balls."

"You are right, Mistress Harrison," said McBride. "The outside husk of the coconut is very hard indeed, and it needs to be. The coconuts often fall into the sea and they need the hard outer husk and shell within to survive sometimes many hundreds of miles adrift in the oceans until they can take root and grow into new trees on a faraway shore. But if you open a coconut you would see why we love their fruit. The inner fruit under a hard shell is as tasty a nut as you could find anywhere and as you get to know Jamaican food you will discover the many different ways we have of using it. But one of the best things about a freshly harvested coconut is the milk inside it."

This time it was Charles who questioned. "Milk! How can there be milk in a nut? Surely milk is only made by animals. Cows, sheep and goats!"

McBride laughed. "Well it's not really milk like animal milk. But it is a milky liquid which is lightly sweet and totally delicious. If we see a roadside trader who has fresh coconuts, would you like us to stop so that you can try it?"

"Oh. Yes, please," said Mellissa, quite forgetting for the moment her dislike for McBride.

And it was only a couple of miles further on that they came across a negro family with a beautiful, and exotically colourful stall, displaying of all sorts of vegetables and fruits, including coconuts. McBride stopped the carriage and jumped down, and Charles and Mellissa got down too. McBride pushed away the woman and children who had hurried up to him, and one of the smaller girls fell down and started to cry. McBride took no notice of the fallen child and went straight to the Negro man. "Well, nigger," he said with a snarl and a sneer on his face. "Are those cocos fresh? I don't want any of your stale, old rubbish."

Mellissa ran to the fallen child, but her mother had already gathered her up and was quietly soothing away the tears.

The Negro father, keeping his eyes lowered, said. "Yes sir. My son climbed up the palms this very morning to get those ones," and he pointed to a heap of green coconuts which, to Mellissa, looked twice as big now that they were down on the ground.

"Give me one," demanded McBride, "and take of the top so that the lady can drink the milk."

The man brought out a huge knife and with one quick movement he swung it and cut the top cleanly off one of the coconuts. Then he tipped out the creamy juices into a small bowl. "I climb up to get the coconuts," said the older boy, "and I made that bowl!"

"Did you?" asked Mellissa.

"Yes. I made it from a coconut shell. Papa, hc peel away the husk and chop the nut into two halves. Mama, she scoop out the fruit, and I rub and polish the two shells. I make that bowl and this one too," he said excitedly, pointing to a matching bowl on the stall.

"You are very clever," said Mellissa. But before she could say any more McBride brusquely took the bowl from the father and handed it to her. With a frown on her face she held the coconut shell very tentatively, brought it up to her nose and smelled the milky liquid, then took a tiny sip. Then she smiled and took a deep drink. "Charles, you have a taste. It's delicious!" she exclaimed. "I don't know how to describe the taste. But it is delicious."

Charles took the bowl from her and gave it a try. "You're right. It is delicious. "Thank you," he said, and gave the Negro a half-penny. "Is that enough?" he asked.

The man nodded without smiling and McBride laughed. "Of course it is enough. He is lucky that you gave him anything at all!" With that he tossed the empty bowl back to the Negro mother and hurried Charles and Mellissa back into the carriage, and they were on their way once more.

Mellissa shut her eyes and laid back amongst the comfortable cushions of the carriage. The coconut milk was nice, but she was still unhappy about the way McBride treated the Negro men and women that they had come across so far. *How did he treat their slaves? What have I come to? She asked herself. Will I ever get used to this place?* She listened as Charles plied McBride with questions about their plantation. The numbers of slaves that he now owned? The state of the crops? Was it all sugar cane? When would harvest time begin? How was the harvesting done and did they have enough slaves to do the work?

The warmth of the day and the motion of the carriage made her sleepy. With her eyes still shut she now heard a hard edge to her husband's voice, a hard edge that she had never heard before. He, too, was now talking about slaves as if they were just cattle. Was this the tender, loving man she had learned to adore in the last few months? Especially the lover who had awakened her senses to passions of her body that she never knew existed.

The thought of her night-time love making with her new husband was making her blush. Under her parasol, still with her eyes shut, her cheeks and neck reddened more and more, and she sank low amongst the cushions of the carriage to hide her shame. As a medically trained woman she knew all about a woman's body, but she had never examined her own before her marriage. Now she had become a thing of the night, each day waiting for the sun to go down so that once more her husband could touch her secret places, when she would become a harlot in her husband's arms. In her sleepiness and semi-dreamlike state she was throbbing and getting quite wet at the very thought of his touch and tongue between her thighs, and her cheeks turned from red to scarlet.

("Sergeant, will you please stop that mobile phone from ringing," said an irritated Dr Akami. "We are trying to adjust her anaesthetic. No noise please.")

She forced herself awake with a start. *I must take control of myself,* she thought, *and stop that mobile phone from ringing. What was she thinking? What on earth is a mobile phone?* She opened her eyes and saw that she had moved her hand from her lap to the inside of her husband's thigh. She quickly removed it, but he had not noticed. Neither had he noticed her high colour and her embarrassment. He was still talking to McBride about niggers, black

45

bitches and sluts. *Did Charles think that she was a slut too?* She sat up and looked around, mobile phones and sluts forgotten.

Charles was now talking to McBride about the daily running of the plantation. "It will be three days that you will have been away from Silver Bay in order to meet and bring us to the plantation, so who is in charge while you are away?"

"We have a freed nigger called George, who is my number one man," said McBride. "He is a big, strong man and all the slaves respect him and follow his orders."

"How come a freed black man, who was once a slave, will oversee black men like himself? The Johnsons never mentioned a second overseer who is employed at Silver Bay," queried Charles. "I wonder why?"

"He ain't exactly employed," explained McBride. "But we do give him a shilling a week."

"Only a shilling! Then what keeps him at Silver Bay? And where does his loyalty lie, with us or with the slaves?"

"Oh! He is loyal enough to Silver Bay," chuckled McBride. "He is married to one of our slaves, Marigold, and they have two boys of thirteen and fifteen called Joe and Paul. It's Marigold and the boys who keep him loyal. He knows that we can sell any of them away from Silver Bay at any time."

Mellissa, who was now wide awake, joined in the conversation. "That is horrible. We would never do that. We would never split up a family, would we Charles?"

"Of course not, Old Girl."

"So," Mellissa continued, "do the slaves marry each other, and who performs the ceremony?"

"Before the Johnsons, the owner of Silver Bay was a Baptist Minister called Sydney Bishop. Funny that, a Baptist called Bishop!" McBride chuckled, more to himself that to his new employers. "He married any of the slaves who seriously wanted to be married. I was even told that he performed the ceremony himself, and provided a simple wedding ring."

"What happens now-a-days if two slaves want to wed?" asked Mellissa.

"Well they just hold a slave party in the compound and declared themselves 'married' in front of everyone, and then they move in together, or build themselves a new cabin."

They had left Kingston far behind now and they were still driving along the coastal road with the most fantastic and beautiful views of blue seas, jungle and soaring mountains. A flock of brightly coloured birds flew overhead and Mellissa gasped at the wonderful colours of their feathers. "What are those birds?" she asked in voice full of wonder and delight. "Brilliant bright reds and blues. And I can see bits of other colours too. They are so beautiful."

"Oh, they're only parrots, macaws actually. There used to huge flocks of them here in Jamaica, but people have been hunting them and now there are not so many," said McBride.

"Why would anyone hunt and kill such beautiful birds?" asked a curious Charles.

"Because of those pretty coloured feathers. The hunters are well paid by traders who sell them back in England to milliners. You know how women like to have brightly coloured feathers, especially in their hats. But just you wait until you see the real beauties of this island, the humming birds. They will make your heart stop with sheer delight."

Mellissa said no more. She was thinking about one of her hats that she had brought from England. It had bright feathers just like those birds, and she had never even wondered where they came from. She felt ashamed.

It was mid-afternoon now, and McBride pulled into a wayside inn. It had a pretty tumbling waterfall running down a rock-face and into a small stream which ran along the side of the building and an abundance of palm trees, their leaves waving in the light winds, planted all around. Abraham, who had been following them in the wagon, pulled in beside them. "Look after the horses," McBride said curtly.

"Yes, Massa," said Abraham. He tied up the four animals and then went off to get some water from the stream. Having had a fitful sleep overnight on the floor of the stables at the dockyard, Abraham was tired, hungry and thirsty, but he knew that he had better water, curry and feed the horses before he could drink or even ask for some food for himself.

As soon as she got down from the carriage Mellissa was, once again ambushed by flies. McBride took no notice of her discomfort and quickly led the way into a small, pleasant looking building. She looked back at Abraham but said nothing as she followed Charles, both of them groping their way through the darkened room with eyes blinded by the contrast between the sunlight outside and the small dark interior. There was only one other person in the tap room, and he was sitting at the bar. "Good day, Jones," said McBride, and he introduced Charles and Mellissa to a young man, thin as a stick and dressed in neat cotton clothing. "Jones is the assistant overseer at the Selhurst plantation, about five miles from here."

"Good day, Mr and Mrs Harrison," said the man called Jones. "I've heard that there was to be a new owner of the Johnston's plantation over at Silver Bay. It's a good plantation, good soil, very workable and very productive. And a fine team of docile slaves. I hope that you will both be happy there."

"Yes," said McBride. "The Johnston's owned and lived on Silver Bay for fifteen years. That's a good long time out here."

"Fifteen years!" exclaimed Charles and Mellissa in unison. They had talked together about living in Jamaica for about three years, four years at the most, making a fortune and going back home, rich! Now they looked at each other and Charles continued, "Well, if they could do it for so long, I am sure that we will make it through this first day!" And everyone laughed.

A barman appeared from the back room and Mellissa was given a drink of watered down rum. "Good health!" she said as she sipped it. "So different from the usual ales and wines, and teas that I am used to, but I like the light sweetness of the flavour."

"That's just as well," laughed McBride. This was the first time that Mellissa had seen a genuine smile on his face. "You will find that rum, which is made from sugar cane molasses, is just about all we drink here in Jamaica! A good quantity of our crop is sold to a local rum maker, and one of the best it is too. They call it the Fire Rum of Jamaica." He turned to the barman. "Have you a bottle of Fire Rum on your shelves. Show it to the lady!"

Mellissa took it and inspected the label, but being ignorant of how sugar is produced and what molasses was, she said nothing. She saw in the corner a black barmaid who was polishing a table and trying to look inconspicuous, and she went over and asked her to show her to the ladies powdering room so that she could relieve herself and be brought some clean, cold water to freshen up her face and neck. On her way back to the men she overheard their conversation as she approached. McBride and Jones were discussing the control of niggers. "I like to use a bullwhip," said McBride. He took out his whip from the back of his waist band and swung it around the room. "It settles well in the hand and it has a long reach, and a crack like a bullet!"

"Let me have a feel of that," asked Charles. McBride handed the whip over with a frown, and Charles took hold of it and swung it lightly. "Yes, it has a good feel to it. I would like to give it a good crack outside," he said laughing.

Mellissa was shocked. Would Charles really like to use such a thing on a man? Then she remembered another conversation which she had overheard a long time ago between Charles and his eldest brother, Jonathan when they had been arguing in the hallway of their home in Oxfordshire. She had been about to descend the stairway, but held back when she heard raised voices.

"Charles," said Jonathan, "we cannot raise production on Blackberry Farm. Jethro Manning has broken his leg and his wife has six small children to care for. She can just about manage to look after the pigs but neither of them can do any heavy work."

"Then just get rid of them. Evict them!" Charles had exclaimed. "There are plenty of strong men out there begging for work."

"We can't do that," replied Jonathan. "The Mannings would starve. Roam the countryside begging and starving."

"That's not your concern," said Charles. "Production and profit. That's all you should be thinking about and acting upon. Profit!" He was really getting his anger up and letting his jealousy of his older brother show. "My God, if only I had been the first born, the one to inherit this land…"

"Charles. Charles. We cannot do that. Those people are fellow human beings…"

"Yes, yes. But this is family, and this estate is being run into the ground because of your and father's soft hearts. The whole family relies on the production of our tenant farmers and if you allow them to fail in production, in meeting their quotas then everyone, including you and mother and father will starve."

"Hardly that, Charles!"

By then Mellissa had retreated silently, back to her bedroom and remained there until she felt it safe to come down. She did remember that Jonathan, much to Charles's annoyance, had rejected his brother's advice and had not evicted the Mannings. He had brought in two young men who had come on his land begging for work. And for the following two seasons they had helped with the pigs and in return were fed and sheltered by the Mannings. When Manning had recovered sufficiently to look after the pig farm by himself, the men had been forced to leave and look for work elsewhere. Work that was not always easy to find when the seasons were bad and crops failed.

The cracking of the whip brought her back to the present. *Oh my God!* exclaimed Mellissa to herself. *Is this really the man I have married? My very own gentle, and not so gentle, night-time lover? Surely the owning of slaves will not turn him into a brute. What* were *all those promises about the gentle treatment of their 'workers'? Had he meant it? Perhaps it would be up to her to take the lead and hope that he will follow.*

Chapter Two

19 July, 1829
Silver Bay Plantation

Nearly home! After a long and tiring journey and an uneventful night spent at the pleasant home of Mr Joshua Jardine, Charles and Mellissa were at last travelling on their own land. They had started out at dawn in the cool morning air and by late-morning they had at last reached the outlying fields of the Silver Bay plantation. The unusually high temperature had cooled to the normal weather for Jamaica, just like a pleasant hot summer's day in England. As they drove along roads dotted with palm trees and cleared through the jungle, they had seen many flocks of parrots, which were so beautiful but very noisy in their continual squabbling and squawking, and plenty of colourful butterflies; but so far they had had no sighting of any elusive humming birds. Now, as it had been for the last few miles, the picturesque vistas of blue seas and jungles had disappeared behind field upon field of sugar cane. The canes, planted row on row, were at least ten feet high and nothing could be seen except the canes swaying in the light winds and a wide roadway running through. Mellissa sighed, sounding like a small child and swallowed her dislike of McBride, asking him how soon they would arrive at their new home.

"We have gone beyond St Elizabeth and we are now only two miles from High View, that's the name of the plantation house, and the slave compound," he replied.

"What sort of town is St Elizabeth and do we at the plantation go there often?" she asked.

"It is probably nothing like anything you know as a town back in England," said McBride. "It is more like a village except it has no village green. Instead you will find small wooden buildings, wooden sidewalks and a dirt road going through it."

"Is there a church and some shops?"

"There is a Baptist church, St Peter's, a plain wooden building with no steeple. In the way of shops there is a general store which sells anything from a candle to a sack of oats, a baker, a small butcher, and a ladies clothing shop, owned by Mistress Gwendoline Smith, where you will find ready-made ladies dresses. Or you can have some made just for you. They also make hard wearing clothing for the slaves of our local plantations."

Mellissa shuddered as she thought of the slaves, some of which she and Charles now owned. "I shall be pleased to visit there. I am sure that we have brought all the wrong sort of clothing for this climate. What else is there in St Elizabeth?"

McBride shrugged his shoulders. "Well," he said, "there is not much more apart from a small hotel with a public bar, and a courthouse presided over by Magistrate Seagrove, a fat and unsmiling man with no humour in his soul. There is a lawyer's office attached to the courthouse and of course there is a blacksmith.

By then they were starting to climb, as the road wound up the side of a hill McBride pointed ahead, "You will see the sea again from the top, and you will be seeing your new home sitting squarely on the crest of the hill and you will have those views of the sea from your veranda. The house is surrounded at the back by tall trees which give it protection and also separate it from the slave compound which is lower down the other side of the hill behind and to one side of the house."

"Why is the plantation called Silver Bay," queried Mellissa, "if we can only see the ocean and not the Bay itself? I thought that the plantation house would be overlooking Silver Bay. All I have seen are the trees of the jungle and fields upon fields of sugar cane."

"We are actually not very far from the ocean," replied McBride. "But when the plantation house was first built the whole of the bay could be seen from it. It was the planting of the sugar canes which obscured the view. If we were to cut all of it down at the same time, you would be able to see the bay again."

Mellissa sighed again and said very quietly so that only Charles could hear, "I am just longing to get down from this carriage, go into a cool house, drink some cool water and climb into a large cool bed."

"It won't be long now, my love," he replied. "I think that I am just as tired as you are. But we will probably have to introduce ourselves to everyone first. McBride has arranged a formal welcome for us. So you will have to hold on a bit longer."

"Oh no," was all she could whisper.

"Come on, Old Girl. Stiff upper lip and all that. We can't let the English down. Got to show the darkies what we are made of," said Charles, with a big grin on his face. And he started puffing out his chest theatrically. Mellissa laughed.

At last, they were climbing steadily upwards and along what was a recognisable avenue of trees, and Mellissa was surprised to recognise them as English oak trees. In the distance they could see a fine, white and very handsome building. High View, at last! As they got closer Mellissa, who was intensively interested in what her new home would be like, saw that it was built like a smaller version of an English stately home, with tall white columns reaching to the upper floor, and a wide white stone veranda at the front. There was a flight of steps leading up to the veranda and the main floor of the house, and underneath this main floor was a semi-enclosed, semi-basement which she supposed was used for storage of some sort.

As they neared the house they could see a sea of white in front of it, and then Mellissa recognised a large garden of white roses, divided by the driveway that cut it in two. Surrounding the rose beds and protecting them from the wind were hedges covered with red flowers. Close to Mellissa could see that most of them were hibiscus, which McBride had pointed out on the drive from Kingston. The other shrubs had long bell-like flowers which dangled down. As they approached the house even Charles became excited. They were holding hands tightly and craning their necks to see more of the beautiful garden in front of their mansion, and then they saw to one side a mass of slaves were lined up in a grotesque parody of the servants of a great English country house lined up to greet a new owner, a new wife or an important visitor.

But when they were near enough to see their faces, Charles and Mellissa were startled to see that there were no welcoming smiles and no enthusiastic chatter, and it took a moment or two for them to realise that these were not friendly house servants, they were their new belongings, their chattels – their slaves! McBride stopped the carriage in front of the house to inspect the three hundred and eighty-two people who now belonged to Charles and Mellissa Harrison. Abraham, who was still following close behind, drove the wagon to the back of the house to set about unloading their luggage.

Mellissa sat up tall in the carriage and stared, open-mouthed, as she looked down upon her new belongings. *These are people,* she thought, *how can we possibly own people?* She started to look at them as individuals. They were mostly men, and mostly well built, strong looking Negro men of varying ages and shades of darkness. She was pleased to see that they all looked healthy and well fed. Their clothing was rough but sufficient for the work that they were required to do. She picked out one man in particular who was standing near the front of the men. He was much taller than the rest, very black in colour and he had what looked like African tribal marks on his cheeks. Unlike the other men who had dipped their eyes in a submissive gesture, he stared straight ahead and made direct eye contact with Mellissa; and it was she who conceded first and looked away. She felt a bit of a shiver down her back and wondered about her reaction to that one man. *I must find out about him* was her next thought as she turned her head to inspect the women. They were standing together in a smaller group, four of them obviously in the latter stages of pregnancy, mostly looking at her with defiant eyes. *No submissiveness there,* she thought.

McBride dismounted and stood in front of the slaves with his hands on his hips and addressed them as one of their masters. "This is your new Massa and Mistress, Massa and Mistress Harrison," he said, in a strong, authoritative voice. "You will obey them in all things as you did with Massa and Mistress Johnston. All things." He looked directly at them and started to handle his whip as he were facing down a challenge.

As a reaction to McBride's voice the gathered slaves seemed to change their collective expressions and looked up with blank faces, faces completely devoid of any emotion except dull acceptance. Mellissa realised that McBride was feared and hated by the slaves. She wondered how soon they would be able to do without him and run the plantation in a kinder way that treated men and women as men and women and not animals.

A tall and very well built and handsome Negro man of about forty stepped forward to stand next to McBride. He removed his hat and nodded in the direction of Charles and Mellissa. "This is my assistant, George," said McBride. "He is the one who has been looking after the plantation while I was away."

Charles acknowledged him with a simple, "Thank you, George."

Then he helped Mellissa to get down from the carriage and they stood side by side, and slightly apart from McBride and George. Looking over his new 'property' Charles said, in what was, for him, a light and friendly voice; a voice that he hoped would reassure the slaves that he would be a good, kind Massa, "I have heard nothing but good reports of all my workers on the Silver Bay plantation.

Mistress Harrison and I will be wanting to get to know all of you soon, and Mr McBride will continue directing your work efforts until my wife and I learn more about sugar production and the management of the plantation."

He did not see the scowl on the face of McBride, only the reaction to that scowl. The slaves could see that McBride was afraid of losing some of his power over them and a slight look of satisfaction came over the faces of some of the work-hardened men.

Mellissa turned to go up the stone stairway and she paused as she reached the veranda to look at the view from the top. It was spectacular. The vast fields of sugar cane were rippling in the wind and looked like the sea itself as waves rippled across the surface. And in the distance there was the sparkling blue ocean again, looking cool and welcoming. She sighed as she turned and walked into the house. She was followed by a big strong and handsome woman, only a few years older than herself, who was much lighter skinned than the other slaves. Two young women and a child of about six or seven, also light skinned, came in behind her. "Hello," said Mellissa, "are you all my house servants? Please tell me your names so that we can get to know one another." She looked over them with a ready smile on her face.

She was expecting a reply in a Jamaican accent or even in the local patois which she had already experienced and found very difficult to understand. Instead the big half-caste woman said in very correct English, with a very English accent, but without any reciprocal warmth or smile, "My name is Lavinia, and I am your housekeeper. This is my daughter Angeline," she said taking the child by the hand, "And these two are Roberta and Chloe, they help me with all that needs to be done in this house. Old Abraham, who is unloading your travelling boxes at the back of the house, does the vegetable and flower gardening and all the outside chores."

Mellissa was a little puzzled. Only three women to look after this large house? She thought of all the house servants that the Harrisons employed in their estate home in Oxfordshire. But of course, there in Oxford, there was always a continual stream of house guests and visitors who needed looking after. Here, it was to be only herself and Charles. She hoped that would be enough for them to be happy.

She looked around at her new home. The very spacious open hallway gave the house light and air. There were doors leading off to, which Mellissa supposed were the kitchen, dining-room and study, maybe even a music room. *That would be nice,* she thought.

She was looking forward to taking a full tour of the house perhaps the next day. All she wanted to do right at that minute was to sit, take a cool drink and go straight to bed! She knew that bedtime would have to wait so she sat down in a very comfortable seating area next to a great stairway to wait for Charles to come in. Mellissa looked up. Each side of the stairs was a hunting trophy of a wild boar's head hung on the fine wooden panelling. She shivered and thought that she would get rid of those as soon as they had settled in.

She turned her head to one side and saw a large hall table with a glass case with a most beautiful display of jewel-like little birds, all stuffed and sitting on various perches and twigs. She was intrigued. Getting up she went over to inspect the display more closely as Charles came in and stood quietly beside her.

"Look, Charles," she said with awe and wonder in her voice, and pointing to the display case, "they must be the humming birds that James McBride was talking about. There must be at least a couple of dozen of them. How beautiful and how sad that they are dead." Mellissa bent even closer to examine the display. The bodies of the humming birds were all tiny, not much bigger than her little finger, but their tails were long, some of them more than twice as long as their bodies. The tails and wings were spread showing to the full their iridescent rainbow-coloured feathers. "It's so beautiful and sad at the same time, isn't it Charles?"

"Yes, I agree," he nodded. "Perhaps we will soon see some live ones in the garden. And we can look in the library to see if the Johnston's have left any books with pictures of these birds so that will be able to recognise them."

"Yes, but that will be for another day. A rainy day, if they have any here," said a tired Mellissa. "I just want a brief look around, then a quick bite and a cool dark bedroom."

She looked up the stairway delicately carved in Jamaican hardwood in an intricate pattern led to an upper gallery which went all around the house. *That gallery is delightful*, thought Mellissa and imagined herself looking down upon whatever was going on below. Opening off the gallery were several doors which were probably for the bedrooms. The carved wooden doors were impressive and welcoming; she wondered which one would be theirs.

Chapter Three

First Evening at High View

It was the end of their first day on their new sugar plantation in Jamaica. At last, they were alone together between the silky smooth sheets of their lovely cool bed, which was screened all around with fine cotton netting to keep out mosquitoes and other flying or creeping insects. They lay quietly in each other's arms, all their senses stunned by everything they had seen, touched, heard, tasted and smelled in their new homeland. Mellissa first thought about all the new things that she had seen since their arrival; the most beautiful vistas, such that she had never imagined; even when she had read descriptions of Jamaica, she had not expected such bright, stunning beauty in the land and seas that surrounded them.

Then there were the smells and tastes of the island. Everywhere, the perfumes of the flowers, shrubs and trees were almost overpowering. And the tastes of the food… Even simple foods such as she had often eaten at home, were somehow more powerful, especially with the addition of Jamaican spices which changed ordinary, everyday food into the exotic. Yes, she must use that word again. Everything here is exotic!

And, then above all, the sounds of Jamaica. The non-stop, overwhelming calls of the birds and buzzing of insects. The cicadas, which started their chirping at dusk and continued incessantly all night. Every night! There never seemed to be a peaceful moment just to relax and enjoy a state of mind that was purely restful.

And finally, touch. Well, everything that she touched somehow felt different. Even flowers that she recognised as ones which grew in England were more perfumed, more sticky, more thorny even. The overpowering smell of the vegetation seemed to stick to the plants themselves and make them feel different. How could she describe it, even to herself? Even the furniture in the house and on the veranda felt different. Why was that? How could she explain it when even her own body felt different? So much more sensitive, vibrating with expectancy. Was it Jamaica, or was it that her sensuous body had come alive since Charles had taught her the delights of love-making?

It was the first time since their marriage three months ago that they had not made love with each other or been intimate with each other in some way or another as soon as they got into bed.

Without saying a word to each other they lay quietly, breathing deeply and listening to the loud and continuous chirping of the cicadas outside, each wondering if they would ever get used to being there.

It seemed silly when there was so much to talk about Mellissa could find no words to express her feelings, so instead of saying nothing she broke the silence between them by talking about inconsequential things. "That delicious fish we ate tonight," she said in a sleepy voice only just above a whisper, "I can only describe it as heavenly. Especially how it was enhanced by that cooked fruit that looked like a small sausage. Lavinia said that it was called a banana. It must have been a fruit to be so soft and taste so sweet. Fish and fruit together, I have never tasted such a thing before, but it was delicious. I will ask Lavinia, if I can ever get her to smile at me, to teach me about Jamaican cooking, and their plants, trees, fruits, birds and animals. I want to know everything about this exciting world that we have stumbled into."

Charles turned on his side and looked down on his wife. He smiled, bent over her and kissed her cheek tenderly. "I was more impressed with the size of our plantation," he said, ever the down to earth, practical one. "It seems to me to be almost as large as ten of our tenant farms back at home in Oxford. From tomorrow I will be getting McBride to show me the whole extent of it. At first sight, the cane fields look the same and uninteresting. Field upon field of waving canes.

But McBride told me that the canes take four years to mature from planting to harvest, so the fields are set out in a rotation of growth. I must find out how he manages the size of the plantation with only three hundred and eighty-two slaves. How do the slaves get to the fields that need to be worked on? I suppose they are driven in wagons. Perhaps like the one that old Abraham was driving today? Did you know that McBride gets up with the slaves at five o'clock every morning to supervise their travel to whichever field they work on that day? He wouldn't go with the wagons, he rides his favourite horse called 'Fireball'. And I wonder how does he manage with only two assistants, they themselves being slaves, to control all the others?"

Mellissa was now stirring out of her sleepiness. "I don't like McBride at all," she said quite emphatically. "I think that we will find that his methods of control are cruel, maybe deliberately cruel. Otherwise, why the hostility with which we were received today. Not just an odd hostile face, but everyone, even Lavinia. If they are the happy childlike people that have been described to us, surely there would have been some smiles of welcome. I will have to tread carefully and be gentle with Lavinia and find out what is going on here."

Charles was on the defensive. "Never mind the hostility," he said, "It is probably that they are worried about changes that we will inevitably make, and how their lives will be altered or turned upside-down by those changes."

"Yes," replied Mellissa, quite wide awake now. "Remember the slave sale that we saw, was it only yesterday? A man and his wife sold away from each other at the order of a heartless owner. And everyone around being totally unmoved by the tears and the obvious terror that the two of them were in. How can we white people become so accepting in our power over these unfortunate black people that we don't even see them as people at all?"

Charles was getting a little bit uncomfortable with the way the conversation was going. The last thing he wanted to do was to quarrel with Mellissa or discuss how they were to treat their slaves. He knew her soft heart, and that she wanted to make a happy plantation, full of happy smiling faces. "But it is not our job to make the slaves happy. We are here to produce wealth for our family, and that wealth will only come from the efficient production of cane sugar, and we need the slaves for that efficient production. End of story." He paused, bent down and kissed his bride again and started to stroke her breasts to arousal. "Come on, Old Girl," he whispered into her ear. "Let's cuddle up and celebrate our arrival in the best way we can."

Mellissa giggled. "Oh Charles," she laughed gently, "you are a very naughty boy!"

Chapter Four

Chloe Cuts Her Hand

It took several days to break down the wall of silence about her. Mellissa inspected every room of their new home and was delighted in what she found. The Johnstons had left what seemed like all their furniture and she loved most of it. There was even a music room with a well-tuned piano in it. Their bedroom with its floor to ceiling windows, finest silk wallpapers and huge dressing room, was the largest and most pleasant of the eight rooms on the upper floor. There were no friendly conversations while she and Lavinia were unpacking the numerous tin travelling boxes that they had brought with them from England. Lavinia, Roberta and Chloe were not unwilling to work in the house, indeed they were always at her side to help, but it was always in silence. They spoke to each other in hushed tones when they were not in close proximity of Mellissa, and they spoke to Mellissa only when she asked direct questions. All the answers given were short and to the point. She would often hear chatter between her house servants, she hated to call them her slaves, but as soon as she entered a room where she heard talk going on between them, the talking stopped. Absolute total silence enveloped her like a blanket of disapproval.

Mellissa decided to ignore the hostility as one by one the travel boxes were emptied, and she busied herself in making decisions as to where the contents of each one should be placed. Firstly, their clothing. Why had they brought their full wardrobes, most of which were impossible to wear in the warm climate of Jamaica? Only the lightest of her summer dresses were of use here and for Charles, only his lightweight cotton shirts and trousers were wearable. What had she been thinking of when she had packed her winter clothes and her heavy silk ball gown? Much to her distress Mellissa had already discovered that there was virtually no social life here, let alone evening entertainment and balls.

Her ten boxes of medical equipment remained unopened in a back room downstairs. She had brought them with her because she wanted to help any of the slaves who were sick or injured. She hoped to gain their trust and to make their lives easier. But for now all she felt from those she had come into contact with were waves of hostility and silence. How long, she wondered, before she earned even just a smile from any one of them?

She made great efforts to acclimatise herself to the island in general and the plantation in particular. After two days when the temperature had returned to its normal level, she decided to explore beyond the house and immediate gardens. Every time she stepped outside she was overwhelmed with the sound of the insects and birds and the overpowering smells of the vegetation and flowers. The nearest she had ever experienced like this before was in an orangery and glass house for tropical plants that she had visited in the large stately home of friends of the Harrisons in Oxfordshire.

Today was the day to start to get to know her way around and she began this exploration by asking Lavinia to show her their homes in the slave compound. Lavinia was perfectly polite and amenable but it was in silence that she was taken to a group of four small houses, more like wooden cabins, which were just behind the plantation house. There were three small ones grouped together; one for Lavinia and her daughter Angeline, one for Roberta and Chloe, and the third for Abraham, whose cabin was next to the stables. McBride lived in a fourth cabin which was a little apart from the other three, and was twice as big as the others. Mellissa, slightly embarrassed to be 'nosy', looked only briefly inside through the open doors and saw that the smaller cabins were substantial enough without having any more than basic comfort.

Then she showed Mellissa the banana grove which was just beyond the cabins. All the trees were kept at a height that anyone could reach up and cut the fruit. And what fruit it was. Mellissa had never seen anything like this before. The fruit which looked like long, curved fingers, were growing together in huge bunches. Some were dark green, some were turning yellow, and some were bright yellow. "Is this what you cooked with our fish the first night we were here?" asked Mellissa.

"Yes," replied Lavinia, without any enthusiasm. "Here, I will get you one to try. They don't always have to be cooked." She reached up and separated a bright yellow banana from its bunch.

Mellissa looked on closely as Lavinia tore back the top and pulled down the yellow skin, to reveal a creamy white fruit. "Here," said Lavinia, with a slight smile, "give it a try!"

Mellissa responded to first display of warmth that her housemaid (she still did not like to call her a slave, even to herself) had shown. She took the fruit and bit the top off. "Oh!" she exclaimed, "I liked the cooked one, but this is even better. It's delicious."

"Well, now you know where to find one any time you would like. But make sure that the fruit is bright yellow, or even yellow with a few spots of black on it like that one." Lavinia pointed to a banana which looked as though it was about to fall off the plant and rot on the ground, as some were already doing. "The green ones are unripe and are totally uneatable," she said.

A pretty stream, which had started its journey to the sea far above in the hills that protected the northern side of the plantation and ran crystal clear over its rocky bed, separated the plantation house, the cabins and the gardens of the upper part of the plantation from the rest. The stream then ran along the half-mile-long pathway which led to the slave compound and the working areas of Silver Bay.

Mellissa was about to set off with Lavinia down that pathway which wound down through the trees to the main slave compound of about a hundred and fifty cabins, when they heard a sharp cry from the kitchen of High View. They both ran in and found Chloe cradling her hand, from which blood was oozing down and dripping onto the floor.

"Oh dear, Chloe," said Mellissa, running to her side. "Whatever has happened?"

"The knife slipped. It slipped and cut my hand," she wailed. "It hurts! It hurts!"

"Lavinia, go and bring me one of my medical boxes, the smallest one," called Mellissa over her shoulder, as she led Chloe to a clean bowl at the back of the kitchen, "and please draw some fresh water from the pump."

She examined the cut hand to check that it was not contaminated with any food or anything else that might cause the wound to suppurate, while Lavinia found the box and brought it to Mellissa with a jug of clean water. She was astonished that her new mistress would bother with any small hurt or pain in one of the slaves.

"Yes, that's good. Pour some of that water over Chloe's hand and into that clean bowl, and now over my hands," she instructed, "and then open the medical box and pass me the little red box which is near to the top. Yes, that one with a picture of a flower on the lid."

"Chloe," she said, "that is a deep cut, and it will be better for you if I stich the edges together."

Mellissa washed the hand and patted it dry with a clean cloth. She opened the red box and Lavinia was even more astonished when Mellissa took out a needle and some waxed cotton thread. "See here," she said to both Chloe and Lavinia, "it's as easy as sewing a dress. As long as we keep everything clean the wound should heal quickly and without too much trouble. I'm sorry, but this will prick just a bit," she said to Chloe. "Lavinia you hold her other hand." And very neatly she stitched up the cut which stopped the blood flow almost at once.

"Well done both of you. Now Lavinia will you look into that brown bag and pull out from it one of those strips of linen and that small pot of salve. Thank you," she said to a dumb struck Lavinia who passed to Mellissa the linen strip. Very deftly Mellissa put a thin layer of salve on the wound and neatly wrapped Chloe's hand around with the bandage. "There, that's done," said Mellissa. "Now Chloe you must keep this clean for the next two or three days. No cooking and no cleaning. Keep your hand clean and keep it dry."

She sat back and looked at the astonished faces of her two slaves. Roberta walked into the kitchen and looked wonderingly at the scene in front of her eyes; both Lavinia and Chloe standing with their mouths open like fish out of water. "Whatever has happened?" she asked; at the same time Lavinia enquired, "Mistress, are you a doctor?"

"No," answered Mellissa, happy to have the opportunity to break the ice between them, "I am not a doctor, but my father, who lives in England, is a very good doctor, and I have learned some doctoring from him. His name is Roger Goodchild and he is well known and respected at home in London where I used to live before my marriage to Master Harrison."

"Is your name God's Child too?" asked Chloe.

The ice between them was indeed broken and Mellissa laughed. "Not God's Child, but it was Goodchild like my father, before I was married. In fact, I do believe that our family name was Godchild a long time ago, but it was changed to Goodchild by my grandfather. He thought that Godchild was a little too pretentious."

None of the slaves knew what pretentious meant, but Lavinia was thinking, *she is God's Child. She must have been chosen by God and sent here to save us. I must speak to the Minister at the next meeting. He is always saying that freedom is coming to us all soon. Perhaps this new Mistress is a sign.*

They left Chloe and Roberta in the kitchen to talk to each other about what had happened, and little Angeline joined them when Lavinia took Mellissa, at last, on pathway which was hidden behind a stand of trees and followed the stream to the main slave compound. The compound was completely hidden from the plantation house by the woodland between them and the pathway down through the woods, which ran alongside the stream, was cool and colourful and exciting to Mellissa. She kept spotting different shrubs, birds and flowers and she expected Lavinia to know the answer to every question she asked of her. "This must be one of the most beautiful places in the world," sighed Mellissa. "I expected blue seas, white sands and palm trees on the coast, but the inland beauty is like a tropical paradise." They reached the bottom of the footpath and arrived at the compound. Most of the slaves were working in the cane fields so it was virtually empty, and Mellissa felt that she could look around without being intrusive.

It was like a little hamlet in the middle of the jungle. Set amongst wonderful flowering trees and shrubs was a double horseshoe shaped open rings of cabins, facing each other with a wide space in between. Some small ones like those of Lavinia, Roberta and Chloe which looked as though they housed maybe up to four people, and a couple or really large ones that could house a dozen people or more. The central space behind the cabins, through which the stream ran, was hard earth, flattened over the years by many feet. The stream, with several little bridges to cross it, gave them all access to its crystal clear water for drinking and cooking, and all washing and clothes washing was done downstream so as not to contaminate the water in the compound. There were several fire pits which served as communal cooking areas, and to one side there were several large hen houses. The hens were free to wander and scratch in the compound and beyond if they wanted to, and each cabin seemed to have a little hen house attached to it too so the slaves could collect eggs daily. Perhaps some had their own pet hens, thought Mellissa.

"I am pleased to see that you are all well provided with fresh eggs," she said. "Are there enough to go around for everyone?"

"Oh, yes and for us, and your home too," replied Lavinia, "and the unwanted cockerels make good eating. The Jamaican way of cooking it, called jerk chicken, is somewhat spicy but very delicious. Would you like for me to cook some that way for you?"

"I'm looking forward to trying all sorts of Jamaican food," replied Mellissa.

They were walking towards one of the bigger cabins when one of the very pregnant women came out. She was a handsome Negro woman, very full in bosom and hips, and in the prime of her life. Mellissa judged her to be about twenty-six years old, and supremely healthy in her pregnancy. To Mellissa's practiced eye she saw that the child would be due in about two or three weeks' time. She went up to the woman.

"Hello," she said. "You know that I am Mistress Harrison. I have already seen that there are a group of pregnant women here. I am the Mistress, but I am also an experienced midwife, and I would like to examine you and the other pregnant women. Do you all live in the one cabin together?" she asked. "First of all tell me your name, and let's go in and have a talk."

The slave girl was reluctant to co-operate but she knew that she had no choice. "My name is Rosie," she whispered, slightly awed to be talking to the new Mistress.

"Do you know when the baby is due? Does your husband also live here with you? What about the other husbands? Oh, goodness," sighed Mellissa, "I have so many questions and so much to find out from all of you. I do want to help you all, but I also need to understand how you all live here."

"Mistress," said Lavinia, "there are four women who are expecting their babies in just a few weeks. There is Rosie here, and also May, Liza and Lulu. And, Mistress, I must also tell you that I am too a midwife. I was trained by my mother who was African, and she was what was called there, a baby catcher. I have been looking after the girls here and I am sure that I will be able to help you when they are ready to give birth."

"Oh," said Mellissa. "Just one more surprise I am learning about you. I'm sure that you will be most helpful to me, and I will be very interested to learn your African mother's methods of midwifery."

Lavinia continued, "But first I must explain what is going on here. These four girls are not married. All the healthy young girls on this plantation were 'encouraged' by Mrs Johnston to make babies; they had little chance to say no. She just wanted to increase the numbers of slaves that she owned, and make money by selling infants."

Mellissa was shocked. Rosie forgot her fear of the new Mistress and spoke out, "Dat M'tress Johnston and Massa McBride dey chose ten of de fittest mens and six of we fit womens to 'visit' at night until de womens was knocked up. We here four womens is de ones now ready for theys babies. We don know which mans is dey father of which baby, and we only be allow to keep us babies if they be girl babies. If they come out as boy babies, we keep them only 'til they is weaned, 'bout two years."

"And then?" Mellissa whispered, holding her breath, knowing in her beating insides what the answer would be.

"And then," Rosie says in the saddest voice, "and then them boys get sold away. Mostly sold away to 'Merica. They mothers don see them babies no more. Like my babies Matthew and Rory," she added, almost under her breath. Her eyes filled with tears and two big fat ones rolled down each side of her face. "And then de mothers must do it all again. The 'visits' with the mens."

Mellissa could hardly speak. "Two of your children! You have had two babies taken from you!" She needed to repeat herself just to really believe that anyone, especially a woman, could steal other women's babies. "It's inhuman!" she burst out at last. "I cannot believe this. It is inhuman." She felt sick. She felt faint and she sank down on the floor. Lavinia was at her side to steady her.

"My baby boy was stolen from me and sold when he was three years old," she said Lavinia quietly, and tears rolled down her face too. "I was allowed to keep Angeline only if I made no fuss about my boy, Jonah is his name, or they would have taken her too."

"Oh, my God," breathed Mellissa. "I cannot take this all in. No wonder that you all hate us. What you are telling me is cruel and inhuman and I mean to stop it right now." She got up with determination. "I want to go back to the house now, Lavinia, and look into this right away."

"You just need to see in the record books. They put everything down in those big books that are in the study." Lavinia was speaking with hope and confidence now. She could at last speak of the secret trading at the Silver Bay plantation. "Both the Johnston's and Massa McBride. They were all working together. Mistress Johnston dealt with the women and the paperwork and Massa McBride took the children to a secret slave dealer from the United States who came once a year to buy slave children for the American markets."

"This story gets worse and worse," said Mellissa as they hurried to get back to the plantation house. "My immediate thinking is that we would try to buy the children back, but if they have been taken to America…"

They were back at the back door of the kitchen. "Just before I go in, Lavinia, I am curious about one of the men I noticed when we arrived. He is a very tall, very dark man with what looked like scars on his face. Was he one of the visiting men, the fathers, I mean?"

Lavinia looked surprised at the question. "Oh, no," she replied. "That's Akami. He is not allowed to 'visit' the women."

"Why not? He looks extremely fit and strong."

"He is too African, he was born there. He is very stubborn." Lavinia was looking very curious and puzzled now at her new Mistresses interest in that particular slave.

"Akami. Stubborn. African." Mellissa repeated.

("Mr Akami, I saw her flutter her eyelids, is she coming round?"

"No, nurse Stevens," he said in his deep dark Jamaican voice, "she's just surfacing a little.")

Akami, my love? My lost love? Mellissa whispered to herself under her breath.

"Yes," Lavinia continued, unaware of the change that come over her Mistress. "He was stolen from Africa when he was a boy. He says that he is the son of an important tribal chieftain. Those are tribal marks on his face to say that he was to be the next chief. He was stolen and sold in a place called Virginia in America. He was given the name James, but he refused to answer to any name but Akami and he was beaten and whipped many times. When they had enough of his African ways, they sold him down to Jamaica. So he is not Jamaican born like the rest of us. He is African and he talks American. He is very proud, very stubborn, very African and very alone!"

"All right, Lavinia. I think that I have the picture and I think that you secretly like him." Mellissa grinned a Lavinia. "Now let us go and find those books."

It did not take long to find Mrs Johnston's three large, leather covered books which were stacked on the study shelves. They were labelled 'Books of Slaves' in bright gold lettering as if Mrs Johnston was proud of her work and her bookkeeping. The first one was a straight forward record of the slaves who were bought with the plantation when her husband George Johnston bought Silver Bay in 1814. Of each slave it recorded:

Name, Sex, Age, Health, Work duties, Value in £'s, Date died, Date sold, £'s received, Children

The second book started after George Johnston bought the plantation and recorded the same details of slaves he then purchased, including their purchase date. This book had over one hundred names which included Lavinia, Chloe, Roberta and Akami and Rosie.

1814, March, Female Lavinia, Age10, Health Good, Child bearing possibilities, Domestic, Price paid £10.

1815, June, Female Rosie, Age 14, Health Good, Child bearing possibilities, Fieldwork, Price paid £12

1815, June, Female May, Age 15, Health Good, Child bearing possibilities, Fieldwork, Price paid £12

1815, June, Female Rebecca, Age 14, Health Good, Child bearing possibilities, Fieldwork, Price paid £12

1816, Jan, Female, Chloe, Age 16, Health not Strong, Children, House/Kitchen, Price paid £10

1816, Jan, Female Roberta, Age 16, Good child bearing possibilities, House/Kitchen, Paid £ 14

1816, Jan, Male James (Akami) Age 16, Health Good, Back scared, Field work, Price paid £20 (Bought from Virginia, US. Good worker but stubborn and needs correction)

1816, Jan, Female Lulu, Age 16, Health Good child bearing possibilities, Field work, Price paid £ 15

1817 This ledger continued to show 6 young females and 4 males in their 20's

The third book recorded only pregnant females, fourteen of them, listed under the headings:

Name, Age, Date baby born, Sex, Health, Health at age 2, Date child sold £ received.

Immediately two names stood out from the rest:

1819, Oct 10, Lavinia, Girl, Good Health, At age 3, Healthy, Walking, Talking, not yet sold

1820, Sept 26, Rosie, Boy, Good Health, At 2 Healthy/Walking, Sold 10/Dec 1822, £12

1821, July 6, Lavinia, Boy, Good Health, Age 2 Healthy/Walking, Sold 6/Feb/1824, £14

The book had pages listing the births of children born, details of their mother, dates when the children were sold, and follow on details of the same mothers with repeated births and sales of their children.

It took a moment or two for Mellissa to understand the full implications of this book. It was true what Lavinia and Rosie had said. And when she saw the recorded listings of Lavinia and Rosie, and their children, she was shocked to the core of her being, and then she cried too. The Johnstons had been farming babies.

Pressure from the abolitionists back in England were forcing the end of the Slave Trade, the capture and selling of slaves from Africa was already forbidden, against the law. This resulted in the value of slaves in the New World, especially in young healthy slaves increasing yearly. Mellissa looked again at the list of slave mothers. Some of them were repeated 4 or 5 times! The slave women were being forced to have children, almost certainly impregnated without their consent, and then their male babies were stolen. Mostly male, but Mellissa could see a few females stolen too – she could only use the word stolen. Stolen from their mothers time after time as if they were sheep and had no feelings for their children after they were weaned. How horrible it all was.

Chapter Five

Stolen Babies

Mellissa had to wait for another three and a half hours before Charles finished his inspection of the cane fields, which were being prepared for new plants at harvest time. Then he would come home for refreshment and rest. He was hot and tired when he came in. Mellissa knew that she should give him time to settle and have a cool drink before she told him about what she had discovered. She tried to bite her tongue but she could not wait.

"Charles," she said almost as soon as he came through the door. "Charles, I found out today that the previous owners and McBride have been breeding babies here, and selling child slaves. It's all horrible. Even Lavinia has had her young son stolen away from her." It was all coming out in a rush and she could not stop even as she saw the look of irritation cross her husband's face. "There is a special cabin where young women are forced to have sexual relations with selected male slaves just to make them pregnant and all healthy boy babies are sold when they are weaned at about two years. Charles, we have got to stop this right now before the next group of women give birth. We have got to assure them that we won't be taking their babies. We have to find and buy back these babies, and we have to dismiss McBride."

She paused to take a breath, giving Charles the opportunity to put his hand over her mouth to stop the flow of words. "Whoa, slow down Old Girl," he said. "I know what is going on…"

"What?" interrupted Mellissa. "You knew. What do you mean you knew?"

"Of course I knew," continued Charles. "I found out everything there was to know about the plantation before we, my father and I, agreed to buy it."

"But you bought it with my money!" Mellissa was indignant now, as well as angry. "I cannot believe you knew what was going on here and you didn't tell me. It is totally disgusting. And that awful McBride, you knew about him too?"

Charles tried to placate her. "Because I knew everything about the plantation does not mean that I agreed with everything and that I will make no changes…"

"What's I, I, I?" interrupted Mellissa again. "This plantation is ours. Mine and yours. For us to make joint decisions. And the first thing that I want to change is the selling of children, and if there are any sales planned that split up families."

"No!" said Charles. "This plantation is not ours, it is mine. It belongs to me and my father, here it is all mine. Mine to make the decisions, and mine to guarantee profits. Not yours or anything to do with you when decisions are to be made about running the business. Your role is to make sure that everything is done that needs to be done domestically and some medical attendance to those who need it. I have not made any decisions about the pregnant slaves. I will probably not sell their babies, but it is a decision for two years' time. I, and I alone, will make that final decision."

"But Charles," protested Mellissa, "even so, it is cruel to leave the mothers in suspense, to suffer every day the fear of losing their babies." She wondered how long he had known about the baby farming. Was that the reason why he had wanted this particular plantation? "If you want to play the hard man and follow McBride's advice, you may end up losing everything – including me! Where is the loving man that I married only a few weeks ago? Who are you now? A business man whose only desire is to make profits, or are you the man that I thought I had married? A straightforward loving human being to whom kindness is the most important thing in life?"

"Mellissa I have no choice," Her husband was crestfallen and his strength of purpose seemed diminished.

"Everyone has choices, and only the good ones count. I cannot stay and fight with you," Mellissa had tears welling up and beginning to overflow. "I will talk to you again later." She turned around and walked out of the room, heartbroken. How was she going to put an end to this awful trade without bitter fighting between them?

Chapter Six

Humming Bird Magic

A wall of silence was built up between Mellissa and Charles. In spite of her body melting with desire for her husband, Mellissa had decided to remove herself from their bedroom with excuse that in the heat it was easier for them both to sleep on their own. They both developed a hardened skin and carried on their daily duties with barely a nod between them. It was Sunday, a day when the slaves had some free time, many of them taking off into the jungle to meet up with slaves from a nearby plantation.

So Mellissa could hear sounds of singing and a few children playing coming from the compound as she was taking a solitary walk in the garden. Suddenly, to her delight, the garden was finally visited by a beautiful humming bird. It was the tiniest bird she had ever seen, not much bigger than her little finger. It was a sort of blackish in colour, with red streaks down its cheeks. And then, it started to hover as it fed, with its long beak and tongue, from the tube-like, hanging red flowers which covered a nearby bush. As it did so, it spread its tail and revealed the most glorious red feathers. Then having had its fill of nectar, it flew away. But even this moment of joy was muted because she could not share it with Charles.

Finally, it was he who called the truce. After five days of hostility Charles decided to relent. He had crept up behind her while she stood alone looking at the fabulous flowering shrubs, hoping that the beautiful bird would return. He whispered in ear, "That was a truly magical moment." She whipped around, and without remembering that she was angry with him, she threw herself in his open arms.

"Oh Charles," she cried, her recent vow of silence forgotten, "did you see it? Wasn't it beautiful? It was smaller than my finger, and its tiny wings were flapping so quickly they were a blur."

"Yes," said Charles, "and you are beautiful too."

"I really do love you," she said softly. "Let's not quarrel any more. We must talk about our ideas for the plantation and who knows, we might even agree on some things."

"Well, I do have something to tell you which I know you will like," he said gently. "Shall we go in and talk while we have some of Lavinia's cooling lemon drink."

Mellissa was so excited that she ran in at once dragging Charles by his hand. When they were comfortably seated in their sitting room, she said, "Come on Charles. Tell me something I want to hear!"

He tried to put on a formal face, but found it very hard to hide his grin. "I have been thinking hard about what you said about the pregnant slaves, and I have come to agree with you that this plantation will no longer sell babies and infants…"

"Oh, Charles," cried Mellissa. "That will be a wonderful start."

"…and," he continued, "we might even start a search for those children that have been sold away from their mothers. But first we, or rather you, could start by telling this to those ladies who are expecting children."

Mellissa jumped up, kissed her husband on his cheek. "Oh Charles, Charles I knew that you had a wonderful heart. Thank you, thank you. I love you," she whispered in to his ear. Then she called Lavinia.

"Lavinia, Lavinia, come here," she called out, "I have some wonderful news for you."

Lavinia came in with a curious look on her face, it was both expectant and worried at the same time. She looked at her Master and Mistress, from one to the other and back again. She was thinking that she was going to be told that they were alright again, and to move Mellissa's belongings back to the Master's bedroom.

"Lavinia it is wonderful news," repeated Mellissa. "There will no longer be babies and children sold from this plantation. And I am going to try to trace your boy, Jonah, and buy him back, if I can."

Lavinia looked stunned, and then she burst into tears. "Oh Mistress, oh Master," she wailed, "I can hardly believe it. Thank you, thank you, thank you." She buried her face in her two hands and cried.

Mellissa hugged her husband, hugged Lavinia and then pulled her into the kitchen. "Well," she said, "I will work to get information about Jonah, but first we must tell the women. Please go into the compound and bring all the women to the garden. Don't tell them anything, it's something I would like to do. Go on, off you go." Lavinia ran.

She was back in twenty minutes, bringing twenty-eight women with her. They gathered in the garden at the side of the plantation house, all of them looking apprehensive. They were sure that the new Mistress had some bad news for them, something that she wanted done which would be unpleasant or hurtful. But the Mistress was smiling!

The women gathered around without any realisation that their lives were going to change for the better.

Mellissa took a deep breath. "I have something to tell you all," she said. "The Master and I have decided that none of you will have your babies and children taken away from you from now on."

There were gasps of surprise, and looks of joy came over their faces.

Mellissa continued, "none of you will be forced to 'visit' with the men any more, and if any of you want to marry and live with any man from this plantation, I will make it possible for you. The cabin that Rosie and the other three pregnant women are presently using I am going to turn into a clinic. Any one, man or women or child will be able to come to me if you have medical problems. I am not promising that I will be able to cure everything, but I mean to help. And Rosie, May, Liza and Lulu, all of you can go back to your own cabins and just come to the new clinic when you babies are ready to be born. We already have Lavinia as your baby catcher and midwife and I am also a midwife, so between us we should be able to catch your babies well."

As she paused a loud cheering, hand slapping and dancing started. Everyone there went wild delight.

But Mellissa had one more thing to say. "I shall be going through the records to see if I can find out where some of your children were sold off to, and try to get them back." Another wild cheer from the women, and when Mellissa quietened them down she went on, "I am not promising anything because I know that it will be difficult, especially if the children were sold away from Jamaica. But with Lavinia's help, I am going to try."

Unnoticed by any of them, slaves or Mistress, James McBride approached the group in the garden. He, himself, did not see

Mellissa, and with a roar, he shouted, "What are you bitches doing here?" He flicked his whip and caught a slave woman called Hannah across the cheek.

She shrieked, and Mellissa called out, "how dare you attack these women who I have called together to talk to?" She came forward and snatched at the whip. She was so angry that she was ready to take the whip from him and whip him too. He realised him mistake and took grovelling action.

"I am sorry, Mistress Harrison," he proclaimed in a humble voice that the slaves had never heard. "I didn't see you. I thought these bitches were making trouble of some kind."

"And you will stop referring to these women as 'bitches'. Mellissa was so angry that she actually hit him. "They are not bitches. They are not sluts. They are women, and they are women for whom we are responsible. You will not be treating them as your playthings any longer. And I shall be talking to Master Harrison about your future role at Silver Bay. Now go away. I cannot bear the sight of you."

McBride was stung and felt embarrassed and humiliated at this treatment in front of the slaves. It was as if the roles had been reversed, and the tormenter had been tormented for the first time in his life. He knew that as soon as the women got back to the compound all the slaves would be told what had happened, and how he had been humbled in front of them by the Mistress. He would lose some of his power over them. The women slaves stood in shocked silence hardly believing what had happened before their very eyes.

Mellissa spoke up again to the women, "I am asking Lavinia to go back to the compound with you and sort out who lives where, and whether any of you want to change cabins. There will no group living unless it is what you want. This will all seem a bit strange to you, and you will have to continue the work that has been allocated to you by Master Harrison or Master McBride, but if I can make your living arrangements better I will try to do so. And Lavinia when you have finished, will you come back to the house so that we can talk about things."

The astounded slaves left with Lavinia, all of them surprised and delighted at what had happened. They were chattering amongst themselves, some of dancing and singing all the way back to their compound.

In the meantime Mellissa returned to house to be met by her husband who was angry once more. "You silly interfering woman," he shouted at her. "I will not have you belittle McBride in front of the slaves."

"He was quick in coming to you to tell tales," stuttered a deflated Mellissa. "But that pig used his whip on a woman right in front of me. He is wicked and cruel, and he controls the slaves with threats and cruel punishments. We will get much more out our workforce if we treat them like people and not animals."

And more to herself she said quietly, "I cannot believe that McBride came snivelling to you behind my back. Charles let's not fight again so soon. I suppose that it will always be about the slaves. You need their work and I want them to be happy in their work. We both want the same thing really. I am sure that they will work better if their life and living is improved."

Charles dropped his belligerent attitude and sighed. He had known all along that the issue of the slaves would always be a bone of contention between them. "Come on, let's have it out right now. I know how you agreed with the abolitionist movement back home. Now we are here as slave owners, you tell me what you think the future of slavery will be."

Mellissa took a deep breath. She knew as well as him that their differing attitudes towards slavery could cause real damage to their marriage. So she spoke quietly with gentle firmness. "You know that England has banned the capture and transportation of men and women from West Africa, and I am sure that it won't be long before the owning of slaves in any English territory will be outlawed too. Already you know that sugar sales are less because people at home are campaigning hard to abolish slavery. They are trying to get people to give up their love of sweet things and sugar, which will hurt the pockets of slave owners, like us.

So why don't we do what we set out to do here in Jamaica? We could start by freeing some slaves maybe, and their freedom could be conditional to them becoming indentured for perhaps five years, and during that time we would pay them a wage for the work that they continue to do."

Charles' first reaction was to reject this idea. He did not become angry or aggressive and replied gently, "No. No. That won't work. Where would we find the money to pay these workers, especially if we are earning less for our sugar?"

Mellissa was expecting that reply and she had a ready answer. "It will become a balancing act. We will save money when we stop supplying food and clothing for the slaves and then we will use that saving to pay wages. And they will have to use their wages to support themselves, pay for their own food and clothes."

Charles tried to stay calm, but he wanted to end this conversation without losing his temper. He said, "As indentured servants, they will not work as hard as when they were forced to work, and we will lose production."

Mellissa had yet another reasonable answer. "On the contrary, we will create a reason for them to be even more productive by paying them more as they produce more. The more they work the more they will be paid, especially the young, strong men. You would see that money will get more from them than the whip."

Charles could no longer hide his impatience, "No. No. No. I will not do it, and I don't want to hear any more of your crazy ideas."

Mellissa knew that she had lost the first battle, and she gave in gracefully. "Well, I will leave my ideas for you to think about. I want to have a word with Lavinia." She kissed the top of his head and went into the kitchen.

Chapter Seven

Lavinia's Story

Mellissa found Lavinia in the kitchen garden and she pulled her to a comfortable garden bench. "Lavinia," she said, "before we start to try to find your little boy, I would like you to tell me your story and how you became a slave."

"Oh. Mistress," she said wistfully, "it is a long story. Do you want me to start with how my mother was taken from Africa?"

"Yes, Lavinia," she replied. "We have plenty of time to talk. I think that you should start with Africa. It has become easy for white people here in the colonies and in America, to accept black people as slaves when they see or hear of them working on plantations in North and South America, but most don't think about them being real people living their own lives in Africa. They do not stop to ask themselves what lives these people had, what languages they spoke and what were their skills in their homelands. All my life I have heard of Negroes being described as niggers, savages, and monkey people living in trees, having no spiritual feeling because most of them are not Christians. Wild savages and heathens who we, the superior white people, have saved by teaching them to become Christians.

You are different from most of them because you have been taught to read and write in English, which makes you an educated woman. From what I hear, most slaves have no proper education and have to pick up English from everyone around them, most of whom don't speak English properly themselves. How they understand McBride's Scottish accent, I really don't know. Even I have difficulty understanding him! So I am very happy to sit back and listen to the whole of your story. I will not interrupt. Off you go!"

Lavinia took a deep breath and started.

"My mother was African. Her name was Nagisso, and she was of the Fulani tribe living in Guinea in West Africa. She had often repeated to me her family story, but only in the most elementary words. She gave me no details of her family village, other than its name, Labe. She said nothing about the huts that they lived in and the river, the countryside and wild animals that surrounded them. It hurt her too much to pull from the hidden recesses of her mind her deepest memories of all that was good and beautiful in her life before she was captured by the hateful Malinke tribesmen from a faraway village, a village from the other side of the wide Konkouré River. These were always strange names that she spoke to me as a child. I always found it hard to imagine her own childhood family and the village that she and her family lived in. She had been apprenticed to her own mother, my grandmother, who was a 'baby catcher', a midwife. When my mother was twelve years old, her village was attacked and raided by those Malinke black slavers. The village of Labe was destroyed, burnt to the ground.

All the elders, including my great-grandparents, were killed and many people were captured. My grandfather tried to protect his family. He ran with his wife and daughter into the bushland but another part of the raiding gang was waiting there and they were all captured. My grandfather tried to fight them and he was killed, his head sliced through with a machete, right in front of my mother's eyes. She was just twelve years and she witnessed that brutal killing of her father. The horror of that vision stayed with her for ever. The horror was so deep that she could never talk about him. All I ever knew of him was his name, Ongoro. My grandmother, who also tried to protect her daughter, received a deep wound in her side which was roughly held together with her own head scarf. She and my mother and some others from our village were forced to walk for many days. They were all tied together with ropes and no one could escape.

They walked like that for two moons through jungles and swamps with poisonous snakes and dangerous wild animals always near them, until they reached the big water at a place called Conakry, where they were sold to white slavers. My mother had never seen a white man before and she was very frightened, they were like 'hants' she said, ghosts in her language. All the captured people were put together into a wooden stockade that had no shelter from the sun and rain. Boiled rice and water were brought each day and left just inside the gateway of the stockade. Only the fittest, who could push away others, had enough food and water to keep them well. It took two more moons for the white slavers to have enough captives to fill their 'big canoe'. During that time, in the horrible conditions in which every man and woman was forced to live (they did not even have any private space to do their necessaries) the whole stockade became a cesspit, and my grandmother died of her wounds. And my mother who was just a child on her own, was not strong enough to fight for a share of the food. She thought that she, too, would die of hunger and thirst, in filth, and pain and sorrow.

My mother could never relate to me the horrors of the crossing of the big water. She would only say that she survived when many others, including friends from her home village, had died and their naked bodies were thrown overboard into the swirling waters to the sharks which were waiting to feed on them. Without ritual burial their souls were lost forever.

By the time the big canoe found land again my mother was sick and near to dying herself, only the stamina of her youth keeping her alive. She told me just the basic details of the next horror, the slave market in what she later learned was Kingston, in a country called Jamaica. Sick as she was, and with her hands and feet bound in heavy chains she was forced to stand on a raised platform completely unclothed. She was forced, with a whipping, to stand still and have her body closely inspected, her mouth and then, to her shame, even her private parts. She was auctioned and sold like a piece of meat.

But if any slave can be thought to be fortunate then she was that one. She was bought by a white man called Michael Winton, and she was given the names Mary, her new first name, and Winton because she now belonged to him. She was Nagisso no more. She was Mary Winton. Her owner lived in a large house in Kingston which was called Heathermoor (where there was neither moorland nor heather), and he also had a sugar plantation not far away. He had bought my mother as a house slave for his wife, Eleanor Winton.

She was treated well, almost as a house pet having her own room at the top of the house instead of living in a slave compound; and with eating good food her health began to recover. She started to learn about how everyone lived in this strange country. Houses with stairs, rooms and kitchens which were so different from the village huts she had been used to. She learned to speak English and, although she was timid at first, she demonstrated her abilities as a midwife when she helped to deliver the occasional baby on the plantation. By the time my mother was fifteen she had become a strong, good-looking and knowledgeable young woman, and that was when Michael Winton took her by force. He was a religious man and although he owned Mary and, by law, had the right to do with her as he pleased, he was ashamed of what he had done. Especially when he realised that Mary was with child. I was born as a result of that rape, and I was named Lavinia by that man.

Michael and Eleanor Winton had no children of their own, and whereas Eleanor resented my mother and me, showing up her own inability to conceive a child, Michael started to take an interest in me, his unrecognised daughter. He could not admit to anyone that he was my father. By the time I was two years old and starting to speak he took up my training and taught me to speak proper English, unlike the Jamaican patois that was the common talk between slaves and difficult for their white owners to understand. At the age of five, he also began to teach me to read and write. In the meantime, I grew up as a house slave like my mother, resented by Eleanor Winton but petted by her husband, my father. To try to put some distance between me and my father, my mother took me aside and began to teach me midwifery, so that I too, would have a useful role on the plantation and not just be a favoured pet who was resented by everyone except my parents.

Michael Winton had promised that soon (how soon was soon?) he would make free citizens of both my mother and myself. Give us freedom papers but encourage us to stay on the plantation; perhaps to give my mother a wage? I do not know. But in early 1813 Michael Winton caught a fever and he died within a week, never having had the time to write and have authorised our manumission papers. As soon as it was possible to do so Mrs Winton sold the plantation and took her revenge on my mother and me. In her spite and resentment against the way that her husband had treated us, especially me, she sold us separately. I was sold privately to Mr Frederick Johnston, and I do not know what became of my mother. I never saw her again.

I was ten years old by then and because I was well spoken, light-skinned and intelligent and Mr and Mrs Johnston took me into their home on the Silver Bay plantation. They were considerate owners, and in spite of my pain, unhappiness at the loss of my mother, and my unwillingness to work, Mrs Johnson let me continue in my education. I was given a Holy Bible to read, which helped me to widen my knowledge of English, and I was soon learning book-keeping as well as housework. I also continued to practise basic midwifery.

I lived as good a life as could be, considering that I was a slave and could make no life choices of my own. I thought that Silver Bay was a 'happy' plantation. That was until I understood Mistress Johnson's slave books, wherein I discovered the hidden pain of my fellow female slaves. It took me only a short while to discover from the women themselves how they had been coerced into making babies. They all loved their children as any mother would do, especially as they had had them with them for two years or more. I cannot forget the howling pain of Rebecca, who still lives here at Silver Bay, when her little boy, Rubin was sold away from her. She begged and begged to be sold off too so that she could be with her son. But it was not allowed because Rebecca was considered good breeding stock who would be impregnated again by any of the healthy male slaves to produce yet another child.

Every woman prayed for a girl child because it was boy children who were wanted, who were easy to sell for a good price. Some of the women were allowed to keep their female children, but always with a provision that they too would be sold if the mother made a fuss about the loss of her male children. It was wicked and it was cruel, and eventually I became a victim of Mistress Johnston's hateful trade in babies.

I had lived on Silver Bay plantation for four years. I was trained as a house slave and cook. I also kept the account books for Mistress Johnston and occasionally I was called to act as a midwife for any of the mothers. It was in the birthing cabin that I learned both the joy and heartbreak of motherhood. The women were happy when it was a girl child, hoping that they would not lose their babies. But when a boy child was born the mother's cry of joy at his birth was turned into torment when she was told that although she would nurse the child and let him grow to be a strong little boy, he would eventually be sold away from her.

Some of the women tried to be cold and unloving to their sons so that they would be able to give them up more easily, but it didn't really work. A mother is a mother and God, in His great wisdom, has programmed all the women of this world to love and protect their children no matter what the cost to themselves might be.

So, when I reached the age of fourteen, I, a privileged and envied house servant, was also sent to the 'visiting house'. In spite of my midwifery skills I knew nothing about a women's body and nothing about mating with men. At first, I fought off the young men who were ordered to 'mate' with me, until I had a whipping from Master McBride. In the end I gave in. The men, not much older than boys themselves, were gentle with me. They too were under orders with threats of a whipping, and dared not disobey. Eventually, when I was well broken in, I accepted the men.

I began to have feelings for one of them named Thomas, and I am sure that it was he who is the father of Angeline. I was allowed to keep her and she has become the sole joy of my life. Two years later I had another child with Thomas. He had joined me and Angeline in my cabin and we were comfortable with each other, we were a family. When our son, Jonah, was born, I knew that Mistress Johnson would sell him before he was three years old, and I was heartbroken, but he was my son and I loved him and cared for him until Master McBride came for him when he was two and a half years old. I became a wild thing and Thomas attacked the Master. He was overpowered by Master McBride who took Thomas to his punishment barn where he was shackled and whipped until he nearly died. His back was dripping with blood and looked like raw meat and the Master ordered that salt be rubbed into it. He wasn't allowed to live with me or visit with me anymore.

I had lost my Thomas who was a bloodied and broken wretch, and now I had to suffer the greater loss of my son who was taken away and sold by Master McBride. I was threatened with the selling of Angeline if I continued to, what he called, 'make a fuss'. Without Thomas's support, I couldn't fight on my own and I had to give in. At last I knew that I was a slave, a thing, a brood mare. And to add to my pain, to my agony at the loss of Jonah, Mistress Johnson made me record Jonah's birth and sale in her records book. I do not know whether she had any human feelings at all, or whether she really thought of her slaves as non-people, no different to her horses."

Chapter Eight

Searching for Babies

Mellissa stood up and went to Lavinia's side, and her Mistress took her hand. Lavinia sighed and said, quite softly, almost under her breath, "So that is my story and I think that almost every slave here in Jamaica will have some story of pain and suffering in their lives. But now I am hoping that the lives of the slaves on Silver Bay will improve because of you, Mistress. And I hope that you and I will be able to trace and find the stolen children."

This time it was Mellissa who had tears in her eyes. They spilled down over her cheeks as she said, "Oh Lavinia. I think that I now understand what it is to be a slave. I am so sorry for you and I will do my best to make your lives happier, but it is my husband who has the authority here and I have no power to go against him. But at least he has given me permission to try and trace the children." Then she added, almost to herself, "But where do I start?"

Lavinia was smiling, "I have an idea," she said. "There is a travelling Baptist preacher called Peter Fellowes but he calls himself Moses. He is a free slave and he lives here in St Elizabeth Parish, on the West side of the island. He comes once a month to our area of the parish, and those slaves with religion are happy to walk the five miles to attend his open air gatherings. These are the only sort of gatherings and meetings that the slave owners of Jamaica allow their slaves to attend. I have often attended these religious gatherings and I have talked to Moses many times. He knows of a fellow preacher called Samuel Sharpe who lives in Montego Bay on the north side of the island. Although Samuel Sharpe is a slave, to a lawyer I believe, he is also a Baptist minister. He is well educated and he is forever pursuing information, coming slowly from England, about the efforts of the abolitionists there to end slavery in the English colonies. Through his contacts both here and in North

America he might be able to start us on the trail of our stolen children."

"That sounds like a good place to start our search," said an excited Mellissa. "First, we must go through the ledger carefully to get as much information as we can about the lost children and their mothers. There may also be some sort of record of this mysterious American slave trader. I am sure that McBride will know some of the details that we need to start our search, but I do not know if he will be willing to help us. He knows that I do not like him, and that I want Charles to get rid of him, so I am sure that he will say that he knows nothing about any slave traders, here in Jamaica or anywhere else," she said to herself more than to Lavinia, "if Charles is in agreement, perhaps I can ask him to try and get information out of McBride."

Chapter Nine

September 1829
Silver Bay

Charles and Mellissa had lived on their sugar plantation for two months. They had become used to the landscape, the weather conditions, the beauty of the birds and incessant noise and annoyance of the insects. But neither of them had got used to owning people.

The four babies of the pregnant slave women had been born without any medical problems. Four happy mothers, Rosie, May and Lulu had boys, and Liza, a girl. The joy of knowing that their children would not be taken from them made the plantation a happier place. Not only for the women themselves but for all the slaves in the compound who rejoiced and thanked the Lord. Mellissa and Lavinia had worked together well as midwives, each approving of each other's techniques, and the shared admiration had brought them even closer together. So much so that Mellissa, in spite of Charles's disapproval when she had discussed the freedom of some of the slaves with him, once more suggested that they free Lavinia and bind her to them with an indenture. Again they could not agree.

Charles was nearer in agreement with James McBride. He did not think of the slaves as workers. They were slaves and they had to obey and do whatever their masters told them to do. They were well fed and housed, and were treated well if they were obedient and worked hard for their masters. Although he still felt uncomfortable when McBride used the threat of punishments, usually whipping to gain their obedience. He had seen the light whipping of slaves just to get them to work harder, and that he could just about agree with, but he had also seen he scarred backs of some of the slaves who had endured whipping as a punishment. And he found that much more difficult to accept.

Mellissa had told him the story of Thomas, Lavinia's common-law husband, and he had been distressed when he saw Thomas with his shirt removed, and had seen the results of that brutal whipping. He had also seen the back of a slave called Akami who had been bought cheaply by the Johnstons as a 'difficult nigger'. Akami had been sold from Africa as a young man into the Americas and had been so difficult to bring to obedience that he had been continually punished. Rather than beat him until he was dead or critically injured, his owners in America had given up and sold him away from while he still had value. And it was because of his near perfect physical body and strength that the Johnsons, who needed the strongest of men for cane harvesting, had bought him, at a bargain price, in spite of his 'difficult' reputation. McBride had learned to control Akami's rebelliousness and to use his strength by putting him in charge of the cane crushing operations. Charles approved of the way McBride controlled the 'workforce', and bit by bit he was getting McBride to slow down on severe punishments.

Mellissa thought completely differently about McBride, and she had come to hate him. She thought that he ruled by fear and cruelty and she could not be persuaded to accept him in their lives.

The more that she felt sickened by McBride's treatment of the slaves the more Charles seemed to approve. They began by arguing between themselves, and by September there was open hostility between them, and Charles forbade her to go into the compound or have anything to do with any of the field slaves other than attend their wounds if they hurt themselves in anyway. If any of them were sick, she was expected to treat them and get them back to work as soon as they were well enough to stand on their feet. Charles very much approved of the clinic that she had opened in the birthing cabin. She found it quite funny that most of her 'patients' were the women who seemed to have the same complaints as that of the society women that she had seen at home in London. If anything proved to her that these black slave women were the same as any 'superior' delicate white woman, then surely it was that their human bodies worked in identical ways. Yet most white people continued to insist that the Negroes were a sub species, barely human beings at all.

Although Mellissa and Charles were at cross purposes where treatment of the slaves was concerned, she was nevertheless mollified by his agreement about the treatment of the pregnant women, even though McBride strongly disapproved. He was privately very angry at the loss of what he saw as his well-earned extras, as he had always received a substantial commission on each sale. She was ready to put into action her search to find the missing children. First she would contact the pastor in St Elizabeth, and she would also call in at the records office there as soon as she went there.

(Staff Nurse Carole Bingham and Student Nurse Julia Radcliffe were gently changing the bed linen of their comatose patient.

"What do you think of her husband?" asked Julia as she smoothed the under sheet below Mellissa's lifeless limbs. "I am so used to seeing him as Inspector Holland it's still hard for me to accept that he is just an actor."

"Yes, but he is still dishy, isn't he? And he positively drools over our Mellissa."

"Do you think that it is real, is it just for show?"

"I don't know. She has been here for ten days now, and he comes every day after filming. It's a long day for him and he must be tired."

"It's a long day for me too," said Julia. "Do you know I haven't been into town since she was admitted. I have just been to the nurse's home briefly for a short kip and then back here. But I need to catch the 82 bus as soon as I can so that I can find a lawyer or solicitor to talk about divorce."

"Divorce? You've only been married a few months."

"I know. But, like her Charlie, he is not the man I thought he was…")

Mellissa was having second thoughts about her loving husband. *He is not the man I thought he was, but he did get the name John Merriweather out of McBride. I will get Abraham to drive me into town. What's a bus? There must be a church in St Elizabeth, with a white pastor, surely? I need to talk about these stolen children. Maybe he will know or know of the slave Baptist Minister called Samuel Sharpe who could spread the word that we are looking for these children. Maybe he might even know how to find this John Merriweather. I'll tell him that the man is an American slave trader who breaks the law by buying and selling Jamaican children into America.*

Chapter Ten

The Punishment Barn

The following morning when Mellissa was walking to Abraham's cabin, she thought that she heard the shriek of a woman or a girl in pain coming from McBride's cabin. What was that? She asked herself. Then there it was again, a woman calling out "No, no, no", followed by that shriek again. Mellissa froze wondering what she should do. Should she go in and interfere, should she call Charles? Then she remembered that Charles and McBride had ridden off together early that morning to inspect one of the outlying cane fields. They wanted to check that it was ready to harvest. He had said that it would take half an hour of hard riding even to get there. So who was in the cabin? She was just about to go in when she heard McBride's voice. "Shut your fucking mouth, bitch. Shut your fucking mouth."

Mellissa was shocked at the foul language, but she was also puzzled. Had the two of them returned already? Before she could decide what to do there was another sheik, then McBride said, "Open your legs, bitch." Then the sound of a whiplash, and another scream. It was all followed by a strange repetition. "Open your legs, bitch." Something was not quite right.

Mellissa could not wait to find help. Although Charles had forbidden her to interfere with the running of the plantation and how McBride ran it, she was so angry that her anger made her bold. Even if she was punished by Charles, she was going to find out what was happening in McBride's cabin. She pushed the door open and walked in expecting to find a cruel scene of brutality and rape; but there was nothing. The cabin was empty. She was astonished. No one in the main room, no one in the bedroom. Then before she could retreat, that voice again. "Open your legs, bitch." And then a piercing screech. This time it came from just over her shoulder. She turned around. A green parrot in a cage! A talking parrot now shrieking like a girl in pain! Mellissa took up a cloth that was lying next to the cage and covered it up. The parrot stopped its noise and all was silent again. But the parrot must have heard these goings on so many times repeatedly for it to have learned the noises and words. It was all too shocking.

With trembling legs, she walked on to the barn standing beyond McBride's cabin, and next to the path to the compound. The door, which was usually shut and barred, was standing slightly open. It was a morning of exploration and discovery of McBride's ways of working. She pushed open the door and saw at once that it was the punishment barn that Lavinia had spoken of. She was shocked again, and she trembled uncontrollably as she took in the several sets of iron chains and manacles set into the wall posts where a victim could be chained up for hours or even days at a time. She expected that there would be little or no food and water for the sufferer while he was left to accept discipline and orders with docility.

But the fiercest and most shocking of all was the cage. It was an iron cage with a solid top and bottom, and solid bars on three sides and a barred door on the fourth. The cage measured about five feet long, five feet high, and three feet wide. When a man was made to get into the cage, he would not be able to stand or lie down and would be forced to sit in a crouched position for the duration of his punishment. Mellissa had already seen an A shaped iron frame outside the barn, and now she saw that the cage could be dragged outside and winched up on chains so that it would swing about three feet from the ground, thus the victim would also have to endure being half cooked in the hot sun for the duration of his punishment too.

Inhuman. Inhuman was all the shocked Mellissa could think.

She waited for the following weekend when she knew that she would have Charles's whole attention, and after Abraham had taken them to the church in St Elizabeth Mellissa decided that she should show Charles the punishment barn.

"Charles," she started rather timidly, "I want to show you something. We have been listening today to our Minister talk about loving kindness to all men, and I did think that, although he did not say specifically who he meant by all men, I'm sure that with unspoken words he did mean slaves too."

Charles sighed. "Oh, you are not going to go on again about treating our slaves like our children. If you cannot think of them as slaves, you must, at least, think of them as workers. Remember how we treated our workers at home in England. They were tenants on our land and in order for them to keep their homes they had to work, and work hard too. There can be no mollycoddling where workers of any sort are concerned."

"Come with me, Charles," she said, pulling him by the hand. She walked him through the gardens without saying anything, and retraced her steps past the top cabins of the house slaves and McBride, and on to the punishment barn. The door was closed but not locked and Charles helped as she struggled to take down the bar keeping the barn doors shut. "Do you know of this place? Have you been here with McBride before?" she asked once they had squeezed themselves in a small opening.

Charles looked around and hung his head a little, and his cheeks reddened up. "You did know of this place," burst out Mellissa. "Is it in use? Did you give that hateful McBride permission to carry on punishing the slaves in here? Please don't say you did," she added, her voice now at a whisper. "Not this. Never like this." Her tears were falling now. "What sort of man are you?" she was almost speaking to herself now. "Who is this man that I have married?"

"Steady on, Old Girl." He was struggling with saying the right words that would satisfy Mellissa. He knew that her heartbroken sobs would move him more that any angry arguments. "Mellissa, darling don't cry," he said trying to take her in his arms. But she resisted his comfort.

"Don't you touch me," she now cried. Her softness was gone and she was angry. "Don't you dare to touch me, you monster."

"Mellissa," he cried, "you haven't listened to me yet. Yes, I have seen this place before, and I did not tell you of it because I knew that you would be horrified. And, yes, I have forbidden McBride to bring any of the slaves here for punishment. I haven't banned whipping altogether because I do think that a threat of punishment concentrates their minds. They are our slaves, and not our peasant workers."

"I thank God that you have forbidden McBride to bring any more slaves here," said a now very calmed down Mellissa. "Can we not strip the barn out and use it for something completely different?"

"That's exactly what we will do when we next need additional storage space up here," he replied. They shut and replaced the bar on the barn doors, and hand in hand, they walked back to High View in silence.

Chapter Eleven

Sheba, the Labrador Puppy

It was the 13th October, 1829, and it was Mellissa's twenty-first birthday. Her special day. The day she became officially an adult. It should have been a day of great happiness for her to share with her husband. Instead she was sitting alone amongst the white roses in an enclosed arbour in her Jamaican garden. She was crying, feeling unloved, unwanted, friendless and alien in this strange land.

It had its magnificent beauty, its plants and especially in its butterflies and birds, but it was not home. Always there was the incessant noise of insects and birds in the air, and the ever present ants that crawled over her shoes and up her legs; so unlike an English garden with gentle heat, and the sounds of a distant cuckoo, a blackbird singing on a top branch, or a bumble bee buzzing in and out of the flowers. She missed home. Yes, even busy and sometimes smelly London. She missed her father most of all. He had celebrated, with fun and games, every one of her birthdays since the day she had been born. Thinking of her father, and then of her long lost mother too, she started crying again. This time she was sobbing with great heaves of her bosom into a daintily embroidered handkerchief which was totally inadequate for the job.

Unnoticed by her, Charles crept up silently. "Happy Birthday, my darling," he called out.

Mellissa looked up, her face all red and blotchy and running with tears. "Oh Charles," she sobbed. "You remembered!"

"Of course I remembered the special birthday of my Best Girl," he said with a laugh. "And I have brought you a gift, which I hope will stop those tears of yours." He produced a large box from behind his back and plopped it down on Mellissa's lap. Before she could take the ribbon of it, the box started moving.

"Whatever is it?" The tears had indeed stopped and a hint of a smile returned to Mellissa's face. She opened the box and the head of a black puppy popped out. "Oh Charles, he's lovely," she cried. "Wherever did you get him?"

"It's not a he, it's a she." Her husband replied in a mock scolding voice. He laughed, hugged Mellissa and helped remove the pup from the box.

"She's beautiful. Oh, so beautiful. I love her already, and I love you for giving her to me. What shall I call her?" Mellissa thought for a moment. "I know. I'll call her Sheba. Just like the beautiful black queen in the Bible. But where did she come from?" she asked again.

"You know when we went into St Elizabeth two weeks ago?" Charles said. "You went off to see Pastor Josiah Smith at St Peter's Church to start your search for John Merriweather and the lost children, while I went to the general store. Well, when I was there Sam Piper, the store owner, showed me his Labrador bitch who had had a litter of eight puppies. They were just delightful, and I knew straight away that you would love to have one. I asked if I could have one for you and when it would be ready to leave its mother, which was this week. I chose this little one, thinking that you would like a girl puppy, and I went into St Elizabeth this morning to collect her."

"Oh darling, she is just adorable. You are so kind and thoughtful," said Mellissa, with all her tears dried up. "I thought that you had forgotten my birthday when you said nothing this morning, and I thought that no one here, so far away from home, loved or wanted me." She was about to cry again, but Charles held her tight and gave her a sweet snuggling kiss on her neck. Little Sheba wriggled out of her arms and jumped down with her tail wagging. They both laughed and bent down to play with her.

Just then a pair of hummingbirds flew down to hover and draw nectar from the pretty red hibiscus flowers of their garden shrub. Mellissa quickly picked up her new pup, and with hushed tones she said, "Look, darling, the gods have not forgotten me either. They have sent me this wondrous gift to enjoy. Lavinia says that they are called Jamaican Mangos." They stood together, with the little puppy snuggling into Mellissa's arms, until the delightful tiny creatures had had their fill of nectar and flew away.

Chapter Twelve

A New Clinic

After her birthday Mellissa set about the building of a new clinic, halfway between the compound and High View. It was urgently needed, she had had already two slaves who had needed her attention. One who had slashed his leg open with his cutlass and the other who had fallen down while carrying some heavy timber, and he had broken two of this ribs. There were also several women in various stages of pregnancy, none of whom alarmed her at present, but now a well provided clean space was essential.

As there was now a lull in the plantation work, before harvesting would begin during November, McBride had grudgingly let her have the use of six men, four of whom were skilled carpenters. Between them they quickly built the frame and filled in the walls. Then they put down a solid hardwood floor and smoothed it and polished it until the new floor shone. They had also cut several windows into the outside cabin walls and created an inner door, all of which Lavinia screened with fine netting so that the air could come in while keeping insects out.

There was room in the new clinic for six beds, three on each side with curtains separating the two sets of beds. The most important place in the clinic was an enclosed room at one end of the hut which had a surgical bed, a desk and several chairs as well as a large screen covered window.

The carpenter slaves installed the six strong beds with wooden frames and sail cloth canvas strapped to the frames, so that they could be washed down when they were soiled. Mellissa had been convinced in London that a clean space to treat patients helped to reduce infection and aid their recovery, so here on Jamaica she tried to reproduce her father's clinic at home. Three cupboards were built to hold clean linen, clean clothes, simple cotton shirts and loose trousers and skirts, and all sorts of swabs and bandages. A chest of drawers was brought down from High View which Mellissa used to keep her medical equipment, her scalpels, needles, threads, forceps, plus her stock of unguents and salves, and anything that needed to be clean and at hand for immediate use.

She also had a desk brought in so the she could store the medical books that her father had given to her before she had left for Jamaica. She read a section from one of them almost daily, learning more and more each time. She kept notes on things that she thought would be of use to her, in particular regarding the sort of illnesses, pregnancies or accidents that might occur on the plantation. She was experienced in all elements of midwifery and she could do simple surgery. But now she was also dealing with things such as snake bites, about which she knew nothing and had to rely on local knowledge from Lavinia, and much as she hated to, from McBride, as well.

Mellissa had already written to her father to send her a whole list of items that she thought might be needed if there were any serious incident or illness on the plantation, and she asked Charles to make a special journey to Kingston to collect the shipment. She also asked him to go to an apothecary in Kingston to buy laudanum, if they had some, and to replenish her salves and buy any snake bite anti-venom if they had any. Either for particular snakes or for use in general for bites which were not poisonous.

Chapter Thirteen

November 1829
Preparing for a Hurricane

"Harvesting should be about to begin but these high winds will make it impossible and very dangerous to start the necessary burning off of weeds growing between the separate lines of the canes." McBride was explaining to Charles the methods used for harvesting the sugar crop, the most important and profitable highlight of the plantation year. He and Charles were inspecting a far off field of canes which had had their four years of growth and were now mature enough to be cut down. "All the men that take part in the burning and clearing of the weeds and deadly snakes that live amongst the weeds…"

"Deadly snakes…?" questioned Charles.

"…but only the fittest and strongest of the men do the burning and cutting," McBride continued without addressing the interruption. "Without that access," McBride continued, "it is impossible to get to each stem to cut it down. And it is essential to burn out the snakes which will have nested in those weeds. It's an ideal place with just the right amount of cover for them to have their babies, and they will be super alert against any danger or threat to their young. Once the fires have done their job and are smothered, the cane can be cut. The rest of the men and women prepare the cut canes. 70% of the canes are topped, tied into bundles, and made ready for crushing, and the rest are cut into smaller pieces for replanting."

"How does that work? Don't we need to crush all the cane that we grow?" asked Charles.

"No. It is essential that we start a new crop each year when we cut the canes that are mature enough to harvest," explained McBride. "We don't plant seeds, we used pieces of the mature canes. Each of the smaller pieces must have at least four buds on them, and they will be planted in the next few days in the fields that we dug and turned over last week. You remember that the remains of an old crop had been left to rot in the ground to enrich the soil. We replant and the four-year cycle starts again."

"So, you don't plant seeds," said Charles, "just part of the adult canes which sprout again into new plants?"

"You've got it," said McBride. "That's exactly what happens."

"Now I can see how it all fits in," said Charles. "How does the crushing work?"

"I'll show you all about that when we start to crush, in the meantime we had better get back to High View and the slave compound and do what we can to protect the buildings in case these winds turn into a full blown hurricane," said the anxious overseer looking up at the skies, and turning his horse towards home.

McBride had told Charles about hurricanes and how destructive they could be. "They don't always hit us directly, mostly they miss Jamaica altogether," he said, "but I think that this time we will be on the edge, which will be bad enough."

"How bad can these winds get?" asked Charles. "I have experienced high winds at home, with trees being blown down over a wide area, but nothing quite like this."

"This wind, at the moment, is just a baby," said McBride, "a full blown hurricane can have rain and winds strong enough to take off the roof of your house. It could blow down any of the structures on the plantation, the cabins, the stores and barns, and even the solid brick cane crusher building."

"Oh, good heavens!" exclaimed Charles. "That would completely ruin our business. Even if we are on the edge, as you say, how bad do think that it will get?"

"I don't know," said McBride. "We will be able to tell in a day or two. These winds will either increase with a huge rainfall over night, or they will turn away from this part of the island and take their rain and destructive force elsewhere until the storm blows itself out over the ocean. Come on, we had better return to your house and start to board up the windows just in case the worst comes to the worst."

Charles and McBride rode their horses at full gallop and they reached the High View before the rains arrived. They were not in the eye of the storm, yet the winds were becoming ferocious, more than anything Charles had experienced before. McBride organised a small team of the strongest men to board up the windows in what looked like a well-practiced routine. Charles looked on as they did their work. It was evident to him that the boarding of the windows had been done many times before. They were quick and efficient in doing it, even with the use of ladders to board the window on the upper floor. Just as they were leaving Mellissa ran out of the house. "Charles," she called anxiously, with tears in her eyes, "I'm so frightened and I can't find Sheba. I think that she is frightened too, and she must have gone to hide somewhere. Please help me to find her."

"Don't you worry, Mistress Harrison, she will be hiding safely somewhere," said McBride. For once he was genuinely concerned about the distress of his employer's wife. "We will all have a look around and I'm sure that we will find her for you." They all went off, Charles included, whistling and calling for the puppy.

A few minutes later a tall black slave, the one with fascinating facial scars, came on to the veranda where Mellissa was waiting anxiously, and he held out the missing Sheba to her. "Here, Mistress," he said with a deep, strong voice with a surprising American accent, "here is your puppy."

"Oh, thank you so much for finding her," said Mellissa, smiling at Akami as she took Sheba safely into her arms. She had recognised the slave as the one who had stared straight into her eyes on the day that she and Charles had first arrived at Silver Bay. As he was turning away from her she asked. "Are you the man they call Akami? Thank you for finding her. Where was she hiding?"

Akami was surprised at the smile on her face and the kindness in her voice. Not only was she thanking him, something that had never happened since his capture many years ago, but she also knew his name. That was astonishing. "I found her sheltering in the log pile." He paused for a moment as he started to go down the stone steps. "How did you know my name?" he asked with amazement in his voice.

Mellissa was a little embarrassed. "I think that I heard it from Lavinia," she said as she turned to go back into the safety of the house. Safe from the high winds and even more, a safe retreat to recover from the thumping of her heart. *What's going on?* she asked herself as she shut the door.

What's going on? Akami asked himself as he walked back to the slave compound? His heart was beating loudly too.

Chapter Fourteen

First Harvest

They were fortunate. The hurricane passed them by and about three days later the winds had sufficiently died down for them to start their controlled burnings of the sugar cane. Charles and McBride were on their horses overlooking the most dangerous part of harvesting. McBride was explaining. "It is a tricky and dangerous procedure. The slaves have to burn and destroy the weeds, and any snakes who have not already left their snug homes. And they have to burn enough of the leaves so that the cane stems are cleared enough to be cut. But they have to be careful that the canes, with their sugary innards which can burn like a torch, do not catch fire completely and be destroyed. So the slaves have to work in small groups doing this dangerous work and we need to be attentive and pull them out if they are in danger." McBride paused.

"We don't want to be killing off our workforce, and we don't want to have to choose between saving the crop and saving the slaves," he added with a wry smile. "They need to be right inside the plants and they have little room to manoeuvre, so they have to burn their way in. Then a slave with a damper, a piece of thick leather on the end of a sturdy pole, smothers the flames when sufficient leaves and weeds had been burnt off. Together they work from patch to patch, so that once the burning off is done and as each patch cools off enough, they can go in with their sharp cutlasses to cut the canes one at a time. It's hard, precise and quick work, full of danger and extremely uncomfortable for the slaves. Sweaty, sticky and sooty, with high possibilities of burns and cuts. But this is the high point of the whole plantation operation so it has to be done the best and quickest way possible."

"You called the machete a cutlass? Is that right," asked Charles.

"Yes, that's what a strong, fierce blade is called here in Jamaica. I suppose it is what has been left over from pirate times. Did you know that in the last century Jamaica was the centre for pirates in the Caribbean?"

"I have heard that. Mellissa has a history book about the island, and she was telling me all about the pirates. Some quite horrid tales and well as stories about treasure and pieces of eight," laughed Charles. "Well, back to modern times. I can see now why only the fittest and most skilled of the men are used for harvesting. I hope that we don't need her, but my wife is a very good nurse, and she will be on standby to help with anyone who is injured from those cutlasses or from the fires." Charles peered again at the first group of slaves, with scarves tied around their faces to cover their mouths and noses, who were setting about their first burning of the day. "I can see who you have put in as team leader, that very tall young man with marks on his face. Is he the most skilled man that we have?"

"Yes, that's Akami," said McBride.

"Akami? What sort of name is that?" asked Charles.

"He's our only African slave," replied McBride. "We bought him from an American, after he had come straight from Africa to America as a young man. He is very quiet, not easily biddable, but he is immensely strong and he is clever too."

"Was that the same American who bought our babies, John Merriweather?" Asked Charles.

"Yes, that's him. He seems to do all the buying and selling from the United States," replied McBride.

"Hm," said Charles, thoughtfully. "Going back to that slave Akami, how do you control him?" asked Charles.

"I have to be a little bit careful and light handed with the whip..."

"Careful with the whip? You?" exclaimed Charles, with a wry smile.

"...light handed with the whip," continued McBride, "because he was over punished when he worked in a tobacco plantation in Virginia, in the United States of America. The deep scars on his back are more that I have ever seen. He has never accepted that he is a slave, but nevertheless he can be a very good worker. So I handle him with care."

"I don't know that I would accept subordination," said Charles. "A slave is a slave. He just has to accept that."

Just then Akami set light to his torch and Charles watched him intently as he started firing a first section of the cane. The flames flared up, twice as tall as the slaves who were standing by to keep them under control. They all jumped back. They waited a couple of minutes while the fire did its work, and then they went forward with their fire dampers and battered the flames until they were put out. They stood back, re-secured their scarves and wiped their foreheads, and then started again on the next patch. Meanwhile a second and third group of slaves, similarly wrapped in face scarves, repeated the same action on other sections of the cane field.

"Wow!" exclaimed Charles, "I have never seen such a thing before. That certainly looks dangerous. How often does it go wrong?"

"Fortunately, not very often. But I have occasionally seen the wind pick up or change direction all of a sudden and set large areas ablaze before the flames could be put out. We have had some nasty and very inconvenient burns which take a slave away from his work for several days. Which is why I take vigilant care so that we don't lose the best workers at the most important time of the year."

The air was becoming heavy with smoke and Charles decided to go back home. "I'll leave you to it," he said to McBride, and turned his horse towards home. He went straight to Mellissa when he got there. "Hello there, Old Girl," he said, grasping her around the waist and giving her a big, noisy kiss on the cheek.

"Charles," Mellissa protested. "Not in front of everyone, please!" and, "Wow, you are sooty and you smell of bonfires!"

He looked around, and then he saw three slave women that he had not noticed before. "Who are these women?" he asked. "Shouldn't they be at the harvesting? They need all hands there."

"No, Charles," she replied. "They don't need everyone, and these are the ladies, Maria, June and Emily, who I have been training a little to help me if we have any casualties that need attention. You should see how we have set up our clinic. I hope that we won't need it, but it is better if we are prepared."

"Yes, I suppose so," he said. "I saw today the start of the cane burning, and it looked hot and dangerous work. I hope no one gets hurt, we need all the men we have to get the harvest in." he paused for a moment, then he said, "I heard from McBride today something that you will be interested in," he said.

"What? Why would I be interested in anything that man has to say?" asked Mellissa, somewhat indignantly.

"All right, I'll say nothing," teased Charles.

"Oh! Come on then," she sighed. "What has the oracle to say that will be so profoundly important?"

"Well," said Charles, "he said that the slave Akami, you know the one who found your puppy, was brought to Jamaica from America?"

"Yes, yes. What about him?" Mellissa was curious, and wondering why her heart rate had started to whizz. "What's he done?" she asked, trying to make her voice sound normal.

"He's done nothing," said Charles. He was deliberately being slow in telling her what McBride had said, just to tease her. "McBride said that he was the one who bought Akami for the Johnstons, and he bought him from John Merriweather."

"That John Merriweather again!" exclaimed Mellissa, getting excited. "He's the one who bought the babies. We must be able to trace him. I will go and see the magistrate in St Elizabeth as soon as we have finished with harvesting and crushing. I must tell Lavinia, and I must ask Akami what he knows of the American slave trader. Lavinia has already been to see her pastor, and he was going to contact the Baptist Minister, Samuel Sharpe, who lives in Montego Bay."

"I don't want you mixing with the slave Sharpe." Charles was worried about her, and his concern came over as an order and she flinched.

"You know that I couldn't go to Montego Bay, even if I wanted to," said an angry Mellissa. "You don't seem to think that I have any sense at all."

"Calm down, Old Girl," said Charles, back to his laughing and friendly voice. "I was only meaning that it would be better if we had nothing to do with this Samuel Sharpe. I have heard that he may become a bit of a trouble maker. He is a slave, and he spends his spare time searching for ways to get all slaves freed on the island. It is my belief that his owner gives him too much free time. He is going to be trouble soon, you mark my words."

"Well, whatever I do," sighed Mellissa, "it will have to wait until after harvesting, and after Christmas too."

"Yes. Christmas," said a smiling Charles. "Our first Christmas together. And it will be so unlike any we have experienced before. Imagine a Christmas without snow!"

"I hope that everything is done on the plantation by then. The canes cut and crushed. The molasses boiled and crystallised into sugar, and the molasses sent to the rum factory. Then so we can give the slaves a memorable Christmas too," said Mellissa with her eyes shining with happiness and anticipation.

"Well, we will have to wait and see," said Charles, not wanting to spoil her happy mood by telling her that he was not going to treat his slaves the way she had treated her maids and servants at home. "And," he added, "don't you expect Christmas trees and plum puddings either. I think that Christmas will be totally different in this climate!"

Chapter Fifteen

Christmas in Jamaica, 1829

Their first Christmas together was going to be a total disappointment. Bad weather had delayed harvesting and cane crushing was still going on. None of the slaves had had any free time and Charles and Mellissa would not be able to celebrate fully either. On Christmas Eve, one the like of which they had never known, with Sheba sitting expectantly at Mellissa's side, they exchanged gifts under the starlight in their perfumed garden.

"I am so sorry my darling," Charles said as he gave his wife a kiss, "that I will have to help with the harvesting tomorrow. Mcbride tells me that it should have been completed by now, but the continual high winds have caused this delay, and if we don't complete the work while the weather is good the crop may well deteriorate." He reached down under the stone bench on which they were seated, and brought out a pretty package wrapped in shiny gold paper tied up with a bright red ribbon.

"Oh. Thank you my love," said Mellissa as she took out her gift. She paused to look at a box covered in green velvet and gasped when she opened it and saw its contents. Even under the dark sky, the stars gave enough light to make the jewels that lay on a bed of silk sparkle. It was an Indian ruby necklace, a family heirloom that he had brought from home, but originally had been obtained at secret cost from a cousin who worked with the East India Company. The necklace was a collar made up of many, many small, glittering rubies and a large, beautifully cut single stone which was suspended from the centre of the collar at the front. "Charles. Oh thank you Charles," she gasped, "it is so beautiful. Please will you put it on for me, I want to wear it straight away."

After he had done so and admired Mellissa, she in turn, reached down for the gift that she had prepared for Charles. "After that beautiful gift I feel a little bit awkward about my gift for you. I did not bring anything from home, I did my Christmas shopping in St Elizabeth, and they have no grand shops there."

"Please don't worry," said Charles giving her a big hug. "I am just pleased to open a gift from you under the Jamaican stars." There were two packages for him to open. The first was a box of the finest Virginian cigars, Charles's favourites. "These are indeed a splendid gift," my darling. "You know how much I love my cigar on the veranda after our evening meals, and these are the best." He opened the second package, and roared with laughter. In it were two very light weight silk shirts, with typical Jamaican colourful designs of flowers and butterflies, that she had had made for him in St Elizabeth. "Steady on Old Girl," he gasped when he had caught his breath, "I know that you want to make me comfortable here, but I didn't know that you wanted me to go completely native!"

Mellissa laughed too. "I know, my love," she said, "but I do see how uncomfortable you get in this sticky heat with your stuffed shirts and cravats. I thought that you might to wear them casually in the evenings when you only have me to admire you." She chucked again. "You don't have to wear them at all if you hate them."

"You're wrong," protested Charles. "I love them. I might even wear one of them tomorrow."

"You will do no such thing, my boy," said Mellissa in a faint scolding voice. "I won't have the slaves laugh at you, or even that dreadful McBride," She was grinning and the both held each other and kissed under the stars. "Merry Christmas, my darling," she said.

"Merry Christmas, my sweetest love," said Charles.

Christmas day dawned and Charles went with McBride down to the cane crushing and sugar boiling house. Akami was already at work with a team of slaves working under his direction. The cane crusher was a simple affair. It consisted of three upright wooden rollers, each made from the trunk of a mature hardwood tree. Each tree had an interlinking gear ring about them at the same height, about eight feet from the ground. The central roller, which was twice as high as the other two, had two opposing long poles attached to it at the top. Where each of these poles reached the ground their ends were affixed to the harness of two strong plough horses yoked together, each team being led by a slave. As these animals walked around in a circle the poles attached to the centre wheel caused it to turn, and the gears on the centre roller engaged with the gears on the shorter rollers, causing them to turn too. The sugar canes were fed between the rollers and were thus crushed, and the liquid that was extracted flowed out through a pipe at the bottom of the machine into buckets. These were collected by teams of slaves who emptied the buckets into boiling vats. The whole operation had to be smoothly run so that the liquid sugar, the molasses, did not overflow from the crusher, and was not left in buckets to spoil before it was processed into sugar.

While the crushing was going on Mellissa had old Abraham drive her into St Elizabeth on her own to attend the Christmas Day service at St Peter's church. She sat quietly in her pew feeling so sad that on this important day in year she was alone. No husband, no friends, no happy smiling children in the streets outside with red cheeks and woolly scarves tied tightly around their necks. She had only happy memories of Christmas at home with both her parents trudging through snow and laughing at her father who so often struggled to remain upright; Christmas mass and then a huge feast in front of a roaring fire. An exchange of Christmas gifts, and gifts too for all the servants. It was always the happiest time of the year. And now here in Jamaica, save for her faithful Sheba, she was all alone.

When she returned to High View, she was slightly embarrassed to give gifts to her house slaves. She wasn't sure if it was the right thing to give presents to slaves. She couldn't possibly make a gift to all the slaves on the plantation, but she felt close to the ones she saw and worked with every day. To Abraham she gave a fine straw hat to protect his balding pate from the hot sun.

"Mistress," he said, with tears in his eyes, "I done never get no present like this in all my days. I just a dumb nigger."

"No, Abraham, you're not a dumb negro," said Mellissa. She was so touched at his reaction to her gift that she was almost in tears herself. "You are a gentle, good hearted man and you have done everything you can to help me feel at home here in this strange land. Thank you."

To Lavinia, Roberta, and Chloe she gave each of them an African styled head scarf, in bright colours. "Oh thank you, Mistress," they said, almost in harmony. Lavinia continued, "We are all so happy that you now live in this house. You have already given us a future to look forward to, which we never had with Master and Mistress Johnston."

"And you made my hand better," chipped in Chloe, and they all laughed together.

Mellissa took Lavinia aside. "I have something here for little Angeline, is she in the kitchen?"

Lavinia called and the little girl came running in and stood at her mother's side. "Look," said Mellissa, "look what I found sleeping on my bed this morning." And she brought from behind her back a large rag doll. Unlike the dolls at home which had pink faces and limbs, this one had a brown face and limbs. It was dressed in a magnificent blue silk frock and had real kid leather boots. "Here, would you like to take her?" she asked a very hesitant Angeline, "I am sure that she would rather live with you than live with me." And she laid the doll in Angeline's arms.

"Thank you, Mistress," she whispered. "She's lovely."

"What will you call her?" asked Mellissa.

"I don't know," Angeline was still timid, but she now started to smile, "maybe I will call her Beauty."

Lavinia was now smiling proudly. "You are so good to us, Mistress," she said, "thank you."

Before Lavinia left the room with Angeline and the others, Mellissa called her back. "Lavinia, I have a little something extra for you," she said, shutting the door quietly. And then with a hug she gave Lavinia a silver ring with a small amethyst stone.

"Whatever is this, Mistress?" asked Lavinia, "You have already given me and Angeline such beautiful presents."

"Lavinia," Mellissa said gently, "You already know that I want to free you and Angeline from slavery. This ring represents from me an assertion that I will do everything that I can do to bring that about. We will say no more at present, I just want you to know that I have not forgotten."

Before Lavinia could say any more, the door was flung open and a hot and frazzled looking Charles burst into the room. "Mellissa, thank goodness you're here," he cried. "You've got to come to the crushing house, there's been a terrible accident."

"Whatever has happened? What do I need to bring with me?" asked Mellissa, almost as alarmed as her husband.

"It's Akami," said Charles. "He's got his hand caught in the crusher. I heard every bone break and splinter. He's screaming in pain. Quick, let's go."

Turning to Lavinia Mellissa said, "Go and get me the large black leather bag, and also the tins with needles and threads, and the bottle of laudanum. Oh, and bring a large bottle of rum, too."

"Charles," she said, she was calm now, the professional nurse part of her taking over from the panicking wife. "I don't think that you have room on your horse for me and Lavinia, and my medical equipment. I'll get Abraham to bring us in the small 'dog cart'. You take this rum," she took the decanter from the sideboard and put it in his hands, "and get Akami to swallow as much as he can. Mix it with the laudanum, it will deaden some of the pain, and hopefully will render him unconscious. Go. We will be following you as soon as I have gathered all we need. Go," she ordered calmly.

Chapter Sixteen

Akami Loses His Right Hand

Charles dashed off and Abraham brought the dog cart to the kitchen door. Lavinia and Mellissa gathered all Mellissa thought that she might need, including more rum, and quickly as he could, Abraham drove them down the bumpy lane to the crushing and boiling house.

Mellissa had not been there while it was in operation and it was like a vision of hell when she saw it working for the first time. McBride had managed to get the two horse teams to reverse enough for a slave called Samson to release Akami's hand as he lay, still screaming, on a board placed across two molasses barrels. The crushing machine was working again, and the shocked slaves were already continuing to feeding it with canes. The vats of sugar were still boiling and steaming. Mellissa approached the injured man. She examined his right hand closely and she could see at once that she would not be able to save it. Every bone was not only broken, but they were crushed flat. The wounds were bleeding heavily, and the blood would never circulate freely in the hand again. If she did not cut the dead hand away, gangrene would set in, poison his blood throughout his body and he would die in agony.

"Akami," she said, "I want to do whatever I can to help you, but I think that the only thing I can do is to remove your hand. It is damaged beyond any possibility of saving it. Can you hear me?" she asked. "Do you understand? I want you to swallow more of this laudanum, it should help with the pain."

Akami was quiet now. He looked at her with deadened eyes, the rum and laudanum that he had taken had partly taken over some of the pain. He nodded to her. "Do it, Mistress," was all he said.

To Charles, Mellissa said. "I am going to do what I can to dress his hand here and make it a little more comfortable, but I won't do the amputation until we get him into my clinic. This is not the right place for him to be or the right place for me to operate on him. I want him tied down on that board and carried to the clinic. Very, very gently. I think that horse or even the dog cart carriage will be too bumpy for him. Will you get the strongest men to do it please? And get some more of the rum down him too, I would like to make him to pass out if we can."

Very carefully Mellissa inspected Akami's crushed hand again. She was sure that she was right in her conclusion that she would not be able to save it, it was much too severely damaged. She used a tourniquet on his upper arm to stem the flow of blood, and dressed his hand lightly so that it would be covered and away from dirt and insects while he was being safely moved. She turned to Lavinia, "Lavinia," she said, "we won't be able to do anything more here. Will you please return with Abraham to the clinic and prepare for me the surgical bed, the instruments and the dressings that I shall be needing. All of them must be new and unused. I shall also be needing lots of clean water, both cold and heated, and plenty of clean towels."

After Lavinia and Abraham's departure, Mellissa and Charles walked with the slaves who were carrying Akami back to the compound and Mellissa's clinic. She ensured that the walk was gentle and smooth, and it took more than twenty minutes to reach the clinic. All the while Mellissa was holding Akami's uninjured left hand and talking smoothly to him. She could see that he was in dreadful pain and shock was setting in. His usual dark skin seemed drained of colour and he looked almost grey.

As soon as they arrived Mellissa went quickly in to check that everything was prepared and waiting for Akami. The slaves held the board alongside the surgical bed then she and Charles gently transferred him. Mellissa now looked up and addressed everyone in the room. "Thank you all so much for your help. I now need just to have Lavinia to assist me to try and save Akami. Please will you all now go, and you as well, Charles, and leave Lavinia and me to start. Thank you."

As they were all leaving, Mellissa was already inspecting her patient. "Akami," she said gently, "can you hear me?"

"Yes, Mistress." His voice was just above a whisper. He was sweating profusely.

"I know that you are in terrible pain, and I am going to have you drink some more of that numbing laudanum and rum. The more drunk you are, the less you will feel the pain." She looked into his dark eyes. The whites were yellow and flecked with blood.

"Lavinia, I want you to trickle the mixture into his mouth. As much as he is able to swallow."

She took up a new scalpel, bent over his right arm, tightened the tourniquet high on the upper arm, and deftly cut his hand away just above the wrist bones which were undamaged. Akami groaned out loud and then screamed.

"I'm sorry, I'm doing my best not to hurt you more than you are hurt already." She said. The blood started to spout out and covered her clean apron. She quickly sewed up the cut artery and then closed the end of his wrist with pads of clean linen. It did not work and the blood was still coming through faster than she could change the cloths.

"Lavinia," she said. "At home, the only way I have seen the sealing of amputated limbs is by dipping the end in boiling tar. I know that we don't have any tar here, but we do have boiling sugar. I think that the only way I shall be able save Akami's life is to do that. Will you call Abraham and ask him to very carefully bring me a kettle of sugar from the crushing house. Then we must set it over a small fire to bring it back to the boil." She looked at Lavinia's horrified face. "I know that it will be the worst pain that Akami has ever known, but it is all I can think of to stop the blood and save his life."

Lavinia left to find Abraham and Mellissa sat with Akami, still trying to staunch the flow of blood. He stirred and groaned. "Akami," she said, more to herself than to him. "Akami, I'm not a skilled surgeon, I'm just a nurse with some medical training. I want to save you and the only way I can think of will cause you more pain. I promise you that I will do my very best to minimise it, but I am afraid. Can you hear me? Shall I go ahead?" She then made a plea to God. "Dear God, what more can I do to save this man. He has already had to bear more pain than any man could be expected to do, yet he still lives. Please God, please help me to save him. Give me the courage and strength to do what needs to be done."

She closed her eyes, and heard a mumbled voice. "Just do it, Mistress. Just you go ahead and do it."

Abraham came in with a kettle full of sugar which he had brought back to the boil on an open fire pit. He was afraid. "Abraham," said Mellissa I need you to be very brave and help me cauterise Akami's arm. He needs to be held down while I do it. Give him some more laudanum if he is able to swallow it, and put a wad of this clean towelling between his teeth so that he does not bite his tongue."

She gently lowered Akami's arm so that it hung down over the edge of the bed. "Are you both ready? She asked. Abraham couldn't speak, he just nodded. Taking a deep breath Mellissa quickly dipped the stump in and out again of the boiling sugar. A scream such as Mellissa had never heard before filled the room. She forced herself to ignore it and working as quickly as she could she ensured that the blood flow had stopped, removed as much as she could of the sugar, and then wrapped the arm and stump with clean bandages.

Akami had fainted, and Mellissa made him comfortable. She knew that as soon as he came around he would be in terrible pain. Although it was warm in the clinic, she wrapped a blanket around him to try to help his body endure the shock.

Chapter Seventeen

March 1830
Akami's Story

It took more than three months for Akami to recover. During that time he lived in the clinic and was visited and nursed daily by Mellissa and Lavinia. Maria and Emily also took turns at attending him, and June stayed overnight. As he improved Mellissa, in order to distract him from his pain, encouraged him to tell them his story. He told it bit by bit and Mellissa, thinking that it would be of future importance, wrote it down.

Akami's story – collected in stages and written down by Mellissa when Akami was in recovery.

Part 1

I was born in Africa the year before the big rains came, which the white people call 1798. I was the fourth son of Chief Oluorogo of the Yoruba tribe, in the land the white people call Nigeria, after the great Niger River.

My father was the son and grandson of well-loved chieftains, who had all held their land and peace from the all-powerful King of Oduduwa, who lived not far from our village in the fortified city called Oyo-Illa. It was to this King that my father owed duty and loyalty, as well as yearly tributes of slaves. It was also demanded by the king that at times of war his chieftains would supply well trained fighting men; so it was my father's duty to be in strong control of his land and to make sure that all the young men of the tribe were trained as warriors after they had undergone their manhood training.

The people of that kingdom were slowly turning away from their ancient gods and were becoming Muslims; following a religion taught to them by the numerous Arab traders who were now more often crossing the deserts to make trade with us and to spread their religion. Some tribes like our own followed both this new religion while still making offerings to the old gods, just to make sure that their prayers were heard.

My father, who had only recently converted to become a Muslim, was an old man of forty-two rains when he first met my mother Yemojo, who was to become his fourth wife. She was young and beautiful, only fourteen rains, and she became the love of his life. She was of the darkest, ebony black, so beautiful in the eyes of our tribes, and in the eyes of my father in particular. She had beautifying tribal marks on her cheeks that showed that she was of the Dahomy tribe, and she had a fine and slender nose showing that she also had the mixed bloodline of Arab ancestry. She had been born of a Muslim father so she always covered her head in the way of Muslim women.

When he had been offered Yemojo in a peace trade with a Chief of the Dahomy tribe, no one thought of her as anything but a slave/servant. No one, not even my mother, thought that my father would have any interest in her.

His other three wives followed only the ways of their ancient gods and they were very jealous of my mother, of her beauty and her different and suspicious Muslim ways. They had been the honoured wives of the Chief for many rains already and they were comfortable with each other. My father's oldest wife, Oluno was more than thirty rains and she had been accepted as number one wife by the other two, and her first born son Odumo would be accepted by our tribe as the new Chief when our father passed over the great river into the land of the gods.

As well as my father's three wives he had more than fifty slave/servants who served him and his wives, each according to their importance within the tribe. He, his wives and his slaves lived in a separate compound in the centre of the village. No one expected my father to even notice his new trade/peace offering, but he did one day when he paused in his tour of his compound and heard her playing an ancient stringed instrument that she called a kora, which came from the far country of Mali. He was fascinated by the beautiful music, the beautiful instrument, and the beautiful girl, and he fell in love with her in an instant. And much to the great anger and jealousy of Oluno, Alana, and Gelado, his three wives, he married my mother in a great and glorious ceremony, when they were given gifts of all types including a beautiful maiden's headdress and armbands which had snakes curling around and

114

looking almost real. These were all made in bronze and studied with precious stones, by the village blacksmith who was also a craftsman in the making of bronze decorations, and fine jewellery.

I have seen many ceremonious gowns and beaded headdresses that are used for special ceremonies. They are beautifully made by the greatest of handcraft workers, both men and women, that they become treasures of the village. The gowns and hugely tall headdresses made especially for my parents wedding were the most beautiful of all. His other wives were made to feel that they had never been so important to him as Yemojo had become, causing yet another reason for jealousy amongst them. My father loved Yemojo so much more than he had ever loved his other wives and she loved him too. And just before the great rains of 1799, I was born.

Each of his original three wives had their own tribal house within the compound of the Chief, and by tradition they were selected in turn to attend and remain in the Chiefs house for a few days at a time. After his marriage to my mother a beautiful house was made for her in a sacred space next to my father's house. And everything changed in the routines of the compound. Against tradition my father spent most of his nights and many of his days exclusively with my mother and me. As a little boy I knew nothing of what had been before, I only experienced the love and company of both my parents almost all the time. But there were days and sometimes as much as a week when my mother and I lived and slept in our own house and I was aware that one or other of his other three wives would be sharing the sleeping mat with my father.

(Mellissa was writing while he was talking. "Akami," she asked, "do you know how to read and write in English?"

"No, Mistress," he replied, "I have never knowed how to read. I never knowed how to write neither."

"This story of yours," she said, "would be more realistic if you could write it yourself. It would be another weapon for the abolitionists to use. I think that it is important for everyone who approves of slavery to realise that slaves are real people, who in their own lives, in their ordinary lives, live a life similar to themselves. How did you learn to speak in English?"

"I just listened. I listened and I learned," he replied.

"Would you like me to teach you? I am sure that you will learn quickly."

"Yes, Mistress.")

The next day he continued his story.

Part 2

It was many years before I realised that I was privileged in my childhood, and during the early years I was included in the games, teachings and early pre-training for manhood with my three older brothers, but I had separate schooling in Arabic and learning to read the Koran. Gradually the hatred felt for me by their mothers was also taken on by their sons and I became almost excluded from their company.

As I was growing up Oluno, the first wife, became increasingly bitter and jealous that her position as senior wife and mother of Odumo, the next Chief elect, was being eroded. She was now also afraid that my father would put aside his first born son and choose me to become the next Chief. In my tribe it was the usual thing that the first born son of the Chief would be the chosen one but it was not always the case. My father had been the second son of his father. His elder brother, my uncle Akami for whom I was named, was not chosen because he was not fit or strong enough to lead the tribe. When he was six years old, he fell out of a tree and the injury to his back became a deformity so that he never walked straight or fully upright again.

My father was well loved by his older brother, they were always friends and playmates and after a time when it became quite clear that Akami would never regain his strength and agility, my father was chosen by the rest of the tribe to be the next Chief. Akami was by then twelve rains old, and was not fit enough to undergo his manhood training, so he not only expected to be passed over in favour of his younger brother, but he was also content with the tribe's decision. He was happy to remain my father's friend and counsellor and this was so for the rest of his life.

He was not treated like the enfeebled ones of the village who were too afraid to undertake manhood training, and who preferred to lie with other men such as themselves. They were despised by the villagers, and when tributes were demanded by the King the elders offered these men as slaves, thus cleaning the village of unacceptable practices.

When I was born, my uncle Akami was still alive but had by then become chair bound. It was an honour for me that I was named for him, and he was still respected by everyone as second to my father. His house was the second largest in the compound and he was served by two wives who lived with him in harmony. They had no children, and all the children, boys and girls of his brother were loved by him and his wives, and treated as their own. My uncle Akami tried his best to make my father aware of the rising hatred and jealousy of his number one wife and of possible danger that I might be in. But although he no longer loved Aluno, my father trusted his first wife and he could not believe that she was a threat to Yemojo or to me. He just laughed it off.

(Mellissa was changing the dressing on the end of his right arm, and Akami was wincing in pain. "I'm sorry to hurt you," she said. "It is looking much better today. There is no sign of any infection and the new skin is growing. I think that when you are telling me your story, it helps to distract your pain."

Akami looked at his ugly right arm and sighed. "You mean that now that I will start to talk about my life pain, I shall forget my body pain!")

Part 3

I was eleven rains old and approaching my twelfth rain and the start of the trials for my manhood training, when my three stepmothers must have started plotting together to get rid of their rival, Yemojo and her hated son, me.

The whole tribe knew about slave catchers and they were regularly warned never to stray far from the main tracks around our village, and never to be alone outside the village walls. In our land and amongst competing tribal villages slave catching, especially during frequent so called wars, which were usually not much more than squabbles between rivals, slave catching was quite common. These captives were either held until a ransom payment was made, usually for a boy, or until they were sold.

Those who were not returned to their villages were nevertheless treated well in their new tribes. Although they were slaves, they were treated like servants, and they worked, lived and often married within their new tribes, becoming, like my mother, completely accepted by the whole tribe as one of them. Indeed, my father's main advisor and friend was a man called Adjani, who had been a captured slave when they were both boys of nine rains. He had become a friend and playmate of both my father and Akami, and during the passing years he had married one of my father's sisters and became part of the Chief's family.

So when my three stepmothers plotted together to sell my mother and me to local slave traders my mother was certain that they thought that we would be cast down from our highly respected positions in life to become lowly servants in another tribe. She did not believe that they would be wicked enough to have us sold overseas into white man's slavery.

My mother was sure that they told the slave catchers where to find us when my mother was taking me to see the arena outside the village where manhood training for me would soon start. All my brothers and I, when we each reached the age of six years, had already undergone facial scaring, when patterns declaring our relationship to the Chief were cut into our faces so that all could see. My elder brother, Odumo taunted me by telling me how much more pain I would soon be facing. He would often pull me aside and tell me in secret, of the terrible things that were expected of those undergoing manhood training, including all sorts of painful trials and the horrors of circumcision. He would show me his scarred and twisted 'toto' which he said was the result of having been cut with a blunt knife.

The real fear of the boys who were waiting for this training to begin was that it was always done in secret and every boy who had become a man had to swear never to tell anyone about what they had undertaken. So Odumo was breaking his oath, but he knew that I would never tell on him. He hated me but he knew that I was honourable. Only the elders were able to talk about what was to happen to each boy in their secret councils, because each time this manhood training happened they discussed each boy individually. They examined the special fears of each boy and what he would have to undergo to find his inner bravery to conquer his fears, and complete the trials to become a man.

("What fear do you think the elders wanted you to overcome?" asked Mellissa as she sat with Akami. "Were you a timid boy?"

"I was afraid of circumcision, but I think that we all were," said Akami. He was moving his arm by now and Mellissa was concerned that he would undo the healing that had already taken place.

"Just a moment, before you continue," she said, "I want to strap your arm close to your body to protect the stump. To begin with most of your right arm was numb, but I think that the feeling has begun to come back now. Can you feel my touch all the way down?"

"Yes, Mistress," he replied with a wince. "I done get better soon. Will I have to go back to the crushing house?"

She used a brightly coloured head scarf to tie his arm across his chest. "You are beginning to heal well, now, Akami." She replied, "But I don't think that you are ready for work just yet." She paused, "now tell me about your secret fears that only the elders knew about."

Akami whispered so low that Mellissa could hardly hear him. "I is afraid of snakes. I done know why. I know they most is no danger to me if I not touch them, but I is afraid of them. I even afraid of they dried skin, the ones they drop on the ground when they gets new skin. I felt sick to look at my mother's beautiful armband decorated with a snake."

Lavinia, who was preparing clean swabs and bandages for the store cupboard, also heard and she said, "We had a slave here who belonged to the Johnstons, who they sold. She was afraid of birds. Any bird, big or small, safe to touch or dangerous. She screamed every time she even saw a feather on the ground, no matter how the Mistress beat her."

"Yes, I have heard of people who are afraid of ordinary things, often things that hold no danger at all. I read in one of my father's books that long ago the ancient Greeks described these fears as 'phobia', that's a Greek word, but I don't really know what it means. I don't know why these fears happen. I understand that you can be afraid of some snakes, especially the poisonous ones. But what harm could dried, dead skin, or a bronze armband do to anyone? It is such a strange thing. What do you think that the elders were going to do with you in order for you to overcome your fear of snakes?"

Akami paused for a while. "I think they may have put me in a deep pit full of snakes, non poisonous ones, and made me stay there until I was able to calm my fears sufficiently for me to work out how to climb out of the pit or until I realised that these ones would not harm me, and I was able to overcome my fear of them."

Mellissa with Lavinia's help, moved Akami onto his side to make him more comfortable. "Do you want to continue with your story now or wait until tomorrow?" asked Mellissa.

"I say it now, Mistress.")

Part 4

It was my mother's intention to calm my fears of the ritual and especially the culmination of this training when each of the boys would have the foreskin of their 'toto' cut away. It was something that every male child in all the tribes of Yoruba had to undertake before he was accepted as a man, we all knew that we had to undergo this, and many were afraid. Most of these boys were successfully cut and their wounds healed after a few weeks of pain and lack of

119

comfortableness, but occasionally things went wrong and their wounds became septic. The fortunate ones died quickly and those less fortunate took several weeks to die.

My mother thought that her three co-wives instructions to the slave catchers were that we were to be taken and sold into a village far from our own so that we would never be able to find our way home. My mother was always generous to them and she truly believed that they had no knowledge of white man slavers.

We were on our way back to the village when we were surrounded and captured by five Dahomy men. No matter that it was quite clear because of my mother's facial scars that she too had come from a Dahomy tribe, they would not relent and we were bound up and made ready to be sold to Arab traders. I tried to be a big boy, I was nearly a man. I wanted to protect my mother and I ran at one of the men with my head lowered. I did manage to surprise him off guard and I rammed him in the stomach. But it was, of course, a useless gesture. He flipped me off as if I were no bigger than a bug, and to my shame the other four men laughed. "We will have to warn our buyers that we have trapped a wild baboon," one of them said as they tied my and my mother's arms behind our backs, and we were helpless.

I was still feeling ashamed of myself for not having been able to protect my mother, and I wanted to die when I realised that I was helpless to save her when night after night in that first week she was humiliated and forced to submit when one after the other the five men took their pleasure of her. They ignored her tears and struggles and justified what they were doing by saying that because she was Dahomian like themselves, she was theirs by right.

Once we had left our lands far behind we were forced to walk for miles through jungles so thick with vines and undergrowth that we all had to use machetes to cut our way through. You can be sure that my mother and I were closely watched so that we had no opportunity to use the machetes to attack and escape our captors. After the jungle there were swamps to be crossed. Swamps that hid deadly snakes, which fortunately for us were more afraid of us than we were of them. We then traversed great open grasslands where we were delighted to have the company of the best of African wildlife, including herds of elephants, gazelles and zebras. Lastly we entered the desert lands where we suffered great shortages of water. By then all of us including our captors, were exhausted.

Eventually, when we had crossed the desert lands we met up with and were sold to another group of Dahomian slave catchers who resold us and thus we became the property of Arab slavers. These slavers already held captive ten men and three women of a tribe whose language I did not recognise or understand, and they were all so exhausted that they looked like the walking dead, ghosts, and we were afraid of them. We were all rested for a day and then, bound together in long line, we were marched north to a small township at the mouth of the Gambia River, and there we were sold to, what I later learned, were Portuguese slave traders. It was many weeks since we had first been captured and I was now twelve of my rains, so it must have been 1810 in your years.

By then England had outlawed the slave trade from West Africa, but the Portuguese were still trading. They had small fast ships that could out-sail the heavy English ships which were trying to stop slaving all along the West African coast. My mother and I, and eight other women, six children and two babies, were put separately in a small holding pen built on the top deck of the ship. My shivering cowardice saved me yet again as I was once more humiliated, counted as a child and kept with the women and children and not shackled up on the bowels of the ship with the men. I knew then that I would never become a man. I had missed my manhood training and my circumcision, my 'toto' was still as a child's, and I was now condemned to remain a child forever. The circumcision that I had so feared was now my most heartfelt desire. Every time I looked at my 'toto' I was ashamed. Not only could I not call myself a man, but I was also unable to follow my Muslim religion, whereby I would now be called an infidel.

The women and children were uncomfortably crushed into that small cage like pen. Because it was on the top deck, not only were we tossed about with every rough wave, but because the sides were open to the elements most of the time we were alternatively soaked with sea water and then roasted in the sun. We were fed through the bars of the cage and had a bucket to defecate into. Once a day, if the seas were calm enough, we were allowed out to exercise on deck and to clean the hold floor and the nauseous smelling buckets. But when, on a few occasions, I came into contact with the men who were most of the time chained below deck I realised how fortunate I had been to be considered still a child.

These men, about one hundred and twenty in number, were chained day and night on a double row of benches with no room to sit up or turn around. Food slops were given to them in wooden gruel bowls, if they turned their heads and refused to eat the slop was forced down them by one of the sailors. Together with spilt food, and vomit they were forced to urinate and defecate on the benches where they lay. They were stinking and covered in muck and shit when they were allowed up on deck to exercise, still linked to each other by long chains, while those who were strong enough were forced with a whip to clean up what they could of the filthy hold. The women and children could see them and even exchange a few words when they were on the top deck, but they were still controlled by sailors bearing whips and guns. They were forced to dance as a sort of exercise. One of the sailors would play a tune on a tin pipe, a Portuguese melody that had no dance connection with our African ways of making music, no rhythm, no drums that we considered as music. In their state of filth, shame and hunger it was almost impossible for them to lift their limbs which were still weighed down with heavy chains, and dance, but that is what they were forced to do. Then the sailors threw buckets of sea water over them as a method of cleaning, and afterwards they were then forced back down into their stink hole to be chained to their benches once more.

Six times during our crossing of the big water one of the men on the lower deck died of filth, hunger and disease. Each time their rotting bodies were left in place until the next time the men were unchained and led up onto the top deck, then the dead bodies were thrown, without any covering, gentleness or shame, overboard to be fed to the waiting sharks. No words or ceremony to catch their souls. Left to haunt the world forever. On one occasion a man, who was the husband of one of the women who were held in our cage, who was dying but not yet dead, was also thrown to the sharks while he was still alive and his screams could be heard above the pipe and dancing. His wife's screams were mixed with his as she called to be allowed to throw herself onto the seas to join him.

(Akami had been in recovery for a week. His wound was beginning to heal, but his body was still in a state of shock. Mellissa, while encouraging him to tell his life story, was deeply fascinated and shocked by what he was relating. Almost all the white people she knew thought of Africans as wild savages, but both Lavinia and Akami talked of arts and culture that go back centuries. Yet at the same time they also have traditions of slavery between the tribes. But it was a very different kind of slavery, a far gentler kind of slavery where slaves became servants and gradually became tribe members, often marrying within their new tribes. Perhaps they even benefited their enslavers by bringing in new blood into small societies. She reflected on white man's slavery, so cruel in America and the West Indies, but that too, especially in the past such as

Roman times, had gone on as part of life all over Europe. Even in the Holy Bible there were several chapters which included slavery between Jews, Egyptians, Persians and other countries of the Middle East. She had even read of slavery in the far eastern countries of Cathay and Mongolia, perhaps, she thought, that it had always gone on in different ways all over the world. But, she concluded, that does not make it right. And our version of slavery seems to be particularly cruel and a horribly acceptable form of slavery.)

Part 5

Akami continued his story. I could not tell, but I think we took about three weeks, maybe more, to cross the big water. When I next saw land, it was the shores of Virginia, in the United States of America. Most of the Portuguese ships took their captives to Brazil in South America, but the captain of our ship had a delivery of barrels of fortified Portuguese wines to take to Richmond, Virginia. So we were taken off the ship in Richmond to be sold there. All the men and most of the women and children were so enfeebled by then that the ship slavers put all of us into a dockside prison where we were fed good foods to get us healthier looking and therefore more valuable as property. We had separate areas for personal cleaning, and we had room to exercise properly. My mother and I, and two of the other women, were fortunate to recover quite quickly and after ten days we were pronounced fit enough to be put up for sale.

We were transferred to a holding pen in Richmond and one after the other the men and women in this pen were taken to an auction platform and sold off to the highest bidder. When it was our turn, we were fortunate enough to be sold as mother and child. Before the bidding started a white man stood up with us and started to describe us in a language which neither of us understood. My mother was forced to remove her clothing and when she hesitated she was whipped. It was a light whipping that did not break her skin, but she still whimpered and to her shame she was forced to stand there naked. It was clear that the trader was saying that she was a good breeder when he pointed to me, a big strong boy, he fondled her breasts, and mauled her between her legs. Once more I rose up to defend and protect my mother, but I was whipped soundly, with such brutality that, unwittingly, a scream was forced out of my lungs. I too, had my trousers taken away I suffered indignity as my 'toto' was pulled and handled roughly by the white slave dealer who stank of dead and rotting meat. I was stunned to inaction and by the time I had recovered myself we had been sold to a Virginian tobacco planter, Rubin Hawkins.

The tobacco plantation was half a day's drive from the township of Richmond, and we were taken there in the back of an old farm trailer. We were the only purchases made by Mr Hawkins that day. I was shackled to the trailer and mother was tied to me. It was dark by the time we arrived at the plantation and without food or water we were transferred to and locked in an outhouse belonging to the plantation house. The next morning an aging white woman opened the door. Although we did not understand her it was clear that she had some sympathy for us, especially my mother.

"Oh. You poor things," she said. "I'm sure that my husband did not mean to lock you up like this. You come to the well and you can draw some fresh water to drink." This became my first duty as a slave, to wind up the bucket. After we had taken a gasping drink we were separated, and did not see each other for several days.

My mother, who had been the equivalent of a queen in her own homeland, was put to work in the kitchens and I, the son of a king, was put with the men to begin my work as a tobacco harvester. I was renamed James but I refused to answer to anything but Akami, and I was often tied to the whipping post and whipped until my skin was coming away. Whipped to make me work, whipped into submission and acceptance of my new status in the world.

("Oh, Akami," said Mellissa, with tears in her eyes, "Lavinia and I have seen the horrible scaring on your back. I cannot understand how anyone could do that to another man.")

Part 6

I did not see my mother again for months. She was taken into the plantation house and I was taken to the slave quarters, and locked into a wooden shed with no windows. Because I was the only field slave who had been brought in straight from Africa, I was treated by everyone, the overseers and the slaves, as a wild savage who had lived in the trees, eating only bananas. I was still only twelve rains, which were called 'years' in America. I was young, angry, and I could not understand what anyone was saying to me. I did not talk but I learned English with every lash of the whip.

It was a small plantation compared with many in Virginia, but Rubin Hawkins was determined to grow the most superior and valuable tobacco, which demanded attention daily from the planting of the first seed to the day when the crop was ready to be harvested.

This meant that all his slaves worked long, long hours, and were forced to work as fast as they could. Those who did not work fast enough were whipped until they bled. We worked in gangs of about ten with lead slaves who worked fastest and encouraged their gang to work as fast as themselves. All gangs were under the direct supervision of two white overseers who were not at all hesitant in using long reaching whips which were flayed at the tips, to encourage speed and punish slackness.

Seeds were planted in seed beds in January. While they were growing we had to prepare the fields where the plants would be grown into small 'hills', one hill for one plant, and there were thousands of hills to be planted with the seedlings in the springtime. During the growth of the tobacco plants, each plant had to looked after individually. This work included watering, weeding, pinching the top leaves off so that the lower leaves grew stronger, taking off each plant any shoot which sprouted between a leaf and the main stalk, they called it suckering. Then worst of all in the hot summer sun we were forced to work all the hours of daylight picking off from the sticky stems, tobacco worms and other insects. And at harvest time each separate tobacco leaf had to be picked off by hand.

During all that time I continued to be stubborn. I could not accept that I was a slave, and I would not let anyone, slave, overseer or Master call me James. I was learning English and I would say, "I am Akami. I am the son of a Chief. I am not James." And I was whipped again and again.

Hour after hour, at the hottest time of the year, from before daybreak to darkness, I made up hundreds of bundles of the tobacco leaves and carried them from the fields to the drying sheds. There was no break for drinking or eating. We took corn pone with us in the morning to eat a bit at a time as we carried our bundles to the drying sheds, and we just were able to snatch a drink of brackish water from a tin cup attached to a water barrel when we got there to deposit our loads. Some of the women slaves worked alongside the men, at an acceptable slower pace, and at harvesting time they worked in the drying sheds. There they were joined by the women slaves from the plantation house. All the women were preparing the cut tobacco leaves for drying and curing and it was only then, when I brought yet another bundle of tobacco leaves to the sheds that, by chance, I next saw my mother.

Something had happened to my beautiful mother. She looked old and sick. Her once beautiful eyes and her shiny black skin looked dry and dull, and she walked slowly and unsteadily.

"Mother, whatever has happened to you?" I cried out in our own language.

"Oh my son, my precious son, I have been praying that I would see you again before I die. I don't really know what I am sickening from," she said, as tears welled up in her eyes, "they say that I have caught an American sickness that won't go away because of my African blood. But to see you again has made me feel happy for the first time since we came to this hateful land."

I did not want to tell her of the beatings and whippings that I had suffered. She was not strong enough to bear that. "Oh mother," I cried. "What evil have we done that our gods and Allah wish to punish us for? I want to go home and I want to take you home with me."

She let me enfold her in my arms. "My big brave boy," she whispered, "I don't think that my body would survive the crossing of that big water again even if I was looked after in the best way. I shall die happy now that you have held me again. My bones will soon be laid in this hostile land and I pray to Allah that my soul will be able to find its way home to Africa."

Before I could say anything more I was pulled away from my mother and sent back to the fields to continue with the harvesting. Two weeks later I heard from slave rumour that my beautiful mother had died. I was not told by the overseer and I was never told where she was buried. My soul died with her and I have never loved again.

(It was Mellissa who was crying now. "Akami, Akami," she cried, "life has been so cruel to you, and I don't know how to make it better. But I will try my best."

"Mistress," said Akami, "you done good already. You is make my life better. I tell of my come to Jamaica, then I done."

Mellissa picked up her notebook again. "When you have finished," she said, "I will write your story up properly and I will send a copy to a man called William Wilberforce in England. I hope that it will help in his campaign to end slavery.")

Part 7

I remained the slave of Rubin Hawkins for eleven years. I never saw him. I never spoke to him. No matter how I was mistreated by the overseer, I worked with deliberate slowness becoming one of the recognised examples of 'lazy niggers'. They thought that I had been whipped into submission, but really I had no care about me or anyone else. I did not converse with anyone and I made no friends with the other slaves who continued to call me a difficult African nigger.

Rubin Hawkins turned out to be a gambler and became deeply in debt, and he decided to sell his difficult slave to pay off some of his debts. He sold me to an American slaver, called John Merriweather, who brought me here to Jamaica. John Merriweather is not a rich man so he cannot buy any slaves outright, he draws on credit notes and redeems them when the slaves are sold. It took two months for us to reach Jamaica, sometimes walking overland, sometimes riding and sometimes taking short trips from port to port on small ships, and during that time I got to know him well. We landed in secret in Montego Bay and John Merriweather was able to hire two horses from a friend. We had to make our way across the island, through the jungle, the wild and impossible Cockpit Country, which is where escaped slaves live, and the rain forest to Silver Bay plantation to Master and Mistress Johnston, with whom he had already had dealings. They were not concerned that I had a 'difficult' label attached to me because they needed the big and strong man that I had become.

They had already two slaves called James, and the overseer also has James as his first name, so they accepted me as Akami, which immediately made me less aggressive and obdurate. I have been a slave here for eight years.

(Mellissa was surprised to hear the name of John Merriweather again. "So you know John Merriweather too. What can you tell me about him?)

John Merriweather is a strange man with white skin and dark Negro hair and eyes. The Americans have devised different words for people of mixed blood. John Merriweather is a quadroon, which means one of his grandparents was black. They even have a silly word for a person who has only one black great-grandparent; it is octoroon, meaning he is one eighth black, and he can still be regarded as a black by a real American white man!

Merriweather's grandmother was an American slave who had a child by her owner. That child with half and half parentage was called a mulatto. She was still a slave, now owned by her father. When she grew up, her father made her a free woman and she was married to an overseer on the plantation adjoining her father's. His name was Thomas Merriweather. John, their child, became involved in the buying and selling of slaves, but unlike most traders he has a gentle heart. It distressed him to see slaves treated as cattle and being bought and sold as beings who have no tender feelings towards their loved ones and children, and he started to decline working for anyone who just wanted to sell their people at auction.

The Johnstons were still ruthless owners, but they differed in that they recognised that they got more work and co-operation from a well-treated slave than one who is continually beaten. They were also determined to sell their infant boys, and although John Merriweather thought that it was a terrible crime against both mothers and children, he also thought that if he could place each child directly with decent owners they would do better than having been sold at auction to the highest bidder, to an owner who had no feelings. I do know that for each child he sold he kept a record of its parents and of its purchasers.

("So," said Mellissa, getting quite excited at the thought of finding Lavinia's son, "if we can find him he will be a direct link to the missing children, and maybe he will help us to find some of them so that we can reunite some of the mothers with their children."

"Mistress, you have a soft heart," said Akami in a low voice, "and I will do all I can to help you to find John Merriweather." She reached out and took his hand, and as before, a small electric shock ran up her arm. She looked at Akami and saw at once that he had felt it too.)

Chapter Eighteen

April 1830

Abraham Gets Some Help

Mellissa, Charles and Sheba the dog were sitting on the veranda watching the sun go down. They were talking quietly about Akami and Lavinia. The cicadas were being particularly noisy that evening. It was almost as if they wanted to drown out the human voices. "Now that you have read their stories," said Mellissa, raising her voice a little so that she could be heard above the dominant insect buzz, "don't you think the abolitionists would find them useful in their campaign? I want to write out clear copies and send them directly to William Wilberforce himself."

"They are certainly very moving, but I don't know how useful they would be to the cause," he said. "I suppose that almost every slave who was captured in Africa would have a similar story. But the trade from Africa has already been outlawed, and most of the slaves we have in the colonies today were born in the colonies."

"Do you really think that makes them less human, less of interest?" asked Mellissa, getting a bit agitated.

"Calm down, Old Girl," said her husband. "I know that you want to free all slaves, but we would be ruined if that were to happen."

"Well I do want to talk about Lavinia and Akami…"

"No," interrupted Charles, "I am not freeing them. And I need Akami as soon as he has healed enough to work again."

"…I am not asking you to free them. I do know that you won't let that happen," said Mellissa. "No, what I want is to have them both help me trace the missing children. Akami knows Merriweather well, and he may know how to find him."

"No," said Charles. It was he that was getting agitated now. "I just told you that I need him to work."

"He will never be able to work again like he did before. He has only one hand now, and a weak left hand at that," protested Mellissa.

"I know, but he can still be a team leader," Charles insisted.

Mellissa thought for a moment. She knew how stubborn Charles would get if she continued to argue against him. "How about this as a compromise," she said a little hesitantly. She wanted to make it look as though Charles had won the argument. "I can see by the way Akami is healing that it will be at least a couple of months until he will be ready to return to working in that hell hole of the crushing house, or even in the fields. And by then it will be the slackest part of the year and he won't be needed quite so much. I know that he is getting fitter by the day and he will very soon want to be active, and not stay in the clinic all day." She paused, she knew that she had to say the right words in order for Charles to accept that her suggestion would be better for the plantation than it would be for Akami himself. "I think that it will be beneficial to all of us to get him strong and healthy again, so my suggestion is that he goes to live with, and help old Abraham for the next couple of months. The poor old man just cannot do the things he has always done, and together he and Akami would work as a good team doing all that needs to be done around the house and gardens."

Charles thought about that idea. He hated having arguments with his wife, and Mellissa knew that she had won as soon as she saw the beginnings of a smile on his face. "All right," he said. "I will let him stay and be mollycoddled by you for a bit longer!" He grinned and reached over to give his wife a kiss. "The sun has gone now, let's go in," he said, taking her soft hand in his, while asking himself, *How do these women always seem to get the upper hand?*

The next morning a refreshed and happy Mellissa asked Lavinia to bring Abraham to the rose garden to see her. She knew that if he were called into the house he would be very nervous. "Good morning, Abraham," she said in a sunny and cheerful voice, trying to allay his apprehension, "Look how beautiful the roses are right now. You know just how to make them bloom at their very best. You work so hard to make all this happen, and now I want to make some changes in your work routines which I hope will help you. Come and let us talk together about your work."

Abraham looked a little frightened. "I's not too old to work, Mistress. I still can do," he said.

"Abraham, I know that you work well and I am happy with what you do," said Mellissa, "but I was wondering if you would help me to make Akami get better faster."

130

Abraham was mystified. What was his Mistress talking about? What did he have to do with Akami's recovery? "Mistress," he queried, fear and strain showing as perspiration ran from his brow, "I not know doctoring. I just a dumb nigger."

"You are not a dumb negro at all, Abraham," said Mellissa. "You are very important to the running of High View and the gardens, and that is exactly how I think that you can help Akami. He is getting better, but his arm is not healed enough for him to go back to his usual work in the cane fields. So, I think that it will help both you and him if, for a couple of months or so, he helps you with the work that you do around the house and looking after the pigs and the garden. Do you think that you could show him what to do?"

Abraham did not look as though he was delighted with what Mellissa was proposing. "I not really know that nigger, Mistress," he asked. "He only got one hand. What he do with only one hand, Mistress?"

"I am sure that you will find that he will be able to almost as much as you can," said Mellissa. "Of course he won't be able to do anything that needs two hands, but he will be able to lift and carry things, he will be able to help you with the gardening, and I am sure that you could teach him to look after the pigs and the horses and drive the wagon."

"Well. I try, Mistress. I try." He sighed. "I jest bring that boy down here to my garden, and I see."

"No, wait until I have spoken to him first," said Mellissa, "then I will send him down to you."

Abraham shuffled off, still looking disconcerted, and Mellissa went to find Lavinia. "I'm going down to the clinic to talk to Akami about him working with Abraham…"

"I think that will be good for both of them," said Lavinia.

"…and I am think that it would work even more if Akami were to live in Abraham's cabin," continued Mellissa. "Come with me and we will go down to the clinic and talk to Akami."

Mellissa was aware that she had some ambiguous feelings towards Akami and decided that she should not spend any time alone with him. Lavinia often accompanied her in the clinic so that there was nothing unusual in her asking Lavinia to come with her. It was an everyday beautiful Jamaican morning, and it was a joy to walk down to the clinic through the beautiful gardens and shrubs. A cloud of multi-coloured macaws were flying from tree to tree and Mellissa had to stop and enjoy the sight. "I still gasp at the beautiful things here in Jamaica that you just take for granted because you have lived with this joy every day of your life."

"But the difference between us is that in miserable England you were and are a free person, bound only by English conventions," said Lavinia, "whereas I, who admittedly have always lived in this beautiful country, have always been a slave."

Chapter Nineteen

23 May, 1830
The Lady Who Has Everything

It was still two months to go, to reach the first anniversary of Charles and Mellissa's arrival in Jamaica, and Mellissa was assessing how the past ten months had gone. It had been an eventful time and a profitable one too. The harvest had been good and the Fire Rum manufacturers were well pleased with the quality of their cane sugar. The only misfortune had been the crippling of Akami, one of the finest and fittest of their slaves. Mellissa was still hostile to James McBride, and he to her, but they both recognised in each other the quality of their competent skills. Mellissa still thought of him as a brutal thug who enjoyed inflicting pain and dominating the slaves, especially the women but she, through Charles, had got him to tone down his aggressiveness. He, in return, recognised her skills in medicine and admired the improvements in the health of the slaves and the nursing of any injuries that befell them. What pleased him the most was that all the additional care that they received made them fit to return to their tasks sooner.

There had been two more births in the new clinic and she and Lavinia had attended both together. Mellissa was satisfied with the competence of Lavinia and was pleased when she offered to train another two girls to learn midwifery and simple nursing. Many of the slaves were eager to exchange their hard lives doing field work for an easier life in the clinic, and finally Rosie and Rebecca were chosen. Rosie was happily nursing her new baby boy with great contentment knowing that he was not going to be taken away from her when he was weaned. Rebecca was daily expecting to be told that her baby boy had been found and bought back, although both Mellissa and Lavinia continued to tell her that were trying to trace the children that had been sold off and they did not know when, or if ever, they would be found.

But Mellissa was proudest of her main achievement, the successful amputation of Akami's right hand, which although for him had been painful in the extreme, had in the end saved his life, saving him either from dying of gangrene or bleeding to death. He and Abraham were now content to work and live together in Abraham's cabin. Akami was treating Abraham as a favourite 'uncle', which brought back memories of his own uncle Akami from his lost life in Africa.

At the end of the month, Mellissa and Charles were once again sitting on their veranda with Sheba sitting quietly next to Mellissa. Her tail was wagging and her mistress was unconsciously scratching her dog behind her ears. She and Charles were drinking a glass of wine and idly discussing the beauty of the island and the events of the past ten months, when they came around to talking about Mellissa's next birthday. Charles pointed to the content Sheba and grinned. "So, Lady Who Has Everything Here in Paradise, what more could you possibly want?" he asked with a smile.

"Charles," she said, "you know very well that it is four months to my next birthday. What on earth are you talking about?"

"Well," he replied. "I was thinking that you might like something to be bought from England. Something to remind you of home, or some sort of home comfort. And that will need some time for me to arrange."

Mellissa took a deep breath. There was something that she really wanted but was afraid of asking for. To achieve her wish she knew that she had to use the right words, spoken in the right tone.

"There is something that I would dearly like, and I really would like it right now rather than wait for my birthday. And I would like you to consider it seriously before you turn me down," she said hesitantly and paused for a moment.

"Go on," said Charles with an audible sigh. He was suspecting that once more she would ask for some of the slaves to be freed.

"I would like you to sell to me so that I would personally own, the two slaves Lavinia and Akami." She held her breath waiting for his reply.

"What?" he exclaimed. "Just because I won't free them you want to free them yourself!"

"No. I promise I won't free them," she said quickly. "You can even put that in as a condition of sale. And I will also agree that you would have priority to call on them both to work for you at harvest time. For the rest of the year I want to be free to use their time as I want without having to ask you or McBride if I can do so."

Charles was puzzled, he scratched his head. "But I don't understand why, and what you want to do with them? He said. "As it is you control most of what they do on a day to day basis."

"Yes. I know that I do," replied Mellissa. "But I am aware that as Akami gets closer and closer to full fitness again, McBride is looming nearby, wanting to get him back to do what McBride considers is his proper work."

"But what is it that you want them to do?" asked Charles once more.

"I want to make a determined effort to find those babies that Mrs Johnston sold away from their mothers. Akami knows John Merriweather well and I am sure that between the three of us, the preacher Moses and a slave in Montego Bay called Rev. Samuel Sharpe we will be able to find at least some of these children."

"I have heard of Samuel Sharpe and I think that he is trouble. Better that you keep clear of him. But, what do you know about him?" asked Charles.

"He is a slave and a Baptist Minister who lives in Montego Bay, with a reputation for helping any slave in trouble, and he knows John Merriweather well. He follows all the work of the abolitionists in England and he anticipates new laws to end slavery. I mean to allow Akami and Lavinia to go about and speak to anyone who can help us, and I would give them papers to carry to show anyone who inquired that they are my slaves and they have my permission to leave the plantation unaccompanied."

"If Akami were to speak to this Samuel Sharpe, he would have to cross the mountains, the jungle and rainforest to get to Montego Bay. What makes you think that he won't run away and join the freed slaves and rebels, the savage Maroons, who live up in the wild mountains of Cockpit Country?" asked Charles. "That's even if I agree to your crazy idea. Why you continue with such ideas, which are totally against anything any of the Jamaican slave owners do with their slaves, their property, I just don't know." He was exasperated, but he did love his wife and he wanted her happiness above all things. He was aware that since she had come to Jamaica she had very little company of any white families, she had had no opportunity to make new friends and she had nothing to do other than the occasional call on her medical skills in her clinic. This finding of the lost babies was filling a void in her life. A deep need, maybe she was even trying to compensate for the fact that she had not yet been able to conceive a child of her own.

Mellissa could feel that that the argument was going her way, so she pressed forward carefully. "Charles," she said gently, "I know how you and everyone else, that is the Jamaican plantation owners, feel about their slaves, and you know that I don't feel the same way. I know that I am the odd one out, but I can't help how I feel. You knew before you asked me to marry you that I had a great deal of sympathy for the abolitionist cause, and since coming here and seeing the reality of slavery, I am even more convinced that it is wrong. I don't think that I am asking too much, but I want to do all I can in a small way to right some of the wrongs that have been done by our own people. And I know that Lavinia and Akami are willing to do everything that they are able to do, within their constraints, to help me to find the babies that have been sold away from their mothers, our slaves. I know that they won't run away. They are both honourable and eager to help, especially as one of the lost babies is Lavinia's and I saved Akami's life."

"You really are an impossible woman!" Charles exclaimed with a chuckle. "You've twisted me around your little finger as usual. All right you can have your way, your own personal slaves! I'll sell them to you for one gold sovereign each and draw up a proper, legal bill of sale."

She decided not to gush. "Thank you, Charles," she said simply. "How well you know me, my love." She left her seat and Sheba came to her side with her tail still wagging. Mellissa laughed and put out her hand to pull Charles up. "Come. Let us go in now before we are eaten up by insects!"

Chapter Twenty

13 June, 1830

Mellissa, the Abolitionist, Buys Two Slaves

It was still two months to go before Mellissa's birthday, but she and Charles were seated at the desk of attorney-at-law Daniel Smith in his office in St Elizabeth. Daniel Smith was a young man, only a year or two older than Charles. And like Charles, he was in his first professional position in the colonies. He was so proud of himself that he wore in his office his courtroom gown and wig, whatever the heat of the day. As Charles and Mellissa sat in front of him, they could see that he was nervous and perspiring profusely. His handsome young face was beginning to redden and glistening beads of sweat on his forehead were threatening to roll into his eyes. He had prepared two Bills of Sale for Lavinia and Akami and put them forward for Charles to sign. Two sovereigns were solemnly handed by Mellissa to Mr Smith, who just as solemnly passed the money on to Charles. "Thank you for these, Mr Smith," said Mellissa, "now will you please write out a pass for each of these slaves to show that they are out on business for Mrs Mellissa Harrison, their owner. I don't want there to be any question of runaway slaves if either one of them is stopped by any trooper, white person or a slave-catcher. If we wait while you write the passes, perhaps your clerk can witness them."

Daniel Smith gave Charles a sympathetic look, but said nothing as he took a fresh sheet of paper to write out the first pass. Charles chose to ignore the sympathy, and while Daniel Smith was writing the second pass, he leaned over to Mellissa, squeezed her hand and whispered in her ear, "Happy Birthday, darling".

She smiled and whispered back, "Thank you Charles. This is a perfect birthday gift, although it is not yet my birthday. I love you."

Akami, who was now fit and able enough to drive the small carriage was waiting for them outside the attorney's office. He did not wear any sort of uniform, but was simply dressed in a clean cotton shirt, overalls and leather shoes. He used his left hand to hold the reins, but otherwise had full use of both arms. As they were driving home Mellissa looked at him with new eyes. *He belongs to me now,* she told herself. *I own a human being. How do I feel about it?* she questioned herself. She didn't like to admit it, but it felt good, good in the way that owning her dog Sheba felt good. *He's not a pet, he's a man and I am determined to treat him like a man. A free man, maybe like an employee.* She laughed to herself and she squeezed Charles's hand in gratitude for his gift, probably the best gift that she had ever received.

When they arrived back home, she asked Akami to come and join herself and Lavinia in the dining room after he had released the horse into the paddock.

"Scuse I, Mistress," he said, "I not have time to clean yet."

Mellissa laughed. "That's all right, Akami," she said. "Come and sit down at the table with Lavinia. I want to talk to you both, and show you these documents." She spread the two bills of sale and the two passes out onto the table.

She took a deep breath. "Now," she said, "you both know that I have great difficulty knowing that my husband Charles owns not only this plantation but all the people that work on it. Much as I would like to free all the slaves you know that it is not in my power to do so, but I am still sure that it won't be long before the parliament in England will make a law that will set you free. In the meantime we all have to live with what is established and make the best of any small freedoms that we have. I will continue to try to make the lives of all the slaves on this plantation as good as I can.

Now for both of you I have some news which I hope will please you. My husband has drawn up these documents to sell you…no, no, don't look so horrified. He has sold you both to me."

Akami and Lavinia looked at each other and both burst out at the same time, and one after the other. "Mistress. How? Why? What is to happen to us? What does it mean? Can you set us free?"

"I know that you will have many questions to ask, and I hope that you will be patient with me," replied Mellissa. "Firstly, I'm sorry that I cannot free you. It was a condition that my husband put upon the sale, that I would own you but I cannot free you. I know that that sounds awful to you. It sounds awful to me, but here is the better part of the deal." She pushed the second set of documents towards them. "I want you both separately and together to be able to go away from this plantation, and not be caught as runaways, whipped and brought back or even worse, sold on to someone else. These papers you will carry about you at all times, and they are to tell anyone who asks that you are owned by me, you are out and about at my command and you are doing what I have demanded of you. In reality you will be doing everything that you can to follow the trail of John Merriweather, and trying to find the children that have been sold from here.

You, Lavinia, I know that you have spoken to Moses, your preacher, and I think that it may be useful if he allows you to go with him to other Sunday meetings in other parts of St Elizabeth parish which are adjacent to ours. Do you think that you could do that?"

"Oh, yes Mistress," smiled an enthusiastic Lavinia. "I will do my best to find anyone who has come across John Merriweather this side of the mountains, and may know where he bought and sold slaves. But how will I get about? Do you want me to walk everywhere, because I won't be able to go that far?"

"I have even thought of that," said Mellissa. "I suggest that you take Bobo, the little brown donkey. He is used to being ridden and he is a willing little animal. Do you know how to brush and saddle him?"

"Oh, yes," Mistress. "I often used him to ride into St Elizabeth for Mistress Johnston, to go the grocery store."

Mellissa was surprised, she didn't know that Lavinia had had that sort of trust from Mrs Johnston. "Oh, I didn't know that! Did you go alone?" she asked, "and did you ever have anyone question you?"

"I always had a note from Mistress Johnston, and a shopping list," said Lavinia. "I was stopped occasionally, usually in the countryside before I reached St Elizabeth, but I was always allowed to continue when I showed my pass note."

"And who were the people who stopped you?" asked Mellissa. She was curious about the policing of slave movements and slave catchers who were rewarded by plantation owners when they caught runaway slaves. The catching and the punishment of runaway slaves when caught was always brutal, and sometimes the slave catchers were brutal to the slaves even before they could produce letters or notes to say that they were away from their plantations for legitimate purposes.

"It was always the troopers from St Elizabeth who stopped me," said Lavinia. "I have never been stopped by any slave catchers, but I have heard of slaves from the Hope Plantation being badly beaten by those people before they even asked for pass letters. Perhaps I was lucky or perhaps the slave catchers don't bother so much with a woman."

"Now Akami," said Mellissa, turning to him, "it will be a lot more difficult for you, because I want you to find out about John Merriweather from the Rev. Samuel Sharpe in Montego Bay. You know them both well and you have travelled on the difficult trail between here and Montego Bay. You must have been through Maroon territory up in the Cockpit Country. What do you remember of that journey you made to Silver Bay when you were sold to the Johnstons? I know that was eight years ago, and I don't think that much has changed, but you may have forgotten a lot about your journey. How is your memory of that time?"

"Mistress, I never forget that travel from Virginia to here," said Akami. "I was happy to leave that tobacco farm in Virginia. I was sad to leave my mother's grave there. John Merriweather was a slaver trader but he a kind man. Sometimes he tied me, sometimes I would go free. We landed in Jamaica in Montego Bay and he took me to Samuel Sharpe. He a good man. He wants to free slaves…"

"But he is a slave himself, isn't he?" interrupted Mellissa.

"…Yes Mistress, he a slave too, but he writes people in that England who make us all free. John Merriweather take a horse and me have a donkey. We go into jungle and up mountains to Maroon village in Cockpit Country. Those people are fierce people, but they like John Merriweather. They don't like white people. They make trouble for white people. They want John Merriweather to leave me there, but he not able, he owes money for me. I say I go with him. I say he is my friend. We travel in mountains and jungle and come to St Elizabeth. I sold to Massa Johnston. I sad to see John Merriweather go. I more happy here than Virginia but I not like Massa McBride."

Mellissa did not want to talk about McBride, but she was curious about his meeting with the Maroons of whom all the plantation owners were afraid. "What are the Maroons like? Why did you not stay with them? I'm sure that they would have freed you from John Merriweather."

"They wild people. Can only live in jungle. John Merriweather my friend. It not honourable for me if he not have money to pay for me," said Akami quite simply.

"Well, Akami," said Mellissa. "I will let you use a horse for this journey and I will give you just enough money to move about the country doing this task. If you have to stay overnight anywhere, I suggest that you ask for the smallest room or even a stall in a stable or a mat in the tack room. If I give you too much money, it will look suspicious, but for all intents and purposes you will be free to choose where you go and where you stay. There is of course a risk that some blackguard will ignore or even destroy your document, and you could be sold on anyway. All I demand from both of you is that at first you don't roam too far from here and you come back here as much as possible. I want my husband to see that you are trustworthy, and I want to be fully involved. I want to find these children as much as you. Do you think that you will be able to do as I ask?"

They were both a little bit stunned, but they answered at once and together. "Yes, Mistress."

Mellissa considered a little. "Akami," she asked, "can you read and write at all?"

"Mistress, I sometimes can read a word, perhaps on a sign, but I not a good reader, and I not do writing."

"Well, I think that you will need to be able to read, even if it is only at a child's level of ability," said Mellissa. She was thinking hard. "Lavinia, I think that if we both teach Akami he will be able to learn more quickly. He is clever and he has picked up spoken English, in a fashion all of his own. Do you have any books from which you can teach him?"

"I have a child's picture book with words in big print which I use to teach Angeline," said Lavinia.

"And I have the Holy Bible," said Mellissa, "which will be a lot harder but I shall try it anyway."

"Mistress," said Lavinia hesitantly, "I think that Akami is of the Muslim faith. They don't believe that Jesus was the Son of God, but the Old Testament is the same as their book of faith. So if you teach him from that it should be acceptable."

"Did you understand that, Akami?" Mellissa enquired. "Shall I teach you from our Holy Book?"

"It all right, Mistress," he replied sadly, "I not know if I Muslim any more. I not pray since I was boy in Africa. Allah has lost me and I not done manhood training. I not real man."

"Of course you are a man, and a very splendid man at that," said Mellissa. But she knew what Akami was thinking about – his uncircumcised penis. *Perhaps I can help him there,* she thought.

Perhaps she could perform the operation and during his recovery they could study Lavinia's picture book and some of the Bible.

Chapter Twenty-One

Circumcision

Akami was lying on the surgical bed in Mellissa's clinic. Several scalpels, swabs and a needle and thread were on a clean, white porcelain tray waiting at the bedside.

"Akami," said Mellissa, "there is a plant that grows in the Jamaican jungle which has special leaves. When you chew it, it deadens the feelings in your mouth and tongue. And I have been told that a soft chewed mass of these leaves can also make numb any tender part of the body. What I am suggesting is that you chew up some of these leaves and we then spread around the end of your penis, your 'toto' as you call it, give it a few minutes to work and then I will quickly remove your foreskin. Shall we give it a try?"

"We do it. Then I am a man," said Akami. He looked a little grey. This little operation was so much smaller that the amputation of his right hand, but it still filled him with the same fear that he had had as a ten year old boy. "Give me the leaves. I chew."

Ten minutes later he was prepared. "Do it." He said, closing his eyes tight. Mellissa held his penis lightly and then, in a flash, it was done and she deftly sewed up the open skin.

"All done," she said. "Did the leaves help?"

"I think, Mistress," he was still wincing as he spoke.

"Well, don't touch it, and leave the swabs on. Better if you stay right here on that bed for a couple of hours until it settles down. I'm sure that there will be some pain and a great deal of discomfort for the next few days, then it will be all over and you can think of yourself as a full man. And tomorrow we will start your reading lessons. How much do you remember of Lavinia's picture book?"

"We looked at it again yesterday," he said. As Mellissa expected, giving him something else to think about was working to dull the pain. "I read some words without looking to pictures. I read apples and ducks and house and lots more."

"That's good," said Mellissa. "Now I am also going to start correcting your words when you speak. I think that once you are away from here looking for John Merriweather, if you can read and speak well you will find that other people, white men and negroes, will respect you more and will be less likely to think of you as a runaway or an 'uppity nigger'. The first thing that we will look at tomorrow is your slave pass. It is essential that if you have to show it to anyone that you are able to read it too, and to make sure that it is correctly returned to you. If you cannot read, it would be easy for anyone who stopped you and took it away from you, to alter it or give you back another piece of paper altogether."

Ten days later Akami was reading; "This slave, Akami Harrison, is the property of Mrs Mellissa Harrison of the Silver Bay plantation, near St Elizabeth. He has the authority of the said Mrs Mellissa Harrison to purchase one or more infants born on the said Silver Bay plantation and sold by Mrs Emily Johnston, the previous owner of the said Silver Bay plantation."

"That's good, Akami," said Mellissa. "You do understand the wording of that document, don't you? It gives you authority and it should keep you safe when you are away from here."

"Yes, Mistress, I understand it all," said Akami, with a wry smile and taking up a cringing pose. "I knows I's no count nigger. I knows I b'long Missy Harrison."

Mellissa laughed. "Don't you dare go back to that humble nigger stuff, not even for fun," she said. "I am so proud of you and what you have been able to learn in such a short time. So, read out to me this other document."

"I, Mellissa Harrison, undertake to give the seller of any infant selected by my slave Akami Harrison a Credit Note of up to £5 (five pounds) for the child. This Credit Note and a Bill of Sale will be honoured by my attorney-at-law, Daniel Smith of St Elizabeth, Jamaica," read Akami in good standard English. "That's it Mistress."

"Good," said Mellissa, quite serious now. "And you have four of these note just in case you find any of these children. With God's, and your Allah's blessings you will be successful." She pressed his hand and once again she felt a sort thrill run up her arm and her heart began to pound. She pulled away at once and looked deeply into Akami's eyes and saw reflected back the same puzzled expression as she had in her own eyes.

When she had got her heart rate back to normal, she reached over her desk and took from one of the drawers a large leather pouch. "We will put all these documents in here," she said in her normal efficient voice. "It is essential that you recognise and read each one. Here is the document saying that you are my property, and you have my authority to be away from Silver Bay, and the four others all looking the same are the Credit Note with which, God willing, you will be able to find and buy any of the children sold in Jamaica. I think that if they were sold into America we will have lost them for good."

Just then an excited Lavinia came bursting into the room. She had been away overnight after going to a church meeting led by Rev. Moses. "Mistress," she cried. "We went to our neighbouring parish, and I've seen the YS Falls. I've lived here in Silver Bay for sixteen years and I have never seen them before. So wonderful. The noise of the water falling in great steps into pools was like thunder. It was so loud I couldn't hear Moses speaking."

"I'm so glad that you went there," said Lavinia. "The Master and I went there soon after we came to Silver Bay, and I remember how we found it truly awesome. One of God's miracles." She was glad of Lavinia's return so she could feel more comfortable with Akami. "Did Moses have any news for us from any of his parishes?"

"He has spread the word that we are looking for babies bought from any of the nearby plantations, but no one seems to have seen a baby without its mother," said Lavinia. "I suppose that it would be too much to hope for that the children would have been sold so close to home, especially as John Merriweather is an international slave trader." She stopped for a moment to think about her own lost baby, Jonah. "But", she continued, "the better news is that he plans to trek over the mountains to visit Samuel Sharpe in two weeks' time. I asked him if our Akami could accompany him and he said that he would be delighted if Akami came. It is a difficult journey and it would be made easier if there were two of them to keep company and help each other in the difficult jungles and rain forest. He also has some kinship with some of the Maroon villagers."

Mellissa looked at Akami. "That would be perfect. Akami is almost ready to start his own adventure and having Moses to guide him is the best possible result. How do you feel about going with Moses, Akami?"

"I'm very happy." He said. "I was a little bit fearful to go on my own, and now I will have the best possible guide."

Chapter Twenty-Two

July 1830
A Trek Through the Jungle

Moses and Akami were following a tough and rugged trail through the jungle. Moses was a short and rather fat man of forty-one years who walked with a decided limp and was pleased to have been given the use of one of the horses from Silver Bay for this adventure. His own horse was rather old not up to the tough journey ahead. Akami, who had started riding only since Mellissa had taken over his ownership, was still a novice on a horse and he had been given a gentle mare who was sure footed. He was strong and fit for walking but he had many difficulties adjusting to the loss of his right hand. So each of them had strength to help with the other's weakness. The trail was mostly open but because the plants grew so quickly there were many parts that were overgrown and had to be freshly cut back. At those places, they had to dismount from their horses and hack at the stems and trailing vines with their cutlasses.

They were making good progress until the afternoon rains fell. There was no shelter. Even the plants with leaves like canopies which held back the rain, giving false cover when eventually they gave way to produce an ever bigger torrent of wetness, almost like standing under a waterfall. Within minutes they were both soaked to the skin and their lack of strong boots hindered every step that they took. The wetness seemed to bring out every creepy-crawling insect from its hiding place. Mosquitoes and flies were buzzing all around, and soon to add to their discomfort, they found leeches clinging to their uncovered limbs, and even under their shirts. The rainfall, although extremely heavy, was short-lived and when it stopped they tied up their horses and rather ineptly tried to light a small fire in a clearing. It was a rather pathetic attempt to dry out, and while they were waiting for the smokiness to become bright, warm flames they sat down, ate some bread and fat pork and talked.

"So," asked Akami, "how come you are a freeman, and how come you are called Moses. He was a slave who led his people to freedom in the Christian Bible, isn't he?"

Moses sat down on a fallen tree to relate his story, "I was born a slave here in Jamaica, and I was a slave for thirty-eight years. My mother, whose name was Belle, was a pretty young house slave on the Braemar plantation near Kingston and my father, John Reynolds, was a slave on another plantation. They met and fell in love during the regular three-day holiday at Christmastime when most slaves were allowed to mix and travel to each other's compound. They asked if they could be married but neither of their respective owners were prepared to sell the one to the other. So for years they lived apart and only met up in the slave's free time on Sundays. When my mother became pregnant, she was still not allowed to marry or live with John Reynolds and eventually she gave up asking. I was born in the slave compound and was named Peter Fellowes. Fellowes was the family name of the plantation owner.

My early life and childhood was happy. I did not even realise that I was a fatherless slave until I was about six years old. My mother worked as a house slave and she was given a semi-basement room in the plantation house, where we both lived. I was an obedient child and I never questioned the authority of my mother or anyone else when I was told to do something. The plantation owners, Josiah and Marina Fellowes, were a white family with two boys, Martin and Luke, about the same age as I was, one a bit older and the other a bit younger than me, and the three of us used to play together all the time in the house and gardens. I hardly recognised that we were different colours or that they were superior to me.

The boys had a tutor, a freed black slave called Moses, and yes, he was named after the one in the Bible. This tutor, Moses, came to the plantation house two days a week to teach the boys to read and write. I was allowed to join in with the lessons and learned quite quickly to read and I was starting to learn how to write. It was less than a year later that Josiah and Marina Fellowes, decided to send Martin and Luke back to England to attend a proper school, and at one blow I lost my two friends, my education and my innocent childhood. I asked my mother if I could go to school too, and then she explained to me the meaning of slavery. Master and Mistress Fellowes no longer had any need of a child to be a playmate for their children and I was sent to work in the fields with the rest of the field slaves.

And that was to be my life for the next five years. I was taken to live in the slave compound and was allocated to share the cabin of two of the female fieldworkers. I was no longer loved, only tolerated and looked upon as a burden. I missed my mother and my former way of life so much that I did not want to learn the new tasks that were expected of me and I went to bed in tears almost every night. But I was soon forced, with a whip, to harden up and obey the overseer. I learned the hard way what it was to be a slave and do exactly what I was told. Like everyone else I was forced from my bed at four o'clock every morning, given a slice of bread and a piece of fat pork, just like this, for my lunchtime ration and loaded onto the farm wagon with the rest of the field workers. Daily we were taken to which ever part of the cane plantation needed to be weeded or prepared for harvesting and were forced to work until sundown. A little less was demanded of me because I was still a child, but I was surrounded by men working as hard and as fast as they could under the constant fear of being whipped. Whenever any of the slaves, male or female, but mostly male, were deemed to be lazy or disobedient they were whipped in the fields as they worked, and any of them who openly and directly crossed the demands of the overseer were punished most cruelly. At the end of the day, he was tied to a whipping post which was permanently set in the centre of the slave compound, and we were all forced to watch as the victim was lashed until he was screaming in unbearable pain and his back was cut to ribbons and running with blood. This was my new life as a slave.

I did not see my mother again until I was eleven years old. That day I had been set to work in the sheds where they boiled the cane sugar when one of the vats was overturned. I did not run away fast enough and the boiling liquid ran over my unshod feet. I was saved by a slave called Alexander who, in spite of the danger to himself, snatched at me just as the shock of my burns made me stagger and ready to fall bodily into that boiling sugar. He saved my life that day, and against the overseer's orders, he carried me to the plantation house and put me into the arms of my mother. Alexander was severely punished for his disobedience and I thank God that I was not forced to watch. I will love and honour that man until the day I die.

It took several months for me to recover and to walk again. During that time I was allowed to have possession of the Holy Bible that had been left behind by one of the boys. I struggled to remember the teaching of Pastor Moses. But I worked hard and eventually I mastered reading and then I copied out the words from that Bible until I could write too. My feet have never truly recovered and to this day I have difficulty in walking so I was given work in the gardens, the stables and the pig sheds and eventually I grew strong again. I was allowed to stay with my mother until I was fully grown and then I was sold.

My new owner was the aunt of Master Fellowes, Miss Joanna Fellowes who wanted a slave as a personal attendant. So although I was unhappy at being sold away from my mother, I ended up seeing more of her when Miss Joanna visited her nephew, than I had done when I was living with the field slaves in the slave compound.

Miss Joanna was already an old lady of nearly sixty and I was her slave until she died. She was thin as a stick and she was always dressed from head to toe in black. What she really wanted was some sort of intellectual companion, but in inland Jamaica there was no single lady, or widow-woman, who could be paid to perform that duty, and she could find no female slave who could read and converse, so she bought me. Someone who would always be at her beck and call. But she was kind to me and never treated me as a slave. She encouraged me in my studies of the Holy Bible and we would read to each other certain passages and discuss what the deeper meaning had been. With her encouragement I eventually I became a Baptist preacher, and I renamed myself Moses after my first teacher and also after the prophet in the Old Testament who led the Jews out of slavery in Egypt. I did not have my own church or parish, but with the gift of a horse and the blessing and permission of my Mistress, I travelled around from parish to parish to become the Minister for all the slaves who lived on the plantations within my parishes. I could not lead them to freedom in this life as Moses had done, but I did try to lead their souls to freedom. As you must already know, the only gatherings that slaves are allowed in Jamaica are religious gatherings.

Although there is an unwritten law that prevents white women to become romantically involved with black men, slaves or freemen, Miss Joanna became fond of me. I don't think that it was a sexual or lustful love, but perhaps it was the sort of love she might have had for a child if she had ever married and produced one. I was thirty-eight when she died and when her will was read, to my surprise I found that she had set me free and she had also left me enough money to continue my mission. Fortunately for me Josiah

Fellowes was an honourable man and he did not contest her will, and I have continued to be a Baptist minister. And so here I am today continuing my mission to help my fellow beings whether they be slaves or freemen, and I hope that together we will able to find your John Merriweather and the babies who were sold away from their mothers."

"So," said Akami, "both of us have to be thankful for our accidents in the cane crusher house for our freedom in being here today. You are fully freed from slavery and I have a gentle Mistress who would free me if she could, and is now giving me a small taste of freedom."

"What would you do if you were completely free?" asked Moses.

"I have often dreamed that I was free to return to my home village in Africa," said Akami, "but if I were really freed I would not know how to go about it. I suppose that I would need much money, and how I would be able to earn that money I don't know. It is probably an empty dream."

"The man we are trying to meet in Montego Bay," said Moses, "whose name is Sam Sharpe, is convinced that very soon the government in England, who govern this island of Jamaica, will make a law to free all slaves in all English overseas territories. But he is also sure that the price of freedom will be indenture for several years afterwards."

"What is indenture?" asked Akami.

Moses sighed and spoke without excitement about the future. "It means that when slaves are freed they will have to agree to continue to work for their former owners for a fixed number of years before they are completely free to leave and do what they will. While they are indentured they would be given a wage, some money every week. It sounds good but they would no longer be housed, clothed and fed by their former owners, who would now be their employers, and probably they would have to pay so much for their cabins, their food and clothing that they would never be able to save any money to leave and live a free life. It would be even harder for those who have children, who would probably not be able to earn enough to clothe and feed a family."

Akami, who wanted more than anything to be freed, was startled by Moses picture of the future. "But we will still be free. We will feel that we are men and women to make our own choices and not be treated like cattle, and our children will be born free.

Even if we are forced to continue to work we will be free in our minds. We will be men."

They were continuing their conversation as they remounted their horses to push forward towards the Cockpit Country. And suddenly the grasslands ended and they were there, riding an almost unmarked trail into a strange landscape of high conical hills and deep valleys all covered in dense vegetation. Not only was the landscape strange and wildly beautiful, it was almost at once displaying the most beautiful birds, flowers and butterflies that Moses had ever seen. They paused to just sit and take in all that they were seeing and experiencing. "Look, look Akami," said Moses in a voice of wonder. "How can anyone disbelieve in the power and love of God when displayed all around us is a place of almost magical beauty? It looks like my vision of the Garden of Eden."

"Yes," replied Akami. "I had almost forgotten the wonder of this place. It was about eight years ago when I came through here with John Merriweather. While I was seeing all this beauty, I was also terrified about what would be happening to me in the following few days. I had had a short time of almost experiencing freedom, or as close to freedom as I had ever had since I had been captured in Africa so many years ago." He stopped for a moment and looked deeply into the undergrowth. "Something I do remember well is snakes. I hate snakes. I have always hated snakes here, in the Americas and at home in Africa. And I do remember a huge snake they called an Anaconda sliding out of a bush and crossing our path. It was longer than a man is tall and the thickness of its body was thicker than the largest part of a man's arm. I was frightened and everyone with us laughed because the Anaconda is not poisonous and it kills its food, mostly rabbits and mammals of that size, by wrapping its body around its victim and crushing it to death."

He started to laugh at his fears when there was a rustling and all of a sudden they were stopped in their tracks by four angry looking Negroes carrying spears and guns, all of the weapons were pointed straight at the Moses and Akami. Their leader, a tall and very well built man dug his spear point into Akami's chest just far enough to cause pain without drawing blood. "Who are you, and what are you doing on our land?" demanded the tallest and strongest looking man.

Chapter Twenty-Three

Cockpit Country

They were surrounded, and two of the men took hold of Akami and Moses, forcing their arms high up behind their backs. But before their leader could do or say anything more, Akami spoke up in a fearless voice, "Hello, Jamal," he said, so very calmly that the aggressors were taken by surprise and stopped what they were doing.

The warrior-like leader looked at him hard. "Who are you? How do know my name?" he said, very suspiciously. He had yet to put down his weapons. The other three men looked on not really believing what they were seeing. No one, not even close friends, stood up to Jamal.

Akami asked, with a lot of bravado that he did not really feel, "Don't you remember me, Jamal?" Repeating the man's name somehow made Jamal uneasy, and Akami pressed home his advantage. "I came here with John Merriweather about eight years ago, and you wanted me to stay here. You were about to be married to your cousin, Mariella."

"Hey, man! I do remember you. You had just arrived in Jamaica and Merriweather was off to sell you to a sugar plantation owner down south." Jamal scratched his woolly head, and nodded at his companions to let go the arms of the two trespassers. "I never did understand why you went off to become a slave again, when you could have stayed here safe from any white man."

"It was the honourable thing to do," said Akami. "John Merriweather had a credit note owing on me. He had to take me to the Johnstons to redeem it, otherwise he might have been re-enslaved himself. Has he been here recently? We are trying to find him. That's why we are crossing your territory. This man is Moses and he is a Baptist Minister working the parishes down St Elizabeth way. We are trying to find slave babies who were sold from the Silver Bay plantation in the last few years. I know that John Merriweather kept a record of all these babies and he will know exactly who bought them and where they are at. We are trying to get to Montego Bay because he is a friend of the Reverend Sam Sharpe. You Maroons must know about Sam Sharpe and his efforts to fight for the freedom of all slaves, even though you may want to stay here in the Cockpits when, eventually, that freedom comes to Jamaica."

"Yea, man, I know of the Reverend Sam Sharpe," said Jamal. "But whatever happens in the future, we Maroons will stay here in the safety of our protected paradise. We want no mixing with white people. They are poison, man. Real poison."

"You certainly are protected by these hills and deep valleys," said Moses. "I've lived in Jamaica all my life, and I have never seen such landscape. It was so difficult for us even to get this far. You and your friends caught up with us so quickly. How did you even know that strangers were making their way into your lands…?"

Akami interrupted, and Moses's question remained unanswered. "Jamal," he said, "we were hoping that we could stay with you in Appleton overnight. And, moreover, we were hoping that you would lead us through your impossible lands towards Montego Bay. I know that it would be dangerous for you to go anywhere near Montego Bay itself, we just need your help to get to the northern border of the Cockpits. Would you be willing to do this for us?"

"Well, man," replied Jamal. "Let us all talk about it when we get back to Appleton." He stared hard at Akami. "And I see that you have lost one of your hands since I last saw you. I guess the result of your slavery? Shall we talk about that too?"

Hostility was now totally withdrawn, and the faces of the four Maroon men brightened with broad smiles. "Let's go," said Jamal. And they all started along the trail leading to Appleton. As Akami and Moses were leading their horses, Jamal said, "We saw John Merriweather only two months ago. He stayed with Mariella and me for four nights, and he was on his way to the western side of Cockpit Country."

Akami was excited. "Do you think that he is still in Jamaica?" he asked.

"I think that it is quite possible," said Jamal. "He was talking about spending quite a lot of time with Sam Sharpe. I think that things have got difficult for him recently in America."

"How long have you lived here in the Cockpit Country?" asked Moses.

"It's been ten years now, and I live with real freedom."

"Are you an escaped slave?" asked Moses.

"Yes. It was more than ten years ago that I escaped from my Master, Edwin Wilder was his name. He is a Sea Captain and I escaped from his ship when we were docked in Kingston. It took me about five months of hiding out and I almost starved to death before I reached safety here," said Jamal. It looked to Moses that he would not be reluctant to talk more about himself so as they were walking along, leading their horses, he continued with his questions.

"I was a slave and I was very lucky that I was freed by my Mistress," said Moses. "Having been an escapee for ten years, will you ever be considered as a free man?

"No." Was Jamal's quick, short answer. "My Master, the English Sea Captain was only due to stay in Kingston for a short while, and that was years ago. He may have been back here since, but I think that he has probably sailed back to India by now, which was where he always said he wanted to return. He will have reported me as an escaped slave to the authorities in Kingston, and there will probably still be a price on my head. I don't think that ever changes however long it is since you managed to get away. But here in the Cockpits, as you know, we are all relatively safe. We are well protected by the difficult terrain and there is a sort of unspoken truce between us and troopers that we stay here in our territory and they stay in theirs. But I will always be a slave, and I will never dare to leave here."

"I was wondering about your name, Jamal," said Akami who had been listening in to the conversation between Jamal and Moses. "You said that he had lived in India, is that an Indian name given to you by your Sea Captain? I have not heard of another Jamal since I have lived here in Jamaica."

"Yea, man," sighed Jamal, "but I was not born in India. I was bought right here in Jamaica, as an eight-year-old child, to be a cabin boy aboard his ship. I was called Joseph then, but my new owner renamed me Jamal. I was his cabin boy for nearly nine years and we had many exciting times on the high seas. We even fought off pirates once, right here in the Caribbean. I grew to like my Master and I am sure that I felt like a son to him, but I was always aware that I was a slave and had no free will to change my life. I knew that I would become nothing more than a common seaman as I got older. So I decided to jump ship at Kingston and find my way home if I could. Captain Wilder trusted me completely when we were docked in port, any port, and he always left me to do as I wanted until we were ready to sail again. I think that he had no idea that I would want any other life than being with him, having adventures and making a living on the high seas. I even think that he would have been more sad than angry when I ran away, even though he must have reported me as a runaway slave. And as for my name, Jamal, although it is a reminder of me being a slave, I did like him and I did like the name, so I have kept it!"

The community in Appleton were a little suspicious of the new arrivals, but then some of them remembered Akami and things eased. They were taken to the chief Maroon of Appleton, a very old man called Michael. His face was deeply wrinkled, and he walked with a knobbed stick to support his bent and crooked back. Moses could not decide if he looked friendly or fearsome with his impressive long flowing white beard, and great bush of crinkled, white hair. He took the two travellers aside and interviewed them. His main concern was that they were genuine travellers and not paid spies for the English troopers and the plantation owners.

The villages all over Cockpit Country were well fortified, most of them in the deep valleys between the conical hills, but they would never be completely safe if the troopers decided to raid with armed forces. Spies were always a threat, a possibility for the troopers to find out any weaknesses in defences that the Maroon villages might have, giving them a chance to take advantage of those weakness. At present, there seemed to be a sort of truce between them and the Maroons, each of them staying out of each-others territories. After an hour or so of quite gentle but perceptive questioning over several cups of sweet herbal tea, Chief Michael was assured that Akami and Moses posed no danger to their community, and he gave Jamal and his three followers the permission to escort them along the north-eastern trail to the edge of the Cockpit Country and point them towards Montego Bay.

After that it was party time at the home of Jamal and Mariella. Mariella had been a pretty girl of mixed race with honey coloured skin and unusually long wavy hair into which she had usually wound some dashing red hibiscus flowers. Akami remembered her well. During the seven years since Akami had last seen her she had matured into a fine looking young woman who was very obviously expecting a baby quite soon, and she greeted them with a big smile. "Come in both of you and let me feed you. I expect that it is a long time since you had decent Jamaican jerk chicken and rice." She was so pleased to see Akami again that she gave him a great big hug and lightest of kisses on his lips. "Whatever has happened to your hand?" she asked. "Are you still a slave? What have they done to you?"

All her questions were coming out at once before Akami could answer any of them. He laughed as he hugged her back. "And what have you been up to since I last saw you?" he asked, pointing to her stomach, still laughing.

Moses joined in, "I do have to admit that we didn't eat properly yesterday or today and we are so hungry that we could probably eat your whole plateful of jerk," he said, he was laughing too. "But I am sure that we will do our best to restrain ourselves!"

The rum was flowing freely as they all sat eating at an outside table looking across the dense foliage of the Cockpit hills, their ears being battered by the prolonged squawking of the colourful but noisy parrots that swarmed in the trees. Mariella turned to Akami and asked him, "now tell me the truth about your slavery at the Silver Bay plantation and how you managed to lose your right hand?"

"It is easier for me than it was when I was forced to work on the tobacco plantation in Virginia, in America, but slavery is slavery whether it is harsh or gently controlled," he said. He had lost the laugh in his voice and talked more quietly now. "And the worst of it, far more than hard work or even beatings, is that it is your mind also becomes enslaved. Your choices are nil and every minute of every day, every action, even every one of your thoughts is controlled by others, whether that control be harsh or kind."

He stopped for a moment and looked down at the stub end of his right arm. "This injury of mine, whilst the most painful thing I have ever experienced in my life, including many whippings in America, has turned out to be the best thing that had happened to me since I was captured as a boy in Africa."

"How could that possibly be? What happened?" asked a timid Mariella.

"It was a most terrible accident that happened to me in the cane crusher house. My hand was pulled into the crusher when I was trying to remove a stone the size of a mango which had somehow got caught up inside a bundle of sugar cane." He paused for a moment and said, almost as if he were thinking of it for the first time, "perhaps it had been put there deliberately by one of the slaves so that the crusher would be damaged?"

"Dangerous," commented Mariella.

"Yes," said Akami. "But I had no alternative as the crushers are pulled by very strong horses, and it is not possible to stop them dead. Without me trying to get the stone out it would have gone in and destroyed the crusher."

"So," said Mariella, "the choice was the risk of losing your hand or disabling the crushing machine. I know what I would have chosen."

"Well, you are not a slave," said Akami with a flat voice. "If I had left the stone, I probably would not have survived the punishment that our overseer, Master McBride, would have inflicted on me. As it is I have only lost one hand and not my life!"

"So why did you say that that horrible injury was the best thing that had happened to you? Why you did not take the opportunity to run away from slavery when you were last here I will never understand," said an exasperated Mariella. "I hope that you will do it now."

"No. It would not be honourable. I have a task to do now that I am honour bound to complete, Mariella," said Akami in a serious voice now. "It is for the Mistress who is also a sort of doctor, and it was she who cut off what was left of my hand to save my life. I stayed in her clinic for months. She visited me daily and we spent many hours together. It was she who made me better, and she who made me a man."

Mariella gave Akami a quizzical look but did not interrupt his flow. "She persuaded the Master to sell me to her so she became my owner. In purchasing me from her husband she had to sign an agreement not to free me, but with her encouragement I am now as free as I could be whilst still being a slave." Akami saw another look pass over Mariella's face, this time it was a look of revulsion. "I know that's it's horrible to speak of having an owner, but that's the reality of being a slave. It was only as my owner that she could give me full permission to leave the plantation with Moses, who is a freeman. He and I are on a mission to find babies, who will be young children by now, who were sold away from their mothers by the previous owner of the Silver Bay plantation. You are about to become a mother, Mariella, you must understand how those mother still cry every day for their lost children. It is worse for them than having their child die. As it is they wonder every day where their children are, and what has happened to them, and what they are being forced to do.

That is one of the worst evils of slavery, that our Masters have the power to destroy families just for profit. Not one of them, except my Mistress, sees us as fellow human beings who have the same love for their husbands and wives and children as they have themselves for their own families."

"Yet you still say that you are honour bound to return," said a disgusted Mariella. The rest of the group of men were now listening intently to the conversation taking place between Akami and Mariella. This time Jamal was nodding in agreement with his wife. "If you do find any of those children, it would be simple enough for you to stay here and for Moses to take them back to Silver Bay," he said quite flatly, without any emphasis.

"No. I have to go back," protested Akami.

"I think that there is more to this than just honour." Mariella was giving Akami a deep, searching look. "What's the real reason for going back? Is it a woman? Is it one of the slave women? Oh no! Could it be your new owner, the Mistress of Silver Bay?"

Akami looked abashed. He fidgeted and stared into the distance. Everyone held their breath and waited for his answer. Finally, he said, "She is so kind and clever and beautiful. She saved my life when she removed my hand. And it was she who has taught me to speak English properly, and to read and write."

Mariella opened her eyes wide in surprise. "You love her!" she exclaimed loudly, and everyone looked at Akami.

"You dare not love a white woman!" cried a horrified Jamal. "This is your Mistress, the happily married wife of your Master." The fun element of the evening had drained away and the atmosphere became charged with fear and danger. "That is certain death, man, even if you don't touch her! Certain death without any defence for a slave and completely without consequence for a Master who kills his slave. Death! And a very painful death too. Even if it is she who wants to do the touching. Even free black men like Moses here would be hanged if they were to lay a finger on a white woman."

"I would never touch her," protested Akami. "And she only touches me for medical purposes. And it is mostly when Lavinia is in the room."

"You must stay away from her," warned Jamal. "Don't go back. Going back would be death for you."

"But I must go back," was Akami's almost whispered reply.

"Well," said Jamal, "You get this adventure to Montego Bay over and done with, then you can have another think about staying here when you are ready to return to slavery!" He stood up, stretched, yawned and lifted his shirt to scratch his pronounced belly. "I think that we should all go to bed now so we can start bright and early in the morning."

Chapter Twenty-Four

Montego Bay

Montego Bay was the busiest town that Moses had ever been in, and they were yet to reach the centre. They were riding through the streets of St James's Parish towards the Burchell Baptist Church where Sam Sharpe was a deacon. They were fearful of being stopped and questioned with demands to show their papers, and the crowds of people in the street were frightening but they managed to find the church and tied up their horses in a yard behind a nearby inn.

"Before we go in," said Akami, "tell me what you know about this Sam Sharpe?"

"I know very little," replied Moses. "He is a deacon of this church and he inspires his congregation with his eloquent preaching. He reads all the newspapers coming from England and they are full of talk about William Wilberforce and his ambition to abolish slavery everywhere. Sam Sharpe tells his followers that he believes that all slaves in the English colonies will be freed soon."

"But he is a slave himself, isn't he?" asked Akami. "How is he allowed the freedom and time to work as a deacon?"

"He is a house slave owned by an English lawyer, whose name is also Sam Sharpe," said Moses. "Well actually, the lawyer is Samuel Sharpe who bought Sam, as a young man from the owners of Sam's African mother and father and he was renamed after his new owner. Samuel Sharpe has encouraged Sam in his education and in keeping up with the news from England. He also allows him as much time as he needs for his religious duties. Like me, although the authorities don't like it, by law all ministers are allowed to preach in churches or in open air religious gatherings, the only gatherings that slaves are allowed to attend."

"It's not Sunday," observed Akami, "is it likely that he will be inside the church?"

"I don't know," replied Moses, "it is possible that he may be in the vestry. We will go and look. If he's not there, we may find someone who is able tell us where to find Samuel Sharpe's Attorney's office."

The simple brick church, spireless and unornamented, was cool and empty apart from a Negress who was polishing the benches. Moses and Akami approached her.

"Good morning, Mistress," said Moses. "Can you please tell me where we might find the Reverend Sam Sharpe? Is he here today?"

"Oh, you have missed him. He left a few minutes ago to meet his Master in the Black Dog Inn," she said, pointing towards the direction from which they had just come.

"Thank you," they both said together. "Shall we follow him there?" asked Akami.

"I am sure that there will no trouble for him to meet a fellow Baptist Minister," said Moses. "Let us look inside and decide whether or not to interrupt him with his Master."

The Black Dog Inn was quiet. There were only five men in the tap room. Two white men, who looked like business men, were sitting together and smoking long pipes with sweet smelling curls of tobacco smoke drifting around them. Between them was a low table which was covered in newspapers, a foaming jug of ale and two half-filled mugs.

A single white man was sitting at another table eating from a plate full of bread and cheeses and a taproom waitress was bringing him a small glass and a bottle of rum.

The two visitors discounted those patrons of the Inn and looked further to see if they could identify the two Samuel Sharpes. Sitting at a round table placed behind a large oak post which supported the ceiling, was a very fat white man in his fifties, with red sweating cheeks. In spite of the warmth of the day he was dressed in a dark suit and white silk stockings, and on his head he wore a lawyer's wig. Beads of sweat were gathering on his brow readying themselves to trickle down his face and neck to settle into his white silk cravat. He was eating from a plate full of meats, and approaching him, with another large jug full of foaming ale and two pewter mugs, was a slightly built Negro man of about thirty, whom Moses quickly assumed to be his fellow Minister. He had the same pure African look that Akami had, with a high forehead, elegantly shaped hair and a bright intelligent face.

Moses approached the table, and he addressed the man he had assumed was an attorney at law, "Excuse me Sir," he said. "I am sorry to disturb you, but are you Master Samuel Sharpe?"

The white man struggled in his seat and eventually turned his obese body towards Moses and gave him a searching look. "I am indeed Master Sharpe. Who might you be? And what do you want of me?"

"My name is Moses," he replied, "and I am a freed slave and a Methodist Minister for the parishes around St Elizabeth. This man," he said, pulling Akami forward, "is a slave from the Silver Bay plantation, near to St Elizabeth, and we would like permission to talk to your assistant Sam Sharpe about an American gentleman called John Merriweather."

"Sam Sharpe is not my assistant, he is my slave." The attorney glanced up at Akami and smiled as he corrected Moses in a mild way. "Does he have travelling papers from his owner giving him permission to be so far from the plantation, Silver Bay you said?"

"Oh, yes. And we also have notes of credit so that we can buy back babies, who will now be small children, sold away from their mothers who are also slaves on Silver Bay. There are twelve on our list and they were traded by John Merriweather. Akami here, who was also bought and sold by John Merriweather, says that Merriweather kept records of where each of the children was sold," said Moses. He did not realise that he was gabbling nervously, and he had gone straight ahead into their reason for being in Montego Bay without approaching the subject privately or carefully.

"Whoa! Whoa! This is all a bit too much to spring on me all of a sudden," exclaimed Samuel Sharpe. "Come, the two of you, sit and join us here and we will discuss this interesting situation." He paused for a moment and signalled to Sam to sit at the table with them. "Sam, what do you know of this John Merriweather?" he asked of his own slave.

Sam paused for a moment and it looked to Moses as if he had to pick the right words to say to his Master. "John Merriweather is an American slave trader. He ought to be hated by slaves and despised by the slave owners he sells to, but he is at heart a very kind man. He is not an abolitionist. His interests in slaving come from a conviction that he has that if the world has accepted that slavery is not only lawful but a good thing, then he will do his best to make sure that at least some slaves will have the best Masters that he can find for the men, women and children he has been commissioned to buy and sell."

Moses and Akami looked at Samuel Sharpe, the Master and Attorney. He did not look angry or upset at the words of his slave. Moses concluded that he was well aware of the support that his slave gave to the abolitionist cause. Maybe, he also wondered, perhaps he secretly supported the cause too, even though he had a slave of his own. Perhaps his clients, most of them being plantation owners and Montego Bay business men would think twice about using his legal services if they thought him a traitor to their views of white superiority and their slave owning status.

Sam Sharpe continued, "He trades very few slaves at a time, and has never been involved with wholesale auctioning. He is not a wealthy man, so he is often unable to buy the slave outright, and his clients, both buyers and sellers have to trust him with credit notes that he has to get redeemed at the conclusion of any trade. He pockets only just enough profit to enable him to live. If he is able to, he selects those he will trade with the knowledge of having just the right person to sell them to. For example, these boy children that Minister Moses has been talking about would have been sold anyway by their unfeeling Masters, so John Merriweather would have taken them to people he knows will be kind to a young child, and bring him up with care and, yes, with love too. He believes that if a Master or Mistress loves a baby then they are more than likely to love the child as he grows into a man.

At the present time, he is having problems with the Authorities in Virginia, America. He reclaimed a child leaving the purchase price for the owner, but without that owner's consent or a Bill of Sale, because he thought that the child was or would be cruelly treated. He has no family in Virginia that he wants to go back to, so he thinks that he will not return there. He is contemplating whether he would be safe if he moved to New York, or perhaps not return to America at all, but stay here in Jamaica."

"Is he still here?" asked Moses. "Is it possible for us to meet up with him here in Montego Bay?"

"I think that at present he is staying at the Baxter Hall Plantation, just along the coast road from here," said Sam. "Mrs Caroline Henshaw, the widowed owner of Baxter Hall, was left with huge debts when her husband Andrew Baxter Henshaw died two years ago and she has been struggling to sell off their slaves so that the house and plantation will not be taken from her by their creditors. It has been said that Andrew Baxter Henshaw and Caroline Henshaw owned as many as two thousand slaves, most of whom are now sold off..."

"Two thousand! That's horrible!" interrupted Akami.

"…It is also said," continued Sam, "that Caroline is terribly cruel to her remaining slaves. She is said to have a dungeon underneath Baxter Hall where she tortures her slaves and she has killed many of them. I do not know if any of this is true, but John Merriweather has gone there to see if he can do anything to help the remaining slaves or buy any of the unfortunates. He said that he would return in a few days' time."

"Well, Sir," said Moses addressing Samuel Sharpe, "if we stay here at the Black Dog would you have any objections if Sam were to arrange a meeting between us and John Merriweather. We have a list of twelve babies that he bought from Silver Bay and we are hoping that he will have matching records of where the children were taken to."

"I have no objection at all," said Attorney Sharpe, with a broad smile. "In fact, I would be pleased to assist you with the legal necessities of any purchases that you are able to make."

"That is indeed very kind of you, Sir," replied Moses. "I am sure that we will have a great need of legal advice. Our papers from Akami's Mistress include an agreement to pay legal fees…"

"…I'm sure that I will be able to waive those fees for this good cause," said Samuel. "Now if you will excuse us, I have an appointment to attend at my office." He was still sweating profusely when he got up and left the Inn with Sam Sharpe following behind. At the door, Sam turned to look at the two men and held up his hand in a quiet wave.

Chapter Twenty-Five

John Merriweather

Four days later a strange quartet of Negro men greeted each other in the tap room of the Black Dog Inn. They were Akami, a tall, well-built, African slave with tribal scars on his face and a missing right hand. Moses, a freed Jamaican mulatto slave of medium height, rather plump, who walked with a shuffling limp. Sam Sharpe, a Jamaican born slave of African parents, he was of slight build and had an intelligent African face. Finally, John Merriweather, a free American quadroon looking like a white man but with black Negro crinkled hair and dark eyes.

John greeted his erstwhile slave, putting his arms around Akami, saying, "My old friend! It is so good to see you again. How are you?" He looked down at Akami's disabled right arm. "Oh dear, friend Sam told me that you had had an accident at the Silver Bay plantation. If it is your wish to tell me about what happened, I would be pleased to listen." The sound of his voice and American accent, so different from the English spoken in Jamaica, took Akami right back to the years he had lived as a slave in America and the time he had travelled with John Merriweather from slavery in Virginia to continued slavery in Jamaica. It was a bitter-sweet reunion for him.

The four men had just completed their introductions to each other when the tap room door opened and a Montego Bay trooper walked in. With his red tunic and shiny pistol showing smartly on his hip, he came forward blinking the sunshine out of his eyes. "Hey! You niggers," he called out, "what are you up to? You know that the law does not allow more than five niggers to meet up and conspire together."

Sam stood up. "Good morning, Trooper Dawson," he said. "As you can see we are only four, and we are not planning to conspire today, and we are not expecting any more company."

"Oh! You are Samuel Sharpe's nigger, ain't you?" said Dawson, not at all abashed, and still challenging. "Well, what are you up to anyway?"

"These *gentleman* and I," said Sam, stressing the word gentlemen, "are discussing the purchase of some slaves from Montego Bay plantations, and my Master, Master Samuel Sharpe, will be completing the legal formalities if our purchases are successful."

"You niggers! Buying niggers?" Trooper Dawson scoffed. "So much for freedom for all slaves! Your usual mantra, is it not nigger Sharpe?" He could not back down without feeling that he had lost some power over the four men. "Well, I think that you three," he said, pointing to Akami, Moses and John, "had better show me your papers, and explain yourselves."

Akami produced his travel permission letter from Mistress Mellissa Harrison of the Silver Bay plantation, St Elizabeth. Moses produced his manumission papers and his registration paper showing him to be a Baptist Minister. And John Merriweather showed his papers showing that he was a freed slave of American birth and citizenship. Trooper Dawson shuffled the documents, which he could not read in detail, gave them back and left the room saying, "I have got my eye on you niggers. Don't you make any trouble here in Montego Bay or free or not free you will find yourselves locked up mighty quickly!"

The four men breathed a sigh of relief as he shut the door behind him. Sam said, "Those troopers are always looking for signs of rebellion from the slaves, and it makes them a bit touchy and sometimes trigger-happy, so it is better not to protest and just accept their scrutiny."

"I will ask the tap room barmaid for a jug of beer and four glasses," said John Merriweather, "then I will tell you how I got on with Mrs Caroline Henshaw at the Baxter Hall Plantation."

"Is she as fearsome as her reputation?" asked Sam. "Is there any truth to the rumour that she is a white witch?"

"I really don't know," said John. "She did grow up in the bayous of New Orleans and it is said that she learned voodoo there, but I didn't ask any of those sort of questions."

"I'm just curious about her, there is a rumour about her and her goings on at the Baxter Hall," mused Sam. "Why did she want to see you? They say that she can be a very difficult woman to deal with."

"She wants to sell the remainder of her field slaves," said John. "After selling as much as she could to prevent the loss of Baxter Hall Great House and the plantation, she no longer has enough slaves to continue production of sugar cane, so she is stopping production completely as of right now."

"And did you offer to buy any?" asked Moses, joining in the conversation.

John turned towards him. "I may go back to buy a young girl house slave," he said. "She is called Maria, and she is just twelve years old. Her mother was sold off a month ago and now she has no mother or anyone who cares for her there anymore. She looks lost and frightened, and Caroline Henshaw is more interested in keeping handsome young men at her side. But," he added, turning to Akami, "I asked her about the child I sold to her and her husband about seven years ago. It was the boy I bought from Silver Bay after I had delivered you, Akami. Do you remember the child called Rubin? He was the child of a slave woman called Rebecca."

"Yes, I remember them all talking about it just after I had arrived at Silver Bay," said Akami. "Rebecca is one of the field hands and her cabin was just next to where they first put me. I used to hear her crying all night, night after night. It took months for her to lose her anger and sorrow, and I know that she still feels the pain of her loss now."

"Well," said John with a melting, sad expression on his plump, shining face, "then I have bad news for her. Caroline Henshaw told me that Rubin had died only three weeks after I had sold him to her. She even had the cheek to ask me for her money back because she said that she had not had any value from him."

"How did he die?" asked Akami.

"Natural causes," she said. "The slave in charge of the little ones said that for the three weeks that he lived on the Baxter Plantation he was uncontrollable. Always running away and always crying. He was probably looking for his mother. On the day he died he was bitten by a snake when he crawled under a bush to hide from his tormentors. He was too small to understand that he had no choices and he was too small to survive," John was looking at Akami as he talked and he saw him shiver in revulsion. He remembered Akami's fear of snakes and this seemed to be proof to Akami that he was justified in his fears.

Akami shivered at the thought of the snake and his fear of them was re-enforced. He pulled himself together. "Poor Rebecca," he said. "She will be devastated when she hears this. She will also be shocked and angry, very angry. I don't know how anyone will be able to tell her that her baby is dead. I hope that it is the Mistress who tells her. She will know how to be gentle, and how to treat her shock."

Moses and John Merriweather then compared the two lists of children bought from Silver Bay, and John filled in the gaps.

"So here we have the lists of twelve children to complete and we will start with Rebecca," said Moses putting the papers given to him by Mellissa on the table.

1. 1819, Rebecca, Rubin born May 21st, sold Sept 13th 1821 to Caroline Henshaw of Baxter Hall and plantation, Montego Bay Jamaica. (£2) died 5th Oct 1821.

2. 1820, Rosie, Matthew born Sept 26th, sold 4th March 1823 to Edward Tyndall of the Brandon Hall Plantation, Montego Bay, Jamaica. (£2)

3. 1821, Lavinia, Jonah born July 6th, sold 10th June 1824 to Edward Tyndall of the Brandon Hall Plantation, Montego Bay, Jamaica.

4. 1821, Mary, William born 18th July, sold 10th June 1824 to Edward Tyndall of the Brandon Hall Plantation, Montego Bay, Jamaica. (£2)

5 & 6. 1822, Lulu, twin boys Victor and Elijah born 6th October, sold 20th January 1825 to Mrs Hope of Hogwell Farm, Virginia, America. (£4 each for twins)

7. 1822, Lucy, Kyle born 4th June, sold 20th January 1825 to Mrs Hope of Hogwell Farm, Virginia, America. (£2)

8. 1822, May, Rory born 25th August, sold 20th January 1825 to Mrs Hope of Hogwell Farm, Virginia, America. (£2)

9. 1823, Liza, Robert born 2nd February, sold 26th January 1826 to Master and Mistress Everdene of Kingston Port Chandlers, Jamaica. (£2)

10. 1823, Rosie, Billy born 14th April, sold 26th January 1826 to Master and Mistress Everdene of Kingston Port Chandlers, Jamaica. (£2)

11. 1824, Lulu, Benjamin born 11th March, sold 28th March 1827 to Mrs Hope of Hogwell Farm, Virginia, America. (£2)

12. 1825, Roberta, Charlie born 2nd January, sold 28th March 1827 to Mrs Hope of Hogwell Farm, Virginia, America. (£2)

"So," said Akami, "we have three living children sold right here in Montego Bay; Rosie's Matthew, who will be ten years old by now, Lavinia's Jonah, and Mary's William, will both be nine. They were all sold to Bassetts of the Greenwood plantation. Do you think, John, that we or maybe you, will be able to persuade Master Barrett to sell them back to Silver Bay?"

"A cousin, Amelia Bassett is in charge of the small children on the plantation. She is the one who chooses the children for purchasing and she organises their living quarters and their schooling. She has incorporated a proper and properly run school right there on the plantation where they all learn to read and write, and other skills that they will need to learn so they will be able to work and look after themselves if, or when, all slaves are freed. But welfare of the children is paramount to their caring and I therefore think that there is a real possibility that the Barrett family would be willing to sell these three children back to us," said Sam. Although they own nearly two thousand slaves…"

"…Two thousand," gasped Akami. "I don't believe it. How can it be possible for anyone to own two thousand people?"

"…They have a reputation of being one of the kindest of Masters in Jamaica. They treat all their slaves well, the adults as well as the children," continued Sam. "They are a really important family in Montego Bay, and have members in the Assembly and they are Justices of the Peace. I'm sure that if we tell them why we want to buy back these young people they will agree without hesitation."

"Shall we all go there tomorrow?" asked Moses. "And what about Attorney Samuel Sharpe? Shall we ask him too? Perhaps he may know the family."

"Before we think about that, John, can you tell us a little bit more about Mrs Hope of the Hogwell farm in America?" asked Akami. "You seem to have sold so many children to her. What's her operation? And is there any chance of us retrieving any of these children? It cannot be that she is using child labour on her farm."

And Sam, who was interested in not just domestic slavery but world-wide slavery too, wanted to know about the Hogwell Farm and slavery in America.

"I have been selling children to Mrs Hope for years," replied John. "The Hogwell farm in Virginia was so called when years ago they bred and sold hogs, but now they farm children and it has become almost a school. Mrs Hope buys children from all over Virginia and Maryland, and some via me from Jamaica. It sounds hard and somewhat cruel but you must remember that these children are put up for sale by their unfeeling owners, and they would be sold anyway. She sometimes has many as twenty-five boys at a time with ages ranging from two to fifteen. The children, after mourning the loss of their parents, seek comfort from each other and become happy together. They all have other children to play with, and as each of them grows up they become the teachers of the younger ones. Three of them are so gifted as teachers that they have been kept on after the usual age of forward selling, to become permanent teachers. The boys are trained to become educated footmen and body servants. All the children on Hopewell farm are well treated, well fed and well clothed. At the age of about fourteen, the young men, who have almost forgotten by then that they are the slaves of Hogwell farm, are eagerly sought after and fetch high prices from clients as far away as New York, and Boston, and even in England and France where they are usually cherished and treated by their new owners as prized possessions.

As the boys grow up they have each other for company and friendship, and they form a sort of elite family. The profit following the sale of each grown up child is well worth the time and cost spent on them. Mrs Patricia Hope is a business lady first of all, but she is also loving and kind to the little ones in her care. I am sure that she sells them for over £20 each."

"Well," said Sam, "we probably won't be able to do anything for those boys from Silver Bay who are now in America, but we can easily reach those living here in Jamaica. We have three living here in Montego Bay, and the other two who live in Kingston."

"Then," said Moses, "will you come with Akami and me to attempt to buy Matthew, Jonah and William from their owners in Montego Bay. We will offer more than their current value to buy them back, and Master Sharpe, being a well-respected Attorney-at-Law, will make sure the payments are made and everything is done legally."

Chapter Twenty-Six

Saturday, 11 September, 1830

The Hero's Return

It was mid-morning as a jubilant group of people returned to the Silver Bay Plantation. Rumours of the great coming home had reached the slaves. They left their work, and much to the annoyance of James McBride, they left the fields to run up to the plantation house to welcome the children home. Mellissa was standing on the veranda of High View and on seeing the well loaded horses plod slowly up the driveway she ran down the stone steps to meet them. Lavinia was at her heels.

"Akami, Moses, how wonderful to see that you have been successful," called out Mellissa.

"Whose children are they? Is my Jonah with you?" called out Lavinia at the same time.

The horses reached Mellissa and Lavinia who were running down the driveway, and the children jumped down into the arms of Micha, Andrew and Rebecca who had also reached the travellers by then.

A crowd of slaves had now gathered around the travellers. "Who are they?" everyone was asking, but Lavinia was quiet, staring hard at one child in particular.

"Is it possible? Are you my Jonah?" she said so quietly that the boy could hardly hear her. "Is it really you?"

He stopped still, then both of them were standing completely still amongst the chaos and excited voices of all the people who were milling around. "Mama?"

"Jonah?"

"Yes! Yes!" And with tears streaming down her face Lavinia gathered the boy up into her strong arms.

Mellissa was watching them. She, too, stood still to let them enjoy the moment and then she put her arms around them both. "I am so happy for you, Lavinia," she said quietly. "So happy because it is you who have made this happen."

"And you too, Mistress," said Lavinia. Her tears were now drying and a broad smile was beaming across her face. Lavinia's daughter Angeline had by now joined her mother and was staring wide eyed at her new-found brother. Hesitantly she put her hand in her mother's, and at once was rewarded with the most jubilant squeeze and kiss. "Look here, young lady," she said, "say hello to your big brother Jonah. You know we say a prayer for him every night, and we ask God to return him to us. And now God has answered our prayers; and here he is!"

Jonah stepped forward and the two siblings stared hard at each other for a moment and then shyly melted into each other's arms. "Hello, Jonah," whispered Angeline. "Hello, Angeline," whispered Jonah.

"So," said Mellissa, turning round to face Akami and Moses. "Oh, well done you two. First tell me who these other two young men are, so that we can return them to their mothers, and then you can tell me all about your adventures over the past two months."

"These strapping young boys are Rosie's son Matthew and Mary's son William," said Akami. But he had hardly got the words out of his mouth when both shouts of joy and a loud, piercing wail made them all jump. Rosie, with her new baby strapped to her back, and Mary pushed forward through the throng of slaves to stand in front of their children. "You must be Matthew," said Rosie picking out a very tall and slim boy. "You's looking just like you gran'pappy. Come here boy and hug you Mammy." As an afterthought almost, she whispered, "I wonder if I's ever gonna see my lil ole Billy again?"

The smaller boy said nothing, and just folded himself into Mary's arms.

But the wailing continued. It was Rebecca. She had been so sure that her Rubin would be returning with Akami, and now all her hopes were dashed.

Mellissa was trying to sort out the hub-bub of the slaves gathering, and she was pleased to see that Charles and McBride were arriving. "Charles," she called out. "Come, see we have had three of our children returned."

"Congratulations, my love," he said. "I really did think that you had sent Akami out on a wild goose chase. In fact, I didn't think that

172

we would ever see him again. I thought that he would run off to join the runaways in the Cockpit Country." He looked at Akami and shook Moses' hand. "Well done, and thank you."

"Now Charles," said Mellissa, "could you and McBride get everyone except all the mothers to go back to the compound. I will be happy to supply two extra hogs and a small barrel of rum so that tonight everyone can celebrate and rejoice on this happy day. What luck that it is a Saturday so that they can nurse their hangovers on Sunday!" She turned around to the triumphant slaves, "Akami, Lavinia and Moses, you three boys, and all you other girls will you all please come into our house so that we can discuss what has happened to all the twelve children who were stolen away from here, and what we shall do from now on." And to Abraham, who had finally come shuffling forward to see what all the fuss was about she asked, "Oh, Abraham, would you please take the two horses and release them in the paddock. I don't think that you will have to do anything for them except to make sure they have clean water to drink. I'm sure that Akami and Moses will be along soon to look after them and feed them. Thank you, Abraham."

"If you can excuse my forwardness Mistress, will you ask Lavinia to take them all in," said Akami quietly, "because I need to tell you something first."

"Of course, Akami, you should never be afraid of speaking to me about anything," she said, laying her hand gently on his right arm. She hesitated for a moment as a buzz of expectation ran up her own arm. What was that she thought? She lifted her hand quickly. Only a second had passed and no one seemed to have noticed the slight change in her demeanour and voice. "Did you hear that, Lavinia?" she said, "Would you take them all in, and Akami and I will join you all in just a few minutes."

When everyone had moved off and Akami and Mellissa were alone, she touched his arm once more, to see if her reaction was the same. The buzz was even more forceful and as she tried to return to a normal, strictly business relationship, she said with a crackling voice, "Now, what is it that is troubling you Akami? Is it something that is to do with the children?"

"Yes, Mistress," said Akami, bowing his head, unhappy to be the bearer of bad news on this happy day. "It's Rebecca's son, Rubin. He is dead. He was bitten by a snake only three days after John Merriweather had sold him to a plantation in Montego Bay. Rubin was taken away from Rebecca at the same time that the Johnston's bought me, and I was with her when night after night she cried for her son. It is seven years ago now, and I know that she has never stopped mourning his loss. I know for sure that she wasn't just waiting for my return with her son, but that she was expecting me to find him and bring him back. She is going to be deeply troubled. For all the other children we have information and there remains two who still live in Jamaica, in Kingston, where it should be possible for us to find them. They are Liza's son Robert, and Rosie's second son, Billy. If we were to bring back Rosie's second son, it will be even harder for Rebecca to accept, especially as Rosie now has had a third child. The other bad news is that John Merriweather thinks that those children who were taken to Virginia, America are all lost to us."

"Oh, Akami," sighed Mellissa, "how wrong I was to think that this is a day of pure happiness. How am I going to tell all this to Rebecca and the other girls?"

Chapter Twenty-Seven

Tuesday, 26 January, 2016, 2:00 p.m.
Wallchester General Hospital

Dr Akami was at Mellissa's bedside checking her vital signs when Lavinia Hobbs entered the ICU Ward 2. He greeted her with a cheerful voice. "Good afternoon, Inspector Hobbs, We've not seen you for a few days. Is your investigation going well?"

"Good afternoon, Dr Akami," she returned in an equally friendly manner. "We are at a bit of a sticking point at the moment. I have at last been able to persuade the local magistrate to give me a search warrant for the marital home, and I want to find evidence that her head injury was sustained there. So how is she doing now? Can you now tell me anything about the wound? How it was inflicted, and what might have been used to inflict it?"

Dr Akami thought for a moment or two. "I do not like making assumptions," he said, "but I would say that according to the bruises on her face, she was slapped hard with an open hand and she fell backwards hitting her head on the corner of a sharp, hard edged unit or cupboard of some sort, probably made of stone or marble. It is my guess that the wounding took place within a clean kitchen with marble work surfaces."

"That's exactly what I had deduced too," said the DI, nodding her head in agreement. "Are you able to bring her out of the anaesthetic yet?"

"We are slowly reducing the quantities that are keeping her under, and I expect her to return to full consciousness in the next day or two," he said, taking her wrist in his hand to measure her pulse.

"I think that she is already responding to you," Lavinia pointed to Mellissa who was lying quietly in her bed with her head covered in bandages. "Look how her eyes are moving under the closed lids every time you touch her. Her fingers are twitching too."

"Yes, I've noticed that," said the doctor. "Perhaps it's because she had become used to my voice over the last few days."

"I think that you are right," she replied. "There is no response at all if I touch her hand. Look," she said, as she gently took hold of Mellissa's hand and rubbed her fingers. "Does her husband come regularly? Does he get any response?"

"The nurses tell me that he comes most days after filming and sits with her for an hour or two. But I am sure that they are drooling over the husband rather that look at his wife's response to him," said Dr Akami, raising his eyebrows and looking upwards, with a soppy expression on his face. "They are still very excited to have a real TV star come visiting, and they haven't told me of any changes or different reaction she has when he is here."

"Just look how she is reacting to your taking her pulse," exclaimed Lavinia. "It is almost as if she is asking you to join her in her dream-state world."

Chapter Twenty-Eight

13 September, 1830

Celebrations at the Silver Bay Plantation

Rebecca ran out of the room, screaming. Akami was about to get up and follow her but Mellissa put her hand on his arm to stop him. Again the buzz! "Akami," she said, "I don't think that you will be able to help her." She turned to Lavinia who was sitting with both her children clinging to both sides of her body, "Lavinia," she said, "she needs the care and love of a woman right now. Is there anyone who she could turn to, someone who will stay the night with her and keep her calm?"

Lulu stood up, the tears had yet to dry on her careworn face. "She my friend, an' I done got lost two chillen in that Viginia. I don gonna see they no more. I go to her. I take her away from de party. We go walk in de woods. Yes, Mistress?"

"Yes, Lulu, you do that," she said with a grateful smile. "And when she feels a little better bring her back here. You can both spend the night here, away from the celebrations in the compound, if that is what you would prefer."

While Lulu hurried out to follow Rebecca, Mellissa turned to the three mothers, Lavinia, Rosie and Mary and their boys. "Well," she said, giving them all a joyful smile. "We have all had an exciting day, and for the children, a very tiring day. I think that you should go and enjoy the fun and celebrations in the compound, and the Master and I will have a talk about what we will do about the children and their future." She shooed them off and they were all happy to run and join the others. Then she called Chloe, Roberta and Winnie, who had recently joined the household slaves. "I am sure that the Master and I will be able to look after ourselves tonight. There are plenty of cold meats, breads and fruits in the larder that we can help ourselves to. After we have had a little bit of lunch, you three can go off and join the others in the compound. So if you prepare our lunch now, you can then go and have fun with the others!"

Having worked with James McBride to organise the hog roast and distribution of rum and extra foods for the slave community, Charles returned to High View. He joined Mellissa on the veranda, hugged her from behind, spun her around and gave her a passionate kiss.

"Congratulations, my darling," he said, as they sat in comfortable chairs with a bottle of wine at hand while they were waiting for lunch, "I never thought that you would be able to succeed with your crazy idea, especially getting Akami to travel to all the way to Montego Bay and return here. He is more faithful to you than is your Sheba, and has the same faithful doggy look in his eyes too." He laughed.

"I did have full faith in Akami," said Mellissa, "but, at the same time, I do have to admit that on occasions during the last two months while he was away I did wonder if he would stay in the Cockpit Country and Moses would come back alone."

"So what's next?"

"Next is lunch, and then maybe a siesta?" she said looking at him in her special way that said that she wanted more than sleep! "Why don't we celebrate in our own way?"

"Woman, you are shameless," he said with a laugh.

It was late afternoon when Mellissa came down to the terrace dressed in her new, shimmering rose silk dress. It was cut in the modern, classical empire line which emphasised her small breasts and showed them to the full, and enhanced by her ruby collar and dazzling pendant which sat perfectly between her uplifted breasts. She knew that she looked her very best; pretty, delicate, and with the additional afterglow of satisfied sex that sat upon her so well. Her private parts were still throbbing from their afternoon of passion and her blood was still coursing excitedly through her body. She stood on the veranda admiring the sunset, with Sheba at her side as usual.

She heard Charles as he came to join her and she twirled around to greet him, her eyes and her rubies sparkling in the rays of the setting sun. He took her two hands in his and studied her. "You have never looked so beautiful as you do right now," he said.

She smiled coyly and laughed. "You said that an hour ago when I wasn't wearing quite so much."

"Your silky skin, your silky dress," he whispered, his lips so close to her ear he was almost nibbling at her earlobe. "You just glow all over."

"It's happiness, Charles," she whispered back to him. "I have never been so happy in all my life, and it is you who has made it all possible. There is only one thing more that I would wish to make our life perfect."

"What is that, my love?"

"I would wish that our wonderful bedroom romps will soon result in me conceiving the child that I know we both desperately desire."

"It will happen one day, darling," he said gently. "I'm sure that it won't be long before it happens." And he caught her to him, held her tight and kissed her once more.

They stood up to toast each other with wine while looking over their veranda towards the sea and the setting sun. Mixed with the usual sound of the cicadas, macaws and parakeets they could hear music, drumbeats and laughter in the distance, and the smell of roasting pig was filling the air and drifting up the hill towards them.

"Do you think that we would be welcome if we were to gate crash the party in the compound tonight?" asked Mellissa, drooling a little and smacking her lips! "After all, I have got my party dress on!"

"Slightly overdressed for a slave compound, my dear!" he laughed. "But it might be fun. And I think that you, particularly, might be very welcome. After all it was you that has made all this happen," he said. "I'm not so sure about me. I'm still the Massa, and I still have to get them all to work as hard as they can every day. Let's see what happens after sunset, perhaps we might get an invite to come down!"

They sat down again, now in deep contentment, enjoying the warmth of the Jamaican evening, and looking at the last rays of the setting sun. While he was in such a good mood Mellissa decided to talk to Charles about the future of the children on the plantation.

She took a deep breath. "Charles," she said in the persuasive voice that he knew so well, "Charles," she repeated, "I am so glad that you are happy about us finding and bringing back those three children, because in a few weeks' time I want to continue to try and find the two children who were sold in Kingston." She continued without a pause so that he did not have a chance to protest. "But right now we will have to settle the three who have just returned. Edward Tyndall of the Brandon Hall Plantation where they have been living, is the most advanced owner on this island in the treatment of his slaves. It is almost incredible to me that any one person can own over two thousand souls, but at least he tries to make their lives as supportable as he can. And he also believes, like me, that he gets more work, more willingness to work from slaves that are treated well than from those who are whipped to force them to comply."

"So how does this relate to our three new children?" Charles already sounded beaten.

"There is a school for the children on the Brandon Hall Plantation. It is for all the children on the plantation. And with two thousand slaves there must be hundreds of children of all ages. They are all taught to read and write, and those that show ability go on to learn other things such as mathematics."

"Don't tell me," said Charles, beginning to sound exasperated again, "that you want to open a school here too?"

"Well, it is an idea that is buzzing around in my head. We have quite a number of small children now, and I think that some of them are too young to be working in the cane fields. They are only there because their mothers are working and they have no one to look after them. We have no old grandmothers here who would look after the little ones as they do on other plantations where the natural order of mothering is allowed to be. If we start a school, not only will it help the children, it will enable the mothers to work harder, to concentrate harder on what they are doing without having to keep an eye open for what their children might be up to. We should start a school. It need only be something small. Lessons for half a day, in the mornings perhaps. Akami knows enough now to be able to teach the little ones basic reading. The three older boys who have come fresh from schooling can show him how their school was set up. Then, perhaps in the afternoons all of them can help Abraham and learn a little about gardening and looking after animals. What do you think?"

"What is all this insistence on learning to read and write? They are slaves and their future will be to work in the cane fields!"

"Yes, right now it is, but you will never look into the future." It was Mellissa now who was getting a bit agitated. "If all slaves are to be freed in the next few years, they will need to know a bit more than sugar cane culture if they no longer have us to look after their interests and they have to start to look after themselves."

"You are so sure that the abolitionists will win, aren't you? Do you realise that even if we are compensated by the English government we stand to lose thousands of pounds if we are forced to free our slaves?"

"Darling Charles, we will only lose money if we lose production. And the best way to secure future production is to look after our slaves. If and when they are freed by law, they will still need to work, like everyone else. And if they are happy here they will want to continue to work here as freemen. If they stay here or even if some of them decide to move on as freemen, wherever they work, whatever they do, just like us they will have to earn their living to pay their way."

"You make it sound easy! Straight forward! All change! No hick-ups!"

"Oh. I'm sure that there will be lots of hick-ups. The slaves will all think that it is easy just to go off anywhere, anytime, and they will find out that they will have to continue to work in order to live. I'm also sure that some will just go off and try to fend for themselves, maybe to come back later with their tails between their legs and ask for work!"

"Well, that's the future," sighed Charles. "What about now? If you open a school, you will probably get children from other plantations wanting to come here to learn, rather like they already come now to get treatment at your clinic."

"Yes. I rather like that. Mostly they come out of curiosity to have little cuts and bruises attended to, but we have splintered a few broken bones and we did save the life of that little boy from the Chamberlain plantation."

"It was a little boy called Samson, wasn't it? I remember you describing the way that his flesh was being eaten away as a result of a bite from a deadly brown recluse spider. Disgusting!"

"Yes. They do have some wonderful birds and animals here in Jamaica, but they have their share of nasty creatures too! In good old England most of our wildlife is rather unspectacular, but at least we can walk out in the countryside without being over-run with stinging and biting insects, or in fear of our lives from snakes."

"Apart from the adders!"

"Oh, yes. Adders," laughed Mellissa. "Actually I have never seen one. Have you?" She stood up. "Come on," she said, holding out her hand to pull Charles from his chair, "let's go in before the mosquitoes get started! I'm afraid that we will have to look after ourselves this evening because I told Chloe, Roberta and Winnie that they could go and join the fun in the slave compound."

"You did what, woman?" said Charles, with mock fierceness. He looked hard at his wife, growled and headed straight for the kitchen. "Is this how the Master of the house, no, the Master of the whole plantation, should be served? I, Master Harrison, who have more than three hundred and eighty slaves at my beck and call, and I have to get my own supper? What sort of Master is that?"

"One who might prefer to eat pig meat straight from the carcass down in the compound?" Mellissa laughed, caught up with him at the kitchen doorway, took hold of him and kissed him until they both felt dizzy. They were just about to select their evening meal from the larder when Chloe came running into the house.

"Massa, Mistress," she called out, "Where are you?" There was fear and urgency in her voice and Mellissa knew at once that there was trouble.

"Chloe," Mellissa answered, "we are here in the kitchen. Whatever has happened?"

"Come quick. It Massa McBride!" Chloe was panting and crying at the same time. "I run all the way from the compound."

"Whatever has happened, Chloe?" pressed Mellissa.

"Rebecca. It Rebecca. She stab Massa McBride," Chloe managed to get out. She was still crying, but a look of terror was beginning to settle on her. "She stab him with pig knife. He bleeding like a stuck pig. Lavinia, she with him."

"Oh my God," shouted Charles. "Come on Mellissa, we will need you. Let's go!"

Chapter Twenty-Nine

Murder at Silver Bay

James McBride was lying on his back on a straw pallet in the centre of the compound. Lavinia was pressing a large pad of cotton wadding against the right side of his chest but the blood was still oozing through her fingers. Mellissa ran to his side and her first thought was that she would be unable to save him, and although she hated him and would, under different circumstances, be glad to see him dead, she nevertheless vowed to try her best to keep him alive. "That black nigger bitch got me," he whispered. "Stuck me with a knife. Got me in between my ribs." Blood was choking off his efforts to talk, and was dripping, in a cloud of bloody air bubbles, out of the corner of his mouth.

"Don't try to talk," said Mellissa. "I want to get you to the clinic to see if I can stop the bleeding." She was sure that his lungs were filling up with blood so she turned him on his side to try to stop him from drowning. A gush of blood foamed out of his open mouth. Then she turned to the slaves who were standing around in shock, looking at their hated overseer. "You, Sammy, and you Louis, get a strong, flat board so that we can take Master McBride up to the clinic. Go. Do it now!" she shouted.

Charles was organising a group of men to carry him up the hill to the clinic. "Where is Rebecca now?" he asked as Sammy brought a cabin door on which they would carry McBride.

Lavinia, who was still trying to help Mellissa, said, "she ran off into the woods. I saw Akami and Moses run after her. Lulu was supposed to stay with her but Rebecca said that she was calm and wanted to join in with the hog roast."

"Let's stop this talk right now," said Mellissa, "and concentrate on getting McBride on to this board and up to the clinic before he bleeds to death."

Charles, Sammy and Louis were guided by Mellissa as they lifted James McBride onto the door and strapped him down on his left side. Then they carried him as gently as they could up to the clinic, almost an identical repeat of the way Akami had been carried there about nine months previously. All the while Mellissa was pressing down hard on the wound in his ribs, and was having some positive effect on lessening the blood flow. The skies were dark by the time everyone reached the clinic and McBride was gently transferred from the makeshift stretcher to the surgical bed cum operating table. Under candlelight and oil flame, with Lavinia assisting at her side, Mellissa worked as hard as she could, using all her medical skills, but it was not enough and the overseer for the Silver Bay plantation, James McBride died, drowning in his own blood.

Sammy and Louis had already crept out to spread the word to the slave community. Mellissa, Charles, Lavinia and Akami were all standing around and staring down at McBride's dead body, looking totally stunned. Charles was the first to react. He could hardly believe what he was seeing. "No. No. No," he shouted. "He cannot be dead. I need him." He looked angrily at Mellissa. "You let him die. Didn't you? It's your fault, you stupid woman."

Mellissa stood there, her beautiful silk dress ruined, soaked in McBride's blood. Her hands dripping with his blood, and even smudges of it were smeared on her face, neck and her ruby collar. She could hardly believe her eyes and ears. "Charles," she protested, "that's not fair. You were standing over me, watching me. You could see that I was doing my very best to save him. You know very well that as a trained medic I have always done, and will always do, my utmost best in the treatment of a sick or injured person, whoever he or she is. It was long ago when I vowed to save every life that I possibly can."

"All I know," said her enraged husband with a snarl, "is that you hated McBride and could not wait until I had learned enough about the plantation to get rid of him. Now you have got what you wanted. Permanently got rid of him." He almost spat out the last words.

"But Charles…"

He stopped further words of protest from her with a completely unexpected slap, a really savage slap, with an open hand right across her face and mouth. The force of his strike, the instant violent pain and the shock of realising that her beloved husband had hit her, knocked Mellissa backwards. She was prevented from hitting her head on the pointed corner of her metal surgical cabinet by Akami, who, without thought that this was his Mistress and he should not touch her person or interfere between husband and wife, instinctively reached out and caught her. Charles said nothing as he turned and left the clinic, leaving Mellissa in tears and Lavinia and Akami stunned and immobile.

They were all suffering from shock, and Lavinia decided that Mellissa needed to return to High View. Akami locked the clinic door leaving the body of McBride where it remained, on the surgical table, and Lavinia gently guided Mellissa back to the plantation house and up to her bedroom.

All the while she had not stopped crying. How could a day that had started so well, and had gone on to become the happiest day in her life, turn, with the flash of Rebecca's knife, to become the worst day of her life? Did Charles really believed that she had deliberately let McBride die? He was convinced that she could have saved him. It was as if he were accusing her of murder, as well as the slave Rebecca. Poor Rebecca, who, for seven long years, had been half out of her mind with grief and loss after the sale of her two year old son, Rubin. She had been so convinced that Akami would bring Rubin home and had now she had been told that he had died almost as soon as he had been taken from his mother's side.

Mellissa was still crying as Lavinia helped her to remove her beautiful dress which had now become nothing more than a blood soaked rag. Lavinia the slave, had no words of comfort for Mellissa her owner and Mistress, so she just held Mellissa in her strong, black arms and rocked her like a small child. "Don't cry Mistress," she said. "It is just the shock. I am sure that he will come back soon to say that he is sorry."

"But he hit me, Lavinia," she sobbed. "He hit me. From the very first day when I met him he has always been so loving and gentle. I have seen him angry before today, but never so angry that he lost control of himself. I still cannot believe that he hit me."

Chapter Thirty

A Burial at Silver Bay

After a fruitless search the in the gardens and grounds surrounding High View and the slave compound with dozens of slaves holding up blazing torches, Charles rode off alone to St Elizabeth to report the murder of his overseer, James McBride. He also reported the missing slave Rebecca, who had committed the murder, and who might be on the run and trying to escape. He returned the following morning with the Minister Josiah Smith of St Peter's church, after his Sunday morning duties and services were completed. In the meantime Lavinia had organised six slave women to wash and prepare James McBride for burial. Apart from the women whom he had forced to have sex with him in his cabin and in the dark, the slaves on the Silver Bay plantation had never seen a white man fully undressed. They found his lower limbs, head, face and neck tanned to a dark coffee colour much like the lighter skinned slaves themselves. But the complete absence of colour on his trunk, hips, private parts and thighs was almost frightening to them. And they could hardly believe that the red hair on his head was repeated under his arms, across his belly and down to his groin. It was like preparing a ghost for the grave. They did the work hastily but carefully and they were pleased, at last, to wrap his body in a winding sheet and place it in the pinewood coffin that other slaves had made in the carpentry workshop.

Deaths happened from time to time on the Silver Bay plantation, but because the Johnstons had made it their business to buy young men and women in the best of breeding condition, and selling off most of their older or injured slaves, a burial on the plantation was rare.

Minister Smith conducted a dignified burial service for the murdered overseer as he was buried in the slave burial ground beyond the edge of the compound. "Did not your James McBride have any friends or family who would have wanted to have him buried elsewhere?" he asked. "You seem to have wanted him buried with almost indecent haste."

"I know of no living relation of his," said Charles. "He was always laughing at me and the attention I pay to my wife's wishes, and he liked to tell me how sweet it was to be entirely free of nagging wives, children and begging relations. He was always telling me how happy he was to be free to do what he wanted, and go where and when he wanted. I think that he had as much sexual relations as he wanted right here with the female slaves who willingly or reluctantly shared his bed from time to time."

The service was completed and a party of slaves filled in the grave. There were no flowers, no mourners and no cross to mark the grave. And without going home or seeking out Mellissa, Charles returned to St Elizabeth with Josiah Smith, leaving instructions with Lavinia to clean out McBride's cabin, and put away all his personal belongings in the storage area under the plantation house.

There were very few really personal belongings in McBride's cabin. A very few books, some pewter jugs and plates, his clothing and the parrot in its cage. Lavinia hurriedly stored away everything but the parrot, for which she opened the cage door and allowed it to fly away to the tree tops. She was anxious to get back to High View to report everything that had happened back to Mellissa who had deliberately stayed in the house and had not taken any part in McBride's burial.

Mellissa was still on her bedroom. She was sitting up in the enormous four poster bed with its new, silk mosquito netting curtains drawn back to join the pink damask curtains which they always left open at night. She thought that the bed looked pitifully empty without Charles at her side. Her loving husband who had rarely slept away from her since their marriage. She looked at his empty pillow and started to cry again. She noticed that Lavinia had already brought in her breakfast on the big silver tray that had belonged to her mother, which her father had given her before she left England. The food was uneaten, cold and sticky on her mother's best china plates, the tea was cold in the matching teapot, and everything in the room, the tables, the comfortable armchairs, the French mirrors, and the wardrobes all looked out of place and as unhappy as Mellissa.

Lavinia knocked on the door and came bustling in. "Good Morning, Mistress," she said, painfully aware that Mellissa was still crying. "Let me tell you what has been happening here this morning. The Master returned home with Minister Smith from St Peter's in St Elizabeth and together they held a short service for Master McBride who was then buried on the edge of the slave burial ground. He asked me to clear our Master McBride's cabin which I did, setting the parrot free. Then he went back to St Elizabeth with the Minister. He said to tell you that he would be back before sundown."

"How can Charles do all this and not come to see me?" she asked, of herself as much as Lavinia, and she started to cry again. "Can he really believe that I could have saved McBride and I deliberately let him die?"

"I think that it was such a shock to the Master who still has so little experience in running this plantation, that he has not been himself since it happened," said Lavinia as she brushed Mellissa's hair and helped her to dress and prepare herself for the day. "Why don't you just pretend that yesterday never happened and start the day anew. I am sure that if you don't confront the Master, he will be as affectionate as he always is with you. He may even feel ashamed of hitting you and will want your understanding and forgiveness. I think that you should do today what you had already planned."

"Well," said Mellissa, drying her eyes, "I did want to talk to you and Akami and the children about beginning a small school, mornings only. I had started to talk it over with the Master yesterday when all these horrible events happened. Will you go and fetch Akami, your children and the others and I will talk to you all in the yard outside the kitchen door."

Fifteen minutes later there were nine children sitting scrunched up together on a long rough bench made from a fallen tree which lined the back wall in the kitchen yard. Akami and Lavinia were writing down their names and the names of their mothers when Mellissa arrived, her face was bruised, but it was well scrubbed and all traces of tears were gone.

"Well who have we got here?" she asked. "I know Jonah and his sister Angeline, and I know Matthew and William who were returned back here to Rosie and Mary yesterday."

"Let me see," said Lavinia, scratching her head and pretending that she did not recognise the other children. "I think that you and you," she said pointing to two pretty little girls of about five years old, "are our famous identical twins Milly and Molly and you mummy is called Henry. Is that right?"

The twins giggled. "Our Mamie is not Henry," they protested, speaking together as one voice. "She's Henrietta!"

"Oh, is that right?" asked Lavinia. The twins were nodding their heads enthusiastically. "Now which one is Milly and which one is Molly."

It was Milly who got in first this time. "I's Milly and I always have a red ribbon in my hair, and she's Molly…"

"…and I always have a blue ribbon in my hair," finished Molly.

Everyone laughed and then Lavinia turned to two little boys of about four who had escaped being sold off when Melissa and Charles had bought Silver Bay. "And you must be Elsa's boy Chuck. And you must be Petra's boy Nelson. Is that right?" More heads were nodding cheerfully.

Mellissa looked carefully at them all. "Well, what a lovely group of children we have here. And enough to start a small school, don't you think Akami?"

Akami was flustered and was quite taken aback as he looked at the dark purple bruise on the face of his Mistress. As yet he had no idea that Mellissa was about to suggest that he became a schoolmaster. "Yes, Mistress," he stuttered. "Are you saying that I will help to start that school?"

"No, Akami," she said with a broad smile. "I am saying that you will become their school teacher, and you will be in charge of the school." She pointed to Jonah, Matthew and William. "You three boys will be able to tell me and Akami all about the schooling you had at the Greenwood Plantation, and I think that it would be a pity for that to stop now that you have come home. Don't you boys? What do you think?" she asked smiling at the three children.

All three were suddenly very shy, and they looked to the ground beneath their feet. "Answer the Mistress," said Lavinia to her Jonah. "Did you like schooling? Have you learned to read?"

Jonah looked up. He was smiling proudly now. "I learned to read and I am best in my class!" he said triumphantly.

"Oh, no you are not," argued Rosie's boy, Matthew. "And I am a year older than you. I know more about everything than you do!"

The challenge was down. "Well, well, well," said a surprised Mellissa. "Do we have rivals for the best learner?"

"And why can't I learn to read too?" asked a little voice piping up. It was Angeline, only seven years old and ready to challenge all the boys!

"I think, Lavinia, we will have to have a talk with the Master about setting up a small school here," said Mellissa. "It would be a pity if all that learning was lost." She looked at Lavinia and Akami. "We have many children here now who will find the future better for them if they can read and write. And some of the adults too might like to start to learn to read. So if we start off small with just these children and if it all works out then we can expand to teach some of the adults too."

Chapter Thirty-One

Who Are the Frobishers?

It was just after the sun had set when Charles returned. Mellissa was waiting for him on the veranda and was about to run down the steps and fling herself in his arms when she saw that he was not alone. There were two men riding up behind to join him at the front of the house. And, curiously they had all approached High View not from the avenue but from the side of the house. Mellissa came slowly down the stairs with a questioning look upon her face. "Hello Charles," she said cautiously, "Who have you brought back with you?" She looked hard at the newcomers questioningly.

"My dear girl," he said in the friendliest of voices, as if nothing unusual or bad had happened between them, "these two gentlemen are Jack and Peter Frobisher…"

The two men dismounted, swept off their hats and all but bowed to her in a mock salute. "Good evening, Mistress," they said in unison, giving her a brazen onceover and taking in the bruising on her face. They were pleasantly handsome young men who looked to Mellissa to be about the same age as her husband, although they were both taller, very much taller and thinner than him, and they looked healthier and stronger too. Two almost identical sets of piercing blue eyes stared right back at Mellissa. If those eyes were indeed able to see properly as they were all but covered under shaggy, and rather dirty, blond hair that was falling forward over their foreheads.

Charles continued, "…Jack and Peter are brothers who until now have lived in St Elizabeth, and I have invited them both be our new overseers. They will take over from James McBride, and they will live in his cabin."

Mellissa was astounded that he had done such a thing without discussing it with her first. She was bursting with questions of who they were, how Charles knew them, how long he had known them, etc. etc. etc. The questions were cramming into her thoughts and gagging her too. She stood there stunned to silence while Charles was acting the gentleman host.

"Do come in, both of you," he said to the two young men, and led the way up to the veranda and into the house, while Mellissa followed behind like a creature struck dumb. As soon as they were all inside Charles took the men into his study and Mellissa called for Roberta and made arrangements for food and drink to be laid out in the dining room. Then she sent for Chloe to make up two beds in McBride's cabin. She joined the men in the study.

"Well, gentlemen," she said, finding her voice at last. She wanted to sit down in her favourite leather armchair, but it was occupied by one of the Frobisher brothers. She was not offered a chair by any of the three men, and was left standing awkwardly. "I can see that you know my husband well, perhaps we should get acquainted too. I am Mistress Mellissa Harrison, and I am the joint owner of the Silver Bay plantation." She saw Charles look askance at that, but she carried on without hesitation. "I have some food and refreshments waiting for you all in the dining room. Perhaps we can talk at table."

"Yes. Why not?" said Charles, with a shrug of his shoulders, and again he led the way for the brothers, leaving Mellissa to trail in the rear once more.

As they were seating themselves Mellissa asked of Charles, "Who exactly are these gentlemen, and what experience do they have with running a sugar plantation?"

Peter Frobisher heard the question and laughed. "What experience have we had?" He laughed again and his brother Jack joined in. "Our father, Michael Frobisher owns the Greenfields Plantation near Kingston, one of the biggest sugar cane plantations over on the east side of the island. I am twenty-eight and my brother Jack is thirty years old. We were born in Jamaica and all our lives we have been learning about every aspect of what is needed to be known about running a successful sugar cane business."

"Then why did you leave home and take employment here?" asked a puzzled Mellissa.

Jack took over the story. "We have yet another brother, a brother who is older than both of us, and recently he has taken over the running of the plantation from our father who is sick and can no longer work like he did before. Our elder brother, Christopher, and his wife Miranda think that they can run the whole plantation by themselves with no help from us. They made life very uncomfortable for us so we decided to leave home and let them get on with it. We will be going back to see the family at Christmastime, just after the next harvest and we shall see whether we are wanted back on the Greenfields plantation or whether we have made you so much extra profits that you will be begging us to stay here at the Silver Bay plantation!"

Charles then joined in with the conversation. "Mellissa, my dear," he said, taking her hand and rubbing her fingers affectionately, "I know that I have rather sprung this thing on you, but neither of us were anticipating the events of the last few days. I had already met Jack and Peter in St Elizabeth and we had had general talks about running a cane sugar plantation, and I had in the back of my mind that James McBride would not want to stay on at Silver Bay much longer and I would at some time be needing some help. Then suddenly McBride is dead and the help I was anticipating for some vague time in the future became needed now. And these boys have volunteered."

"That's all very well," said Mellissa, who was studying the thin, rather cruel looking, faces of the two men who were making themselves so comfortable around her dining table, "but can we afford to employ two overseers?"

"This is the arrangement that I have made with Jack and Peter," said Charles carefully. He was always the owner and boss of Silver Bay, but he knew that it was with his wife's money that the plantation had been bought, so he felt somewhat obliged to at least acknowledge it by giving her some say, or letting her think that she had some say, in the big decisions on how the plantation was run. "We had a very good harvest last season, much better than McBride expected, and these boys are so assured that can make us an even better profit that all they ask for as payment is for the same wage as we paid McBride to share between them, and then after harvest time we give them half of the extra profit they make above what we earned last season. That sounds like a good deal for all of us, don't you think?"

"Well I suppose so," said Mellissa reluctantly. She would much rather have had this discussion in private with Charles, but she realised that she had not much of a choice and had been presented with a 'fait accompli'. She said no more for the present and changed the subject completely. "Is there any word of Rebecca? Has Magistrate Oliver Seagrove in St Elizabeth arranged for any searches to be made of the countryside between here and St Elizabeth?"

"Oh! Rebecca!" Charles replied with a false air of surprise in his voice. "Did I not tell you? We have found her. She was hiding amongst the hibiscus bushes on the outskirts of St Elizabeth, and we brought her back to Silver Bay with us."

"You've found her!" Mellissa was astonished. She was ready to jump up from the table. "Why didn't you say so? Where is she? Shall I go to her? She must be very frightened. She is very sick, but she must know that she has done wrong. She will be expecting some sort of punishment, but I hope that Magistrate Seagrove will be considerate when you take her back to St Elizabeth."

"Of course she has done wrong! She is a murdering bitch," Charles almost shouted at her. "And right now she is locked up in the punishment barn, shackled to the wall. We will decide what to do with her on the morning."

"Aren't you going to take her to the Magistrate for him to punish her?" asked a very unsettled Mellissa. "You promised me that you would never use that punishment barn!"

"No," said Charles, and an almost gleeful look came upon his face. His eyes were gleaming in anticipation. Mellissa was shocked to realise that he was expecting to take a part in whatever punishment was meted out to Rebecca. She recoiled in horror and was only half listening when Charles continued. "Magistrate Seagrove has already decided and told me that if I find her, I should punish her myself, in any way that I choose."

The two strangers were silently watching all these exchanges between husband and wife and deciding which of them was the more powerful, or even who of these equal partners would win this particular power struggle. Reflecting on the wife's bruised face, they decided on the husband, and Jack, the elder brother spoke up. "Mistress Harrison," he said with an ingratiating smile, "my brother and I will make it our first mission on this plantation to deal with the slave Rebecca. She will be punished and we will make our position, our new positions as overseers, known and felt by having all the slaves witness that punishment. Strong discipline is the only way to control slaves and get the best out of them."

Mellissa looked at Charles. "You don't mean to have her whipped, and in front of all the slaves, do you?" with her face now a mask of horror. "You cannot do that. That's savage. We have a plantation where we treat our slaves with care and consideration and as a result they are willing to work hard to give everyone, ourselves included, the best life possible. You cannot allow this to happen, Charles." She was almost begging him.

Charles was somewhat abashed, but he stood his ground. "This will be the best possible way to show all the slaves that Jack and Peter Frobisher are the new overseers, and that they mean business. I know that you won't like it, but Rebecca has to be punished."

"Wickedness! Wickedness! And I will not stand by and let you do it." She was speaking directly to her husband and then turned to the new overseers and repeated, "I won't let you do it!"

With that she stood up and left the room to retreat once more to her bedroom.

Chapter Thirty-Two

Rebecca Is Punished

Mellissa was woken up by a sort of rough scraping noise outside. She looked at the other side of her bed to see what Charles made of the noise, only to see that he had already got up and had left the bedroom. She was very troubled but she was determined not to start crying again. Perhaps he had stayed up very late and had thought not to disturb her this morning. She rang for Lavinia to come.

"Good Morning, Mistress," said an unhappy looking Lavinia. "The Master has had his breakfast and has already left the house."

"Do you know where he has gone, or what is that noise I have been hearing?" asked Mellissa, as she was getting out of bed.

"I do not know exactly what is going on," answered Lavinia, "but I do believe that it came from the area beyond Abraham's cabin and the stables."

"That's where the punishment barn is! Oh, I did hope that Charles would change his mind about what to do with Rebecca," said a startled Mellissa. "I was hoping that he would take her back to Magistrate Seagrove in St Elizabeth after all." She ran towards her wash stand and clothing. "Never mind breakfast, Lavinia, just help me to get washed and dressed quickly. I want to see what is going on, and I want to help Rebecca if I can."

Within ten minutes Mellissa, with Lavinia at her side, was making her way towards the punishment barn. She stopped up short outside it to see that the metal A-frame, that she had seen soon after they had arrived at Silver Bay, was being hauled away from where it had rested, unused, for all that time. Charles was there overseeing the overseers, who had a small team of slaves dragging the heavy metal frame away.

Mellissa went to her husband's side. "What is going on?" she cried, her voice almost drowned by the noise that the removal was making. "Where are they taking it, and why?"

"Morning, Old Girl," said Charles giving her a hug and a peck on her cheek. He was pleased to see her as he wanted to make things right between them, and to seek approval for what he had decided to do. "I am not going to keep Rebecca chained up in the barn. She is going to be punished for killing James McBride, but it will be done gently, and in front of the other slaves."

Mellissa lost hope that she would be able to help Rebecca. "Then what is that A-frame all about? She asked.

"We are moving it to the flat area behind the compound cabins and she will be tied there for a whipping that everyone will witness," said Charles. "But I have ordered the Frobishers, who will be administrating the punishment, to do it lightly and not break her skin. But she will be given fifty lashes."

"Oh, Charles," cried Mellissa. "Not so much. She is a sick woman and I am sure that she did not plan, or mean to kill McBride. I was hoping that the Magistrate would punish her by giving her a sentence in the St Elizabeth prison."

"My Dear Girl," said her exasperated husband, "if you saw the prison in St Elizabeth, and how the prisoners are forced to live in there you would realise that this is much the better option for her. It won't be pleasant, but it will be over and done with and then we can all go back to normal living."

Mellissa sighed. She knew she was beaten. "Well can I go to see her now, before she is taken down to the compound?" she asked.

"Yes, you go on in." said Charles. "It will probably help for her to see you. She is probably in a high state of anticipated fear. You may be able to calm her down."

"Has she been given food and water since you brought her in last night?"

"I ordered that she should have some when we arrived, but I don't know if anything has been taken to her this morning."

Mellissa entered the barn. Her eyes did not adjust quickly from the bright sunshine outside to the darkness within, so she did not at first see Rebecca, but she did hear and smell her. The noise outside had covered what was going on inside the barn. When Mellissa's eyes had adjusted to the gloom, she saw that Rebecca was shackled by both wrists to the back wall of the barn with her arms raised high above her head, and she was wailing. A continuous, non-ending long wail. Her eyes were swollen and closed, and she had soiled herself. Mellissa was gagging as she approached the terrified woman, and it was evident to her that Rebecca was not only extremely uncomfortable, but that even if there had been water and food available to her it would have been impossible for her to reach it.

"Rebecca," called out Mellissa. "It is your Mistress come to see you. I want to help you a little if I can."

"Mistress, Mistress," Rebecca started crying anew, "Mistress get I free. Get I arms down. I not run away no more."

The crying, the obvious pain and discomfort was very difficult for Mellissa to see. There was very little that she could do make any difference until Rebecca was freed from her chains. With tears streaming down her face she ran outside to her husband. "Where are the keys to her shackles, Charles?" she cried. "Have you seen how they left her all night long? Her arms are almost pulled out of their sockets, and she has had no food and drink. Not even a sip of water, I think, since you brought her back."

"I don't think I have the keys," said Charles as he ran back into the barn with Mellissa. "Oh, my God!" he exclaimed when he saw his prisoner. "Mellissa, I swear that I did not know that she had been left like that."

He looked around for the keys of Rebecca's shackles and eventually found them on a hook high on the doorframe of the barn. He reached for them, brought them over to Mellissa and Rebecca, and unlocked the padlock that was chaining Rebecca to the wall. She fell to the floor as soon as she was released, and Mellissa laid her down on a straw bale. "Charles," she instructed as she started massaging the fallen slave's arms and shoulders, "will you please see if you can dribble some of that water into her mouth. Not too much, that would choke her. I will see if I can rub some life back into her wrists, arms and shoulders."

Charles was ashamed that he had allowed this to happen. He had been all for the punishment of Rebecca, but when it came down to it he realised that he did not have the stony heart to inflict that punishment himself. He saw her as she was now; a broken, terrified and pathetic woman who soiled herself in her discomfort and fear.

After a while Rebecca was able to sit up and take her water herself. Her arms were still very painful to move and she could not stand unaided. "What you do to me Massa?" she cried. "I not mean to kill Massa Bride."

"Yes, but you did kill him, Rebecca," said Charles quietly. "And the Magistrate in St Elizabeth has said that I must punish you."

"Not whip I, Massa. Not whip Rebecca." She started to cry again, but before Charles could reply Jack and Peter Frobisher came in the barn. They looked at the scene in front of them and realised at once that it was Mrs Harrison who now had the upper hand, and that Mr Harrison was as changeable as the wind in his strength and control. Jack decided that the only way that he and his brother would have the authority to work in the way they believed brought the maximum profits was exclude Mistress Harrison from any conversations that they had with Mr Harrison, and force him to take their side. For the moment they had to tread carefully.

"Mrs Harrison," he said in his most gentle and pacifying voice, "we will take the slave Rebecca now, and I suggest that you return to your plantation house. I expect that for legal reasons your husband will need to be a witness to her punishment."

"Not whip I. Not whip I," repeated Rebecca. "Mistress not let the mens whip I?"

"Rebecca," said Mellissa in a kind and gentle tone. "You must go with these men now, and the Massa will take care of you."

"Charles. Promise me," she said as she left and was again in tears by the time she reached the barn door. "I want no more of this. It is all too horrible." Mellissa and Lavinia were making their way back to High View when Mellissa realised that however light the punishment that was meted out to Rebecca she would need some help to recover. "We had better go and open up the clinic," she said to Lavinia. "I have never experienced this sort of savage behaviour in all my life, and I don't know what Rebecca will be suffering. Whatever they do to her I want her brought to the clinic immediatcly. Will you please go back down to the compound and give my instructions to the Master."

"Even if they are light handed I know that it won't be pretty, Mistress," said Lavinia, with deep sorrow in her voice. "I have seen a few beatings in my life, and it was never less than terrible. I will go and I hope that the Master will listen to me."

"And I also want you to find Akami and get him to take the small children into the cabin he shares with Abraham. I don't want them to see or be in anyway part of Rebecca's punishment. He can pretend that they are going to start school there." Mellissa was in a hurry to shield the young ones from the reality of slavery, and to help those she was unable to protect. "When you have done that I want you to, go to Rebecca and see what you can do to help there." But it was only a minute or two after Lavinia had left that Mellissa first heard the screams. Piercing screams that were carried on the wind all the way from the slave compound to Mellissa's clinic. She shivered and swore that even if they lost money she would try her hardest to end slavery. First right here on their own plantation and then give encouragement to people like Sam Sharpe to end all slavery on the island.

Lavinia was back within twenty minutes. She was flustered and crying. "Mistress, Mistress," she cried, and she started wailing almost as loudly as Rebecca had done in the barn. "Mistress, they have all but killed her!"

"Oh! Dear God. Charles promised that it was to be a light punishment," cried Mellissa. "What have they done to her?"

Lavinia took hold of herself. "They used rope to tie her by the wrists to the cross bar of the A-frame so that her feet did not touch the ground. Then they took off all her clothes above the waist, and then those two new men whipped her in turns. Her body was twisting around with each lash from where she was hanging and she was cut and bleeding all around. Her back, her sides and her breasts. I have never in all my life as a slave seen anything as cruel as this. I have never seen a woman whipped on her breasts."

It was Mellissa who was sobbing now, but Lavinia had not finished her story. "All the slaves watching were too shocked to cry out, or too afraid to cry out in case the whips were turned on them. When those men had counted up to fifty lashes, they called for two of the men to cut her down and lay her on the ground. I thought that they would give the command to carry her up to you here, but no! They ordered young Michael, who is only just sixteen years old, to take hands full of salt from a pot ready and waiting, and to rub it in every bleeding wound. Rebecca started screaming again and young Michael, under the threat of a whipping himself, was screaming too as he was forced to do as he was bid."

"What sort of monsters are these men?" cried Mellissa. "And what monster have I married who allows such things to happen in his name? Shall I run down to her or is she being brought up to me, Lavinia?" Mellissa was about to pick up her skirts and run down to the compound.

"Stay here Mistress," cried Lavinia. "Those monsters, as you rightly call them, have ordered that she stay untouched in the hot sun to let the salt burn her wounds for one hour before she is brought up here to you."

Mellissa was shocked, sickened and angered in turns. "We shall see about that," she said with determination, and then she did pick up her skirts and ran. She could hardly believe the spectacle that met her eyes. Even in the most terrible and grimmest of places in London where she has seen the poorest of Londoners in the most terrible of conditions she had never seen such an appalling sight. Rebecca, or what was left of Rebecca, lay on the ground. She was no longer screaming because she was unconscious. Her upper body looked like a piece of meat ready to hang up in a butcher's shop. In places her flesh was cut to ribbons and her blood was still running freely. Flies, ants and other insects which were not put off by the salt were crawling all over her body. The slaves and especially young Michael, who still had his hands bloodied, were standing around mute and ridged in horror, as was Mellissa's husband Charles. The only ones who did not seem at all concerned were Jack and Peter Frobisher who were standing by chatting to each other as if everything were perfectly normal.

Mellissa ran up to her husband, and shook him out of the trance he seemed to be in. "How could you let this happen?" she screamed at him. "You are the Master here, not those two monsters that you have brought back here. You are the Master!"

"You two," she said, pointing to the two nearest and strongest looking slaves. "Pick her up gently and carry her up to my clinic." The Frobishers were about to stop them saying that her time in the sun was not yet completed, when Mellissa rounded on them. "Don't you dare countermand my orders. Who do you think you are coming here on my plantation and causing such pain and terror. I don't care what my husband has agreed with you, I want you to go. I want you off this plantation now!"

She left Charles and the two Frobishers looking at her in amazement as she walked back to the clinic with the slaves who were carrying Rebecca. They were unable to lie her down because she was wounded on all sides so they held her securely on a stool in the shade outside the clinic. Then Mellissa got Lavinia to organise the same slaves to haul buckets of water from the stream so that she could rinse all the salt from Rebecca's wounds. Even as a practiced medic and nurse Mellissa had never dealt with someone who had such extensive cuts all over her upper body where some of her flesh was hanging in strips like ribbons, and never such cuts on a woman's breasts. It made her shiver with horror and shame that this had been done on her plantation. She knew that Rebecca had killed a man, yet it seemed to Mellissa that Rebecca should have been tried for murder and if she had been found guilty, then she should have been rightly hanged or imprisoned for manslaughter. This cruel punishment of a sick woman should never have been allowed by the

Magistrate. He should have dealt with Rebecca in the name of the law and justice.

By the time Rebecca was stirring back to consciousness most of the salt had been washed away and the bleeding had stopped Mellissa was spreading a salve on the open wounds. Many of the cuts were superficial, some were deep, and a few, where the flesh was torn away completely, were open. "I hurt," was all Rebecca could say.

"I know, Rebecca," said Mellissa, holding her hand gently. "I know you hurt, and I am sorry for you. Lavinia and I will try to make you comfortable, and I want you to stay here. It will be difficult for you to lie down in a bed so I will have you moved inside the clinic to a chair with arms so that you can sit comfortably without any part of your bandaged front or back coming into contact with the chair and making the bandages stick."

Abraham brought a dining chair from High View and placed it in a cool place in the clinic. Then he and Lavinia managed to get Rebecca to walk to it and sit.

"That's right," said Mellissa. "Lean forward and support your weight on the arms of the chair. I will tie your arms to the arms of the chair with soft bandages, and I will have someone sit with you for the rest of the day and the night to make sure that you don't fall off." She looked around for the two men who had carried Rebecca, and then turned to Lavinia. "Will you get back the two men who brought her up here, I do not know their names, and I will get them to stay overnight and help Rebecca."

Chapter Thirty-Three

Damaged Love and Another Death

Three months had passed since the punishment of Rebecca and the lives of almost everyone living on the Silver Bay plantation had changed, from the owners to the smallest of the plantation slaves.

Charles had managed to persuade Mellissa that Jack and Peter Frobisher should stay on until at least the end of harvesting. Mellissa hated them with a force that she did not know that she had within her, however, for the sake of peace between them she agreed with Charles. Nevertheless, although peace between them had been restored, the love that Mellissa had for her husband had been damaged but not the physical attraction. She still questioned herself as to how she could still want to make love to someone who had proved himself to be a blood-lusting, soulless man with the same disregard for the slaves as almost every white person she had met in Jamaica. Her respect and regard for him had diminished, and her dream of owning a plantation where the wellbeing of the slaves was of utmost importance, was shattered.

She still shared the same bedroom and bed with her husband, but she had begun to think of the plantation house as just that, and not as a home. There no longer existed those gentle feelings of love and comfort and shelter that a real home provided. But at night she was ashamed at how her body still responded with full force to all the sexual performances that Charles did to make her want him, and she would quake in expectation every time they lay in bed together. Starting with deep kissing, his lovemaking from gentle caresses to full arousal of her breasts to her vagina still made her shiver with expectation, and when he plunged himself deep into her she could only surrender to a climax that was always both loud and long.

In the daytime, however, she began to withdraw her involvement in the daily running of the plantation other than her continued interest in the welfare of the slaves. Rebecca had recovered in body from her whipping. Her wounds had healed leaving her upper body scared but with physical movement uninjured, but her mind was even more unstable than before. She made everyone, including the slaves, feel uncomfortable to be with her, because of her continued weeping and wailing over her dead child. No one knew what to do with her, and everyone, even her close friends, lost sympathy for her. The Frobishers wanted to sell her but neither Charles or Mellissa would agree. She was no longer fit to work in the fields, the clinic or the plantation house. Mellissa thought that the best way to use her and to help her would be to give her a job that was all her own and where she would not have to mix with the other slaves.

So Mellissa decided to give her work that included some dedicated caring for small creatures. She had two slaves who were skilled carpenters build a wooden enclosure of about twenty feet by twenty feet, with walls which were three feet high. It was built next to the patch of banana trees, and within it were built sixteen rabbit hutches. Then she sent Lavinia to market with Abraham where they bought four big crates of baby rabbits to fill the hutches, and two large bales of hay and straw for them to sleep on. When the rabbits were settled in, she brought a whimpering Rebecca to see the new enclosure. "Rebecca, do you think that you could help me look after these rabbits?" she asked. "They will need fresh water every day, and lots of green leaves and carrots to eat every day. They will need their straw bedding changed every week, and they will need their fur brushed to keep them looking nice and silky." Mellissa picked one of the rabbits up and held it towards Rebecca. "Here," she said, "why don't you take this little one from me and see how warm and soft it feels. I am sure that it would love you to cuddle and brush it."

Rebecca took the animal from her Mistress and all at once a change came over her. "It soft baby, Mistress," she whispered. "It need food and love."

"Yes, Rebecca," said Mellissa quietly. "That is all it needs, food and love. Do you think that you will be able to give that to all of these baby rabbits?" Rebecca nodded enthusiastically. "And you must make sure that you always keep the enclosure door shut, otherwise the rabbits will get out and run wild all over the plantation." She nodded again. And from that moment Rebecca was a problem no longer. Her cabin was deconstructed and brought up from the compound, reconstructed and put alongside the rabbit enclosure, and from that day every moment of everyday a happy Rebecca could be found amongst her rabbits.

Mellissa asked Lavinia to take on, amongst her new responsibilities, the supervision of Rebecca, which she did by giving advice in such a caring and subtle way that Rebecca just thought of Lavinia as a friend. Her new world contained just her rabbit babies and she had no idea that she was being controlled at all. At the back of her mind, she knew that as they grew some would be taken away, and even killed for food, but as there were always more babies being born she was content to blot out this negative part of her enterprise. Within a week Rebecca stopped all her weeping and wailing and could now be heard talking and even singing to her rabbits.

The greatest change in the plantation was the changes brought in by Jack and Peter Frobisher. They set up home in a new cabin on the edge of the slave compound, and the one that had been McBride's became the new school. Gone was the relaxed way the slaves were organised. The way the Frobishers organised every hour of their days made the rules of James McBride's seem like happy Sundays. With McBride they were getting up at five a.m. and had to be ready to climb onto the wagons which would take them to the work fields by half past five. Now they had to be ready to mount those wagons at four a.m. The whistle for the end of the day's work now sounded at six-thirty p.m. instead of at five-thirty. It meant that every slave was both getting up and going home in the dark.

They worked hard all day in the hot sun with only a few minutes allowed to eat whatever lunch they had prepared the night before, and snatch a drink from whatever casks of water were available in the fields where they were working. If any of them were deemed to be slow in their work or not working hard enough, the whip was now a reality, and not just a threat as it had been in McBride's time. The women were treated only a little less harshly than the men. They were given the easier tasks that needed less skill or less strength, but there were times when the whip was laid on their shoulders too.

At the end of each day, all the slaves were too exhausted to do anything more than cook and eat, prepare their food for the next day and haul their tired and aching bodies to bed. All children under the age of fourteen were now released to attend Akami's new school, which was set up in McBride's unused cabin, but as soon as they reached fourteen they were forced to join the adults in their hard day's labour.

Lavinia and Akami were very soon to be so happy that they were both owned by Mellissa, and therefore escaped the new regime that had been put into place by the new overseers. It was with unexpected ability that Akami threw himself into his new role as a teacher. With the help of Lavinia, who was now the supervisor of High View, the clinic and Rebecca, Akami soon learnt to write and spell and was immediately able to pass on the same lessons to his pupils. The three boys, Jonah, Matthew and William were the star pupils and also helped with the teaching of the younger children, who were coming to the classroom almost as soon as they could talk.

Mellissa had convinced Charles that as it had been her money that had bought those three boys from Richard Barrett of the Greenwood plantation, then they were under her ownership and protection, so there was no fear that as soon as they reached age fourteen that they would be made to become field workers. All together there were fourteen children who went daily to the school, and as soon as the word spread a few children from neighbouring plantations began to arrive. Included in these was young Samson from Thomas Chamberlain's plantation who Mellissa had treated and saved from the spider bite. And bit by bit each new pupil started to bring others, as long as they were able to walk the distance from their plantation to Silver Bay they came, until Mellissa had to regulate the numbers and insist that they could teach no more than twenty. At first, some of the parents wanted to learn to read and write too, but under the new regime forced on them by the Frobishers they had no time or energy to go to school, even in their free time on Sundays. They just needed their rest.

Mellissa filled her time with her involvement with everything that was going on in and around High View. She loved organising the school and the clinic, and she was also closely involved with Abraham and his work in the gardens and the piggery. But she was saddened to notice that he was beginning to become forgetful and frail.

She approached him one day while he was deadheading the roses in the rose garden. "Abraham," she said, "as you know all our small children are schooling every day and sometimes it is difficult for Akami to teach them all with such a difference in ages." Abraham was beginning to look a bit uncomfortable. He did not like to work with other people, and he did not like small children in his gardens.

"You not want old Abraham to teach too? He asked in a trembling voice.

"No, Abraham," said Mellissa in a soft and gently reassuring voice, "I thought that you could help Akami if you took two or three of the boys from the school and get them to learn what you do too." Before he could protest, saying that he needed no help or he could not teach his work Mellissa continued, "I have seen how well you and Akami get on, and he has often said to me how like an old uncle you are to him. I just thought that you would want to make his teaching classes easier." Abraham was about to protest again, and then he sighed and nodded his head.

Ever since the arrival of the Frobishers Mellissa and Charles always seemed to be at loggerheads whenever they talked about the plantation, so later that day when they were talking on the veranda Mellissa was very tentative when she spoke to him about Abraham. "Charles," she said in an unchallenging and non-demanding way, "I am seriously worried about old Abraham. I want him to accept help, but he is too proud to admit that he is becoming quite frail. And his memory is going too. How do you think that we should handle him?"

Charles paused for a moment. "What exactly are his chores?"

"He sets his own day, but he is busy all day long. His main duties are the horses and the stables. Akami does most of the town driving now, but Abraham still looks after and feeds the animals. He also looks after the pigs, the chickens, the flower gardens and the vegetable gardens."

"That does seem a lot for an old man. Do you know exactly how old he is?" asked Charles.

"I'm not sure, but he must be well into his seventies. I have been asking some of the children to help him, and it works well for things like weeding and feeding the chickens, but some of his other tasks need ability and strength."

"Well," said Charles, who was pleased to have a pleasant conversation with his wife without the usual disagreements. "What about if we could find one of the older children who are now working in the fields to be re-allocated to work with Abraham?"

"Oh, Charles that would be splendid. I know that it is a busy time for everyone now that harvesting is about to start, but if a boy could be spared…" she paused, as if she was thinking. "I know. How about young Michael. You know that boy who was forced to rub salt into Rebecca. I know that he is a timid boy and it might help him to grow more confident and stronger too."

Charles was hesitant. He wanted to please Mellissa, but he knew that Jack Frobisher had picked Michael out to be a fire damper when the firing was to start. "Jack Frobisher wants…" He got no further.

Mellissa could restrain herself no longer. "What Jack Frobisher wants!" she exploded. "Who is the Master on this plantation you or Jack Frobisher?"

Charles backed down immediately. "You are right. I will choose the way the slaves are selected to work, and I will make sure that young Michael comes to report to you tomorrow."

Mellissa was delighted. Before starting the conversation, she had already chosen Michael, and somehow she had now managed to persuade Charles that it was his idea. All anger subsided, she jumped up and hugged her husband. They had not been so comfortable together for weeks. "Sheba," she called to her dog, who was ever at her heels. "Come on, and you too, Charles, let's go for a walk around the gardens before the mosquitoes get busy!"

It was only a week or so later, three days before Christmas, that Lavinia came softly into Mellissa's bedroom and woke her up gently. "Mistress," she said. "Mistress, Akami is in the kitchen. He says that he needs to talk to you."

Mellissa was puzzled, but she was aware that something important must have happened for Akami to ask Lavinia to wake their Mistress. Mellissa got out of bed and saw at once that Charles had already got up and left to busy himself with the harvesting. *Perhaps,* thought Mellissa, *there has been another accident in the firing fields or the cane crushing house.* This year, because of the speed at which the Frobisher brothers were forcing the slaves to work, there had been many more injuries to the slaves. Mostly it was cuts to the legs where a cutlass had been swung too far after cutting down the canes, and had caught a tired slave before he could jump out of the way. There had also been a few minor burns that Mellissa had dressed in the clinic. Burns from the firing and from boiling sugar. None of these had been life threatening, but some were still quite nasty. And there was no resting for these patients. As soon as Mellissa had tended their wounds and covered them up securely, the injured slaves had been required to re-join their fellows and continue their work in the harvesting.

Mellissa had protested to Charles. "You know that these wounds, only small in themselves, could get infected and become life threatening if the slaves don't have a day or two off to let the healing start."

"I know what is ideal," Charles had replied, "but this is harvesting time when we need every hand available. It is only because I am the Master that I have stopped Jack Frobisher from forcing Akami, Lavinia and the house slaves to join in too!"

Mellissa was brought back to the present by Lavinia. "Mistress. Mistress, here is your dressing gown. Shall we go to Akami in the kitchen?"

They went down and Mellissa saw immediately from Akami's face that there had been a tragedy. "Mistress," he said, with tears in his eyes, "I woke up as usual and tried to wake Abraham, who is usually up and dressed before me, but I could not wake him. I believe that he has died in his sleep."

"Oh! Akami. I thought that he had been looking frail. But I hoped that with extra help he would get more rest. I am so sorry," said Mellissa, and her tears made those in Akami's eyes overflow too. "Will you go and tell the Master. And I will need Rosie and Liza to lay him out and prepare him for burial. He is the oldest slave here and I believe that he has lived on Silver Bay all his life. First I want to say goodbye to him myself. Will you come with me, Lavinia?"

Abraham was buried the next day in the slave graveyard next to the slave compound. Akami had driven Lavinia into St Elizabeth and they had managed to persuade a busy Moses, who was preparing for Christmas, to bring his old horse and come back with them. It was a simple ceremony and only a few slaves, Akami, Lavinia, and Charles and Mellissa attended. He was laid into the earth with love, care and sadness too that he had no family to say goodbye to him. Mellissa had picked a huge bouquet of the best of his roses and laid them on his grave.

It was the day after Christmas when Mellissa was sorting out the few possessions that Abraham had left, she first found a small child's picture book and then a handsome wooden box that had been tucked out of sight under his bed. She sat on the bed and with shaking hands she opened it. Tears welled up once more as she took out a very old and pretty cotton shawl. Wrapped up inside it, she found a very thin gold wedding ring and a little wooden horse and cart, carved skilfully from a colourful piece of hickory wood. There was also a grave marker with the names 'Anna' and 'Michael' written in faded ink, and a simple date: '22 Dec. 1810'. "Oh! Akami," she said, with tears running down her face once more, "did you know that Abraham had a wife, a properly married wife, and a child? He must have been married by Sydney Bishop, the former owner of Silver Bay. Sydney Bishop who was a Baptist Minister."

"No, I never knew that he had been married," said Akami. "He never said anything about his life here in all the years that I have known him. And I believe that I had become closer to him than anyone here."

"Well, he did have a wife and a child called Michael, and they died twenty years prior to the day that he died. He must have been thinking of them and just let himself go. Akami," she said, through her tears, "look at these things that he kept for all those years. And he never said anything about them to you, even when I asked our young Michael to work alongside him? That must have caused him to bring back memories of his own child. I wonder how old his Michael was when he died, and what they both died of."

"No, he said nothing to me," repeated Akami, coming to her side. And without thinking he did the forbidden thing and he put his arms around her to comfort her. At first, Mellissa held herself ridged with shock, but then she relaxed into his arms, laid her head against his powerful chest, and cried with an outpouring of grief that she never expected. She cried for Abraham, and she cried for Rebecca, and she cried for the loss of love and respect that she had had for her husband.

It took a minute or two before she could pull herself together, and they were both a little shocked and embarrassed to find themselves in each other's arms. Mellissa disentangled herself first and with a shaky voice, she asked Akami to go and find Lavinia. She wanted to be alone for a while. She wanted to think about her strange reactions to Akami, her slave. Why had she had those 'electric' feelings before when they touched? And now the sensation of coming home when he had put his arms around her. She knew that, although he had disappointed her recently, she loved her husband. Yes, she loved her husband dearly, but her reactions to Akami were almost as if she were in love with him too! No, he was a slave, a Negro. Any decent white woman would never have feelings of that sort for a black man. Surely not! Yet. What was that buzz she felt? Love? Surely not. It must be because she felt supremely sorry for him, sorry about Abraham, sorry about everything! But what had she done with Akami?

He's a nice man, a good man, but he is also a black man.

She got up, ready to go back to High View. *I'll see him again tomorrow, then I'll sort it out,* she thought. Though why did she have butterflies in her stomach just at the thought of seeing him again? "Come on, Mellissa, control yourself," she said as she mounted the steps up to her veranda. "I'm coming, Charles," she called out as she entered her home.

Mellissa told Charles about Abraham's box and showed him the contents. "What shall we do with it?" she asked. "There is no one who we can give it to."

"Why don't we fold the book and put it in the box. Then we can bury it at the foot of Abraham's grave," suggested Charles.

"Oh, Charles," she said, "I think that yours is a lovely idea. We have no way to find the graves of his wife and son, and as he slept with his memories under his bed for twenty years, it is as well that he will have them with him into eternity."

Chapter Thirty-Four

Mellissa Has an Adventure

Christmas 1830 had come and gone, and once more it had been a bumper harvest. Jack and Peter Frobisher had proved themselves to be all that they had said, and Charles and Mellissa who had just returned from a long New Year's Day walk with Sheba, Mellissa's dog, were talking about the brothers when they had settled in their comfortable chairs on the veranda. Charles was all for making their overseers positions permanent at a joint salary of one-and-a-half-times the amount they had paid James McBride, plus the same extra bonus next harvest.

Mellissa was unhappy. "Charles," she cried, her desperation showing on every line of her face, "I agree that we did have a superb harvest, and your father, at home in England, will be delighted when he hears about it, as are all our customers here. Especially the makers of the Fire Rum. They are particularly delighted with the quantity and quality of our sugar and molasses. But at what cost, Charles? At what cost?" she repeated. Before Charles could get in any sort of reply Mellissa continued with her voice getting sharper and more forceful with every sentence. "Every single one of our slaves is exhausted, ill and covered in all sorts of sores and wounds. The mothers of young babies have had their milk dry up, and those very babies are being fed on coconut milk and crushed bananas to keep them from starving. And rather than give them a few weeks to recover, the Frobishers have already started on their own routine for planting the new crop. It cannot go on, Charles. We will soon have slaves dying of exhaustion in the fields. Is that what you want?"

"Don't be so silly and so dramatic, Mellissa," said Charles. He was getting annoyed now. "You know very well that I still hold the slave's welfare to be of the utmost importance on this plantation. But we cannot be running a slave's playground here. They have been born, or bought and brought here to work, not to take part in a charity-inspired and fanciful, fun life where they can make their own choices and work when they feel like it. And you, my Girl," he said, gesturing a pointed finger at her, "are encouraging these unsettled feelings with all your games of playing school, and how are you feeling today? Do you know what I think?" he queried, with the beginnings of a nasty, sneering look upon his face, one that he had never before shown to Mellissa. "I think that your clinic should only be open to those who are really ill, and not to any of the slaves who hold up a cut finger and cry that they cannot work. And I also think that we should shut down that silly school of yours which is filling the children's heads with all sorts of nonsense about freedom and life choices which they will never have," he repeated himself almost spitting the words at his astonished wife. "They will never be free. And the sooner they learn that and go back to helping with weeding and such, the better it will be for everyone!"

"Oh, Charles. You cannot really mean what you are saying," cried a horrified Mellissa. "Don't you dare go back on your word. The sacred oath that you swore to me on the day that we were married. That we were coming to Jamaica to make a new life for ourselves and a better life for our workers."

"They are not our *workers*!" shouted Charles. "They are our *slaves*. And slaves they will remain. Doing everything that they are ordered to do by you, me and the Frobishers. Especially the Frobishers who will be staying on. I have decided!"

Instead of returning fire with fire, Mellissa's anger became hard and cold. She said no more and to an astonished Charles, who was already feeling guilty about what he had just said, and how he had said it, she just got up from her chair and with Sheba following at her heels, she went inside shutting all doors behind her with a loud crash.

And so life on the Silver Bay plantation continued. Charles and Mellissa quarrelled about how the plantation was run, then they made up and made love. But every time they quarrelled, the making up and making love was a little bit more strained and a little bit less loving.

One Sunday morning in February while they were contentedly eating a relaxed breakfast of boiled eggs and toast, Mellissa suddenly blurted out to Charles, "I have been in correspondence with Mistress Everdene of the Kingston Old Port Chandlers, and she has agreed to let me buy back the two children she bought from the

Johnston's. They are Robert, who is Liza's child and Billy, who is Rosie's child. Both of them are now eight years old."

"Oh dear!" exclaimed Charles, in a perfectly amiable voice, "you're not continuing with that nonsense, are you, Old Girl?"

"Yes, I am," declared Mellissa, "and not only am I continuing with 'that nonsense', as you call it, I am also going next week to Kingston in person to buy them back!"

"You," he spluttered, almost choking on his piece of toast, "going in person! How and when did you decide that without asking me? How do you think that I can drop everything and go gallivanting off to Kingston when we are so busy planting the new canes?"

"I am not asking you to come with me," said Mellissa, defiantly. She was expecting a huge protestation from her husband. "I am going with Lavinia and Rosie, and Akami is going to drive us there. In fact, I am looking forward to the adventure. Do you realise that since we first arrived in Kingston over eighteen months ago, I have not been any further than St Elizabeth, and I have hardly had any company or decent conversations with any white women of my rank?"

"Well, I am not going to stop you," said Charles with a sigh. He knew that she was right and he had been secretly surprised that she had not complained before about being so shut off from other women with whom she could have an equal relationship. Mellissa was pleasantly surprised, she was expecting to have a fight with her husband. She found it strange and somewhat frightening that he had given in so easily, and she wondered what he was up to. Did he have something in mind of which she not only knew nothing, but would also disapprove of if she did know? Now was not the time to investigate.

"When are you planning to set off? And how are you going about it?" he asked, genuinely interested in what she had planned. "You know that it will take you at least four, maybe even five days? And what about the thunderstorms that we are expecting any day?"

Mellissa was a little excited now. "If we were to start off next Monday, that is eight days from today, it will give me plenty of time to make arrangements with the school and the clinic. Would you like to accompany us as far as St Elizabeth? Then I plan to ask Moses to accompany us for more of the journey, perhaps the whole way."

"Yes, I can do that," nodded Charles. "But what about overnight feeding and sleeping for all of you? I will be very worried about your comfort and safety. Perhaps I will come after all."

"Oh! Yes, Charles," said a smiling Mellissa. "Please do come. At least you could come as far as the first overnight inn to make sure everything is clean and safe for us."

"Do you intend to go back to the inn where we stayed on our first night in Jamaica?"

"Well," said Mellissa, happy now that things were turning out to be unexpectedly easy between her and Charles, "I know a lady, called Gwendoline Smith, who has a dressmaking establishment in St Elizabeth. She is the one who made those fancy silk shirts that I gave to you. For her main work, she and her workers make the burlap trousers which we buy for our field hands. Did you know that burlap is called crocus, here in Jamaica? Strange word to use, isn't it? Nothing like a spring flower! And they also make the homespun cotton shirts that we buy too. Now Gwendoline has a sister called Georgiana, who is married to an innkeeper, Thomas Roberts. Their inn is situated in Maryville, which is almost exactly halfway between here and Kingston. Gwendoline tells me that their inn is very popular with people from St Elizabeth for that very reason. She says that it is a good clean establishment with rooms for the gentry and adequate accommodation for travelling companions and slaves. I have already asked her to send a message to her sister to say that I will be needing some rooms next Monday and Thursday nights. I thought that I would spend two nights with Mistress Everdene to give us and the horses a rest."

Charles let out a long whistle between his teeth, a habit of his that usually irritated Mellissa. "Good Gracious!" he exclaimed. "I suppose that I should have known that a clever woman, such as you, would have had all this worked out. I am truly surprised, but I am pleased too!"

"I am so happy myself. I dreaded another angry scene with you and I will be delighted if you came with us, even if it is only half way to Maryville. And you will be able to check out the inn of Georgiana and Thomas Roberts."

"What a set of names those sisters have, Gwendoline and Georgiana. I wonder if there are any more, perhaps Geraldine and Geofforina?" He laughed merrily and Mellissa giggled, happy to join in.

"I do so love you, Charles," she said, quite simply. Then she went to him and embraced him in her soft loving arms.

So it was all arranged. They set off the following Monday in the carriage which had a hood that could be pulled over if the thunderstorms of the past week returned. Charles's nut-brown horse, Brandy, was tied up behind the carriage and trotted along perfectly happy to be out and with no burden to carry. Rosie sat up in the front seat with Akami while Lavinia shared the carriage with Mellissa and Charles. They did not stop at St. Elizabeth because Mellissa decided that she no longer needed Moses, as Charles was coming half way, and she had already completed the negotiations with Mistress Everdene for the two boys.

It was almost like a new honeymoon for Charles and Mellissa as they retraced their first journey, but in the opposite direction. They remembered their shared delight with everything that was so very new to them as they had journeyed into the interior of the island. "This is where we first saw macaws, Charles. Do you remember?"

"Yes, and I remember how you told me afterwards that you were ashamed because you had brought along with you to Jamaica a hat, bought in London, a highly fashionable hat that had macaw feathers to make it beautiful."

"I have never worn it since, but I keep it as good reminder that we humans foolishly think that everything and every bird and animal that lives on the earth is there just for the taking, just to make our lives easier or prettier."

"No lecturing today, Old Girl," said Charles, squeezing her hand. "After this bit of road I think that we will be driving along the coast again. Yes, look through those trees. Can you see the sea?"

"Oh! It is so beautiful, Charles," she sighed. "We are stuck on the plantation and we never experience the real beauty of Jamaica. Everywhere you look, in every direction it is all so beautiful! Lavinia, have you ever seen the coastline between here and Kingston?" Mellissa asked, without thinking that any travelling she may have done before she was a Silver Bay slave, journeying from master to master.

"Like you, Mistress," said Lavinia with such a sadness in her voice that Mellissa felt ashamed for asking her question, "I travelled along these roads only once before. I was only ten years old and I had been sold away from my mother. Sold to Mistress Johnston who took me to Silver Bay. I only remember that I was crying all the way. I did not look around at the beauties of the island. I remember Mistress becoming annoyed with me for my continual crying, and she pinched me hard on both of my arms. I slept overnight in an inn somewhere, and I was made to sleep on the floor tied to Mistress Johnston's bed."

"Oh! Lavinia," cried a mortified Mellissa. "I am so sorry. Sorry to have asked that question which brought back such hurtful memories to you." She looked at Charles who shrugged his shoulders and said nothing. There was silence in the carriage for the next few miles, then they saw the signpost for Maryville.

"Look!" exclaimed Mellissa, all excited once more. "Maryville. Gwendoline said that if we drive along the coast road and through the town, the inn will be straight in front of us. It is on high cliffs which overlook the bay below." It was only a village, rather than a town and they were through it in only a few minutes later. "There it is," shouted Mellissa. "It looks every bit as nice as Gwendoline said."

They pulled up outside, and everyone got down from the carriage with stiff backs and legs, and were glad for a stretch of all their limbs. Robert and Georgiana Thomas were waiting for them and came out immediately to welcome them. "Well, well, my dears," said Mistress Thomas. "Do come in and make yourselves at home. You must be tired and thirsty after that long drive. We have some cool lemonade for you all to drink, and then we will settle you into your rooms before we bring you your dinner. We have a table for you coloured folk here," she said pointing to the back of the tap room, and for Master and Mistress Harrison I have a small table for you in my private parlour."

It was a successful and happy visit for Mellissa. She and Charles had a very pretty bedroom which overlooked the bay, and after their evening meal they retired very happily to spend the night there. Lavinia and Rosie were given a back bedroom and Akami slept in an outbuilding next to the stables.

The next day, after breakfast, Charles reluctantly mounted his horse ready to ride home leaving a happy Mellissa to continue her 'adventure' with her three slaves. "I'm so sorry, Old Girl," he said, with a real look of disappointment on his face. "I wish now that I had made arrangements to come with you for the whole journey, but I have already arranged with Jack Frobisher for him to show me a different method of planting, and according to him, it should have been done last week and can wait no longer."

"No matter," said Mellissa. She was excited now that she alone would be in charge of their expedition. "I am sure that with the help of Lavinia, Rosie and Akami, I will be able to find the Everdenes, buy the children, and come back home safe and sound. I will be back on Friday. Goodbye, my darling!" And a saddened Charles, sitting comfortably astride Brandy, set off with a wave of his hand.

As soon as he had gone Mellissa went into the inn to collect Lavinia and Rosie. "It's another beautiful Jamaican day outside, and I hope that we will all enjoy the rest of our journey without any rain. You, Rosie, must be so excited at the thought of seeing your boy, Billy again."

"Mistress," she said, with huge tears in her eyes, which started to flow down her face. "I's happy to be you slave for the rest of my life. You done give me back my babies. I never knowed it could ever happen. You's surely a saint!"

Mellissa blushed and laughed awkwardly. "Lavinia," she said, wanting an excuse to escape from Rosie's emotions, "will you see to it that my overnight bags are got ready, and I will go to the stables and check with Akami that all is well there."

Within minutes they were off and ready to complete their journey to Kingston. All four of them, Mistress and slaves, were happily pointing out pretty scenes and places that caught their eyes. Akami and Rosie had never been beyond St Elizabeth, and even Lavinia was no longer sad to be returning to Kingston. They approached the town as the sun was low in the sky, ready to set, and easily found the Kingston Dock Chandlers, and then onto the Everdenes' home which was one of the grand houses which lined the coast road going eastwards out of town.

Chapter Thirty-Five

February 1831

Lucy Everdene

Mistress Everdene was waiting for them and greeted them all, Mistress and slaves with warmth and invited them all in. Rosie looked around eagerly for her son Billy but he was not in sight.

"Welcome Mistress Harrison, welcome everyone," she said, smiling broadly and giving Mellissa an unexpected hug. Mellissa heard an accent, which she recognised as one from northern England, but she could not exactly say which town Mistress Everdene came from. They entered the house and were standing in an open hallway which was flooded with light from a large window at the back. The house seemed to be perched on a wide rock, as the front of the house was level with the roadway but from the window Mellissa could see a sandy bay and blue sea way down below.

Mistress Everdene was just like Mellissa's idea of a perfect grandmother. She seemed to be at least sixty years old, and was warm, plump, and small with her grey hair drawn back behind her head in a fat bun. "I am so pleased to meet you at last," she said to Mellissa, "and I am looking forward to a good talk later." She turned to Lavinia, Rosie and Akami. "There is a light meal and some refreshments waiting for you three in the kitchen, and there might even be someone waiting to see their Mamie! Perhaps we should all go down to the kitchen."

She led the way down a winding staircase to the lower part of the house. Mellissa followed with Rosie, Lavinia. Akami was occupied with looking after the carriage and horses. It was not at all like any basement that Mellissa had ever known. Through the open doors she could see that all the rooms had a golden glow and were bright with the light from the setting sun coming through large windows which opened out onto views of the sandy beach and coconut palms. They could hear excited chatter coming from the room at the end of the lower hallway. "Robert, Billy," called Mistress Everdene, "there are some people here who have come to see you."

Two brightly eager boys rushed out of the kitchen. Although there was only two month's difference in age between them, they looked totally different. One was almost a foot taller than the other, and he looked fit and strong. The other seemed frail and weak in comparison, and looked at least a year younger. They pulled up sharply when they saw Mellissa, then Rosie came forward and stared at the boys. "It you, innit Billie boy?" she said pointing to the tall, strong looking boy.

The smaller boy piped up, "he's not Billy, I am! He's called Robert."

Rosie looked again. "'Course you is my Billy. I's only joking!" And she bent down and took her 'baby' into her arms, while her face flooded with tears. "It be nearly six years since you was in my arms. But you be in my heart every day."

Robert looked at Lavinia. "Are you my Mamie?" he asked expectantly.

"No, my dear," she said, and she put her arm around him. "Your mother is called Liza, and she is waiting for you back home in the Silver Bay plantation. She told me to give you a big hug, and she says that she cannot wait to do it for herself."

"Why didn't she come too, to find me?"

"She wanted to," said Lavinia. "She really did want to come, but there is not enough room in the carriage for everyone to fit in. You will be seeing her in just two days."

"Now," said Mistress Everdene, "will you two boys help Billy's mother and the others with their refreshment while I take Mistress Harrison back upstairs?"

"Yes, Mistress," they said together.

Five minutes later Mellissa was sitting with Mistress Everdene in her parlour, sipping cold tea. "I am so pleased to meet you. I think that it is wonderful that you are trying to re-unite children who were sold away from their mothers when they were just babies. I have had no children of my own, and I so wanted the opportunity to have children around the house. I have often felt that I had done the wrong thing when I bought those children, but John Merriweather…"

"Oh, I know John Merriweather!" interrupted Mellissa.

"…said that their owner, Mistress Johnston, was determined to sell all the boy babies on her plantation, and it did not matter to her who bought them. So I decided that at least if I bought them I could make sure that they would be allowed to grow up with kindness and with only light demands made upon them. It will be quite hard for me to say goodbye to them."

Mellissa was a little timid about what she was about to ask, but she took a deep breath and went ahead. "Mistress Everdene, do you mind if I ask you a personal question?"

"My name is Lucy, please do call me Lucy," she replied, smiling broadly. "Yes you may ask me whatever you want if it is about the children."

"My name is Mellissa, and I am very happy to call you Lucy," said Mellissa. "The question I want to ask you is about slaves. My husband and I have nearly four hundred slaves who are needed to work on our sugar plantation. We have owned Silver Bay for a year and a half, and four hundred slaves always seemed a lot to me. I was worried about being responsible for four hundred people. Then I heard about much bigger plantations on the north of the island that have up to two thousand slaves, *two thousand*. How can it be right for any man to own two thousand souls? So my question to you is how many slaves do you and your husband have, and if it seems to you so wrong to own small children, how do feel about owning adults?"

"Well, that is a deep question, indeed, to ask someone you have only just met!"

"I'm sorry," said Mellissa, and she blushed with shame and awkwardness. "I suppose it's because since I have been here in Jamaica, I have not yet met any white lady with whom I can talk to frankly, and I only met you for the first time a short while ago. I'm so sorry to embarrass you, please, forget what I have just asked."

"Don't be sorry, Mellissa," said Lucy. "I quite understand. I suppose that you are shut away on your plantation and never see anyone else."

"That is just how it is. I see the shop keepers and the Minister in St Elizabeth every few weeks, and I see our new overseers, Jack and Peter Frobisher, who I dislike entirely, and apart from them and my husband, Charles, I never see a white face. That is why I am so pleased to make this journey to Kingston to meet you."

Lucy Everdene looked shocked and curious at the same time. "Did you just say Jack and Peter Frobisher?"

"I did, yes. Do you know them?" asked a surprised Mellissa.

Lucy pulled a face. "I do not *know* them," she said, "but I do know *of* them. Oh my Goodness! You have not employed those two, have you?"

"My husband, Charles has employed them. For myself, I cannot tolerate them. They are cruel."

"Cruel! That is not the word for them. They are murderous fiends!" exclaimed Lucy Everdene.

"Whatever is it? What have they done?" asked Mellissa. She was really worried now. Was it even possible that Charles might be in danger?

"They killed one of the slaves on the Greenfields Plantation, which is owned and run by the Frobisher family. They beat the man to death with paddles which broke almost every bone in his body."

Mellissa was so horrified and distressed she could hardly speak. "Beat him to death? With paddles?" The realisation of what a long and painful death it must have been made Mellissa cringe and shrivel inside herself. She was shaking with horror when she asked in a voice so low that Lucy could hardly hear her. "Why? Whatever had the slave done?"

"He had attempted to prevent them from ravaging his daughter. His eight-year-old daughter. They were pinning her down and taking turns…"

"Don't! Don't say any more," gasped a horrified Mellissa, holding both her hands to her face. After a moment she sipped her tea and recollected herself before she exclaimed softly, "No wonder they had been thrown out of their home by their brother. My poor, gullible Charles cannot have realised that he has let two monsters into ours."

"…the poor child died, too," said Lucy, and a single tear slid out of each of her eyes. "She was so cruelly hurt that she died of shock and of blood loss." She stopped for a moment to wipe away her tears, and then continued. "Even the local slave owners, who are usually hardened about the mistreatment of slaves, were horrified. But the local Magistrate would not prosecute because he said that slaves are property, the property of their owners and cannot be treated as people, which I think is a horrible indictment of the cruelty of owning slaves. The good people of Kingston shunned those two Frobisher boys and drove them away."

"So, you too, Lucy, think like me, that it is wrong to own slaves," said Mellissa tentatively. It was not the norm to criticise out loud the practice of owning slaves. "What can we do to help them until abolition is made law. It will be made law soon, I am sure of

222

it. My husband disagrees with me, so all I can do at home is to treat those that are not under the direct control of him and the Frobishers, as well as I can."

"As soon as I received you letter enquiring about the two children, Billy and Robert, I had a good feeling that you would be someone who is sympathetic to the plight of slaves," said Lucy. "I am too, and because we live and work in the main port of Jamaica, we get mail and newspapers direct from England. I follow all the news that reaches us about the work of William Wilberforce and the abolishment movement, and I am sure that the good people of England will soon force their parliament to make these laws. In the meantime we must do the best we can."

"I, myself, sent to William Wilberforce two testaments, the stories of two of the slaves who have accompanied me here to Kingston. And he kindly wrote back to me, thanking me. Now I cannot believe that I am hearing the words that I am hearing from you," said Mellissa. "I have come to think that I am the only white person in Jamaica who thinks like this. Although we live quite far apart I feel so happy that I have found a friend in this foreign land." The two women who were so different in age and status stood up and hugged each other anew. They sat in silence for a minute or two and then Mellissa asked, "Do you know of a slave called Sam Sharpe who lives in Montego Bay?"

Lucy shook her head. "Should I? Although Montego Bay and Kingston are both important ports in Jamaica, probably the most important ports, we don't have any direct connection with Montego Bay. So who is Sam Sharpe, and why do you think that I should know him?"

"Although he is a slave, he is a very educated one, he is a Baptist minister, and he is the slave of a lawyer, Samuel Sharpe, who gave Sam his own name when he bought him. Like you, he reads all the English newspapers that come to the port there. He follows everything that the abolitionists are saying and doing in England, and he, too, is convinced that slavery will soon be abolished."

Lucy shook her head again. "I don't know of him, but I will keep my ears to the ground to see if his name comes up here in Kingston."

"Well, before we go downstairs again I would just like to ask you what do you think I should do about Jack and Peter Frobisher when I get home? I'm sure that my husband won't believe anything I say against them, and I am really worried about how they are able to influence him. He thinks that because our profits have increased that those two are wonderful!"

"I have a copy of our Kingston newspaper, the Gleaner, which reported the story of Jack and Peter Frobisher and what they have done," said Lucy Everdene. "I will look it out and give it to you to show your husband, he will have to believe you then. But before we re-join the others I will answer your first question. Yes, my husband and I do own slaves. He has sixteen adult men who work with him in the Chandler's business, and I have two women and a girl who help me run the house. My husband is not at all an abolitionist and he always laughs at me and my 'silly' ideas."

Mellissa smiled. She knew what it was like to believe in the abolishment of slavery and to have a husband who thinks that she is living in a dream world where everything is pretty and lovely. She looked at Lucy, with a knowing look, "One day," she said, "and hopefully, one day soon, we will all be rethinking about our attitudes towards slavery. I hope that when it happens the English government will give the slave owners enough compensation so that they accept the emancipation of their slaves without complaint."

"But," Lucy sighed, "I don't think that their attitude towards these black men and women will change much. I know that my husband will never think of them as equal citizens. He does not even think that they are capable of thinking and learning."

"Well, said Mellissa, "he has not met my Lavinia. I believe her intellect is equal to my own, and if she had had the education that I have had, I'm sure that we would be real equals. Did you teach Robert and Billy to read?"

"Yes I did, much against my husband's approval."

"When did you start, and how are they getting on?" asked Mellissa.

"I started two years ago when they were both six. I started with the alphabet and a child's simple picture book, and they soon learned. And I am pleased to say that they can now read the Holy Bible. Well, most of it. There are some words that I struggle with myself!" She paused for a moment, then she said, "Shall we go down to them so that you can meet them properly?"

"Before we do that I think that we should get the formal business done," said Mellissa, "I have had the documents of sale drawn up properly by my attorney at law. I have signed them and have the ten pounds, five pounds for each boy, ready to hand over to you. Will you please sign the documents as well… Just here," she said, pointing to a dotted line on the document. That was quickly done and the sales papers and money were put away without further comment. They both felt slightly contaminated by the buying and selling of the children, the reality of everyday slave owning in Jamaica.

Mellissa then followed Lucy down to the kitchen once more. Lucy's three household slaves were there seeing to the evening meal, and Akami had joined them, so the kitchen was comfortably full. Akami was showing the boys the stump of his right arm where his hand had been amputated. They had never seen anything like it before and instead of being upset or horrified, they were fascinated. Robert was asking Akami, "Can you feel it when I touch the end?"

And at the same time Billy was asking, "How do you manage to pick up anything that needs two hands?"

"It has been a year now since my hand was cut off, and I have got used to my hand not being there. I have some feeling at the very end of the stump, and I am now able to use it to pick things up quite well. Do you see our Mistress over there?" he asked, pointing to Mellissa. "Well, it was she who did it…"

"The Mistress. She cut your hand off," said Billy, and he looked so scared as he looked at his new owner.

"Yes, she did it to save my life. She did not want to do it," said Akami and he looked up at Mellissa and gave her a huge smile. "I had damaged my hand in one of the machines on the sugar cane farm and I was bleeding to death. She saved my life by cutting off my hand."

The two boys were not convinced and they backed away from their new Mistress. Lucy was the one who was most surprised. "You did not tell me that your education included surgery," she said. "Wow! How did that happen?"

"I actually had quite a busy life before I was married and came to Jamaica," she said. "My father, Roger Goodchild, is a doctor whose patients are the gentry of London but he also works for free with the poor folk of London in one of the hospitals there. I was his assistant for many years, and it was he who taught me doctoring. At Silver Bay, we have set up a small clinic and I see to most of the medical problems on the plantation. Lavinia was trained as a midwife by her mother and she now assists me with simple dressings for cuts and burns, and childbirth problems as well as straight forward deliveries. Akami's hand amputation was the worst thing I have ever had to do, and I pray to the Lord that I never have to do such a thing again!"

"Well," said Lucy. "It is about the time when my husband returns home, so I think that we will leave everyone here to enjoy their evening meal, and we will go back upstairs so that I can introduce him to you."

Master Everdene, whose name was John but known to everyone as Johnny, turned out to be a pleasant and jovial man. Like his wife, he was small and round, and about the same age too. In spite of his conviction that slavery was a good thing and was there to stay, he was as kind as his wife towards his slaves. Johnny and Lucy had owned a small chandler's shop, in the port of Liverpool, in Northern England, selling everything one could need to supply a sailing ship, from huge ship's anchors down to the smallest brass screw. Six years previously they had taken the risk to sell everything and move to Jamaica and now their business had become an important part of Kingston docks. From simple beginnings they were now relatively wealthy.

Johnny was very happy that his wife had made a friend amongst the gentry, and it would be an important factor in a decision that they were soon to make. "My wife and I," said John Everdene, "have been talking about retiring. The great question between us is whether to remain here in Jamaica, leaving the Chandler's to be run by a manager and live off that income, or whether to sell up everything, business, home and slaves, and return to England, where our profits would give us a comfortable life for the rest of our days."

"I have recently been longing to go back home to Liverpool," said Lucy, wistfully, "but I love the climate here in Jamaica, and I haven't forgotten the cold, dark and dank days of an English winter."

"Not just winter," mused Mellissa. "I can remember, even in the warmer south of England, waiting and waiting for spring to come. Sometimes even until the end of May! I don't envy you having to choose. I feel the pull of home too, but I know that I will miss the good things of this island when we return home."

Chapter Thirty-Six

Another Happy Return

Five days later, a very happy carriage-full of people turned into the long avenue of trees that marked the entrance of the Silver Bay plantation. Rosie was once more sitting up front with Akami and the children were sitting inside the carriage with Mellissa and Lavinia. After their upsetting and very sad leave taking from Lucy, they had similar broken hearts when she had said goodbye to the boys who had not really been her slaves, but more her foster children, they were now bouncing with excitement with the expectation of seeing their new home. And Robert was additionally excited and curious knowing that he was about to see again the mother he had all but forgotten.

Charles had been on the alert for them, and came galloping down the driveway to meet them, with Mellissa's dog, Sheba, running not far behind. Akami stopped the carriage and Rosie jumped down from her front seat and opened the carriage door for Sheba to jump in. The dog was so happy to be re-united with Mellissa from whom she had not been separated for even a day since she had been a puppy, and with panting tongue and wagging tail she flung herself on Mellissa's lap.

Charles laughed. He knew that Sheba was always first in line for Mellissa's attention. "Hello, Old Girl. Good to see you," he said to Mellissa. And then to the slaves he said, "I am pleased that you have all travelled home safely. I see we have two more little boys to add to our collection," he added with another laugh. "Liza is waiting in the schoolhouse for her son. Which one is hers?"

"I am, Master," said Robert. Although he was a big, confident boy, suddenly on seeing Master Charles, he became a little boy once more.

Charles trotted alongside the carriage until the High View came in sight. "I will be home in ten minutes," he said to Mellissa, and he rode off towards the slave compound. Mellissa was curious about his behaviour, but she said nothing. Akami took the carriage to the schoolhouse where Liza and all the other youngsters were waiting for them. The children jumped out as soon as Akami opened the carriage door. Robert ran to Liza. "You are my Mamie, aren't you?" he said as he rushed into Liza's open arms. Rosie was already introducing Billy to his brother and sister, and Lavinia was also gathering up her own children, so no one was paying attention when Akami put out his hand to help Mellissa down.

Once more it was as if an electric shock ran between them and her heart began to thump so loudly she was sure that everyone could hear it. Mellissa was shocked. How many times had this happened? And what did it mean? While she had been away from home she had made sure that she had never been alone with Akami because of this very reaction every time they touched, even accidently. Akami, too, was deeply aware of the strong, forbidden feelings that continued to draw him towards his Mistress. For a moment or two, their eyes were locked together, and Mellissa felt a deep attraction and connection to Akami. She almost threw herself into his arms, but somehow she retained enough composure to remind herself that she was married to Charles, and this man, this black man, who was helping her down from her carriage, was her slave. Mellissa turned to see if any of the others had noticed anything. No. They were all talking together. She stayed for a few minutes to see Liza and her lost son. With tears brimming over, she hugged him, and her first words to him were, "My, oh my! How tall you have grown. You just like my own Pappy."

He hugged and kissed her too. "Mamie," he asked, "am I gonna live with you now? Will I still go to school with Billy?"

"Lavinia," Mellissa asked, "will you look after everything here, and see that Rosie and Liza can settle in with their children? I need to go back home to talk to Charles."

With her heart still thumping, and her blood rushing through her veins, she went back home and waited for Charles to join her. Within a minute or two he came striding in. "Well, Old Girl," he said as he hugged her tightly. "It's only been four days that you have been gone from me, but I can't tell you how much I have missed you. Did you miss me too, or were you having too much of an adventure to do that?"

He said it with a laugh, but Mellissa could sense a bit of a challenge there, so she laughed too and said, "My dear Boy, you know very well that I miss you every moment that we are apart. Just feel how my heart is thumping!" Blushing guiltily as she spoke, she followed that up with, "Especially at bedtimes!"

"That's my Girl," he chuckled, putting his hand on her bosom to feel her heart beat, "we can soon rectify that little problem!"

"Oh! Charles, let us have a drink and our evening meal first. And anyway," she said with a sigh, "I have something I need to talk to you about."

"What? Is there a problem with the children, you have just brought back?"

"No. It is nothing to do with the slaves," She hesitated, because she knew that he did not want to hear anything derogative about the Frobisher brothers. "It's the Frobishers."

"No! Mellissa, No! I don't want to hear you complaining about them again." Charles lost at once all the pleasure he had had at Mellissa's homecoming. He knew that they would soon be quarrelling. "Let's have a nice evening together, and talk about your misgivings again tomorrow? Yes?"

"All right, Charles." Mellissa too wanted a quiet evening and a little loving overnight. She glowed with pleasure and expectation.

She was still glowing the next morning they sat down to breakfast, but both of them were wary at the thought that soon there might be cross words between them. While they were eating their toast and marmalade, rather than say anything to Charles, Mellissa passed him the copy of the Kingston Gleaner that Lucy Everdene had given to her. Charles was crunching his toast as he read the article about the Frobisher brothers, and then he put the paper aside.

"Well?" asked Mellissa, in a normal voice. She knew that Charles would defend the brothers, and she was determined to stay calm whatever his reaction.

"I do not believe it," said Charles, quite simply.

"How can you not believe it?" queried an astonished Mellissa, still keeping her voice low and level. "It is there in black and white. And Lucy Everdene was living right there in Kingston where it happened. The whole town knows what happened on the Greenfields Plantation."

"Something happened, but this is all exaggerated," countered Charles. "It is a rag of a newspaper that has written a sensational story out of a simple act of slave correction."

"Slave correction! Whatever are you talking about?" asked an astonished Mellissa, with her voice suddenly raised in spite of her determination to keep calm.

"Jack Frobisher told me all about it months ago. The slave, Jacob, attacked both of them with a cutlass when they were having rough and tumble with a young woman, an adult young woman, that Jacob had set his eyes and his heart upon," said Charles. The bravado of his stance was telling Mellissa to accept this explanation and not to push it further. "They were able to wrestle the cutlass away from him without serious injury. And, yes, they did punish him. They only hit him a few times with paddles, and he died suddenly of a heart attack."

Mellissa was scathing. "A heart attack! So they are doctors too, I suppose! Oh! Charles, you are so gullible," she said, softening her attitude towards her husband, and lowering her voice once again. She sighed, "Why is it that you believe everything they say, and nothing that I say? You don't have to believe me, you saw with your own eyes how savage they were with Rebecca, and she had nothing to do with them."

"Mellissa, I know you hate them. You have done so ever since you first laid your eyes on them. You have never given them a chance," he said. She noticed there was not an 'Old Girl' this time. He hardly ever addressed her as plain Mellissa. "It does not matter what you say, I am not getting rid of Jack and Peter Frobisher. Their methods work well and the plantation is blooming under their supervision. And I am always here to control them and their excessive actions and reactions."

Mellissa started to cry. "You are determined to ignore everything I say, aren't you? I just cannot talk to you when you are like this."

She got up and ran out of the room, and ran blindly out of the house. She did not stop until she reached the school house, thinking that Lavinia would be there as she usually was each morning getting it ready for the day. But Lavinia was not there so she sat down at the desk, put her head in her hands and cried her heart out. She did not hear him approach, but she knew that it was Akami as soon as she felt his hand on her shoulder.

"Whatever is the matter, Mistress?" he asked in a soft and gentle voice. And without thinking she stood up and let him put his arms about her. This was different. Achingly different. Her body was not on fire demanding fulfilment; it was not throbbing with lust. But it was as if a gentle glow of light was infusing within her. She melted into Akami's arms and put her face up to be kissed. His soft, plump lips were so different to Charles' thin tight ones. Those lips of Charles that she had yearned to kiss as soon as she had met him in his father's home all those years ago. Here and now this kiss of Akami's, so soft, warm and undemanding, was drawing her deeper and deeper into a world of floating sensations. A place where she had never been before. A strange lost world with no signposts, no indications of where she was or where she was to go next.

It was now Akami who was taking the lead, although this was all totally new to him too. He had never in all his thirty-two years held a woman this way, and beyond a gentle brush of lips he had never kissed or been kissed before. Mellissa's mouth opened under his and it was as if the sweetest flower in the garden was opening its petals to him, and he was tasting its nectar. There was no thrusting of tongues, no demanding of deeper encroachment into each other's bodies. It was as if the world of lovemaking was being made anew just for the two of them. After the longest of kisses they stood back from one another, both of them completely overwhelmed, astonished and dumbstruck at what was happening to them. They looked deeply into each other's eyes and without saying a word, they started to kiss again. This time it was different, during the long, soft kiss their hands began to move. Hers holding him tighter and reaching up to his shoulders as if to draw him even closer to her body, and his single hand was exploring the round softness of her bottom and her angular hips, which without warning were suddenly thrusting towards his groin. He found his 'toto' swelling in response and now she could feel it between them, hardening and demanding.

They broke off and it was Mellissa who found words first. They came out as words of quiet wonder, and not of admonishment, "Akami. We must not do this. It is wonderful but it is not right and we must stop."

"I am so sorry, Mistress," he whispered. "I don't know how this has happened or what is happening to me. I am lost."

"I am lost too," she said. And she turned around and fled the cabin. Suddenly she was blindly running, running anywhere and everywhere until she reached the hidden safety of the arbour in the rose garden. Abraham's beautiful rose garden, where she sat down and tried to let her heart and emotions settle back to an everyday beat.

It was there where Charles found her a short time later, thinking that she had run there directly from the house. He looked at her tear-stained face and his heart melted. "What are we going to do to keep the peace between us?" he asked as he sat down beside her and put his arm around her. Her immediate reaction was to pull away from him. She was thinking about Akami and wishing that it was he who was sitting next to her, and not Charles, but Charles thought that she was still angry with him.

She pulled herself back from dreamland to the present. She looked around at her beautiful garden, and watched a spectacular hummingbird feed on a pretty red flower. For a fleeting moment she wondered how it was that something so beautiful that had made her gasp with wonder only a few months ago, now had become just a part of everyday life.

She took another moment and then she replied to the question. Looking directly at her husband she said, "The only way we are going to keep the peace between us is for you to get rid of the Frobisher brothers. I believe the story as told to me by Lucy Everdene and written up in the newspaper. I believe those men to be vicious, cruel monsters. And I believe that everyone on this plantation is in danger from these men."

"Then we are not going to get this resolved. I am unable to run this plantation without expert help, and I believe that the Frobishers are teaching me what I need to know." Charles was determined to have his own way, but he still wanted to resolve the problem between himself and Mellissa. "What if I restrict their access to the compound and only that part of the plantation, plus of course the cane fields and the sugar production buildings? I will keep them away entirely from the cabins up here, the clinic and the school house. That will protect all the vulnerable women and children."

"You can do that, but it will not work," said Mellissa, with a sigh. "I am just as sad as you that we cannot resolve this. I think that we are going to end up with each of us doing what we need to do, and the harmony and joy we had of trying to create a plantation as an example of profit with care, will be lost."

"It was always your dream, not mine."

Mellissa did not want to continue the argument, so she left the arbour and returned to the house. Charles sat on alone feeling deflated and angry. He considered that he had done his best to make a workable compromise, and she had thrown it back in his face without any deep thought or consideration.

For the next week Mellissa's head was in a spin. She knew that she loved her husband, she still enjoyed making love with him, but she also felt that she was in love with Akami, and she had dreamed of making love with him. How could that be possible?

She felt guilty and avoided Akami as much as possible. In the meantime, Charles had done what he had suggested, and had had one of the better cabins in the compound made larger, made more comfortable and better furnished, and the Frobishers had moved themselves away from the work areas near the plantation house.

Charles was still trying to make Mellissa feel more comfortable about the continued employment of Jack and Peter Frobisher, and he offered Mellissa to build an entirely new school next to the McBride's cabin which was currently used for the schoolroom. "It will not only be bigger and better than the one you are using right now," he said amiably, "we can have it properly refitted with benches, a large blackboard that everyone will be able to see, and have small slates and chalks for the children to use. How about it? We can use the other one as a school store room."

Mellissa accepted the olive branch that was being held out to her. "You can always twist me around your little finger, Charles," she said.

"I accept. But I want you to promise me that you will supervise those monsters so well that they will be unable to inflict pain or punishment on any of the slaves, no matter what fault they have done. Will you promise me that?"

"Of course, Old Girl," said a cheerful Charles. "I won't let them hurt even a hair on anyone's head!" he chuckled.

Chapter Thirty-Seven

March 1831

Poppy

It was on a Sunday afternoon two weeks later and everyone on the plantation was enjoying a well-earned rest when Lavinia ran up the steps to the veranda, where Mellissa and Charles were dozing in the warmth of the Jamaican sun.

"Mistress, Mistress," she called softly, not wanting to wake Charles too.

"What is it, Lavinia? What has happened that is so important that you want me to stop being lazy, and get out of my comfortable armchair?" Then Mellissa looked at Lavinia's troubled face, and she realised that something bad had happened. Her silly heart started to thump and her silly head immediately thought that Akami was in trouble once more, but before she could form a question, Lavinia spoke up again.

"It's one of the young slaves. Her name is Poppy and she is sixteen years old. She has cut her arm deeply, and I cannot stop the blood flowing. I think that it will need stitches."

Mellissa was wide awake now, and Charles was beginning to wake too. "Where is Poppy now? Is she in the clinic?" asked Mellissa.

"Yes," replied Lavinia, "she is there with Roberta. I have tied a tourniquet on her upper arm."

"Good girl, I'll come at once." Mellissa was halfway down the steps by then, and Charles, having awoken and fuzzily aware of the conversation between his wife and Lavinia, he called down after her. "What's up, Old Girl? Do you need me to come too?"

"No, my love. It's a medical emergency. I'll be back soon and tell all," she called back.

Mellissa and Lavinia hurried down to the clinic and found the situation just as Lavinia had described. The young girl was sitting in a chair and Roberta was holding her hand. She was said to be sixteen, but she was small and delicate, and so very under developed for a Negro girl that Mellissa thought that she looked to be only about twelve. Although the tourniquet had been applied properly, blood was still flowing from her thin wrist. Mellissa quickly washed her hands and asked Lavinia to do the same and then to get and prepare the medical needle and thread. "Whatever has happened to you, Poppy?" asked Mellissa, as she gently examined her patient. "And who did this to you?"

Poppy started to cry. "I done it to me," she said between her sobs. "I done it myself."

Mellissa had seen that the cut was clean and was beginning to stitch it up, but she was mystified. "What do you mean, 'you did it yourself'? Why ever would you do such a thing?"

"I want me to die. I don't want those mens, those Massas, to hurt me no more. I don't want to be in they bed. But they, the Massas, I got to do what I told. All three of the Massas do it before. An' last night, they Massas do it more. They whip if I tells." And she sobbed even harder. Mellissa finished the stitching almost automatically while she was trying to make sense of what she was hearing. She spread some salve on Poppy's arm and covered the wound with clean cotton bandages, then she made a simple sling out of a cotton square and got Poppy to wear it to support her arm.

"You will have to wear this for a few days to give your wound a chance to start healing, and I want you to stay here for the rest of the day and sleep in the clinic tonight. I will come and see you again tomorrow," said Mellissa.

Turning to Lavinia she said, "I want to get to the bottom of this. What does Poppy mean by saying that she does not want to be with the mens, the Massas? Is she being forced to have sexual relations with the Frobishers? She is too young and too small for any of that, especially rough sex. Is it just Poppy or are there other girls being forced to give their bodies to these men?" She paused for a moment, and then she asked, "What did she mean when she said three Massas?"

It was Roberta who answered. "Them two Massas have pretty new cabin. It not in slave compound, it been built where no one see it, no one hear them make noise in it." She lowered her eyes and studied the floor. She could not look Mellissa in the eye. "It was all three Massas last week," she said in a voice only just above a whisper.

Mellissa was beginning to get a bad feeling. Was this true? And how much did Charles know about it? Could it really be that he was involved? Surely not. "Is this right, Lavinia? Have you seen this new cabin that has been built for the Frobisher Masters? Do you know what goes on inside it?"

"I have only heard stories…"

"Poppy," said Mellissa, "I would like to examine you, I would like to see where you have been hurt by the men. Will you let me look?"

Poppy was scared, but she nodded. Mellissa and Lavinia helped her up onto the surgical bed and Lavinia held her hand as she lay down. Mellissa lifted back her skirt and saw that she was not wearing any underclothes. She gently examined her vulva and vagina, and Poppy winced. "It is all right Poppy," she said gently, "I just need to take a look at what has been done to you." Mellissa was horrified. She could see how bruised her inner thighs were, her vagina was torn and her vulva was very swollen and still bleeding slightly. She cleaned away seminal stains and dried blood that remained, and once more applied the salve. That was all she could do to make the child more comfortable.

"Lavinia, I want Poppy to stay here in the clinic for the next few days, and we will need someone to stay with her. Do you think that Mary would do that? Perhaps her William can stay with Akami. Would you ask him?" Mellissa stopped for a moment and suddenly her anger returned. "Look after everything here, Lavinia!" she said sharply and she started running back to High View and Charles as quickly as she could. She was panting when she reached him and she could hardly talk.

"What's up, Old Girl?" he asked. He was acting nervously because he suspected that the emergency might have something to do with what was going on in the cabin in the woods, and what he had done while Mellissa had been away.

"Please say it's not true?" She gasped as soon as she could catch her breath.

"What's not true?" he asked with an innocent sounding curiosity.

"Those monsters!" spat Mellissa. "You have let them build a cabin in the woods for them to molest the young female slaves. Far enough in the woods so that no one can hear them calling out or screaming." Mellissa was angry now, more angry than Charles had ever seen her. "And you have been there too." It was not a question, it was a statement, which Charles did not deny. Still consumed with anger, she started to cry. "I have a sixteen-year-old girl, Poppy, in the clinic who has cut her wrist to try to save herself from being attacked again. I have seen what has been done to her private parts. I am a medic and it even shocked me. And on top of what had happened to her, and I *will* call it rape, Poppy was threatened with a whipping if she told anyone what is going on in that cabin. Is this how you want to make extra profits on this plantation? Is this really what you want, because if it is, then I want out. I am ready to leave this whole place to you and go back home to England."

For once Charles did not have a ready answer. Mellissa glared at him and went inside. He came in half an hour later, hoping that Mellissa had got the worst of her anger out of her system. Instead he found her upstairs with Chloe, removing his clothing and personal items from their shared bedroom. "What are you doing?" he asked with genuine surprise, as Mellissa flung his favourite shirt and blue silk cravat onto a pile of his clothes that were already on the floor.

"What do you think I am doing?" she asked, not expecting a reply. "You do not think that I want to sleep with you after you have had sexual relations with one, or is it more, of our slaves?" Charles cringed. "Four nights! Just four nights I was away from you, and you did that. How can you think that I will ever want you in my bed again after that?"

"Where do you expect me to go?" asked Charles miserably.

"There are eight bedrooms in this house. You can choose any of the other seven! Chloe will take your things there."

"Please, Mellissa." Charles was almost in tears. "Please Mellissa forgive me. I was stupid."

"You were not stupid," came back Mellissa's quick reply. "You were evil, as evil as those hateful Frobishers. Little Poppy is a child. She may be sixteen, which I doubt, but she has the fragile body of a child. Three grown men forcing themselves on a small child, whether she be a slave or free, whether she be black, white, pink or purple, it is disgusting! Disgusting, wicked and evil! However do you expect me to forgive you? How?" And Mellissa broke down in floods of tears. Chloe had already, discretely, left the room and Charles went forward to comfort Mellissa. She shook him off and screamed at him, "Don't you dare touch me. Get away! Get away from me. I do not want to feel your grubby hands on my body, and I do not want to see your stupid, evil face again."

Charles was crying too. "Please, Mellissa. Please!" he sobbed.

She felt herself weakening, and said in a normal, tired voice, "Just go away now Charles. I may talk to you again tomorrow."

The following day, ignoring her much subdued husband, she visited Jack and Peter Frobisher in their cabin. She took along with her, her own slaves Lavinia and Akami, who she knew would not be intimidated by them and could not be ordered about by them.

The two men were sitting in rattan chairs outside the door of their cabin. They were both casually dressed in shirts which were open almost to the waist. They were unshaved and unwashed and even from a distance, smelled strongly of rum, dirt and sweat. Mellissa first inspected the outside of the cabin. It was indeed well enclosed by protective trees, far enough away from the slave's compound for anyone there to be aware of what was going on there. The brothers both looked at Mellissa and her two slaves with an insolent regard, and did not invite her to join them or sit down.

She, nevertheless, pulled herself up to her full height and pointed her index finger at them. "You two men," she said in her most authoritative manner, looking them straight in the eyes, "are employed here to run a profitable sugar plantation with the help of slaves. That is all you are here to do. That and nothing else. Those slaves do not belong to you and are not your toys and playthings. You do not have any authority over them other than while they are working. You do not have authority giving you the rights to use and abuse their bodies. I have seen what you have done to Poppy and you disgust me. If I were able to do so, I would whip you myself. Even if you persuaded my deluded husband to join you in your devious and disgusting pursuits, it still does not give you permission to please yourselves, or pleasure yourselves with any of them. These slaves belong to me as well as my husband, and I do not give you permission to use and abuse a single one of them. Do you understand me?"

The Frobisher brothers were truly startled. They knew that Mellissa was a powerful woman but they also thought that if they could control her husband they would be able to control her, via him. Now they realised their error and they were at risk of being thrown off the plantation.

Jack Frobisher stood up. At first, he tried to excuse himself. "The girls here are all adult and willing," He said with his lazy Jamaican drawl. "Some even offer themselves up hoping for extra favours – less work, more food. You know the drill."

"No. I do not know the 'drill', as you call it," spat out an angry Mellissa. "All I know is that I have in my clinic a little child whose vagina is so torn up that she can hardly walk, and who attempted to kill herself rather than submit herself once more to your murderous, degrading and depraved assault. If you had done this to a white woman, nay, a white girl, both of you would have been tried by the courts, found guilty and hanged!"

"We will promise that we will no longer bring any young girls…"

"No women at all. Unless they come to me personally and beg me to allow them to spend the night in your cabin!"

Mellissa was trembling by the time she had finished her tirade, and she didn't want them to see the state she was in, so without another word she turned her back on the brothers and walked away, with Akami and Lavinia, who had said nothing at all during the confrontation, following in her wake. No sooner than she had got out of sight of the cabin she almost sank to her knees with delayed shock and fear. Akami and Lavinia were at her side at once and they both put their arms about her to support her. At that very moment, Charles was approaching the cabin on his own way to confront the Frobishers. He was not at all pleased to see Mellissa being supported by Akami, ignoring that fact that Lavinia was also holding her Mistress in a firm embrace. He was well aware that Akami, who was nothing but a Negro slave, doted on his wife, and he was outraged and jealous.

"What is going on?" he spluttered. "Akami, take your filthy hands, I mean hand, off the Mistress."

"Don't be silly, Charles. I have just spoken to your wonderful overseers and have made them understand what they can and cannot do with our slaves," said Mellissa, still shaken by the experience. "I hope that you will back me up this time. Before you talk to them, I want you to take over from Akami and help me back to the clinic before my legs give way entirely. I want to see how Poppy is today and I want you to see her too."

Charles felt very ashamed about facing his 'victim', as Mellissa had described her, and he felt guilty too. He knew that he had done wrong and he was deeply uncomfortable about seeing Poppy.

By the time they had reached the clinic Mellissa had recovered her strength. It was she who entered the clinic first. Poppy was up and walking about the room, her arm was rested and still in the sling. She still looked small, very young and very vulnerable, but now there was a new sparkle in her pretty eyes. "Are you feeling better

239

today, Poppy?" asked Mellissa. "Does your arm still hurt, and do you feel more comfortable below?"

"Yes, Mistress," she said, "I's better today. I go work now?"

"No, Poppy. I don't want you to go back to working in the fields. I want you to help Rebecca with the rabbits today. And then the Master and I will decide what we want you to do next."

Poppy, until then, had not seen Charles enter the clinic. Now, she looked up and immediately a look of fear passed over her face and she shied back. Charles spoke up. "You don't have to be afraid of me now, Poppy." He could not find it within himself to say sorry to a slave, but he did his best. "And I will make sure that the Massas will leave you alone in future."

It was five days before Mellissa felt calm enough to talk to Charles again properly, and another six days before she let him come back to their bedroom. She did not exactly forgive him, because what he had done was horrible even though he had been encouraged by Jack and Peter. Mellissa felt that he should have been strong enough with his employees to stop the abuse that was happening. But he did not and instead he had joined in, and only felt guilty when he was found out. However, Mellissa too, had her own guilty conscience about the kiss she had shared with Akami, so she did not think that she had the right to judge her husband.

So the two of them returned to their usual life and routines, but were each of them treading carefully about each other. They still loved and wanted each other, but it was not the same as before. By the beginning of March, Mellissa was acting normally, but the residue of her anger against Charles had not yet melted away. She forced him to check up on the activities taking place in the Frobisher cabin, and was satisfied that he was telling the truth when he reported back that all was calm. Mellissa knew though the chain of slave gossip that although there had been some visits to the cabin, the women who had taken part in any sexual games had done so without being forced. Jack and Peter Frobisher were subdued and found that they had lost some of their authority over the slaves, who were beginning, at last, to realise that the Mistress was their champion.

Poppy was now working with Rebecca in the rabbit run. Rebecca had had a complete change of heart. Looking after the baby rabbits had made her feel loved and needed. She was now able to grieve quietly and gently for her dead child. When Mellissa had taken little Poppy to Rebecca, it seemed that all her mothering instincts were transferred to the care of Poppy, and she even invited

Poppy to move into her cabin with her. And Poppy was happy to have a new protector, a foster mother, having lost her own mother to an unknown sickness when Poppy was only nine years old.

Mellissa now divided her time entirely between the clinic, and all the activities surrounding High View. There was Michael and some of the older children who were now competently performing the tasks that had been Abraham's: caring for the horses, the stables and the pigs and chickens, doing the gardening, both flower gardens and the vegetable plots, and the drawing of water from the well for all those activities and for the plantation house. Akami was now a competent and well liked schoolteacher. Rebecca and Poppy had their rabbits. Chloe, Mary and Winnie were good cooks and house servants, and Lavinia as well as working most of the day in the clinic, where Rosie was now a competent nurse for minor problems, was here, there and everywhere supervising and advising everyone in this the upper part of the plantation.

Chapter Thirty-Eight

An Artist Is Discovered

It was another Sunday morning when Lavinia came to Charles and Mellissa as they were taking morning coffee on their veranda. "Master, Mistress," she said, "Akami has a small problem over in the schoolroom. He would like you both to come and see it."

They were both comfortable and would have preferred to remain at ease where they were, but curiosity won the day. At first, when they entered the school room, they saw nothing, not even Akami. But then they heard his deep African voice. "Master, Mistress. Just look this way, if you please!"

They turned at the same time, and they were both astonished at what they saw. The whole of the back wall of the schoolroom was covered from floor to ceiling with the most fabulous paintings and drawings, some in bright colours and some in charcoal. Mostly, they were of beautiful Jamaican birds and flowers, and then Mellissa gasped; here was the very face of Lavinia looking through a jungle of plants and wild flowers. And there was an absolute reproduction of Akami, complete with the tribal markings on his face.

"How? What is this?" Mellissa managed to get out. And then she saw herself, it was as if she were looking at her reflection in a mirror! How had the artist managed to catch her likeness, the very essence of her being, without her 'sitting' or even being aware that someone was sketching her?

It was Charles who spoke next. "Akami," he said, "this is the most wonderful display of talent that I have ever seen. Who is the artist?"

Just then, a young slave girl entered the schoolroom, and shyly went to stand at Akami's side. "This is Melanie," he said, reaching out and holding her hand. "She is the daughter of Thomas and Eliza, and for the last few weeks she has been coming to our little school.

She has not yet learned to read and write, but I discovered her amazing talent as soon as she held a slate and chalks. When we went to St Elizabeth last week for supplies, Lavinia and I bought some paper and paints with some of the money that you, Mistress, gave me for the school. And this outpouring of artwork is the result."

"Well, Melanie," said Mellissa. "I am astonished at the wonder of your paintings, they are magnificent. I don't think that I have even seen such beautiful paintings in the art galleries of London, the biggest city in the world. However did you manage to do that portrait of me? You could only have seen me as I walk around the plantation. It is amazing!" She went to Melanie and took her other hand, but Melanie continued to look only at the floor. Mellissa tried again to get her to look at her. "I would be so pleased if you would make another for me," she said, smiling, "and maybe one or two of the bird pictures for the Master and me to put in our home. Would you do that for me?"

Melanie was lost for words, and she nodded her head, and remained looking at the floor. Charles then spoke up. "Melanie, I do believe that you would be able to sell your paintings in St Elizabeth, and maybe even in Kingston. We will let you keep the money and then you would be able to buy all the materials you like to create more artwork. Would you like me to arrange that for you?"

Melanie's head remained bent towards the floor, but just for a moment she lifted it, gave Charles a lovely, girlish smile, nodded once more and looked again at the floor.

Akami spoke up. "There is just one problem, Master. Melanie is fifteen years old, and she will be sixteen in three weeks' time, when she will be expected to join her mother and father in the cane fields…"

Mellissa quickly interrupted. "Oh! We cannot let that happen," she said. She thought very quickly, and before her husband could say anything, she asked, "Akami, Melanie still needs to learn to read, but I was also wondering if you could use an art teacher in the school?"

Charles smiled. He knew when he had been presented with a *fait accompli*, he had done it to Mellissa when he had presented her with the Frobisher brothers, and now the tables were turned, but he was happy to agree. Akami smiled, he knew that he had won. "Mistress," he said, "it would be the best thing you could do. Melanie will continue to learn, and she will also make a very good teacher. What do think Melanie? Do you have something to say to the Master and Mistress?"

At last, Melanie found her voice. "Thank you Massa. Thank you Mistress. I like to teach please." And, at last, she managed to look them in the face, and smile. Charles and Mellissa stayed a while longer studying Melanie's artwork, and as they left to go back to their lazy Sunday on their veranda Mellissa said to Lavinia and Akami, "I have something to show you two which is in the clinic. I would like you both to meet me there at the end of the day tomorrow."

"Yes, Mistress," they replied together, both wondering what their Mistress was going to tell them, or ask them to do.

Charles was equally inquisitive. "What are you up to now?" he asked as they were strolling back to their house.

Mellissa took a deep breath. She knew that what she was about to say and do would not please her husband, but he need to know before she saw Lavinia and Akami the next day. "I feel that your recent behaviour, you know, in the Frobisher's cabin, has given me the right to break one of my promises to you…"

"Whatever are you talking about? What promise?" stuttered Charles. The last thing he wanted on this pleasant and sunny Sunday afternoon was to be reminded about what he had done. But he couldn't remember any promise except that he would not go there again. But that was his promise, not hers. "What promise? He repeated.

"It is the promise I made to you when I bought Lavinia and Akami."

"What promise?" Charles was completely thrown. He had forgotten all the details of the sale of Lavinia and Akami to Mellissa.

"Well, I'm glad that you don't remember my promise, so perhaps you won't be upset at my breaking it."

"I'll break your neck in a moment, if you don't tell me what you are going on about!" Charles was getting exasperated, but he was making fun, not getting angry.

"When I bought Lavinia and Akami," said Mellissa, slowly dragging out her story, "I promised…"

"What promise?" Charles spat the words out between his teeth.

" I promised not to free them," she said so quickly that it came out as one word.

"What?"

"I promised not to free them."

"Is that what you've done? You have set them free after all we have talked about, after you promised not to do that?" said an exasperated Charles. "When did you do that and why, for heaven's sake?"

"It is not exactly done yet." Mellissa was relieved, she thought that she might be getting away with what she had done. "I have had the manumission papers drawn up by our attorney-at-law, Daniel Smith, in St Elizabeth. Lavinia and Akami have both proved so loyal I think that they deserve freedom from slavery."

"You! You think that they deserve freedom. So you just went ahead without asking me?" Charles' reply was almost calm.

"Was he too calm?" she asked herself.

Mellissa had been surprised at her husband's reaction, but she was a little bit concerned about the calmness. Was he now giving himself a licence to do something to which she would not agree? She thought that she had better quickly explain to him the full terms of freedom for her slaves. "I have not yet told you everything about the manumission papers. I have specifically made their freedom subject to them staying to work for me for at least three years before they can choose to leave entirely."

"So you think that that helps?" asked Charles. "You still went behind my back."

"Yes I did. Firstly, because you did more than that behind *my* back, and secondly, because I think that Lavinia and Akami will be even more loyal with their freedom.

"I thought that you said you would not talk about what I did again," said a sullen Charles.

"I don't want to. All I want is for the both of us to be happy once more. Happy like we were only a few months ago. Please, Charles, let us call a truce and love one another again?"

Charles gave in. "I suppose you have only half freed them. And who knows where we will all be in three years' time?" He sighed. "All right, Old Girl," he said. "Let's love one another again!"

Chapter Thirty-Nine

Illicit Love

Lavinia and Akami were walking to the clinic together after the day's chores were done. They had been talking together and they were both curious about their mysterious summons. As they were approaching the clinic Lavinia said, "I am sure that our Mistress had nothing to tell us that we would not like."

"Yes," said Akami, "I know that we are both slaves, but I think that we have the best Mistress in Jamaica. I always want to be here, and I know that I would do anything for her."

"Be careful, Akami," Lavinia advised. "I think that you are falling in love with her, and that would be most unwise of you."

Their conversation stopped at that awkward point as they reach the clinic. Mellissa was waiting at the door, and she was smiling as broadly as it was possible for her to smile.

"Come in, Come in you two," she said happily. "I have something to show you."

They all sat down at the table and it was almost like a repeat of the time when she had showed them the papers revealing that she had just bought them both. This time she gently gave to each of them their freedom papers. They both read them slowly.

"Can this be true?" Lavinia gasped. She was expecting something good, but never as good as this.

"Oh, my dearest Mistress," Akami sobbed, "I've been a slave since I was a boy in Africa, and I never thought that I would ever be free again. And now I have it I know that I don't want to be free from you."

Mellissa laughed. "You haven't read the document properly. Akami. You are free, but both of you still have to work for me for another three years!"

And then she was also starting to cry. "Well, I am so happy that you want to remain with me. I have made legal copies of your freedom papers, which, I am sure that you will want to keep. All I ask of you is that for the present you tell no one, not even your children, Lavinia, because it might cause the rest of our slaves to become unsettled. But I have fulfilled the promise made to you, Lavinia, when I gave you that ring."

Lavinia looked at the silver and amethyst ring that she wore every day on the third finger of her right hand. "I do look at it every day and I remember your promise, Mistress," she said in a subdued, but happy voice. "But now you have given me my freedom I know that I, also, do not want to be free from you."

"I promise," said Akami, "that I will tell no one, and I will keep my copy safely, maybe on my own person. I will make an inside pocket in my shirt, and keep it always next to my heart!"

"I promise too," said Lavinia, still crying. "And I will keep mine in the locked box in my room, but perhaps I will keep the key on a chain around my neck and next to *my* heart!"

Mellissa was attempting to dry her tears, and to bring everything back to normality she tried to be funny, saying in her version of a Jamaican accent. "Come now, Lavinia, you still be my slave. Where my dinner at? What you cook for me today? None of that spicy jerk. I want fish and banana. You git going an' do what I tells you, you no 'count lazy nigger."

Through their tears they all laughed. "All right, all right, Mistress," said Lavinia, picking up her copy of her manumission document. "I's going. I not lazy nigger. Don't whip I!" she said. Pretending to cringe but still laughing, she left to supervise the evening meal. Akami was just about to do the same when Mellissa stopped him.

"Akami," she said as she was looking at the main manumission papers and gathering them up into a leather pouch. "I have a problem with my records of the slaves. I am ashamed to say that I knew nothing about Melanie, or her parents. And I don't know how many young people we have, who might miss out on schooling because they are more than fourteen." And then she said to herself, "Who might be in danger from the Frobisher brothers?"

"It is a big task. What I would like you to do for me is to collect and give me full details of who lives in which of the one hundred odd cabins in the main compound, what their ages are, and what work they do on the plantation. Of course, I am familiar with those who live near High View at the top of the plantation, but it is the rest that is not detailed." At last, she looked straight at him and smiled as she ignored her beating heart. "Do you think that you could do that for me?"

Akami felt the same thing too, and he was lost for words. He could not bear to be alone with her, and was just able to stutter a "Yes Mistress", and he turned once more to leave. Once more Mellissa stopped him.

"Akami! You have blood on the back of your shirt. What have you done to your back?"

"I am all right, Mistress. It is only an old scar which has never healed properly. It does bleed from time to time, but it will stop soon. I will wash it away when I get back to my cabin."

Mellissa was all medic now, and since they were in the clinic where she had the means to check the wound and clean it, she said. "Sit down, Akami, and take off your shirt. I want to take a look at your wound."

Akami hesitated. He was afraid to let her come near to him, especially in a state of semi-undress. But old slave instincts of obedience were too strong. He took off his shirt and sat on a stool. Mellissa had seen his back before, but she was once again horrified to see the deep scaring which covered the whole of it, reminding her of the wicked way he had been whipped and beaten as a slave in America. One particular small area up on his left shoulder blade, was infected. Pus and blood were oozing slowly from it.

"Your back is infected!" Mellissa exclaimed. "Did you say it often weeps blood? Why did you never ask me to attend to it?" Akami made no response while Mellissa was cleaning the old wound and applying her special salve. She did not know how to cover it other than place a bandage over his shoulder and under his arm. As she started rubbing his scared back he turned around to her and held his arms around her hips. It was too much for both of them and without thought he stood up and started to kiss her. As before the softness of his lips against hers melted her insides. She returned his kiss with the full force of desire and before they knew what was happening they stumbled up against one of the clinic beds.

Without thinking about the rights or wrongs of what they were doing, or even checking that the door of the clinic was locked, they fumbled with the strangeness of each other's buttons as they undressed each other with passion. For a moment Mellissa was stunned at the beauty of his African body. She had seen him undressed as a medical emergency, but now she saw him as a man.

Apart from his deformities, he was a magnificent specimen. His strength, his muscle tone, and yes, his manly genitals.

Akami, in turn, had never in his whole life seen a white woman undressed. For a second or two he had a flashback to his village in Africa. He remembered the young women and girls with their beautiful ebony skin, and coal-tipped breasts that pointed straight at him. This was another world to him, indeed, it was the other side of the ocean, and this fabulous woman was nothing like a ghost or a dead fish as his people describe white people. She was like a lustrous, shining pearl, and he was blinded with love and desire. Her soft breasts with their rosy nipples were as inviting as a sugar stick to a child. Without words he bent his head and took her nipples into his mouth, first one and then the other. She in turn reached out to hold his genitals, and especially his hugely engorged 'toto', which was already up and inviting, and then became stiff as ramrod.

They slowly, oh so slowly, sank down upon the bed and then Akami mounted his Mistress, his one and only love. Her legs parted and lifted to curl themselves around his back, inviting him and he plunged himself deep inside her. Her eyes opened wide with surprise and almost as soon changed to a look of sensual pleasure. Her body arched as again and again as he almost withdrew and returned with such force that she climaxed again and again until with both of them coming at the same time they shouted out loud together. He slowly sank down on her relaxed and tender body and they both slowly waited until their heartbeats and breathing returned to normal.

They were both speechless as they cleaned themselves and hesitatingly fumbled with their clothing to dress. "I love you," she whispered, as she held him close.

"And I adore you," Akami whispered back. "I can never be a freeman, because you will always be my Mistress, and the Mistress of my heart."

"I shall dream of you tonight, but I must go now, goodnight my dearest Akami," With that she was gone, to walk on unsteady legs and with throbbing insides, back to High View. She walked as slowly as she could so that she could recover her normal senses before she re-joined her husband.

Charles noticed nothing. "So, how did it go? Have you got two extremely happy slaves?"

Mellissa's only reply before she retreated to her bedroom was, "They are indeed both very happy, and both of them avowed that it would make no difference and they would stay with me always."

Charles muttered under his breath, "I am sure that that big black buck did!"

Mellissa continued as she was making her way to climb the stairs to look down on him from the upstairs landing, "I am thinking of bringing them both back with us when we return to England. I'm sure that we will want to do that before their three years are up." With that she was gone, leaving a slightly stunned Charles in her wake.

Chapter Forty

Poppy Is with Child

During the next few weeks, life on Silver Bay returned to normal, that is as normal as Mellissa could make it. She still saw Akami most days, but apart from a secret smile when she was sure that no one was looking, she made no further moves towards him. Every time she saw him she was filled with desire, but she knew that love between them was impossible and she vowed that she would never be alone with him again. She even got Rosie to check his back and change the bandages.

One afternoon Mellissa came to join Charles, who was standing on the veranda, the smoke of a pipe-full of Virginia tobacco was curling all around him and filling the air with its special aroma. Putting her arms around his waist she said, "I was thinking of asking Lucy Everdene to come and stay with us for a few days. What do you think? Would it disturb you?"

Charles was pleased. "I think that it would be a nice idea. I know that you get lonely for a woman friend, and it is good for you to meet up with other white women living here on the island."

"You do know that she is not of land owning gentry, don't you?" said Mellissa. "She's is just a simple tradeswoman from Liverpool, and she speaks with a Liverpool accent!"

"I know. You did tell me, but if you like her, then I'm sure that she will suit me too. Would you like me to send a messenger from St Elizabeth when I go there tomorrow?"

"Yes, please," said Mellissa, giving her husband a hug and a little kiss. "I shall look forward to having a friend to chatter to."

But before Lucy arrived, another big change was about to happen in the Harrison household. One morning Mellissa was checking up on Rebecca and Poppy, and she found Poppy being sick in the corner of the rabbit enclosure. "Oh dear, Poppy," she said, "have you eaten something that disagrees with you?"

Before Poppy could answer, Rebecca joined them. "She has been sick like this every day this week, haven't you Poppy?"

Poppy was still recovering, and could only nod.

Immediately Mellissa guessed what was wrong with her. "I think that I would like to examine you, Poppy," she said. "Will you come down with me to the clinic so I can do it properly?"

Rebecca was disturbed at the thought of her protégée being taken away from her. "Shall I come too?" she asked.

Mellissa could see the fear in her eyes, and did not want the unstable Rebecca to start worrying again. "You can come if you like," she said. "But I want both of you to wash your hands first, and put on some clean clothes and shoes. I don't want any of these rabbit droppings in the clinic."

The examination confirmed Mellissa's suspicions. There was no doubt that little Poppy was with child. Mellissa was dumbstruck, she just told Rebecca to take Poppy back, and she gave her some tonic telling her to give a spoonful to Poppy every morning. Then she returned to High View to wait for Charles' return. Her thoughts were going around and round in her head. Who was the child's father? Was it one of the Frobisher brothers? Or could it be possible that Charles was the father? They had been married for almost two years now, and in spite of them making love several times a week, the longed for conception had never happened. Was it her fault? Was it his fault? Even if Poppy had a mulatto child, they still would not be able to say for sure who the father was. The Frobishers had long limbs, long thin heads and faces, and they both had very blue eyes, and Charles had a small, round head and face, and his eyes were green. Would that help?

Charles returned in the late afternoon. He saw at once that Mellissa was agitated. "Let me have a quick wash, a change and a drink before you tell me what you obviously are dying to say," he said.

Fifteen minutes later they were sitting in their favourite seats on the veranda. "Now then," sighed Charles. "What is it this time?"

"Poppy is pregnant," she came out with a blunt statement.

"Poppy. Pregnant?"

"Yes, and there will be no way of telling who the father is," said Mellissa in a flat voice. "It may be one of those brothers." She could not even say their name. "But, of course, it may be yours. What shall we do about it?"

252

"Mellissa, I just do not know what to say. I only did it once, and you know well that we have made love hundreds of times and you have never conceived." He was almost crying. "I have been longing for you to become pregnant, and I have begun to think that I might be at fault."

"I have been having the same thoughts, thinking that it is my fault," said Mellissa, who at seeing her husband weep, started to weep too. "What shall we do?" There was no reply from Charles, so she carried on. "It is also plain to me that Poppy is such an underdeveloped child that she may not be able to carry a child to full term. She will need very careful attention in the next few months. I don't think that she even knows what is happening to her body. I will have to explain it to her in the next week or so, and I don't know what to tell her. She may not even know how this has happened to her. Whatever shall I tell her?"

"And she now lives with the unstable Rebecca," said Charles. "What shall we do about that?"

"I think that it will be best if I talk it over with Lavinia, and we can pool our expertise on pregnancies." Mellissa paused for a moment to pull herself together. "When people start to ask questions, I think that we must assume that the child has been fathered by one of the Frobishers. We will not know, even if we ever know for certain, until well after the child is born."

"If everything goes ahead healthily and normally, when will the child be due?" asked Charles.

"Well, it was at the end of February when I went to Kingston, so we must assume that the child will be born sometime in November.

I think that I will, with help of Lavinia, tell Poppy tomorrow."

"And what about Rebecca?" asked Charles.

"It is best that we include Rebecca," said Mellissa tentatively. "I think that she will either go straight into a grandmother role, or she will revert back to the time she was expecting her baby, Rubin, who died in Montego Bay. I will pray to God that it is the grandmother role she takes, then she will actually be useful in the overall care of Poppy."

"I am so sorry, Mellissa," said Charles, who was tearful once more.

Mellissa, thinking about her lapse with Akami, came to his side and held him lovingly in her arms. "I think that we will speak no more about your part in this. We will assume that it is the child of one of the Frobisher brothers, and hope that Poppy does not want to

253

question what we tell her about how a baby is made. And you must make sure that the Frobishers agree that the child is theirs. Tell them that they will be dismissed instantly if there is any talk about you."

"I really do love you, Old Girl."

"And I love you," returned Mellissa. "Now let us talk about Lucy Everdene who will be arriving in three days' time. We did not expect all this when we invited her, so we will have to just go along with the 'happy plantation full of happy slaves!' stories."

In the end it was Lavinia who did most of the talking and explaining to Poppy. She was much more experienced with young slave girls who knew virtually nothing about their bodies and how they worked. Rebecca, too, turned out to be as concerned and grandmotherly as Mellissa had hoped.

"When will I have my baby?" asked Poppy.

"It will be a long time yet," said Lavinia. "It will grow inside you just like the rabbits have babies that grow inside them, but because you are so much bigger than a rabbit, it will take a lot longer. I think that it will be ready to be born just before cane harvest time."

"That a long time," agreed Poppy. "So I have time to fix on baby name for my baba. When I knows if it be a boy or a girl?"

Rebecca chimed in this time. "Sweetheart, you won't know what it be to be until it born."

"That all right," said Poppy, and she went away smiling to herself and talking quietly to her tummy. "You be a good baba for you Mamie, won't you?"

Chapter Forty-One

April 1831
Lucy Pays a Return Visit

Lucy Everdene duly arrived, very hot and tired after a long journey. Her usual immaculate bun on the top of her head had slipped, and her pretty flowery cotton dress was all crumpled and stained. One of her husband's slaves, Joe, was her driver, and after he had been given refreshments by Chloe, she took him to Akami's cabin where he was to stay for three nights. Mellissa and Lucy were immediately and happily reacquainted, she had a quick, refreshing drink of lemonade and then she was shown her room by Roberta. She was back downstairs within fifteen minutes very much refreshed with yet another pretty cotton dress. She looked every inch a grandmother. Round, jolly and talkative.

Charles, who had been introduced to Lucy soon after she had arrived, joined in with the two women as they drank tea in the dining room, while they were waiting for supper to be brought in. He was amazed to see them both together. He had never seen Mellissa with friends chatting about this and that, and just general female gossip. And he realised at last how starved she had been of ordinary female companionship since they had been in Jamaica.

"How have you been since your boys left you?" Mellissa was asking. "I expect that you will be happy to see them again tomorrow."

"Oh, I cried for two whole days after they were gone," said a sad faced Lucy. "I know in my heart that they will be better off with their mothers. Maybe they will think kindly of me as they grow up. I hope that it will not be too long before they become freemen. Perhaps they might even travel to Kingston for work. I'm sure that we will find some for them if they ever wanted to work in a Chandlers' shop, that is if we are still in Jamaica."

"Have you and Johnny had any more thoughts of selling up and retiring to England?" asked Mellissa.

"We have talking about it endlessly since your visit," said Lucy, "but we haven't been able to make a decision. I'm not getting any younger, and as you know, we don't have any children of our own and I miss my sister and her children and grandchildren back in Liverpool. But life is much easier here in Jamaica than it ever is in Liverpool, especially I love the beauty of the island and the wonderful climate."

"What about doing both?" suggested Mellissa. "You could go back to Liverpool for an extended visit. Perhaps for the whole of one summer, then you both might find it easier to make your minds up."

"You are a very clever lady!" exclaimed Lucy. "Now, why did I not think of that? If my Johnny could only find someone he trusted to look after the business without robbing him for that time, that is exactly what we could do."

"Why! Have you been robbed before?" asked a shocked Mellissa.

"Oh, yes," replied Lucy. "He had a manager last year, Andrew Kershaw was his name, and he robbed us blind while he was working right alongside my Johnny."

"How did he manage that?"

"Johnny caught him taking money for goods and not recording the sale. He saw him putting the cash straight into his pocket. All the while, Johnny had been wondering how his stock levels were going down without money coming in."

"I can see why your husband is cautious about taking on a new manager," said Mellissa. "What happened to that Mr Kershaw?"

"Well, Johnny was too embarrassed at his failure to monitor Kershaw to report him to the local Magistrate, so he just made Kershaw give him back everything that Johnny worked out that had been stolen, and he sent him on his way."

"He was very lucky not to be imprisoned or even hanged," said Mellissa.

She turned to Charles, who had just been sitting by enjoying the women's conversation. "What would you think about having a manager if we were to return to England for a holiday?"

Charles was serious as he answered, "As you know, we were expecting to be here for about three years, and I am not sure yet about the plan for when we want to return. I think that my father had in mind that we would sell up rather than leave everything in the hands of a manager or overseer."

"I don't think that we should talk about overseers while Lucy is with us," said Mellissa, with a wicked smile. "You know that she knows all about the Frobisher brothers. Have you heard anything more about them since we last met?" she asked, addressing Lucy.

"Well, I hate to tell you," said Lucy cautiously, "but everything that was written in the Kingston Gleaner was true. By chance, at a church meeting, I met up with Miranda Frobisher, the wife of the older brother, Christopher, and she told me that it wasn't the first time that the 'boys' had savagely attacked one of the young female slaves on the Greenfields Plantation. It was only because they had also killed the father that they had been reported to the Magistrate."

"I know. I know," sighed Charles. "I have been having wars with my wife constantly since she came home from Kingston. And I reluctantly agree with you both that I must make alternative arrangements about my overseers. Unfortunately, I agreed with them that they stay on until after the next harvest. I know that I could dismiss them sooner, but I have been unable to find suitable a suitable replacement." He looked at Mellissa, "I promise you that as soon as I can I will replace them. And even if I keep them until harvest time I will certainly dismiss them afterwards."

Mellissa looked somewhat mollified. "Let's change the subject," she said. "You must be tired, Lucy, after that long journey. I know that I was when I did the same journey in reverse. How about we all go to bed as soon as we have had supper. Then you can have a good rest and be ready to meet Robert and Billy bright and early tomorrow morning."

"Yes, indeed. I am so looking forward to seeing them again that I will want to jump straight into bed after supper!"

It was actually mid-morning by the time that Mellissa, with Sheba at her side, and Lucy were ready to go to see what was going on in the schoolhouse. Before entering they peeped in through the window. Akami was surrounded by a group of girls, eight of them all told including Lavinia's Angeline, and he was reading them a story from a children's simplified version of the Bible. Matthew and Jonah were working with some of the younger boys, showing them how to form letters of the alphabet on their slates. Melanie was nearest the window where the light was strongest, and she was showing Robert and Billy how to draw a dog.

Billy looked up and saw Lucy looking in the window. "Mistress, Lucy!" he called out, his face beaming with happiness.

257

"Oh, Mistress Lucy, you came to visit me. You came!" By then Robert had also seen Lucy at the window, and they both rushed out to greet her, and ran straight into her arms, which were being held wide to receive and hug them.

"Well, well, well! I do believe you have both grown since I last saw you," she said, with tears in her eyes, and still not letting go of them. "Whatever has Mistress Harrison been feeding you on?" Now she was laughing as the boys dragged her into the schoolroom.

Akami greeted her with a smile. "Good morning, Mistress Everdene," he said. "Robert and Billy are a real credit to you. They have already started showing the little ones how to do their lettering. And they also enjoy helping Michael with the chickens."

"We collected fifteen eggs today, Mistress Lucy," said Billy. "We didn't drop any this time."

"Oh dear!" she exclaimed. "Does that mean that you dropped some yesterday?"

"It was Billy's fault," chimed in Robert, "I told him not to run!"

Rosie and Liza then came to the schoolroom to meet Lucy. As soon as they saw her they both started to cry. "Mistress Lucy, thank you for my baby, my Billy," said Rosie quite simply, and to her surprise, Lucy gave her a hug.

And then Lucy hugged Liza too. "My Robert. Big boy now. I thinks I never see him no more. You good Mistress Lucy."

Mellissa and Lucy stayed on for a while with Rosie and Liza and then left Akami with the job of calming all the children down. After leaving the schoolroom Mellissa showed Lucy around the upper part of the plantation, first they walked to the banana grove and the rabbit enclosure. Rebecca and Poppy were feeding the little creatures who were all hopping around and coming forward to be fed.

"Poppy," asked Mellissa, "how are you feeling now? Has your sickness passed?"

"I much better now, Mistress," said Poppy. "I not sick no more."

"That's good. You make sure that you come and see me again if have any more problems. Any problem at all," she said. Then she added, "Rebecca, will you make sure that she goes regularly to the clinic. She must be checked up regularly by Lavinia or myself until she is ready to have her baby."

"Yes, Mistress. I make sure."

As they walked back towards the rose garden Lucy said, "That little lady seems to be very young to be having a baby. How old is she?"

"She is said to be sixteen," said Mellissa, "but I am sure that she is no more than fourteen. We will have to watch her closely because she is so underdeveloped. I am hoping that her little frame will be strong enough." Without thinking about Charles' involvement, she said, "Guess who the father of her baby is?"

Lucy gasped. "Not one of the Frobisher brothers, is it?"

"Not one, but both! One or the other! It happened while I was visiting you. The poor little thing was violently attacked by them. And, as you know from last night's conversation, I have been trying my best to get my husband to get rid of them." Mellissa realised that she should never have told Lucy that Poppy was pregnant. She was even wishing that she had not taken her to see the rabbit enclosure or spoken about the child's father. She did not dare to mention that her Charles had been there and that he was also one of the possible fathers.

Mellissa was now feeling very uncomfortable. She did not want to lie to Lucy and she very much wanted to change the subject. "Here we are at the rose garden," she said in an almost overly cheerful voice. "Isn't it beautiful? It was created by Abraham, one of our slaves who died recently. He was a lovely old man who had lived on Silver Bay all his life. He was born a slave here and Silver Bay was always home to him. I loved him," she said simply. Then she took Lucy to sit in the arbour where Sheba spread herself out under the cool stone bench.

"It's wonderful. It's like sitting in my idea of heaven," said Lucy, taking a deep breath, "and the perfume is totally delicious." Just then a hummingbird came to take nectar from a pretty pink rose, from a rose bush which was overflowing with blooms. Lucy gasped. "Oh, Mellissa," she whispered, so as not to frighten the bird away. "It is so, so beautiful. A miracle. How could I ever think that I would be happy in England without the magical sights that this wonderful country has to offer? This really is heaven on earth."

Bit by bit, Mellissa showed Lucy the whole of the plantation, including the slave compound, the sugar workshops where Akami had lost his hand, and the cane fields, and the three days of Lucy's visit passed very quickly. The evenings sitting on the veranda and eating in the dining room with Charles in top form were also fun for them all, and there was no more mention made of the Frobisher brothers.

Robert and Billy were sad to see her go, and Mellissa could see that the two children had really been more like foster children than slaves to her. "I will look after them too," said Mellissa. "Just like the three other children that I brought back from Montego Bay, they actually belong to me, not my husband. And I shall make sure that they are freed before we leave Jamaica. That is if Emancipation has not become the law by then."

"I am so happy that your kind heart led you to my door. I hope that we will be friends forever," said Lucy, giving Mellissa a kiss on her cheek as they climbed into the Harrison's carriage.

Charles joined Mellissa and Lucy in the larger carriage for a part of Lucy's return journey, with her slave driving the smaller one behind. When the time came to part, Mellissa and Lucy had a long hug and said their goodbyes with tears in their eyes. "I will keep in touch by letter as often as I can," said Mellissa, "and I will keep you updated about the progress that Robert and Billy are making."

"And don't forget that you can come and stay with us at any time, any time you like, and Johnny would like to meet you too," she said, looking at Charles.

"I might take you up on that. It is about time I took my wife for a holiday, and we have hardly seen anything of Jamaica." He was about to give Lucy a formal handshake when she startled him by giving him a hug, as she had given to Mellissa. When he recovered, he said, "I would like to meet your Johnny, and see something more of Kingston. When we first arrived in Jamaica, we were so tired of travelling, we hardly saw anything at all. And our driver, James McBride, whisked us through the town as quickly as he could."

As she was driven away she was saying to herself, "My Johnny used to know a James McBride. I wonder if he is the same man." She twisted herself around in her carriage and called out, "Goodbye Mellissa, Goodbye Charles. Please come to visit us soon."

Chapter Forty-Two

Another Pregnancy at Silver Bay

It was three weeks later when Mellissa found that she was with child! She was not a mother already, but as a well-practiced medic and midwife she knew the first signs, tender breasts and a missed period of menstruation. For a minute she was delighted and was about to rush to Charles and tell him the news. At last! At long last, after two years of marriage. Charles so wanted a son and heir! Then she paused and pulled herself up mentally. She remembered Akami. It was just four weeks ago that she had had that moment of madness and had made love with Akami.

Suddenly she did not know what to do, and the only friend she had to talk it over with at Silver Bay was Lavinia. Perhaps she would wait another month for her next menstruation to be absolutely sure. But she had to tell someone, and someone who would understand what she had done. She had to tell Lavinia. It still took another week of bouncing backwards and forwards between fear and delight, before she could summon up the courage to speak. It was a workday morning when Charles had already got up, breakfasted and left the house. Lavinia came into Mellissa's room as usual with her breakfast on a tray.

"Good morning, Mistress. It's a lovely day outside!" said Lavinia, with her usual ironic morning greeting.

"Lavinia, you know as well as I do that every morning is lovely in Jamaica, except during the winter storms, and even they are usually over within a week. Every day here on the Silver Bay Plantation is usually lovely too. It's only people that make things go wrong," Mellissa ended sadly.

"Oh! Mistress, whatever has gone wrong? It must be something big for you to be so downhearted," said Lavinia.

"Lavinia. I'm pregnant!" said Mellissa, and she started to cry.

"Mistress, why are you crying? You have been telling me, ever since you came here to Jamaica, how much you and the Master want a child."

"We do. I do," cried Mellissa. "But I have done a terrible thing."

"What have you done? And how can I help?"

"I have fallen in love, Lavinia. I cannot help it. I love my husband, but I also love…" she could not quite say his name.

"Oh! Mistress," said Lavinia. "You cannot love him! He is a slave! Even if you have given him papers to set him free, he will always be a black man."

"I did not say his name…"

"I know it," said Lavinia. "I will not say his name. It is impossible. How did it happen? You should never have let it happen."

Mellissa was desperate. "I love him," she wailed.

"Oh, my dearest Mistress," said Lavinia, who sat down on the bed and held a weeping Mellissa in her strong arms. Both of the women were silent for a while then Lavinia said, "You must let me think about this, and I will talk to you later."

Reluctantly Mellissa pulled herself together and Lavinia left the room. It was almost as if the slave/mistress roles had been completely reversed. With the thoughts in her head going around like a whirlwind, she collapsed on the bed and did not make herself ready for the day until it was almost time for Charles to return home.

Mellissa was in her usual comfortable chair on the veranda with Sheba at her side. Stroking her beloved dog was the only thing that was keeping her calm. Then Lavinia came to see her. Immediately she was flustered again. "Sit down, Lavinia. Do sit down. What have you been thinking? Have you come up with a solution? Of course, you haven't, it's an impossible situation. Tell me what you think I must do."

"Mistress, you must calm down. It is not good for you or the baby for you to be so agitated," said Lavinia as she took her place at Mellissa's side, "You do not need for me to tell you that you have been very foolish, but I know that love can make us all foolish. I have been thinking about your problem all day, and I think that I may have found a solution."

"A solution! What solution?" Mellissa gasped. It was if she were visibly clutching at straws. "Tell me what I can do to get out of this terrible mess I am in?"

Lavinia took a deep breath. She knew that the answer that she had come up with would hurt, and she wasn't sure if her beloved

Mistress had the strength to accept it and go through with it. "First. You will not be able to hide your condition, so you must tell the Master. He will be very excited and very happy, and you must act excited and happy too.

Second. You do not need to tell me because I know, you make love regularly with your husband. So there is a great possibility that the child is his, much more so than it is the other man's. You told me that you only did this once with Akami…"

"I did not say his name. How did you know…?"

"…You only did it once with Akami," Lavinia repeated. "So it is more than likely that the child will be the Master's."

"But we have been married for almost two years, and as you say, we make love all the time, even when we are cross with one-another, and it has never happened. Much as we wanted it to, I just haven't conceived. Why would it happen just now? The one and only time I have made love to someone else?"

"It often happens with married people. They want a child and they try and try and almost give up, and suddenly the wife conceives. And only the Lord God knows why. So it is entirely possible this child could be the Master's, especially as you have said that you only made love with…him…on one occasion.

"Now this is what I have thought that might solve your problem. It seems that the baby was conceived in March, so it will be due in December, probably around Christmas time. You will not know until the child is born whose child it is, so for the next eight months you will have to relax, be happy with your husband and enjoy your pregnancy. When the time comes and you go into labour, we must both make sure that only I will be there to be your midwife. If the child is white, we will know that it is your husband's." She paused for a moment because she knew that what she was about to say would distress her Mistress once more. "But if the baby is dark skinned, I will take it away immediately and have it fostered amongst the slaves. I will prepare someone to be on standby to accept that baby. It will make you unhappy, but it is the only way…"

"But what will I say to Charles…?" Mellissa interrupted once more.

"…the only way will be for you to tell the Master that the baby was born dead."

"Dead?"

"Mistress, if the child is born black it will be dead to you anyway. Do you not understand? You will either have a healthy white baby, or your baby will die at birth."

263

The reality of the situation became suddenly evident to Mellissa. She opened her eyes wide and mouthed the word 'dead'. Then once again she collapsed in tears. She knew for certain that what Lavinia had said was the only solution, but the thought of having to give up her baby, Akami's baby, was for the moment, more than she could bear.

She was still weeping softly when Charles was due to return, so she hurried upstairs and, fully dressed, she went to lie on the bed. She was still crying when Charles, forewarned by Lavinia, burst into their bedroom a few minutes later. "Whatever is the matter? What has happened Old Girl? Tell me," he said with complete loving and tender concern.

Mellissa, who all day had not been able to decide what to do, suddenly, in that very instant, made up her mind. "My dearest Charles, I am feeling unwell, and I am feeling so very well. I am feeling unhappy, and I am feeling so very happy," she said, caught through tears and laughter. "I am expecting a baby!"

"A what? A baby!" Charles was stunned for just a moment or two, and then he cried out, "My dearest Girl! Are you sure? What is it? When will it be here?" He rushed over to her and as she was lying on the bed he scooped her up in his arms, and crushed her to him. He laughed. She laughed.

"Do be careful with me. Put me down," she said, giggling and laughing. "I say, put me down, sir! I am a pregnant woman!"

"Sorry! Sorry! I forgot. I must be careful with you from now on."

"Don't be silly, I am only playing with you," said Mellissa, still laughing. "I am a healthy young woman. I am not at all fragile, at least, not yet. Are you pleased? Are you happy?"

"Oh! My Darling Girl. I am beyond happy. I am ecstatic!" He put her down carefully and he looked deeply in her eyes, while holding her close to his heart. "You have made me the happiest man in the world! I love you. I do so love you." Then looked at her again. "And when is this perfect being expected to make his arrival?"

"You have already decided that the baby will be a boy, have you?" She laughed as she hugged her own body and twirled, and twirled around the room until she was dizzy. "It is going to be my very own New Year's present to you!"

Chapter Forty-Three

More Problems with Rebecca

The next few weeks flew by in a whirl. Mellissa was completely healthy and well, with not even a sign of morning sickness. Her secret was being kept by both Charles and Lavinia, and she decided not to tell Akami until her body made it evident that she was with child. But every time she was with him, she longed to take him by the hand, and hold it to her stomach. She knew that she should want the baby to be her husband's, but secretly, impractically, she longed for it to be Akami's baby. She longed to be with Akami. It was an impossible longing, but she longed for it just the same.

Poppy was also blooming. Her conception had taken place one month before Mellissa's, and the change in her little body was there for everyone to see. Rebecca was taking great care of her and not allowing her to do any heavy work, or any work at all apart from feeding their beloved rabbits.

Akami had noticed that Poppy was expecting a baby, but he asked no questions. Soon, via the rumour machine that worked so well in all slave communities, everyone knew that Poppy was pregnant and questions were being asked about who the father-to-be was. The finger was even being pointed at young Michael, who strenuously denied that he had ever been near Poppy. But he, nevertheless, started going to see her daily at the rabbit enclosure, and the two of them could be found giggling and holding hands together. Mellissa thought that if it did not upset Rebecca, it might be a good idea to foster that relationship, so that when the child was born the baby could have a recognised 'father'.

Meanwhile Jack and Peter Frobisher, forewarned by Charles, said nothing. They were not at all concerned, having planted their seeds in many young girls on their father's plantation, fatherhood and responsibility meant nothing to either of them.

Rebecca brought Poppy down to the clinic for a routine check-up by Lavinia. Rebecca was fussing about her like a mother hen, and Lavinia could see that Poppy was beginning to tire of the constant prohibitions and was struggling to be free. Even without young Michael in the picture Lavinia could see trouble ahead.

"Rebecca," said Lavinia, "would you just stay here for a minute or so while I take Poppy into the surgical room to examine her."

"I want to hold Poppy hand. She got my baby inside," stated Rebecca with the full intention of coming into the surgical room too.

"No, Rebecca. I want to examine Poppy alone. In fact, I think that the Mistress should look at her, too. Will you go and tell her that I would like to see her here."

Rebecca went off unhappily, and as soon as she had gone Lavinia took Poppy into the surgical room. "I do not think that there is any problem with you and your baby," she said, after examining her. "Its little heart is beating strongly, and your tummy feels like everything is in the right place. But I want to ask you how you feel about Rebecca. When I saw you with her yesterday, I thought that you looked as though you wanted to get away. Is that right?"

"Becca, she good to me, she want my baby come soon, an' she say it her baby," said Poppy, "She not like me go see Michael. I like Michael. I want be with him."

"I thought that was the problem," said Lavinia. "Does Michael…"

Before Lavinia could ask more questions Rebecca had already returned with Mellissa. "Stay here Rebecca," said Mellissa, pointing to a chair in waiting area of the clinic, and she went through to the surgical room, shutting the door behind her.

"Good morning to you both," she said, "Lavinia, is there a problem with Poppy's pregnancy?

Lavinia shook her head and whispered, "I want to get her away from Rebecca for a while. I need to talk to you about her." Then she said quite loudly so that a listening Rebecca could hear through the door. "Mistress. Would you please check the baby's heartbeat, I wasn't quite sure that it sounded right when I examined Poppy?"

"Poppy, will you lift your skirt again so that I can listen to baby." Mellissa did an examination of Poppy's tummy and said in a low voice. "Yes, she is fine." Then in a loud voice that Rebecca could hear, she said, "I agree with you, something is not quite right. I think that she should remain here for a day or two so that we can keep an eye on her."

Mellissa left the room and went to Rebecca. "I am a little concerned about Poppy's baby, and I am going to keep her in the clinic for a few days. You can go back now, Rebecca."

Rebecca started to protest. "But, Mistress…"

"Rebecca, do not argue with me," said Mellissa. "Go. Now!"

As soon as she had gone, Lavinia joined Mellissa in the waiting area, leaving Poppy in the surgical room. Then she spoke quietly to Mellissa. "The problem is not with Poppy, it is with Rebecca. She is behaving like a watchdog. She hardly lets Poppy out of her sight, and I think that she believes Poppy's baby to be hers. She is preventing Poppy from doing what she wants or going where she wants, especially now that she has made a friend of Michael. I think that she might become dangerous again. She might even try to kill one or both of them. What shall we do?"

"The Master is at home today. I want you to lock the door and stay here with Poppy, while I run back and ask him what he thinks we should do."

When she reached High View, Mellissa went straight to the study where Charles was looking at the account books. "Charles," she said, panting hard, "Lavinia and I think that we have a problem. I need your advice and help."

At first, Charles made light of what she was saying. "That will make a first when you ask my advice," he said, laughing.

"Charles, I am serious," insisted Mellissa. "We do have a problem. It's Rebecca!"

"Not that woman again," sighed Charles. "What has she done this time?"

"It's not what she has done, it's what I think she may do." Mellissa told Charles about Rebecca's recent behaviour, her possessiveness with Poppy, her jealousy of Poppy's new attachment to Michael, and now her apparent appropriation of Poppy's baby, as her own. "Both Lavinia and I are convinced that she will attack and probably kill either Michael, or Poppy if she thinks that Poppy won't give up her baby."

"Where is Poppy right now?"

"She is safe, locked inside the clinic with Lavinia."

"And where is Rebecca?"

"I sent her back to her rabbits."

"The first thing we must do is to get Michael out of harm's way," said Charles, completely serious now. "Do you know where he is working to day?"

"Yes. I saw him with Angeline and one of the boys, I couldn't see which one, when I was on my way here just a few minutes ago. They were working on the far side of the rose garden."

Charles got up from his desk. "Let's go there straight away, and hope that Rebecca has not had the urge to strike right now because Poppy has been kept away from her."

They both ran down the steps from the veranda towards the rose garden. And they saw at once that they were too late. Rebecca was already approaching from the other direction. Mellissa could see the sun glinting on a knife that she was carrying in her right hand. Charles called out, quite calmly in order not to panic Michael and the children. "Michael, come here. I need you now, and bring the children with you."

Michael looked up. He was puzzled, the Master never usually spoke to him other than to say how nice the gardens were, or how well the horses looked. "Yes, Master," he said, and began to round up Angeline and her brother Jonah.

"Right now, Michael. Hurry!" called Mellissa.

He was almost too late. Rebecca's arm was up and she just missed Michael's left shoulder by a whisker as she slashed downward, aiming for his back, as he ran towards the Master. Charles was also running towards them to try to stop Rebecca repeating the action. He caught up with her, and wrestled a large kitchen knife out of her hand, but not before she had swung the knife down onto his arm and sliced it to the bone. Charles felt pain but he did not realise how deep the cut was. He turned and caught her arms as Michael joined him, and between the two of them they managed to subdue the now frenzied Rebecca. Mellissa joined the struggling threesome and together they were able to get Rebecca down on the ground and tie her hands behind her back with Mellissa's silk scarf.

It was only then that Mellissa saw the blood running down her husband's arm. "Darling! You are injured. She cut you!" she cried. "We must get you to the clinic at once."

While Michael alone was holding down the still struggling Rebecca, Mellissa tore off the sleeve of Charles's shirt and tied it tightly around the wound. Akami had heard the rumpus from the schoolroom, and he came running, after telling all the children to stay inside. He saw at once that Michael was not strong enough to hold down the frenzied Rebecca, and he gathered her up and caught her to his chest in his strong arms.

"What shall I do with her, Mistress?" he called to Mellissa.

"I must get the Master to the clinic straight away, Akami," she said. "Can you and Michael manage to take Rebecca to the school storeroom, and lock her in while I look after the Master? I'll be back as soon as I can."

"Yes, Mistress. We will do that. Do you need any help to get the Master to the clinic?" he asked Mellissa. The urgency of the occasion took away, for the moment, the frisson of love that was usually so strong between them.

"No." said Charles. "I will be fine."

"And Lavinia is there already. She will help us," smiled a grateful Mellissa.

Charles was leaning heavily on Mellissa and somehow he managed to walk to the clinic without fainting away. "Open the door, Lavinia. Be quick, I have the Master here and he is injured." Lavinia unlocked the door and helped Mellissa get Charles inside. Poppy just stood there, open mouthed.

By the time they got him on the bed in the surgical room Charles had almost passed out. His wound was deep and he had lost a lot of blood. Mellissa quickly removed the ripped-off sleeve and after assuring herself that the cut was clean, she deftly stitched and bound up the wound.

Poppy made Charles a hot cup of tea, and Lavinia laced it with a little rum. "Here, Master. Drink this," she said, "it will help to revive you."

Charles sat up and Mellissa made him support his damaged arm in a sling. Looking around and still a little dazed at what had happened, he took the cup and started to drink. "Well, Old Girl," he said. "I have always admired your work from afar, and now you have had to treat me, my admiration is even stronger."

She came to him and kissed him. He was a patient no longer, just her loving husband.

"I am so glad that I am able to treat you, my darling," she said. Taking the hand of his undamaged left arm, she led him to one of the patient's beds and encouraged him to lie down. She didn't want Poppy to be involved in the discussions about what to do with Rebecca, so she called Poppy to her side. "You can go back now to the rabbits. Rebecca will not be there to trouble you again today, and I will come and see you later."

Then, sitting on the bed next to Charles she said, "Now we will have to decide what to do with Rebecca. We cannot keep her permanently locked up, and we cannot free her. Whatever shall we do?"

"I really do not know," said a tired Charles. "At home, we would probably take her to a lunatic asylum, but I don't know if they have one here. Do they Lavinia?"

Lavinia shook her head. "I do not know of one in St Elizabeth, Master," she said. "Perhaps there is one in Kingston."

"I hate to say it," said Mellissa reluctantly, "but we may have to ask Jack Frobisher for help in this matter. Shall I leave that to you?"

Charles was just about to agree when she changed her mind. "No!" she said. Once more the medic in her was taking charge of the situation. "You are not strong enough to do that. You certainly could not walk down to the compound. Lavinia, would you please go and find Jack Frobisher and tell him that the Master wants to talk to him in the clinic."

Lavinia found George, the assistant overseer, in the slave compound and she was able to convince him that Jack Frobisher was needed by the Master, and that it could not wait until the end of the work day. He set off on his horse to pass on the message, but it was still nearly an hour before the hot and sweaty overseer reached the clinic. Her features curling in disgust, Mellissa reluctantly let him in.

"Whoa! What has happened to you, Master?" was the first thing he said when he saw Charles lying on the bed.

"My arm has been slashed with a knife, but my clever wife has attended me well, and I shall recover quickly. Now. Here is the problem," said Charles, and he told Jack the whole story.

Jack sat down and listened, then whistled through his teeth. "All I can say is that it is a pity we didn't hang the nigger bitch when we first came here!" he said.

"That's not very helpful," said Charles. "We need to decide what to do now. Do you know if there is a lunatic asylum in Kingston? I know that there isn't any sort of place like that in St Elizabeth, except a lock up prison."

Jack had a think. "I believe that the hospital in Kingston, in North or West Street, has a separate building where they keep mad bitches like yours, but I have also heard that the place is little better than a stable. The 'patients', if that is what you want to call them, are treated like animals. They live in cages and sleep on the floor which is covered with filthy straw that is hardly ever changed. The inmates would probably be better off in a prison, and that is bad enough!"

"Thank you, Jack," said Charles. "You can go back to work now. I will talk it over with my wife, and then we will decide what to do with Rebecca. If we do decide to take her to Kingston, I may ask you and George to drive her there."

After Jack Frobisher had left, Mellissa said, "Even in her deranged state I would hate to trust Rebecca's welfare in his hands. My thinking at the moment is that we should take her to the Magistrate in St Elizabeth and make him deal with her, as he should have done before. But right now I want you to rest here for the remainder of the afternoon. I will go, with Akami and Lavinia, to see to Rebecca. I want to make sure that she has calmed down, that she is restrained properly, and that she has food and water."

Charles was sleepy and cold now as a reaction to all that had happened, and Mellissa covered him with a warm blanket. "All right, Old Girl," he said as he settled down on his bed. "Come back soon and…" And he was asleep.

Leaving her husband in the care of Rosie who had been working at High View that day, and had been sent down to the clinic by Lavinia, Mellissa hurried to the school store room. Akami was standing outside and Lavinia was just approaching with some freshly made bread and a jug of watered rum.

"Is she quiet now?" Mellissa asked.

"Yes," said Lavinia. "I went in with her when we brought her up here. I don't think that she has realised that she has hurt the Master. She just sat down on a chair saying over and over again, "where my Poppy? Where my baby? Where my Poppy?"

Before opening the door, Mellissa wanted to see what Rebecca was doing, and why she was so quiet, so she climbed up onto the bench outside and looked in through a widow which was set high in the wall, and was just big enough to let a little light into the storeroom. She screamed. And screamed again. "Lavinia, she's hanged herself!"

Akami opened the locked door and they all rushed in. Rebecca was indeed hanging by a cord from the roof beam. "Cut her down! Quickly!" cried Mellissa. "We may be able to revive her."

But they were too late. The troubled Rebecca was dead. She had found a cord, thrown and tied it over the roof beam, tied a noose around her neck, climbed onto the chair and kicked it away.

Chapter Forty-Four

26 July, 1831

Anniversary

"Two years to the day since we arrived in Jamaica!" said Mellissa. "What shall we do to celebrate?"

"It's not as if we can have a party here. There is no one we can invite to celebrate with us. I wasn't even able to do something special for you on our wedding anniversary last month. And really there's nothing I want to celebrate except that we are having a baby. And I want to celebrate that every day!"

"Everyone will know soon. It's beginning to show now. And…" Mellissa stopped mid-sentence, and an unsure, little smile began to spread across her face.

"What's the matter? What's happening?" cried an alarmed Charles.

"I have just felt it. The baby. I've just felt it move," said Mellissa, in hesitant wonder. "It was only the tiniest of movements, just like having a butterfly trapped inside me."

"Darling! How wonderful!" breathed Charles, now also caught up in the wonder of the moment. "Could I feel it too, if I were to put my hand on the right spot?"

"No! No! It's too soon to feel it from the outside. The flutter I felt has gone already. But as the baby grows big enough we will both be able to feel it from the outside," said Mellissa. Then she added coyly, "especially at night when we are lying together with no clothes to get in our way."

"My beautiful darling. I just cannot wait!"

"Our own baby to come has set me thinking of the babies that I have delivered in these last two years, there have been nine of them, did you know?"

"No. What are your thoughts? I think that I know, but tell me anyway."

"I want to think that the children that I have delivered into this world are free, and not slaves. And the five boys that I managed to buy back for their mother's. They will still be small children by the time we leave Jamaica, so it will make little difference to us. Will you agree with me, this time without a fight?"

"How can I refuse you anything, my dear girl, when you are giving everything I ever wanted?"

"You are too good to me!"

Mellissa was now living in that dream bubble that so often takes over the life of a pregnant woman, especially when it is her first child. She saw Akami quite regularly in the course of their everyday work, and each time she felt her heart begin to beat rapidly. She had lost none of her love and yearning for him, but she knew that it was a hopeless situation. And she had almost convinced herself that her baby's father was Charles.

It was just a few weeks after the second anniversary of her arrival in Jamaica, two years since Mellissa had first laid her eyes on Akami, and had felt that strong pull of attraction to him, that she somehow found herself alone with him once again, this time in the schoolroom. Usually there was at least one of the children or Lavinia there at the end of the afternoon lessons. Even Melanie, who seemed to spend every waking hour doing her drawings and paintings, was not there that day.

"Oh! Akami," she stumbled, fully aware of her thumping heart, and her words were coming out all at once. "I thought that Lavinia was here. I wanted you both to check up on the schoolroom stores, because I am going to St Elizabeth tomorrow. We are going to see our attorney. I want him to draw up manumission papers for all the children that I have delivered since we came here, and the five boys who we rescued between us. I want the boys and my babies to grow up to be free men and women." She was aware that she was gabbling, and that she was blushing deeply too.

"Mistress. Mistress, you must slow down," he said. "There is no need for you to be afraid of me. As always, you have such a very kind heart. Their mothers, and Mistress Lucy, will be so happy."

"Afraid of you? That is just it," replied Mellissa, as she walked towards him. "I am afraid. I am afraid of what I might do every time I see you, or even hear your voice. I am afraid because all I want to do is throw myself into your arms and kiss you."

273

"Mistress!" was all he said as he did exactly that. They kissed deeply and felt each-others body quiver in heightened expectation. Then Akami stepped backwards and gave Mellissa a questioning look. "Mistress," he said again. "I can feel that your body has changed. Is it possible that you are going to have a child?"

"Oh! Akami," she gasped, "I was hoping to keep it from you for a little longer. Until I could no longer hide it from you."

Akami was saddened. "The Master must be delighted," he said in a low, beaten voice.

"Yes he is, Akami. He is delighted that I am having a baby. And so am I, except for one thing."

"What is it, dear Mistress?"

"Akami," she said, stepping forward and holding him close to her once more. "Akami. I don't know whether the child is his or yours!"

"But, Mistress, we only…"

"I know, Akami. But it only takes one time to conceive. And I knew that I was with child only three weeks after you and I…"

"It cannot be, Mistress," Akami was now fully aware of the possibility that Mellissa might have a mulatto baby, his baby, growing inside her.

She kissed him once again, and they melted into each other's arms. "I know that I sound very silly and very frivolous, but I do love my husband, Akami, but I also love and want you too. How can I truly love two men at the same time? But I do! It is all too impossible." And she started to cry.

Akami was too stunned to say anything, he just put his arms around her and held her close. After a while Mellissa calmed down, and she was able to explain to Akami, Lavinia's solution to the problem. Akami had a little think and then he nodded his head. "I am sorry to say it, but I think that is the only way we will be able to solve this problem. I think that I, too, will make sure that I shall be nearby when you have the baby. I shall also look to see if any of the other women are having babies, and if one of them would be the right one to foster our baby. That is if it is our baby!"

"There is Poppy," said a cautious Mellissa. "That is, if she remains healthy and brings her baby to full term. She is only one month ahead of me. We can tell her that another of the slaves in the compound was raped by the overseers, and that she does not want to keep the baby. If she has a safe delivery, she could easily feed two babies."

"And what if the baby is the Master's?"

"Then we will tell her that the woman changed her mind after the child was born."

It was mid-November, and quite late in the afternoon, when Poppy went into labour. In spite of her tiny size, she had managed to remain healthy and all was normal. With Michael at her side, she made her way to the clinic where a very pregnant Mellissa and Lavinia were waiting. All the while she was struggling to deliver her baby, Mellissa was reminding her and reassuring her that her baby would be born free, as were now all the other babies that Mellissa had delivered. Mellissa was also aware that Poppy's baby might possibly be Charles's baby, and as soon as the baby was born, Mellissa looked at him hard. He was fine looking new-born, with light chocolate coloured skin, long limbs and a very long, very thin face. To her relief she was quite certain that that the child was a Frobisher.

In spite of his conception, it was quite clear that Poppy had all the natural instincts of a mother. She held him close and kissed his little wrinkled forehead. "Look," she said to Michael, who had come in the delivery room as soon as the baby was born. "Isn't he beautiful? What we call him?"

"I think Pompey fit. I hear that name someplace. What you think?"

"I think it grand. Most Poppy and a bit Michael? Pompey. Pompey. Is good. He be Pompey."

Mellissa left Lavinia to continue with the care for Poppy and as she walked back to High View, she was wondering how her own labour, soon to come, would be. She was also terrified of the result. A little bit of her wanted the child to be Akami's, but she knew that life would be so much easier for her if the baby was white, undoubtedly Charles's baby.

She met Charles, who was walking down to the clinic to meet her. "Well?" he asked. "Did all go well? Were you able to tell who the father might be?"

"Oh Charles," she sighed, "you can breathe easily. I definitely think that he, it is a boy by the way, is a Frobisher. He has exceptionally long limbs and a very long, thin face. Just like them. Poppy is delighted to be a mother, and Michael has already stepped in as a father. They have called him Pompey, would you believe?" And they both laughed.

"I will tell the Frobisher brothers, but I doubt that they will be interested," said Charles.

"That's just as well," said Mellissa. "It would only unsettle Poppy if they were to take an interest in the baby."

It was two weeks later when Mellissa was next able to have a conversation with Akami. It was outside the schoolroom where some of the children were running about, so they were unable to share any intimate moments. He was pleased to see that in spite of her size, she looked fit and well. "Good afternoon, Akami," she said, managing to keep her voice quite normal.

"Good afternoon, Mistress," he replied. "Are you keeping well, and when will you be having that baby?" he asked.

"Oh! It will be at least three weeks from now. It could even be a month."

He looked at her and gave her his secret smile, and said quietly, "I want everything to go well for you, Mistress, better for everyone if it is the Master's child." And in a louder voice that anyone nearby could overhear, he said, "I heard something interesting from Moses when I saw him last Sunday. Sam Sharpe of Montego Bay is convinced that England is about to free all the slaves in their territories very soon, and he is suggesting that the slaves in Montego Bay should strike after Christmas, just at the busiest time for harvesting, so a strike could be really costly for the plantation owners."

"Why would he do that? What purpose would it achieve, other than make the plantation owners angry?" asked a puzzled Mellissa.

"He thinks that if the slaves started asking to be paid for their work, the Masters would be forced to give in because of the need to harvest the cane."

"But how would paying them help?"

"He thinks that the Masters need to accept the freedom of their slaves, and start to pay them for their labour."

"Well, you know how much I would like to see all slaves given their freedom, but I'm not sure that is the right way to go about it. I think that Sam Sharpe is talking dangerous talk, and I also think that you had better have no connection at all with either him or Moses. I don't want any state troopers coming here and asking questions of anyone who knows either of them."

"But that Moses, he is a good friend. I am sure that he would never encourage any of the slaves living in our St Elizabeth parish to do anything that would provoke the Masters."

"Yes," said Mellissa. "I feel sure that freedom is coming soon to all the slaves in Jamaica and other English territories. But it has to be best for them to wait patiently for just a bit longer. And I

276

repeat; I think that it would be better if you stay here at Silver Bay for the present and stay well away from Moses or anyone who is tempted to follow Sam Sharpe's lead."

Chapter Forty-Five

New Year's Eve 1831

The expected freedom announcement in the English newspapers reaching Jamaica did not happen, and Sam Sharpe's strike, which had been set for Boxing Day, turned into a full scale revolt. At first, it was contained in the Montego Bay area, but it spread like lightning, and within a few days, there were pockets of revolution over the whole island, terrifying all white people, and especially plantation owners.

By New Year's Eve, it had reached the parish of St Elizabeth. So far, Silver Bay was quiet. The slaves all loved the Mistress and, for her sake, they tolerated the Master. Because the nursing, caring Mistress with her kind heart, had found and returned as many of the stolen children that she could find, and freed them all, as well as all the babies that had been born on Silver Bay since she had arrived, she was almost revered by the slaves.

But things did not remain the same. On 29th December Peter Frobisher was attacked and killed, with wild sweeps of many cutlasses, by a group of slaves from the neighbouring Chamberlain plantation, but they were led by a Silver Bay slave called Lucas. He had no sick wife or child at school to make him feel grateful for the care that the Mistress gave her slaves, and he hated the Frobisher brothers, who had made him feel the sting of their lashes almost daily, for what they called stubborn defiance.

Immediately Charles and Jack Frobisher joined the white militia in order to catch and kill Lucas, and to help to quash the local uprising. Although Mellissa was about to give birth any day, Charles felt that with Lavinia at hand and Silver Bay quiet, and the traitorous killer slave was on the run, it was his duty to help find Lucas and put down any other troublemakers in the local community before they too became killers.

Mellissa was therefore on her own and unprotected when a large gang of men and women, chanting and banging loudly on drums, came from the Chamberlain plantation to set fire to Silver Bay. They started with the sugarcane crop which was being stored, ready for crushing, and with cutlasses, they hacked to death three of the Silver Bay slaves who tried to protect the store house. Then, satisfied with their wicked handiwork, they moved on to crushing the house.

It was sunset, and Mellissa could smell the burning before the dense black clouds of smoke reached High View. "Lavinia, Chloe," she called. "We are not safe here. Lavinia, get everyone out of the house, and collect your children, collect all the children. Chloe, you make sure that Poppy, Michael and the baby leave their cabin, and that he leads everyone down to the slave compound. They will not attack the compound."

"But, Mistress," cried a very confused Lavinia, "I must stay with you."

"No, Lavinia. You look after your family first. I will have Akami to protect me, and I will meet you in the clinic when everyone who lives around High View is safe."

After everyone had gone, Mellissa called for Sheba, who was afraid but ran to her side. She left the house to find Akami just as the mob were nearing High View. Akami was nowhere to be seen, so she started on her way down the track to the clinic when Sheba, who became terrified, darted back towards her favourite hiding place: the log store. "No, Sheba," called Mellissa. "No! Come this way." But Sheba was beyond hearing and understanding.

Mellissa ran back, but found that she was too late. The chanting, drumming mob had reached their goal. Still looking out for Akami and Sheba, Mellissa hid behind the tallest and fattest oak tree that topped the avenue leading to the terrace. She, who had remained calm until then, was suddenly caught up in the terror. She stayed hidden behind the oak tree and watched in horror. The mob was being led by Lucas, the very man that Charles was hunting and had abandoned her to catch! And next to him was a man Mellissa recognised from the Chamberlain plantation. He was Jonathan, the man whose child Mellissa had saved soon after she had arrived at Silver Bay. For a moment or two, Mellissa suppressed her terror in surprise and wonderment that a man, who had expressed his profound gratitude and love for her, could betray her like this? In her terror she could still ask why?

"Sheba! Sheba! Akami!" Mellissa was calling softly. But by then the mob had surrounded her home and had begun, one after the other, to throw firebrands into it. It only took a moment or two for the fire to catch and take hold. Mellissa was about to turn and run when at last Sheba left her hiding place and started to run towards her. But before she could reach Mellissa, one of the men grabbed hold of her. Mellissa held her breath and prayed for him to let her dog go, but no. He took his knife and with a great, savage cry, he cut her throat. She died quickly with a soft bark which just reached Mellissa's ears above the chanting of the murderous mob. Mellissa nearly screamed out loud as first he, and then all the others, the women included, dipped their hands in Sheba's blood and smeared it all over their faces and torsos. Looking like painted savages, they shouted, ululated and danced in triumph around the flaming building.

All of a sudden, with a rumble and a sort of popping noise the roof crashed inwards. Sparks and flames flew high into the darkening sky and the top of Mellissa's oak tree started to burn too. Too terrified to run, Mellissa crawled backwards into the hibiscus bushes which formed the edge of the garden, and it was there at last where Akami found her.

"Akami! Akami, my love," she cried as he gathered her up into his strong arms. "You have come to save me. Where were you? Why did you leave me alone to face this mob?"

"They caught hold of me too, as I was running to find you. But I managed to get away from them," he said as he was carrying her as quickly as he could down to the clinic.

She was sobbing onto his shoulder, "They killed my dog, Akami. My lovely dog Sheba," she howled and then continued, "they smeared her blood all over their bodies. How could they do it, Akami? A lovely, innocent dog who never hurt anyone?" She was still sobbing when they reached the clinic, only to find that that had been destroyed too.

Lavinia was waiting outside. "What shall we do?" asked Akami. "Where is it safe to take the Mistress?"

"I think that the safest place for her is in the slave compound. We can hide her in one of the slave cabins." To Mellissa, who had stopped wailing, but was gently sobbing, she asked, "Can you walk now, Mistress?"

"Yes, I am all right now. You can put me down now Akami. Thank you both for saving and protecting me," she said quite simply. But as she spoke her water broke. "Oh dear! Lavinia," she said, "my baby is coming. It's not due yet, but all this must have made it come early."

Akami picked her up again and the three of them made their way down to the compound and found Rosie's cabin. Rosie was inside and her children were hiding under her big bed. "It de Mistress! She hide here."

"Yes," said Lavinia, "but she is also about to have her baby.

"She have baby here. I help," insisted Rosie.

Mellissa and Lavinia were in no state to argue, Rosie sent the children off to stay with Liza's family, and four hours later the babe was born. And there was no doubt that he was Akami's son. Rosie gasped in surprise and she was sworn to secrecy. A secret that she kept until she was an old woman and the secret no longer had any importance.

Mellissa and Akami held their baby, kissing him and passing him from one to another. They named him Akami, for his father, and did not dwell on his immediate future. Akami was delighted in the little creature that was his son. He inspected every one of his little fingers and toes and swore that even accounting for his light coloured skin, baby Akami looked just like his mother Yemojo.

"Oh! Akami. He is so beautiful I cannot bear to give him up," cried the new mother.

"My dearest Mistress," he replied. "You must not worry. When this is all over, you will be able to see him every day. Poppy believes that she will be looking after the baby of another of the overseer's victim, and she will be proud and happy for you to take such an interest in him. Maybe the Master might even let you adopt him when everything has returned to normal."

Remembering the story that she was going to tell her husband Mellissa called Lavinia. First she could not resist the pride that all new mothers have. "Lavinia," she said. "Isn't he just beautiful? Have you ever seen such a beautiful baby?"

Lavinia indulged her. "Yes Mistress, truly, he is the best and most beautiful baby I have ever delivered!" she said with tongue-in-cheek laughter. "Now that we have safely delivered the afterbirth, you must sleep."

"I cannot while there is so much to be done."

Lavinia held her hand and asked gently, "What is it you would like me to do?"

"Oh yes," said Mellissa, becoming serious again. "Will you go and find Michael and ask him, if the mob have gone and it is safe out there, to find my darling Sheba and dig a grave and bury her in the rose garden, if that still exists. I will be telling the Master that our baby died at birth, and she is buried in that same place. I shall be able to visit Sheba's grave and cry for the loss of both her and my baby, because he, too, will also be lost to me."

It was not long before Lavinia came back with serious and dangerous news. "I met a man, a stranger to Silver Bay, and he said that the militia are now hunting down anyone who has had connections with Moses or Sam Sharpe of Montego Bay. That is both Akami and me, Mistress. What shall we do?"

"Lavinia, you should not worry. You have had no direct connection with Sam Sharpe, and only religious connections with Moses. Both the Master and I will be able to protect you." Turning to Akami she said with renewed tears in her eyes, "You know that you will be my one love forever, but right now I want you to leave Silver Bay and go and find your friends in the Cockpit Country where I know that you will be safe. They have killed the horses in the stables, but there must be one of the working horses in this compound. And you must take with you your freedom papers and no one should question you. You may still be able to return when…"

"No! Mistress. No!" cried Akami. "I cannot leave you in such a state. Not when you have just given birth to our baby. I will stay here with Lavinia and her family. I will keep my head down, and I will be safe."

"Akami! You won't be safe! Remember Peter Frobisher was killed by Sharpe's rioters and his brother will be seeking revenge."

"But I did not kill him, Mistress. I will be safe and at your side where I belong to save you and protect our baby."

"Akami. You are my slave, and I order you to leave. You must leave without delay."

"Mistress. Mistress," said Akami gently. "Did you not give me papers that say I am a free man? Well, this is my first choice as a free man. I will not leave you."

"Oh! Akami," was all she could say, and in spite of Lavinia's presence, she flung herself into his arms once more. They held their baby close and cried together.

Chapter Forty-Six

Revenge and Retribution

It was all over by January 5th, 1832. It was early morning two days after High View had burned down, and Mellissa's baby had been born, when Charles with Jack Frobisher finally returned to Silver Bay to find his home and all the cabins, workshops, pigsties, and stables all of which had supported the plantation house, all blackened ruins. Charles was shocked and then he panicked. He did not care about High View, that could always be rebuilt. But where was Mellissa? What had happened? Had his baby been born? He howled and suffered guilty regret that he had not stayed behind to protect her. Instead, he had been happy to prove himself a man by chasing all over St Elizabeth parish capturing, punishing escaped slaves, and hanging the guilty ones.

He searched for Mellissa at the schoolroom, and the clinic, and found them both burnt down. Eventually he found her in the slave compound, in Rosie's cabin, still crying for the loss of her baby, who, for safety's sake, she had not seen again since he was born and passed on safely into Poppy's care. "Oh! My darling," he said, taking her in his arms. "I am so sorry that I left you, especially at this special time. Tell me what happened, and where is the baby?"

Mellissa's voice was flat, devoid of emotion. "You deserted me, Charles. Deserted me in my time of most need. It was Akami who saved me from the mob and the flames and it was Lavinia who delivered our baby. She was born early and she was born dead! She is buried in the rose garden. I cannot feel it in my heart to forgive you for your betrayal. If you had been here to protect me, I wouldn't have been so terrified and maybe the baby would have born at the right time and would have lived. The mob also killed my darling Sheba. They danced around the house daubed in her blood. They burned the horses to death in their stables. I can still hear them

283

screaming now. They burned down the pigsties and I can still hear the pigs squealing too. That's what happened while you were away." She did blame him, but she was also very conscious of her lies about the baby, and she felt ashamed of herself.

Fat tears began to fall from his eyes and he clung on to Mellissa in a passionate and agonising storm of despair, sorrow and self-blame. "Tell me more about the baby. Did you say that it was a girl? "What did she look like?" Was there a sound of slight relief in his voice? Only a girl. Not as important as a boy!

Mellissa's voice was still flat. "She was just a tiny new-born baby, like every other new-born baby. She was small, red, wrinkled – and dead! I only held her for a moment and then someone took her away, and she was buried straight away." Then she was sobbing once more and clinging onto Charles in genuine grief at the loss of her child, who she had not seen since the day of his birth. Charles was suffering too from the loss of his child, but all the while, his own grief and guilt was jealously turning to anger and blame towards the very ones who had been there in his place, protecting his wife.

Charles stood up abruptly. "So!" he said in a completely different mood and tone. "So? Where are they, Lavinia and your precious Akami? Do I need to thank them or turn them in as traitors?"

Mellissa roused herself out of her lethargy and sprung to their defence like a lioness protecting her cubs. "Traitors? What do you mean by traitors? I have never in my life had more loyal servants," she cried. She was beginning to be afraid for them both. She knew that Charles could be vengeful, and she recognised that he was starting to change his guilt into blame for the others. "The Silver Bay traitor was Lucas, who you were supposed to be catching. He was the leader of the mob of slaves from the Thomas Chamberlain plantation that attacked us. I saw him with my own eyes when I was hiding, terrified, behind the oak tree next to our home. Did you manage to catch him?"

Charles was mollified. "We not only caught him, we hanged him from a tree in St Elizabeth."

"Good. He and his horrible mob killed my Sheba. If I could have cut his throat like they did to Sheba, I would have done it myself!"

Just then, Jack Frobisher knocked on Rosie's cabin door. "Master Harrison," he said, "I think that you and Mistress Harrison should move into our, I mean my, cabin until you know what you want to do next. I will move into one of the empty ones."

"Thank you, Jack. The Mistress and I have not talked yet of what we want to do next, but we will probably move into St Elizabeth until we can decide on our future…"

"No! Charles," Mellissa interrupted, she could not bear to think of being so far apart from Poppy and her baby son, so she had to think quickly of reasons not to move away from Silver Bay. "I need to stay here to reorganise the rebuilding of the clinic and the school, and the housing of Lavinia and Poppy's families, and all the other house servants…"

"They are not servants!" cried Charles, interrupting in his turn, and once more turning to anger against his wife. "They are slaves. Slaves! When will you get your head around the fact that we live on a plantation in Jamaica and our workers are slaves? We do not live on some kind of gentleman's country estate worked on by farmers, estate managers and house servants."

Jack Frobisher was standing by listening to the near quarrel between his employers, and he tried to press home his advantage to get the Master on his side and do his bidding. He was still throbbing with anger himself over the murder of his brother and he was seeking to take more revenge against Silver Bay slaves. Not knowing that Akami belonged to Mellissa, and had been freed by her, he said, "Master Harrison, I think that after Lucas, the next biggest troublemaker here on Silver Bay is that fancy African nigger who calls himself Akami. I have heard that he has even met up with that Sam Sharpe who started all this rumpus. Don't you think that we should take him into St Elizabeth for questioning?"

Before Charles could say anything, Mellissa shouted out, "No! No, not Akami! He has done nothing but try to save and protect everything and everyone on Silver Bay."

Her face gave her away. Blood had drained away leaving it as white as a sheet. And then Charles knew for sure what he had suspected for quite a while. Somehow, against all nature and natural feelings, Mellissa, a white woman and a Mistress had formed some sort of attachment to her big black nigger slave. He did not shout in anger but said very quietly and forcefully, "Yes, Jack. That's exactly what we will do. But we won't take him to St Elizabeth, we will question him ourselves. Here." He looked directly at Mellissa waiting for her to challenge him.

"You can ask Akami any question you like. I know that he has never been involved in any rioting or stirring up of resentment of any of our slaves against their enslavement," she said calmly, but with her stomach churning in fear. "But just remember that he is now a free man, and he is no longer answerable to you or any other man. But I am sure that he will talk to you because he is an honourable man, and he will want those involved in the burning of Silver Bay and the killing of the three slaves who were trying to defend our land, to be caught and punished." Mellissa was trying not to betray her emotions any more than she had done already. She hoped and believed that Charles would do no more than simply ask him what he knew about the uprising, and she knew that Akami was totally innocent of any plotting or any involvement at all.

Unfortunately, she did not realise that this cold talking Charles had become like a serpent about to strike. "Yes, Jack. You go and take some reliable slaves to get hold of him and bring him here. We will question him together."

After Jack had left, Mellissa spoke to Charles, trying not to show her mounting fear. "Charles," she said, calmly and sweetly. "You really don't need the two of you to ask Akami questions. He will be quite willing to tell you anything that he knows. Which will only be knowledge of what happened here after the rioters arrived and started with the burning of our sugar cane."

Charles turned on Mellissa. "Just you be quiet, woman," he said with a snarl. "If anyone has been a traitor around here, I believe it to be you! Now you will see what I can do with my 'questioning' of your pet nigger."

Mellissa started to cry. "Please Charles, Akami is innocent."

"Innocent? But you love him?" Charles was only just realising the depth of his wife's feeling for her former slave.

Mellissa was now terrified for Akami. She needed to deny her love in order to save him. "No! Charles. I love you. You know that. I have loved you from the day that we met. I am very fond of Akami, but I am not in love with him. That would be ridiculous. I love you!"

"Well! We will see how much you love me after I have finished with the questioning."

They sat in silence, with Mellissa suffering agonies of fear which she dared not show. How had he guessed her feelings for Akami? She would continue to deny her love, more to protect him than herself. What would Charles do to him? Surely he would not whip him? She didn't dare say anything more in his defence, in case it made Charles even more vengeful.

It was a full half-hour before Jack Frobisher returned. "Here he is, Master. Plain as you like out there playing football with the children. Looks as though he would never hurt a fly. But we know better, don't we nigger?" he said, as he gave Akami a vicious punch in the stomach.

Akami was unprepared for the blow and he doubled up in pain. Mellissa was terrified. She knew now that Charles was not going to question him gently, and she tried to divert his cold, unjustified anger. "Charles," she said, without showing any of her fear, "I don't think that beating Akami will help you find out anything. Why don't we all try to discover what really has happened here, and why our slave Lucas turned against us? It was he and not Akami who led the mob from the Chamberlain plantation to kill and burn."

Charles ignored her, and Akami could feel her inner terror. He wanted to send a signal to her to tell her not to worry about him, but he couldn't.

Jack Frobisher pushed Akami towards Charles. "What do want me to do with him, Master?" he asked as he turned his sneering face towards Mellissa. He has guessed that the problem was nothing to do with the burning of Silver Bay, but the jealousy of his employer of his wife's feelings towards her slave.

"Well," replied Charles, with vindictive, cold intent in his voice, "with that hand missing, we cannot tie him up by the wrists to the A-frame, so I think that the 'cage' would be appropriate."

Mellissa had to interject. "Charles! That is cruel. You cannot put such a large man in that cage!"

"Don't you tell me what I can or cannot do, woman," Charles all but shouted at her. "Frobisher, you get that cage dragged down from the top to the compound. Now!"

The cage was about the only thing that survived the burning down of the punishment barn. Charles knew that he was being wicked and cruel, but his jealousy was sweeping him onwards. He forced Mellissa to watch as the cage was placed under the A-frame and chained to it so that it swung nearly three foot from the ground. Then, at knifepoint, Akami was forced to climb into the cage. It was not high enough for him to stand and not long enough or wide enough for him to lie down, so the only way he could position himself was to crouch. In that position even after only a few minutes all his muscles in his legs and back were screaming out to be released.

"Now," said Charles, "would you please be so kind Master 'freemen' Akami, to tell me what instructions you have received from that rebellious fiend, Sam Sharpe?"

"No instructions, Master Harrison," said Akami, loudly and strongly, defying the pains of his caged joints and muscles. "I have not heard anything from Minister Sam Sharpe since I last saw him well over a year ago. That was when we, Moses and I, brought the three boys back from Montego Bay." He tried his best not to be afraid, but seeing Mellissa being forced to watch made him afraid for her. He did not want to break down because he knew that it would be too much for Mellissa to bear, and if she were to start to cry, then the Master would know immediately that she had strong feelings for him. He did not know that Charles had already guessed, that his wife had more than a deep friendship with her slave, but fortunately, as yet, her husband could not even imagine that her child could have had any other father than himself.

Charles was not satisfied with Akami's reply. "Well, I think that you have been in league with him all this while, and I will instruct the authorities in St Elizabeth to bring in that other so-called minister, Moses, and question him too. I think that we will let you think about Sam Sharpe and your association with him, and I will ask you more about him later this afternoon. You will not be released from that cage or be given anything to eat or drink until I am satisfied that you have no more to tell me."

And leaving Akami caged in a cramped metal box which dangled in the sun during the hottest part of the day, Charles dragged his wife back to the cabin which he had decided to accept after all from Jack Frobisher.

It was four hours later when Charles and Jack returned to the cage, Akami had all but fainted from the heat and lack of water. Mellissa had been not forced to return for the questioning of Akami. She just heard the screams! The metal cage was now too hot for Charles to touch, and he could see that wherever Akami's flesh touched the burning metal it was beginning to blister. His eyes had rolled back into his head and his tongue was swollen and hanging out of his mouth. Jack Frobisher threw a bucket of cold water over Akami which should have revived him, but the contrast between the heat and cold was shocking and he shouted out in agony. His body was also so cramped that he could not feel his legs and feet, but when he moved each tiniest movement caused an agonising cramp and pain.

Charles spoke first. "So how is our own home-grown traitor now after a little cooking in the pleasant Jamaican sunshine? Do you have anything new to tell me now, Nigger?"

Akami could hardly move his mouth or tongue and he gurgled a reply while shaking his head.

Jack Frobisher now took his turn in questioning. "I think that our lover-boy…"

Charles was startled at the use of the word 'lover-boy'. "What do you mean?" he asked Jack, looking him directly in the eyes.

"Oh! I just heard that one of the black bitches around here has had one of his babies," he said casually.

"Which one? Who?" asked Charles, almost giving way to his suspicions about Mellissa. *Surely it could not be. No! She might be more than normally interested in her slave, but surely he knew her well enough not to suspect that. No! Never! That would be indecent for a white woman. No! Mellissa might be strong minded for a woman, but above anything, she was a decent woman.*

"Oh! I don't know," drawled Frobisher. "I just heard something on the jungle drums. It don't mean nothing." He looked at the shocked face of his employer and knew that he had touched a nerve. *Well,* he thought to himself. *Surely not?* But it could be a big stick to force Charles to do what he, Jack Frobisher, wanted. That was for the Harrisons to go back to England and leave the running of Silver Bay to him alone. Lots of profits to find their way into the Frobisher back pocket!

"Let's stir up the big nigger bastard," said Jack. "I think that a little more encouragement might help." With that he fetched some kindling wood from a nearby pile and set it under the cage, which still continued to twist and turn in the late afternoon winds.

"You don't mean to…?" whispered a shocked Charles. He could be cruel, but he was not naturally vicious.

"Yes I do," said Jack. "Now you can sit back and hear the bastard scream. It don't matter now if he has anything to reveal or not. It will sure make the rest of them jump to do what they are told." And he set fire to the kindling. Within seconds it caught light and Jack added larger pieces of wood. He kept the supply of wood to a minimum level to keep the fire burning slowly and hot.

Akami started to scream. "Master! No!" is all he could mumble through his swollen lips and mouth. And he continued to scream as his skin burned and peeled away. Then any part of his body that was touching the cage started to cook. He fainted and Jack Frobisher threw more water and more water into the cage to revive him, each time succeeding to prolong his agonising suffering until finally he became unconscious. It took him another two hours to die the most horrible death that anyone could imagine.

Charles was in a state of shock and denial at what he had allowed his overseer to do. He could hardly face Mellissa when he returned to their cabin. She already knew what had happened. Akami's screams and the awful smell of burning flesh told her everything. Every agonising scream had seared through her like a knife slicing through her own body, her heart, and her very soul. Through her shock and tears she said to Charles, "I will never talk to you or sleep with you again. I am going to arrange to go back to England. You can come with me or stay here as you want, I don't care. This is the end for us. To think that I loved you! I have loved a monster! And now I hate you with the deepest hate I ever felt." And she lay down on the bed and wept.

Chapter Forty-Seven

March 1832
The Return Home

Dear Lucy,

I, we, have lost everything. I have lost my baby who came early during the firing of our plantation, and she was born dead. We lost High View, all the cabins, workshops, stables and the schoolroom. We also lost the clinic, and all the uncut cane, cane stores and sugar crushers. All gone! But worse than the loss of property, I have lost my baby, and I am heartbroken. I am also living in a state of shock and terror because of what my husband has done.

We are leaving Jamaica and as soon as we reach England I am leaving Charles. I cannot bear to be his wife any longer. I will go back to work for my father as Mellissa Goodchild once more.

Charles, my charming husband, turned out to be a killer. He murdered my Akami. He murdered him in such a monstrous way that I cannot bear to put it down on paper.

But I must! Yes, I will write of it to make a record as one of the monstrous things that were done here in Jamaica after the revolt was put down. I shall also write to William Wilberforce himself so that the people of England can be told just how much the sugar that they put in their tea costs – in blood! Indeed, I will make my first duty to visit William Wilberforce to tell him face to face all that I have seen and experienced here in Jamaica and I sincerely hope that my testimony will help to put an end to slavery for ever.

But Lucy I must force myself to tell you about my dearest friend, Akami. They roasted him, Lucy. They roasted him alive! My husband and that Jack Frobisher roasted my dear, sweet Akami. My poor innocent Akami, who did nothing but protect me from a wild, killing mob, as Charles should have done. They put him in an iron cage and suspended it from an iron frame. After leaving him in the hot sun for hours they set a small, slow burning fire underneath the cage, and they roasted him alive.

After it was all over the Frobisher monster wanted to set about my Lavinia. But Charles's blood lust was done by then. "Leave her be," he said very wearily, "my wife needs her". I did indeed need her that dreadful day, and I need her still.

But I am leaving Lavinia behind to bring up Akami's son. Yes, he had a baby son. I have freed him, and Lavinia and both of her children, as well as all the babies that I delivered, who were born on Silver Bay while I was there. As soon as Akami's baby is weaned, Lavinia will adopt him and bring him up as one of her family. So I am not bringing her to England even though she and all of her children are free Jamaicans. She wants to remain in Jamaica to teach them and baby Akami about their country, and I hope that very soon all enslaved men, women and children will be freed and have children born in freedom.

I have also freed the five children that I bought back to Silver Bay, including your Billy and Robert.

As soon as I can arrange transportation to Kingston I shall come and stay with you, if I may that is, until we set sail for England. I shall be sad to leave you, the only real friend that I made in Jamaica, apart from Lavinia and Akami.

I send my affectionate love and hope to be with you soon.
Mellissa

(Akami. Akami. Where are you, my sweet love?)

Part Three

Chapter One

Wednesday, 3 February, 2116
Wallchester General Hospital

Mellissa Wakes Up

(My poor, innocent Akami.)

"Look!" exclaimed Nurse Bingham, "Look doctor, I think that she is mouthing your name. I think that our Mellissa is waking up."

Dr Akami came to Mellissa's bedside. He took her hand and patted it gently. "Mellissa. Mellissa," he said quietly. As a single tear rolled down her face, Mellissa opened her eyes for a second or two. The first thing she saw was Dr Akami looking down at her.

"You're alive!" she gasped. "How can that be? You're alive! Oh, thank God!" And then she went back to a deep, natural sleep.

"I wonder what that was all about. But good," he said, "she is waking naturally now. In a day or two she will be fully back to consciousness, and we will be able to assess her mental capacities. Her head wound is healing well, and I have high expectations that her brain is undamaged. Nurse Bingham, will you please call DI Lavinia Hobbs and let her know that Mellissa will soon be able to answer her questions."

"What did she mean about you being alive, Dr Akami?"

He laughed. "Of course I am so wonderful and handsome, that she has been dreaming of me all this time! And perhaps she dreamed that I had died!" And they both laughed.

When Mellissa next woke up, Dr Akami was standing at her bedside next to a Jamaican-looking lady. A stranger, but one Mellissa felt she recognised. "This is Detective Inspector Lavinia Hobbs," he said. "She wants to ask you a few questions about how your head was hurt."

"Lavinia? You are here too?" muttered Mellissa. "Have you got my baby with you?"

Dr Akami had already explained to the DI that she should expect Mellissa to be confused, so she said gently, "No, I haven't got your baby with me. I have come to talk to you about your husband Charlie Harris."

"He's not Charlie Harris. His name is Charles Harrison, and I don't want to be married to him anymore."

DI Hobbs wasn't sure if Mellissa was quite taking in what she was saying. She tried again. "Do you remember your Charlie? He plays DI David Holland on the television?"

Mellissa was trying to remember. She screwed up her face. "Detective Inspector David Holland? Yes, I remember him now. He hit me."

"Yes," said DI Hobbs. "I think he did. Do you want to tell me all about it? About what happened?"

"It was nothing much. We were in the kitchen and we were arguing about our holiday to Jamaica. And he slapped my face. I think that I hit my head on the kitchen unit. That's all. I don't think that he meant to hurt me. But was it Charlie Harris or Charles Harrison who hit me? I think that they both did."

"Well, the only one I know about is Charlie, and he did hurt you. You could have died. Do you know that you have been unconscious and in hospital for the last two weeks?"

"Yes," said Mellissa, "the doctor told me. I don't remember anything after falling in the kitchen. I just remember dreaming about living in Jamaica a long time ago. The doctor was there and so were you!"

"Well, Mellissa," said Lavinia Hobbs, "your husband has already been charged with GBH, that's grievous bodily harm."

"But I don't want to give evidence against him. He didn't mean to hurt me."

"Mrs Harris, we have collected enough evidence from your home to bring a case against him, and I believe that he intends to plead 'guilty', so you will not be asked to give evidence. Do you know what he did after he hit you? Do you know where you were found?"

Mellissa was puzzled. "The doctor said something about you finding me in Westover Woods. I don't know how I got there."

Lavinia Hobbs started to tell Mellissa how she had been dumped in the woods and left for dead, but after a few minutes her eyelids fluttered shut, and she was asleep again. As the DI was leaving, she bumped into Dr Akami. "Your patient seems to be well on the way to recovery. She's asleep again now. She told me that it was her husband who hit her, and I will take a statement from her when she more fully awake. We have enough evidence for the moment to continue with our prosecution, and we will complete the details while he is out on bail."

"You mean that he can't escape prosecution by being such a famous TV star?"

"He's got very expensive and very good lawyers, but yes, we will see him face a jury charged with GBH."

"Good!" said Dr Akami. "She is a sweet girl. I'm sure that if she had her way she would let him off."

"No way! It doesn't matter who you are these days. Domestic violence is taken very seriously now. No one can evade the law or buy themselves out of trouble, and we don't have to rely on the victim's statement if there is enough forensic evidence. It doesn't matter if the victim says that he or she doesn't want the perpetrator charged, we still go ahead if the evidence is strong enough."

Chapter Two

Things Turn Full Circle

Three months later after Mellissa had fully recovered and had been discharged from the hospital, she and Dr Akami, whose first name she had discovered was Alexander, were walking together on Hampstead Heath.

"So, what happened with your husband?" asked Alex.

"Well, he pleaded guilty, so he had a very quick trial. He was fined quite heavily and he was given one hundred hours of community service to do. And he has got a new contract for the next series of DI Holland, so he didn't lose his job, after all."

"I think that he was very lucky to have got off so lightly," said Alex. "You do know that if that cut had been just a few millimetres deeper you might have been brain-damaged for the rest of your life."

Mellissa sighed. "Well the cut wasn't deeper and I wasn't brain-damaged. So it's no good for me to be feeling vengeful against him. We are separated now and our divorce proceedings have started. I think that the community service will be good for him and the schools that he is to go into."

"Schools? He's going into schools with a GBH record? What is he going to do?

"He is an East End boy, and he knows of several poor schools in the East End which have no money or facilities to teach the kids drama, so Charlie is going to divide his spare time, what spare time he has, teaching the kids, giving them drama lessons. Because he is famous, they all want to do it, and I think it will help to keep them off the streets and away from gangs."

"Anyway," said Alex, turning to face her and take hold her hand. "Let's try to get our personal histories to coincide and see what was real about your 'dreams' and what you put together out of conversations you overheard whilst you were unconscious, but aware of what was being said and done around you. Or, perhaps you really did go back and re-live a life that you may have had nearly two hundred years ago. If you and I were lovers in that time, then today we must be distant cousins of their children, both descended from that same Mellissa! Me from that Akami, and you from a boy child she must have had when she returned to England. Perhaps her husband Charles, or maybe she did divorce him and marry someone else? But she seems to have kept the Goodchild family name going. It's a magical coincidence that we have met up again in this life."

"Who knows! But I can tell you that I am happy living this life just as it is right now." Then taking both of his hands in hers, Mellissa leaned forward and kissed him. And Dr Alexander Akami responded happily…

The End

This is a work of fiction. All characters are fictional except Sam Sharpe, a minister of the Baptist church in Montego Bay, who was an inspirational slave who led the Christmas 1831 rebellion in Jamaica – sometimes called the Baptist War. During the ten days of the uprising of about 60,000 out of more than 300,000 slaves in Jamaica, fourteen white people were killed and 207 slaves. The uprising was put down in ten days by the Jamaican militia and English forces led by Sir Willoughby Cotton. The reprisals were brutal. After the rebellion between 300 and 350 slaves were killed, mostly hanged, some even for minor crimes. Sam Sharpe was executed in the Market Square, Montego Bay, on 23rd May 1832. His last recorded words were, "I would rather die upon yonder gallows than live in slavery."

When the British public read about the harsh reprisals of the uprising in Jamaica, they were so loud in their condemnation of slavery that it became a big contribution to the arguments against slavery leading to the laws that made all slavery in the British Empire being outlawed within two years.